CHEATING

A DOUBLE EDGED SWORD

by
Robert M. Wade

CHEATING
A DOUBLE EDGED SWORD

by
Robert M. Wade

Harrison House Publishing

San Antonio, Texas

Cheating: A Double Edged Sword
All Rights Reserved
Copyright © 2011 Robert M. Wade
v2.0
Edited by Ronda Wade Anderson
Cover Art designed and layout by J. Alexander, Genesis Productions©

PUBLISHER'S NOTE
The publisher does not have any control over and does not assume any responsibility for author or third-party Websites or their content.

Harrison House Publishing
www.theharrisonhousepublishing.com
info@theharrisonhousepublising.com
Paperback ISBN: 978-1-4675-0677-9
Library of Congress Control Number: 2011945587
Harrison House Publishing and the "HH" logo are trademarks belonging to Harrison House Publishing.

PRINTED IN THE UNITED STATES OF AMERICA

DEDICATION

This book is dedicated to the loving memory of my beautiful parents: Joseph Harrison Wade and Zelma Maedella Holmes-Wade.

Daddy and Momma, although you are not here to rejoice in my moment of triumph I know you are watching over me and sharing in this dream come true. Thank you for teaching me the power of love, humility, forgiveness, patience, benevolence, and preparing me for the trials of marriage and fatherhood.

I love you and miss you

ACKNOWLEDGEMENTS

My Father in heaven, without Your love and guidance I would not have been able to reach this dream, for I am nothing without You.

I also acknowledge my wife, Sun Hui, of 30 + years, who are the wind beneath my wings. And I personally Thank my fans for supporting my previous works: Patriotism: Red, White, Blue, and Sometimes Black; and, Reparations: Erasing The Stain From America's History.

Other Harrison House Publishings
by Author Robert M. Wade:

Patriotism: Red White Blue & Sometimes Black

CHAPTER #1

As Dominique walked pass their bedroom, he overheard Tashiana whispering into the phone. He looked at his watch, it 8:45 p.m. The time would not have mattered if not shortly afterward she said a friend needed to talk to her. When he asked her who the friend was, she said someone from her office he didn't know. The answer angered him because he knew Tashiana was lying, but he said nothing. Dominique knew you didn't whisper when you're talking to a friend in need. The calls from these unknown friends, he didn't know, were increasing daily.

"How long are you going to be gone?" he asked.

"I don't know. Probably a couple of hours," she answered.

"Why didn't she call earlier? Doesn't she know you have a family who want to spend time here at home with you?" Dominique asked. He said "she" because he didn't want to let on that he knew it was a man she was talking to.

"I'll tell her not to call me this late anymore. Ok?" Tashiana asked.

"Make sure you do," he said, knowing it didn't really matter what Tashiana told her so called friend because her life would end this night.

Dominique knew she was meeting her lover. He waited an hour before leaving the house to find the rendezvous spot where they met. If they stayed true to the adultery protocol, she would park her car in a prearranged location and they would leave together in her lover's car. When he found Tashiana's car, he would wait in the shadows for her lover to drop her off. While driving around looking for Tashiana's car he couldn't help but notice San Antonio was a beautiful city at night. The lights flashed, glimmered, and bounced off the windshield of his car. He had found nothing but happiness in this city in which he had lived for the past four years. Now, he was about to commit a crime that he was sure would land him on death row. Texas has a habit of frowning at people who commit premeditated murder. They say putting murders to death deter crime, but he would show them just how much the death penalty would deter him.

Dominique reached over and took the 357 Magnum from underneath the passenger seat. The weight of the gun felt good in his hand. Six brand new hollow point shells rested in its chambers. While in the military, he had learned to hit whatever it was he shot at, whether it was moving or standing still. Tashiana and her lover would never know what hit them. He replaced the pistol underneath the seat and continued his search for their rendezvous spot. Dominique checked the rendezvous spots he had heard people in his office talk about using when meeting their lovers. Tashiana's car was in none of those locations. As he continued his search, he pictured in his mind what was going to happen upon their return to her car. There was no doubt that he would locate the car. They would be so engross in each other, they will not bother to see if anyone was watching them. He would simply walk to the edge of the shadows and blow their heads clean off their shoulders. Lover man would be taken out first, and then his darling sweet wife. Dominique wanted to see the look of terror on Tashiana's face as she watched lover boy's body lifted off the ground by the impact of the hollow point slug. He wanted to see the fear in her eyes as he appeared from the shadows with the "to death do us part" maker in his hand. He wanted to see that look of disbelief on her face upon feeling the hot searing lead going through her body, ending her cheating life. He could already feel the recoil of the gun in his mind as it spit forth the death for which it was made.

Remembering Tashiana had mentioned stopping by a cute little boutique several days earlier behind Sunshine Park Apartments, which were not far from their house, he decided to check it out, and sure enough her car was parked in front of the shop. Dominique got out of his car walked up to hers, to make sure it was her car. He couldn't have wished for a better location. The boutique was located adjacent a military surplus store. The only lighting in the area was from the apartment complex on the south side of the military surplus store, leaving the boutique almost in complete darkness. To make matters even more convenient, there was an alley running between the two buildings. He backed into the alleyway and waited.

Dominique had no regrets about what he planned on doing. However, he did regret that he wasn't going to be around to watch his children grow up. It was amazing how important time was to an individual who was about to change his life forever. He wanted to remember the exact time his life, as he knew it, ended. At 11:15 p.m., a car headlights flashed by the alley and pull in beside Tashiana's car. Dominique got out of his car and eased up along side of the boutique, peeped around the corner of the building, and watched as lover man came around and opened the car door for her. After closing the car door he took her into his arms.

"You know we can't keep sneaking around like this, huh?" Lover Man asked.

"I know, but what can we do. I'm not ready for a divorce and your wife won't give you one," Tashiana said.

"I think we should say to hell with the both of them and skip town. We could start a new life some place else. What'd you say?"

"I'll think about it. Dominique is a good man, but he just can't satisfy me for some reason."

"No one can lay the pipe the way I do, huh?" Lover Man asked.

She never got the chance to respond to his question. The anger upon hearing the crude remark heightened the murderous desire he felt in his heart. The anger traveled from his brain, through his heart, down his arm, and out through the barrel of the gun. The roar of the 357 was deafening as it roared into action. The hollow point round caught him right between the eyes. The back of her lover's head exploded, spewing brains, hair, and other matter against the side of his car. Tashiana's eyes were wide with surprise and fright at the realization that his life was no more as his body slid down the side of the car. Tashiana turned toward the alley as he stepped into the little light that the apartment complex provided. She attempted to say something to him, but was silenced forever as the gun again roared into life. The impact of the bullet lifted her onto the hood of the car. Her legs were spread wide, causing her skirt to rise up almost around her waist. *What a fitting position for you to be found in. Maybe he can lay the pipe to you in hell*, Dominique said to her lifeless body. He calmly walked to his car, got in and left. He would explain to the children that mommy had been a bad girl and he had to punish her for it. He didn't know what he would say to them when the police led him away in handcuffs, but he was sure he would think of something. The shooting incident had taken all of one minute. At 11:16 p.m., he was officially a wanted man. Dominque drove home whistling an old favorite tune of his "What a Fool I've Been."

Tashiana Goodman is looked upon as the Black Venus in her neighborhood in San Antonio, Texas. Not only is she beautiful, she has the body of a Greek Goddess. She is so beautiful, and well portioned, that *even* homosexual males give her a second take as they pass her on the streets. The compliments about her body and beauty, by men and women alike, never cease.

Growing up in rural Arkansas, overly protected and somewhat secluded socially from the outside world by her parents, Tashiana didn't realize the influence her beauty had on those around her. Tashiana was driven to and from school functions, school socials, school dances, and sporting events by her parents until her senior year of high school. They wanted to prevent her from hanging around with the bad girls, and boys, that were going down roads that led to nowhere. For the same reason, Tashiana was not allowed to date until her senior year of high school, and then only if her parents approved of the boy asking to date her. Because of the parental domination, Tashiana developed an automatic rejection of situations that her parents would probably disagree with her getting involved in. However, that did not prevent her from helping her friends, on the high school cheerleader team, to meet boys As for herself, Tashiana was very rude to any man, young or old, who made a pass at her. But her rudeness didn't deter them from the chase, still they would tell her what they would do for her if she would only talk to them. She found men to be unbelievably stupid when trying to impress her. The men who thought they had a rap made promises that was obvious lies that no woman in her right mind would believe. The shy men who felt intimidated by her beauty, said nothing, but stood around grinning like blooming idiots. To further delay the knowledge of how she could use her looks and body to gain power and favor over men, she fell in love and got married. Tashiana had been married several years when the realization of how she could use her sexuality pushed itself to the forefront of her psyche. Therefore, her manipulation of the men who catered to her desire came later in her life and was done under the cloak of darkness and secrecy.

After moving to San Antonio, Tashiana established a reputation as a good mother and a good wife who went out of her way to help those in the community who were less fortunate than her self. She was also the owner of a small legal assistance business, which gave her the title of being a professional and responsible woman. So in the eyes of the community Tashiana was the ideal mother, wife, and professional role model that young women should emulate. Now she found herself in a three way love affair that would probably not only ruin her reputation in the community but would probably lead to a divorce and the lost of her family and friends. Since she had always rushed to help those in need in her community she hoped they wouldn't judge her too harshly when the news of her infidelity became public knowledge, but she knew that there would be very little sympathy when they found out this affair was not her first. She prayed that, at the least, her friends wouldn't take joy in seeing her shame bared before the world. Where she had once considered her beauty an asset, she now looked upon it as the curse that pushed her vanity buttons and cause her to go astray.

Tashiana had been a devoted young mother and wife when she entered the work force while living in Alaska. It was there she acquired the attitude of an independent woman when her income became sufficient enough to support the children and herself. Her wages exceeded that of her husband's. It was also while in Alaska, she discovered the majority of the male species of the world would do almost anything to get close to a woman as beautiful as she. And it hadn't helped that her husband, Dominique, was a homebody of whom she came to view as wimpy and boring.

Whenever she felt adventurous and wanted to do something crazy, or to see some of the tourist sites Alaska had to offer, Dominique always had an excuse why they couldn't go. They couldn't find a babysitter, or the trip was too expensive was his usual complaints. When Tashiana insisted that she wanted to see a tourist site, Dominique would tell her to go with one of the tourist agencies. After several of these tours alone, Tashiana became quite comfortable at pretending to be single because she was able to flirt with the male tour guides, and other men on the tour. She still pretended to be upset whenever he suggested these outings alone, but it was really how Tashiana had preferred it. It gave her a chance to experience life to its fullest while she was still young without having him or the children in tow. Live for today and tomorrow would take care of itself had been her secret philosophy. As far as the children were concerned, she felt she would have time to be with them when life slowed her down. Dominique knew if he wanted to hang with her he had to find a babysitter that was willing to be called on at any time day or night, but he didn't. He preferred spending his time with his children. It was not until they moved to San Antonio, TX, Tashiana finally realized that affairs has their pit falls and valleys waiting to devour the unsuspecting who fell into that void.

Running the streets was fun while she was young, but the

years took their toll on her, both mentally and physically. Over
the years, she came to realize that while she had thought her
husband was wimpy, boring, and a tight wad, he was trying to
establish a financial future for their family. The time he spent
with the children was to establish a strong family bond between
parent and child. She felt guilty it took her so long to realize what
he was doing, and for not listening when he told her she should
be doing the same. Now that her 14 year old daughter, Shantel,
was interested in boys and came to her for advice, it caused some
awkward moments. It was advice she couldn't give with a clear
conscience. Every time Shantel asked what type of man she
should look for in a husband it was always Dominique who came
to mind. It didn't help she hadn't been close with her daughters
during their younger years. She had been busy chasing her own
dream world, a world that barely included them. A world where
her main concern was getting men to give her all their worldly
possessions while she in turn gave them nothing, a world where
she would remain young and beautiful forever, a world that exists
in the mind of those who wish for immortality. Unfortunately, time
stands still for no one, Tashiana included.

She now stood naked in front of a dingy, steam covered motel
bathroom mirror staring herself in the face. The soap and water
hadn't washed away the guilt she was feeling. It was time to put
an end to this affair, and set the proper example for her children,
if she could. Tashiana knew it wouldn't be easy because she had
true feelings for him. She didn't know if it was love or not, but
it was as close as you can get to love. After drying herself and
getting dressed, she re-entered the room and sat on the bed beside
Ahmaad, who was still naked under the covers.

She said, "Ahmaad, I'm not going to see you anymore after

tonight. The guilt of cheating on my husband and lying to my kids about where I go all the time is starting to take its toll on me."

"Not again, Tashiana," he laughed, "You've been saying that for six months. You know I'm not going to let you walk out on me like this, not after all the risks I've taken to build this relationship to what it is today. Whether you accept the fact or not I've fallen in love with you. I know it wasn't supposed to happen, but it did. And there isn't a damn thing I can do about it. If you even think about dumping me, I'll be forced to tell Dominique what a hot little number you are in the sack. And tell him how much of his money you spent on me," he threatened.

"You wouldn't dare! What difference does it make if he found out from you or me? We'll probably end up divorced anyway, because if this sneaking around continues we are going to get caught eventually. Beside, I'm tired of this sneaking around. Everywhere we go I'm scared someone we know is going to recognize us. You do whatever you think is right. If I can find the strength, I'm going to tell Dominique about us and hope he can find it in his heart to forgive me again. You have threatened me for the last time. You knew the only way you could keep me was by threatening to tell Dominique about us. Well, let's give the devil his do."

"Tashiana, you can't mean that. I love you. I'll divorce Laquan, [his wife of seven years], and marry you, if that's what you want. We know this threatening to tell each other's spouse is a pretense. Hell, you've been calling me more than I've been calling you lately. I know you feel as much for me as I do for you, please reconsider. You know I wouldn't do anything to hurt you, or your family. You know that," he pleaded.

"Yes, I guess I do, always have. I got disillusioned with this relationship also. Always telling myself the only reason I kept sleeping with you was because you'd tell my husband about us. I finally faced reality and realized it's a lie. A lie I'm no longer willing to live with. So if you don't mind, take me to my car so I can go home. I don't know if I'll ever get up enough nerve to tell Dominique about us, but I do know we're finished," she said.

No further words were necessary. Ahmaad showered, dressed, and dropped her off at her car. He drove away without a backward glance. He knew the relationship wasn't over, not by a long shot. She always acted that way whenever she got a case of the guilties. In a day or two, she would call and apologize for what she said and ask him to meet her some place.

"God, she's sweet," he said.

Ahmaad Tate is what people call a high yellow pretty boy. He is six feet tall, muscular, and fair skinned, with stringy hair like white people, and a thin mustache. He hadn't lied about being in love with Tashiana. He would dump his wife in a heartbeat if Tashiana asked him to. He realized all too well that she enjoyed their set up the way it was. They had fun, but made no commitments. Besides, she had one of the most beautiful families in the state of Texas. He knew she wasn't ready to give it up yet, but he had tried to convince her otherwise. Ahmaad tried numerous times to convince her that the two of them would be much happier if they divorced their spouses and married each other. He lost count of the number of times he made this proposal. The conversation was always the same.

"Tashiana, you know how much I love you. I like to think you love me, although you've never said so. We should divorce our spouses and run off to Alaska, or some other place far away. I know Laquan will want to keep Ahmaad Jr., and Dominique will probably want to keep your kids. That would leave us free to start a new life together. God knows he love those kids more than he does you. What do you say?"

"Ahmaad, how many times do I have to tell you? Although I'm sleeping with you, I love my husband very much. You're just an outlet I use when I start to feel I'm not appreciated at home, nothing more. Besides, I could never marry you because we're too much alike. I could never trust you, and you would never trust me. Let's enjoy what we have while it last. We may get caught the next time we're together and that would be the end of our little escapades," she always answered, and that would be the end of the conversation.

CHAPTER #2

Tashiana stared straight ahead as she drove home from what she hoped was her last motel rendezvous. How she would tell Dominique, and the children, about her infidelity she hadn't the slightest idea. Dominique, especially, since this was her second affair since they had been married. She had to if she was serious about putting an end to her sleeping around. Otherwise, things would only get more complicated because she felt more for Ahmaad than she was willing to admit.

How many times have I told myself I have to put an end to this affair? She thought. *How did this sneaking around start again anyway?*

Tashiana had guilty feelings before, but this night her guilty conscience worked over time. Her sub conscience provided her with the answer as her past flashed before her eyes.

She and Dominique had attended a party hosted by one of his co-workers and got separated for an extended period of time and she had no idea where he was. Like the majority of the other party goers at 1 a.m. in the morning she was pretty wasted and wanted to see how much longer Dominique was planning on staying at the party.

"Have you seen Dominique?" Tashiana asked Claire Jones, as she staggered by.

"The last time I saw him he was headed upstairs with that bitch

Charlene Tillman. If I were you, I'd go up there and see what the hell's going on. She screws every man who asks her for it. It doesn't matter if the man is married or not. She certainly doesn't give a damn that she is," Claire, chastised Charlene.

"How long ago was it you saw them go upstairs?" Tashiana asked, becoming angry.

"I don't know. Maybe half an hour, give or take a few minutes," Claire answered.

Everyone in their neighborhood had heard the rumors that Charlene was the biggest whore in San Antonio. Some whispered that she and her husband were active members in a local wife-swapping club. Since her husband wasn't at the party, Tashiana figured it was Charlene's big chance to screw as many guys as she could before calling it a night.

As Tashiana started for the stairs, Dominique and Charlene were coming downstairs holding hands and whispering as if they were sharing a secret they didn't want anyone else to hear. Knowing Charlene's reputation, Tashiana jumped to the conclusion that they had been to bed. She didn't know they went upstairs at the same time but not together. On his way back downstairs, after his trip to the john, he heard someone crying in one of the bedrooms and he went to see who it was. There sat Charlene, crying her eyes out because her marriage was on the rocks. He talked to her until she stopped crying. Once he realized how much time had elapsed, he told her to pull herself together. He wanted to get back downstairs before someone thought they were doing something they had no business doing.

Tashiana was furious. She swore she would screw the first man who came along. Dominique's explanation fell on deaf ears.

"Hey, you missed me?" Dominique asked grinning.

"Oh, have you been someplace?" Tashiana quipped sarcastically.

Dominique could tell she was upset about something. Then it dawned on him it was because she saw him and Charlene come downstairs together. He also knew about Charlene's reputation.

"Alright, what's wrong? I guess it's because Charlene and me came downstairs together. Nothing happened between us. Really, she was up there crying her eyes out because her marriage is breaking up and she needed someone to tell her troubles to, that's all," he explained.

"I bet", Tashiana said in a huff

"You think I'm lying, don't you?"

"I don't know what to think, to be honest with you."

"Do you really think I'd be stupid enough to sleep with a woman with you right down stairs? Come on for Christ sakes, give me credit for being somewhat intelligent," Dominique said angrily.

"I wasn't up there. I don't know what you did. You certainly were up there long enough to have done something," Tashiana snapped.

"Look, I'm not going to stand here arguing with you about something that never happened. You want to go home?"

"No not yet. I guess I over reacted because of her reputation. Let's stay a little while longer. Okay?" she smiled, thoughts of revenge running through her mind.

"Sure honey. You need anything?" Dominique asked.

"No, I'm fine."

"You're sure?"

"Yes, I'm sure."

"Okay, I'll be back in a few minutes. Greg has something he wants to talk to me about," he said, thinking the matter was settled and would be forgotten.

After Dominique left, Ahmaad appeared out of nowhere. "Hey pretty lady. Who was dumb enough to leave you all alone?" he asked seductively.

"My darling husband was dumb enough to leave me alone, that's who," Tashiana answered.

"Is your husband the jealous type who'll try to beat me up if he sees me talking to you?"

"No, he's not," she assured him.

"What if he sees me dancing with you?"

"I don't think he would mind, as long as you keep your hands to yourself."

"Well, may I have this dance?" Ahmaad bowed at the waist, and ushered her toward the living room floor where other couples were dancing. "If I may say so, you don't look very happy. Is anything wrong? Maybe I can help," he said once they were on the dance floor.

"I feel so alone. Dominique, my husband, is so busy talking politics it's as if he has forgotten I'm here. But, that's not your problem" Tashiana sighed.

"I'll tell you what. I'll make sure you don't feel alone the remainder of the night, or ever again if you want. How does that sound to you?"

With the vision of Dominique and Charlene still fresh in her mind she said, "I'd appreciate that. Mr.

"Mr. no one, to you its Ahmaad."

"Okay, Ahmaad it is. I'm Tashiana."

"I know. You're the fantasy of almost every man's dream in the neighborhood," he informed her.

"Really?" Tashiana asked.

"Really," he assured her.

They talked off and on the remainder of the night when Dominique wasn't around. She found him to be very funny and interesting.

He was nothing at all like Dominique. Dominique's passion these days was politics. His idea of romance was watching a congressional debate on C-span, or world events on "This is CNN."

At 3:30 a.m. Dominique was ready to go home. As he was getting their coats, Ahmaad came up behind Tashiana and handed her a piece of paper.

"That's my work number. If you need a friend don't hesitate to give me a call," he smiled.

"I might do that," Tashiana responded, still thinking Dominique and Charlene had been to bed.

Tashiana called Ahmaad on Thursday the week after the party and asked him to meet her at the club on Lackland Air Force Base that Friday night. He said he would be more than happy to meet her.

When Tashiana arrived at the club for their first encounter, she was so nervous she almost turned around and went back home. What she had done when they lived in Alaska crept into her mind. After parking she forced herself out of the car and into the club. She might've backed out of the meeting if Ahmaad's table hadn't been close to the entrance. He waved to her as soon as she entered the club. She walked over to his table and sat down.

"Hi beautiful, I was beginning to think you weren't going to show. You said about 8:00. It's 9:15," he pointed out.

"I'm sorry I'm late. I started not to show up at all. I'm new at this sneaking around," she said nervously. It was true as far as San

Antonio was concerned.

"After a while, there's nothing to it. Believe me."

"I guess you're an old pro at this sort of thing, huh?" Tashiana asked, wondering if she was making a mistake by meeting him.

"No not really. But, to get a chance to be with a woman as beautiful as you are, I would risk everything I own in this world," he complimented her.

Had she been a white woman, her face would've looked like a traffic light stuck on flashing red, she blushed so. Although she enjoyed his flattering compliments, she knew from past experience that regardless of what a man said, he was after one thing. She wondered if she could control Ahmaad, and his finances, as she had controlled Harvey's.

Tashiana had never dealt with a man who had been playing the seduction game a lot longer than she had, a man who was an expert at catering to a woman's every desire until he got what he wanted from her.

Ahmaad, on the other hand, had never met a woman like Tashiana. The end result was they ended up on a roller coaster ride in which they had very little control.

During the course of the evening, he said all the right things, which made Tashiana feel more of a woman than she had felt since arriving in San Antonio. Sure Dominique complimented her on her beauty all of the time, but hearing Ahmaad say it was more romantic somehow. She had forgotten what a thrill it was flirting with danger. She responded to his praise as no other woman he'd known. As they continued to talk, the sexual attraction they felt became overpowering. The first slow song they danced to, she became putty in his arms. It was stimulating beyond belief as Ahmaad grind against her. She matched him grind for grind. She became so excited she could feel the sticky wetness running down the inside of her thighs. The way Ahmaad was breathing, she was certain he was about to explode inside his pants. When the dance ended they walked back to their table on unsteady legs.

"Excuse me Ahmaad, I have to go to the little girl's room," she breathed.

"Yeah, me too," he panted.

They both laughed, knowing he meant the men's room.

She entered one of the stalls and removed her panties and cleaned herself off. The seat of her panties was as wet as if she had dipped them in water.

God, give me the strength to get through this night without doing something I may regret in the future, she prayed. God had nothing to do with what she ended up doing.

Never in her wildest dreams did Tashiana think it would be so easy to forget or not care, again, that she was a married woman with four children. Not to mention she was setting herself up to be a cheap one-night stand. While she was in Ahmaad's arms the only thing that mattered was the warmth she felt between her legs. If he had laid her right there on the dance floor and seduced her, she would've giving herself willingly. Tashiana knew what was going to happen before the night ended. She had lost her will power and was ready to do whatever he suggested. Tashiana asked herself if that wasn't the reason she had met him there in the first place. Ahmaad was back at the table when she returned.

"I don't think I can handle another dance like that unless we made plans for later on this evening," Ahmaad confessed.

"I know what you mean. I'm not sure if I'm ready for this at this point in my life," Tashiana lied.

"No one ever thinks they are. The only way to find out is to do it. If the guilt is too much to handle, then you can say you're not ready," he said. Ahmaad's confidence grew because he sensed she was fair game.

"I don't know. Maybe after another drink, or two, I'll be able to make up my mind."

Ahmaad stopped the first waitress passing their table and ordered fresh drinks. While handing the waitress his empty glass he dropped his straw. As he leaned over to retrieve it, he happened to glance under the table in her direction. He almost fell out of his chair upon seeing she wasn't wearing panties. After the waitress left the table he could hardly speak.

"If I did something to you out of the ordinary, would you slap my face?" Ahmaad asked.

Tashiana didn't know what to make of the question, or what caused him to speak in such a strange tone of voice. She was searching for the proper response when she felt a stocking foot sliding under her dress. The touch was like an electric shock. Tashiana jerked back so violently she almost tipped her chair over. Although only a couple of people glanced in their direction, she felt the whole world watched the incident on closed circuit television.

"Ahmaad, please don't do that again," Tashiana said in a hoarse whisper.

"Aw, come on, you beautiful creature. Move back up to the table and let have some fun. I'll make you feel like you've never felt before. Come on, you'll see," Ahmaad pleaded.

"When did you take your shoe off," Tashiana asked huskily, moving cautiously back up to the table. This was the most exciting game she ever played in a public establishment.

"When I noticed you weren't wearing any panties," he smiled.

"How did you know.....Oh shit, I should've known you noticed something when you picked up your straw by the way you sounded afterward. I don't know if I can play this game, with all these people around," Tashiana said. She looked from one table to the next to see if anyone noticed what was going on at their table. Everyone was entrenched in their own drunken, lust filled worlds to care what was happening at their table.

Ahmaad didn't wait to make his move, fearing if he hesitated too long she would talk him out of playing the game. It was also his first time attempting anything that bold, therefore, he was just as excited as she was. When his stocking foot slid under her dress and he started caressing her with his big toe she closed her eyes and let out a small inaudible moan. In seconds she was a mass of quivering flesh. When she climaxed, the sensation was so intense she became dizzy. Her breathing was so ragged a passing waitress asked if she was okay. She could only nod her head, indicating she was fine.

After the sensation passed, and she was able to speak again, Tashiana said, "I guess I owe you one. You were right. I've never experienced anything like that in my life. It was beautiful."

With a wide grin Ahmaad said, "The fun doesn't have to end here. You'll get even more pleasure once we're in bed. I hate to brag, but satisfying beautiful women, is my whole purpose in life. And I must admit, I'm the best," he bragged on himself knowing he had her right where he wanted her, hot and ready.

"After how you made me feel, I don't doubt it. Where do we go from here?" she asked.

It was what he had hoped would happen. He reached into his jacket pocket and produced a motel room key.

"I guess you know me better than I know myself," Tashiana

said, feeling like a push over.

"No not really. I hoped you had reached that point in your life where you were ready for something different. I was prepared to get on my knees and beg you to go to a motel with me tonight. Ever since I laid eyes on you, I haven't been able to think of anything other than how good I believe you are in bed. If you take your shoe off and place your foot in my lap, you'll find that I'm just as excited as you are," Ahmaad invited.

"No thanks. I'll take your word for it. Let's go before I change my mind," Tashiana said. She couldn't have backed out at this point even if she wanted to.

During the drive to the motel, her mind was racing at break neck speed. *God, please forgive me for what I'm about to do. You know the flesh is weak. I'll never do this again as long as I live. I swear it.* Tashiana tried to convince herself rather than the Almighty.

"What're you going to do if Dominique finds out about you being unfaithful again, Tashiana?" a voice in her subconscious mind asked.

"I'll plead for his forgiveness and hope that would be the end of it," she answered the voice.

"How will this sleeping around again affect the kids, Tashiana?" the voice persisted.

"Damn you. I know what I'm doing," Tashiana scolded the voice. "Hell, he forgave me once, he'll forgive me again."

"We shall see, slut," the voice said, getting in the last word.

Tashiana was sure what she was doing was worth the risk. As Ahmaad took her into his arms, all was forgotten except the warmth running through her body. She acted like a starving homeless woman who had found a neatly wrapped roasted ham sitting beside a dumpster. She thrilled to the sensation of his probing tongue, the rolling of his hips as he tried to penetrate her through her clothing. She became unbelievably excited as he shoved the top of her dress down to expose her breasts. He took one nipple, and then the other, into his mouth. She almost reached that magical moment just from his manipulation of her breasts. The only time she could remember being that excited was the first time she and Dominique made love in the back seat of his Dad's antique '59 Chevy.

Tashiana met his every movement. Licked and kissed every part of him within her reach. She moaned at the touch of his hot fingertips as they danced over her hot throbbing body. Her knees became weak, and she had to sit to keep from falling on her face.

"It has been so long since a man made me feel this way. Please, don't stop," Tashiana, gasped.

He undressed her and blazed a trail of hot kisses from her head to her toes. The closer he got to the center of her being, the more she squirmed. Tashiana was sure if the pleasure got any better, she would die from a heart attack, and the world would know she died in the arms of a man not her husband. When she could not stand the sensation any longer, it was her turn to show him she was also capable of giving pleasure, as well as receiving it.

Tashiana pushed him onto his back and undressed him. Her hands trembled as she took his member into her hands. She massaged him hesitantly, knowing what he expected of her. Although Tashiana was raised to believe oral sex was taboo in the black community, she heard her parents whispering that it was going on anyway. The women were call cocksuckers and the men cat-lickers. She didn't necessarily want to do it, but knew all men, black and white, loved for women to do it for them, although she had refused to up to now. She'd never had a man this way before, not at home, nor while they lived in Alaska. But in San Antonio it would be a different story altogether. She didn't know what sensation to expect. Tashiana chalked it up to being in the sexual experimental stage of her life.

With this in mind, she gave him the pleasure he sought. His eyes rolled back in their sockets. He moaned as if he was experiencing the greatest sensation he ever experienced in his life. The way he reacted to her handling of him, gave her more confidence than she knew she possessed. Tashiana had often wondered what it would feel like to perform oral sex on a man, but never in her wildest dream had she wondered what it would be like to bring a man to a climax that way. She had no intention of doing so now, but she got so carried away by their animalistic passion, the unthinkable was happening before she realized what was occurring. It was too late to pull away. To her surprise, she felt neither nausea nor remorse. It was give and take all the way.

For a quick moment, Tashiana thought of Dominique begging her for a moment such as this, but during their fourteen years of marriage she had refused to accommodate him. The thought left as quickly as it had entered her head. After such an intense climax, she was pleased to see he was still ready to fulfill his promise. He rolled her onto her back and satisfied her wanton desire.

Tashiana never forgot that first encounter. As she drove home, she was scared she wouldn't be able to lie to Dominique about where she had been, not with a straight face. To help with the lie she was going to tell him Tashiana called her girlfriend Janet from the motel.

"Janet, this is Tashiana. Has Dominique called there looking for me?"

"No, why?" she asked sleepily.

"If he calls before I get home, tell him I just left your house and I'm on my way home. If he asks you tomorrow, or whenever, where we went tonight, tell him we went to Lackland, and after the club closed we decided to have breakfast before coming home. He'll be too pissed to say much to me when I get home tonight. But he'll try to find out from you, sooner or later, what kept me out so late. You got that?" Tashiana asked.

"Yeah, I got it. Tashiana, you little devil. Who is he?" she asked excitedly.

"Tell you about him later, okay? Gotta go now, just don't forget what I said."

As planned, Janet saved the day, although she knew nothing of what happened between Tashiana and Ahmaad that night. When Janet came over to visit the following day to get the scoop on who it was Tashiana was fooling around with, the first thing Dominique ask her was where they had gone last night. Like a good little trooper Janet stayed with the script. It was the first lie of many she would tell to cover for Tashiana over the next two years.

The affair Tashiana had with Harvey Kitchen when they lived in Alaska was nothing compared to the one with Ahmaad. She knew from their first encounter she was getting into a relationship for which she had very little control. Tashiana had been willing to ride out the waves for as long as they lasted. Now the waves had turned into an undertow that was pulling her down and threatening to drown her. It was time for the ride to end.

What a damn ride it has been, she said returning briefly to the present. Heaven help me if Dominique ever finds out I'm being unfaithful to him again.

As if Tashiana wasn't feeling guilty enough, her mind took her

back to that earlier affair in Alaska, when she questioned herself
as to whether she wanted to stay married to Dominique. She had
considered him a wimp and a loser for putting up with a tramp like
her. She changed her mind when he took a stand and she thought
she was going to lose him and the children.

Early one Sunday morning, Tashiana lay awake watching him
and listening to Dominique snoring. What in the hell did I ever
see in him, she wondered. Then she remembered how, when they
were dating and early in their marriage, he use to send flowers
to her job with little "I love you" notes cards attached. How he
used to take her to fancy restaurants. Dominique made her feel
she was the only woman alive. And when they made love, he
wouldn't stop until she said she had had enough. It had been years
since he took the time to romance her. Now, when they did have
sex it was over in minutes. At first his excuse was he didn't want
to wake the kids. She went along with that rationale when the
kids were young, because they would come screaming into the
bedroom at all the wrong times. When she suggested a babysitter
a couple times a week so they could be alone, he rejected the idea
as a waste of money. Tashiana didn't doubt his love for her, but
he refused to acknowledge that over the years their lives were
starting to resemble two magnets repelling each other. When she
mentioned this he said if they were moving in opposite directions it
was because she had become too materialistic and wasn't thinking
about the future.

Tashiana longed for those exciting high school days when
the boys catered to her every desire. She knew being a married
woman and having kids hanging on each arm didn't exactly show
her sex appeal, but she had a lot to offer any man who would

dare take the chance to explore the curves of her neglected body. Besides, she was in the sexual prime of her life and wanted to experiment with different ways of receiving and giving pleasure. The preacher's wife she was not.

Tashiana knew as long as she was a married woman, she wasn't free to do every thing she wanted to do before she got too old. The only way was to get out of the marriage, but she knew he would never agree to give her a divorce. Whenever the subject came up, Dominique would profess his love for her and threatened to kill her if she left him. So he left her no alternative, but to figure out a sure fire way of getting rid of him without being caught. The children would mourn for a while, but they would eventually get over their lost, especially if she hooked up with a good man who had lots of money. When she told her best friend about how she felt about her marriage, her friend's advice was that she should get out of the marriage as soon as possible. She told her friend it was not that simple. Her friend handed her a card. *Whatever problem you may have in your life, come and see Madame Comuchie, the voodoo lady who lives in cabin #5 in Seward, Alaska. I will free you of all your burdens.* Her friend assured her Madame Comuchie was not a joke. Tashiana didn't believe in the occult, but what the hell, these were desperate times. That weekend she and her friend drove up to the Seward and talked to Madame Comuchie.

"What can Madame Comuchie do you young lady?" she asked.

"I'm tired of my marriage and want out, but my husband won't let me go," Tashiana explained.

"So, you don't love him anymore," Madame Comuchie said.

"Not enough to stay married to him," she answered.

"Understand me woman. I only provide permanent solutions to the problems of the people I help. Are you sure this is what you want?" Madame Comuchie asked.

"Yes," had been Tashiana's simple answer.

Tashiana got up and went into the kitchen to cook breakfast. After everything was prepared, she reached behind the spices and took out the little vial of clear liquid she bought from Madame Comuchie. Madame Comuchie guaranteed her that the solution was undetectable by all the world forensic experts, because it came from deep in the Amazon jungle where man dared not tread. She was instructed to put a drop in his coffee every morning for five days. After the fifth day if she were not rid of him, she would get a full refund. Tashiana wanted Dominique out of house, when whatever was going to happen to him happened, so she started putting the solution in his coffee on Wednesday. Sunday was his golf day, so right after breakfast he would be out her life forever, she hoped. Tashiana was somewhat worried because after four days of drinking the portion there was no change in his health or his demeanor. Have faith the voodoo lady had told her.

As they sat around the breakfast table eating, Tashiana was surprised no one noticed how nervous she was. Her heart beat faster with each sip of the coffee he took. She got through breakfast without having a heart attack. When she kissed him on his way out the door, a pang of guilt gripped her heart because her children would be fatherless before this day was over, or so the direction she had been given said. She looked at the clock. It was 9 a.m. She wanted to remember the last time she had saw him alive if the police began an investigation.

Tashiana went about her daily routine, but expected the phone call to come at any time to inform her she was now a widow, or her husband had run off with some bimbo at the golf club. As the day passed and no phone call came, she wondered if the old lady had lied to her about the poison. Half an hour before the time he normally came home from his golf game the phone rang. It was the Anchorage Police Department informing her that her husband had a massive heart attack on the 16th hole and was being rush to the hospital even as they spoke. Tashiana gathered up the children and they went to be with their loved one at Elmendorf AFB Hospital. The look on the doctor's face told her all she needed to know. She prayed to God that no one could see the relief in her eyes through the tears, or the happiness surrounding her heart. Free, Tashiana whispered to herself as she left the hospital to start making funeral arrangements.

Tashiana and Dominique had been married for nine years before moving to Alaska. It was while living there that she got her first taste of what it felt like to be financially independent. She liked it more than she would have ever imagined possible.

Soon after they arrived in Anchorage, she got a job as a legal assistant with a well to do law firm, Brown, Greer, and Brown. Being the daughter of a lawyer, and a policeman, plus having an associate degree in legal aid, Tashiana proved to be an invaluable employee to the firm. There was very little she didn't know about how a law office should be run. Her mother had taught her how to write, and type, common motions and legal briefs to be filed with district and Federal courts. Therefore, the firm saved a great deal of money, and time, by not having to train her. The Browns, and Mr. Greer, told her if she didn't go back to school and become a lawyer she would miss her calling, because of the advice she offered on several cases the office handled. All three were totally professional at the office, so she didn't have to worry about them trying to corner her at work. However, they did compliment her on her beauty and body stature.

The senior Mr. Brown, David, was 5' 9", 62 years old, forty-pounds over weight, and very laid back. He had a habit of slicking back the hair he no longer had.

Mr. Greer, Harold J., was the other senior partner at the firm. He was 6', slim, 61 years old, and a workaholic. It was common for him to work until midnight several nights a week. Mr. Brown constantly told him the only reason he worked so much was to make people think he was the better lawyer.

The senior Brown and Greer attended Harvard Law School together, and graduated the same year. However, it was ten years after they graduated before they decided to pool their resources and start their own firm in Alaska. Mr. Greer had a bad habit of repeating the question he was asked before answering. It drove senior Mr. Brown nuts. Tashiana smiled remembering one such incident.

"Harold, when is the Thomas trial set to begin?" Mr. Brown asked.

"When is the Thomas trial set to begin? I think it starts in a couple of weeks, but I have to check the docket," he answered.

"Do we have everything in order?" Mr. Brown asked.

"Do we have everything order? I think so, I'll check to make sure," Mr. Greer answered.

"Harold, do you realize how annoying it is when you repeat every question you're asked before you answer it?" Mr. Brown asked.

"Do I realize I repeat every question I'm asked before answering it? I guess I do, but it's not to piss anyone off. It's a habit I find hard to break," Mr. Greer said.

"Well, I wish you would try harder because it's really

annoying," Mr. Brown informed him.

"I don't understand why it still annoys you. I been doing it since we met in college," Mr. Greer said.

"And I have been telling you to cut the crap out since college, but do you listen? Hell no. I may as well be talking to that damn wall behind you," Mr. Brown complained.

"You may as well be talking to this wall? Keep griping about my habit and you can have this damn office to yourself," Mr. Greer threatened.

"I can have this office to myself? For goodness sake, just shut up and make sure the Thomas case is ready for trial," Mr. Brown directed.

Mr. Greer started to say something but Mr. Brown held up his hand and pointed toward the file cabinet. Mr. Greer mumbled something under his breath but did what was asked of him.

David Brown II was a perfectionist. Everything had to be exactly the same at all times, and no paperwork left his office until he approved it. He was 6'3", 40 years old and in excellent physical condition. His wife was 46. He said he had to have a woman mature enough to give him what he needed. Mr. Brown Sr. said junior was trying to replace a mom who died when he was twelve.

Another reason they liked Tashiana was because she never complained if she was asked to work late whenever they needed her to. Dominique had no problems with her working late occasionally because he worked late occasionally himself. Tashiana felt blessed at being hired by such an affluent law firm, and having white bosses that was a joy to work for. After six months on the job, Tashiana was promoted to assistant supervisor in the legal aid department. To her surprise the majority of her white co-workers accepted her being promoted over them with little or no hostility, because Tashiana's knowledge of the law was impressive. Along with the promotion, her confidence grew by leaps and bounds. No one could tell her anything. It was during this realization of her value to the world she hooked up with females in her office who were accustomed to bar hopping, and cheating on their husbands. Tashiana manage to resist the urge to go bar hopping with them in the beginning, choosing instead to have a couple of drinks with them after work and then going home.

After more than a year of prodding they finally convinced Tashiana she could run the streets, and still maintain a healthy household. She knew it was a lie, because the majority of the workingwomen she knew who ran the streets in Alaska were divorced. Still, she threw her hat into the ring. The ringleader where Tashiana worked was Jessica Clark, her immediate supervisor, white, classy, and a divorcee with no kids.

"Mrs. Goodman, all you ever do is work, work, work. Have a couple of drink afterward sometimes and run home to hubby and the kids. Are you ever going to go out with us to unwind and let your hair down?"

"No, I'm doing fine thank you. I have four kids and a husband to take care of once I leave this office. I don't have time to be going out and letting my hair down, as you call it," Tashiana said seriously.

"Damn, home girl, you sound like you are scared to do anything without hubby's approval. I have four kids and a husband to take care of," she mimicked Tashiana.

"Well, I do," Tashiana, said weakly.

"You act like one of those old stuck-up pretty bitches who think she is too good to hang out with the rest of us. Are you?" Jessica asked with hands on hips.

"No I'm not. I'm married, and have children that need me at home that's all," Tashiana explained.

"I thought maybe it was because you're the bosses' favorite girl, and you don't want them to see you hanging out with the office tramps," Jessica said.

"Why would you think something like that? This is not the first time you asked me to go out with you guys, and I tell you why every time you ask me. So why are you sweating me?" Tashiana asked.

"Sorry if that's the vibes you're getting from this little conversation. We just want everyone in the office to be one big happy family, that's all," Jessica explained.

"In that case, I'll see what Dominique has to say," Tashiana said giving in to the peer pressure.

"I bet when you tell Dominique you're going out with the girls from the office to unwind, he won't mind at all. You wanna bet?" Jessica asked.

"No, I don't wanna bet. I'll tell him I'm going out with you girls this coming Friday, how about that?"

"That's a girl. I'll pick you up around eleven. We don't start the party here in Alaska before eleven-thirty," Jessica said.

"Who else is going with us?" Tashiana asked, wondering how Dominique was going to react to her telling him what she was going to do as apposed to asking him if it was ok as she had in the past.

"A couple more old married broads. They're going to show you the ropes it takes to have fun and take care of the home as well. These women get more than I do, and they're married. Do you believe that shit? Well, anyway, you be ready now. And don't come up with this, I got a headache shit. I'll pick you up around eleven, okay?" Jessica asked.

"I said I was going, didn't I?" Tashiana said.

Jessica doing the driving was fine with Tashiana, because she was terrified of driving on icy roads. Tashiana was so afraid she refused to drive during the winter months, unless there was an emergency and she had no choice. As a result of that fear she rode the bus to and from work. Dominique tried to get her to drive so she could get over the fear of driving on ice, but Tashiana refused. After the first snowfall in Alaska, around the end of October she placed her drivers license in a glass case with a note that read 'in case of an emergency, break glass and use driver's license to drive your self where you need to go.'

That Friday night was the beginning of her search for that perfect world. The world that would allow her to do whatever she wanted in life without having to answer to anyone and not have to pay a price for any consequences that arise as a result of her misadventures.

When she told Dominique during dinner, Thursday evening, that the girls at the office had asked her to go out with them Friday night he didn't even miss a bite.

"Sure baby, that's fine with me," was all Dominique said.

Tashiana wondered if it really was possible to live a secret life and maintain a happy household. She would soon find out for herself.

The other two ole' married broads were Julia Crystal, white, and Carrie Sinclair, the other black chick in the office, both were very attractive and amply endowed. Julia had been married sixteen years, and Carrie seven. They were dressed to impress men. As far as Tashiana was concerned, they were only a sneeze away from being hoochie mamas. If either one bent over you could see their future. As soon as they entered the "Gold Dust" club, men scrambled around their table like a pack of male dogs finding a bitch in heat. It was obvious that these fair weather maidens were well known in this establishment. Jessica, Julia, and Carrie, all played the innocent fair maidens role well. However, being the new slab of meat on the grill, Tashiana received the most attention from the girl's regular pack of hounds. Each wanted the bragging rights, of who got a taste of this juicy morsel first. The special attention Tashiana was receiving didn't go unnoticed by her newfound friends.

"Damn, home girl's getting all the action," Carrie said, as Tashiana was asked to dance for the fourth time since they sat down. The three of them had been asked once each.

"Don't go getting all jealous and shit Carrie it was the same when Julia and I brought you out with us the first few times. When they find out she is not going to give up any trim, they'll back off," Jessica said.

"How do you know she won't give it up if she met the right guy?" Julia wanted to know.

"Believe me I know when a bitch is in heat. She's not there yet. All she needs a little help from friends like us," Jessica laughed. "Beside, Sal and Allen will be here before long, to snatch your asses out of here anyway," she finished.

"Still, it would be fun to get some of the attention from these bastards until they got here," Julia complained.

Tashiana was still on the dance floor when Allen arrived. When she returned to their table Allen asked, "Hey, what do we have here?" He stood and took her hand.

"This is Mrs. Tashiana Goodman. Tashiana, the leach that is holding your hand is Allen Burnside," Julia introduced them.

"Hi, how are you doing?" Tashiana said trying to retrieve her hand.

"Just fine, now that I have met you, pretty lady," Allen said.

"You can let go of her hand, and put your tongue back in your mouth, before you bite it off," Julia said.

Allen laughed and sat down. To keep from pissing Julia off, any further, he danced with her, Jessica, and Carrie before asking Tashiana to dance. While they were on the dance floor he asked her why she was getting mixed up with women like Julia, Jessica, and Carrie.

"What kind of women are they?" Tashiana asked.

"They tease the men they don't like, and screw the ones they do," he said, matter of fact.

"I guess you're one of the ones Julia like. Huh?" Tashiana asked.

"Guilty as charged. It's just that, you don't look like the club scene type. Hell, what you're wearing right now look as if it's the same dress you wore to work today. So, what's your story?" he asked.

"We all work for the same law firm. Jessica asked if I would like to hang out with them tonight. I said sure. So here I am. End of story," Tashiana said.

"Be careful who you hang out with, is all I'm saying. You don't want to be guilty by association. If you know what I mean," Allen warned.

"And what heinous crimes have they committed?" Tashiana asked. Curious as to why he was telling her to stay away from the woman he was sleeping with.

"Just take my word for it. If you want to be labeled as an easy lay, keep hanging with them," he advised. After the dance ended

Tashiana thanked him for the advice.

When Mr. Salvatore Spencer arrived, there were snickers all around the table. He was so proper, and he was a very articulate individual. It was easy to tell he was use to bossing people around. It wouldn't have been so comical if he hadn't been 5' 5" in stature. He sounded so proud of himself when he told the new woman in the group that he was the most powerful black stockbroker in Alaska. People came from around the world to get advice from him about different stocks. To Tashiana, he was a black clone of Felix Unger of the Odd Couple.

Carrie admitted it was the money that attracted her to him. Her husband didn't know that Sal had set her up a bank account, in which he insured the balance was never below five thousand dollars. He had been asking Carrie for months to divorce her husband and marry him.

When ask why she didn't divorce her husband and marry him, Carrie would laugh and say, "Can you imagine having to put up with him seven days a week. Why do you think his other three wives left him?"

As it turned out, Sal could be very charming when he wanted to be. He tried his best to impress Tashiana. He wouldn't let anyone at the table pay for anything. It irritated Allen to have Sal throwing his money around that way, but he said what the hell, he's saving me a buck or two. Allen was by no means a poor man, himself. He was doing very well in real estate. It amazed Tashiana to learn, with all their money, these were two of the most insecure men she'd ever met in her life. Julia and Carrie treated them like high price, fragile, toys. Something you show off every now and then. Then you put it away until it was time to show it off again.

Tashiana had never been the type of woman who could be

easily won over with money. It didn't mean she didn't respect men with money, just that an asshole was an asshole, rich or not. Also, men with money had a tendency to want to control the lives of the women they are involved with. Therefore, Tashiana found it surprising that Sal and Allen allowed themselves to be controlled by their lovers.

Tashiana had a really good time, and she loved the attention she received from every man who asked her to dance. She didn't dare let Julia and Carrie know how much she enjoyed the attention the men showed her, including Allen and Sal. Seeing the jealousy in the eyes of Jessica, Carrie, and Julia as the night progressed Tashiana knew, eventually, she would have to strike out on her own if she was to experience the power of her sexuality. She also knew it would probably be more fun if she clubed alone. However, it would take a while before she built up the nerve to do so. She hung with Jessica, Carrie, and Julia for a couple months before she started making the rounds solo. Tashiana knew it was time to break the bond with Jessica after she made a blatant pass at Dominique at an office party.

While approaching Dominique and Jessica, where they were deep in a conversation, Tashiana hesitated long enough to overhear Jessica saying to Dominique, "If anything ever goes wrong between you and Tashiana, you can always depend on me to help you through your pain and disappointment".

"Are you trying to tell me something?" Dominique asked.

"Not really. It's just that I've noticed that Tashiana has started hanging out at the clubs quite a bit these days. It's best to be prepared than sorry," Jessica said.

"Well, if anything comes up I'll let you know," Dominique said with a laugh.

"Dominique, I'm serious. You may think you have everything under control, but there is a situation developing in your marriage that you're not aware of. If you stop by my house we can talk about it," Jessica said, placing her hand on his arm.

"Look Jessica, I don't know what you're implying. I do know one thing though. I won't need your help even if something does happen between Tashiana and me. Beside, it would be foolish for me to run to the girlfriend who got her started clubbing in the first place. Don't you agree?" Dominique asked.

"Just keep the offer in mind," Jessica said demurely.

"Yeah, excuse me, I see someone I need to talk to," Dominique said and walked off, leaving Jessica with naughty thoughts going through her head

Tashiana knew Jessica was a whore, but she never thought she would be that damn bold. After Dominique walked off Tashiana when to where Jessica was standing and asked, "What the hell do you think you're doing hitting on my husband?"

"Chill-out home girl. I just wanted to see if your shit is tight, that's all," Jessica lied.

"Next time ask me. Don't go rubbing your ass all over my man," Tashiana warned her.

"I'll remember that, until you start giving it up at the club. Whether you want to admit it or not home girl you're game. So don't be surprised when poor Dominique finds out about it, and I'm the one offering him a shoulder to cry on," Jessica advised.

Although Jessica was right about her starting to fantasize about being with other men it didn't give her the right to disrespect her. "Until that time, you keep your horny ass to yourself," Tashiana said.

Jessica smiled and said, "Until that time pretty lady."

"By the way Jessica, Dominique doesn't do white meat," Tashiana said and walked away.

After the incident with Dominique, Jessica and Tashiana's friendship cooled considerably. They were still cordial at the office but they no longer hung-out together after work. Tashiana was right about it being more fun being at the clubs by herself. The guys gave her their undivided attention. They didn't have to pretend they liked her friends. Dominique accepted the fact that partying most weekends was what most people did in Alaska, if that was your thing. He wasn't a party animal as most of his friends were, and Tashiana had become. He never attempted to lock her away, or chastise her for partying until it started affecting their marriage. In the beginning their main disagreement was about their finances. Then she started pushing him beyond his limit by staying out later and later when she went out partying on weekends. In addition to her weekend jaunts, she started going for drinks with her girlfriends several days a week when she got off work.

Dominique dealt with her running the streets, without too much heartburn. What upset him most was, they were making enough money to have a decent bank account. Instead, they found themselves living from paycheck to paycheck, wasting money that should've been set aside for their children's education. It was spend, spend and spend, until they were almost completely broke. They had furniture meant for a mansion, enough crystal to start their own business, and they had eaten out so often at expensive restaurants the kids were happy when they got plain old hotdogs. Although Dominique disliked the life style Tashiana wanted to portray, like an idiot, he went along with whatever she wanted to do, trying in vain to make her happy.

On a Friday night, which turned out to be the beginning of her unfaithfulness, Tashiana said, "Darling, there is a new disco club opening on Mountain Street tonight. Let's go," she suggested, knowing he probably wouldn't because he had to work at the clinic that weekend.

Tashiana's real intention for asking Dominique to take her dancing was to make him feel guilty for neglecting what she wanted to do. She used his refusal to become a party animal as an excuse to justify why she always partied alone. Therefore, Tashiana could mess with the heads of the men at the nightclubs without feeling too much guilt. It was fun getting them all worked up thinking they were going to get her into bed, and then saying her good nights, I hope to see you later. Tashiana knew Dominique wouldn't allow her to do that sort of thing if he was with her, plus she was feeling bitchy.

"I don't want to go to a disco club tonight. Besides, I have weekend duty tomorrow, and have to get up early. You know that," Dominique said. Going to nightclubs was all she wanted to do lately.

"You're a very boring person. You know that? Maybe I should find someone who enjoys doing the same things that I do," Tashiana said.

"Yeah, like yourself, who forgets or doesn't give a damn that they have kids to take care of. All you do is get off from work every evening and weekends, and hit the road, leaving the kids to find whatever they can to eat. If I didn't cook around this damn place the kids would probably starve. If you did find this prince in shining armor what would you do with the kids put them up for adoption?" Dominique asked. He tried to make her feel guilty because she'd been neglecting the children. She was not swayed.

"I didn't say anything about not including the kids in my life. Hell, they would probably be happy to have someone who would take them some place other than McDonald or Kentucky Fried Chicken. And you're always trying to save every damn penny you get your hands on," Tashiana snorted.

"McDonald and KFC is a welcome relief from that overly expensive shit we're always eating at Captain Cooke's Seafood Shack and all the other restaurants you call your favorite places to eat. Besides, what the hell are we going to do for money when these kids grow up and start high school and then college? All of that shit cost money you know, or are you thinking that far ahead? Do you want them to grow up and become legal assistants or x-ray technicians? Apparently you haven't given it much thought, or you're so blinded by the streets you don't give a damn. Do you realize that you're wasting money as if you're a millionaire, or some rich assed jet setter with money to burn? You'd better wake up to the real world before you find yourself out on the streets competing with the rest of the homeless bitches with no families to go home to. But knowing your mind set right now, you'd probably enjoy having only yourself to worry about."

"I haven't forgot how expensive it is to raise kids. That's why you're no longer the only breadwinner in this family. You don't have to give me any of your money if you don't want to because I make enough to take care of myself, and the kids. You know the majority of the money I spend is on the kids, or the house, anyway. But, it's not the kids or the money you're concerned about. Is it? You know men will do anything for a woman as beautiful as me, huh?" Tashiana smiled, and continued. "You have probably guessed by now that I love making those stupid fools do whatever I tell them to. You men are all alike. You'll do anything a woman tell you to, as long as you think you have a chance to get in her pants," Tashiana finished.

"Almost all men," Dominique corrected her. "Then there are those men who know your beautiful face and body isn't going to last forever. What then, Tashiana? Are you going to be like the other old broads who hang around the nightclubs, hoping some man will think you're pretty enough to buy you a drink? And maybe later take you to bed? How would you explain to your children why you chose the streets over them?"

"Damn, I don't believe this long ass lecture is because I ask you to take me dancing. Why do you have to make everything so damn complicated? I love you, and the kids, more than I do the streets. I just want them to have all the things I never had, and have a little fun during the process. What the hell is wrong with that?" Tashiana asked, becoming angry.

As usual his resistance began to fail him when she used that logic, because he too wanted the same things for the children, but he was looking at the long-term expenses of raising the kids. Tashiana was talking about instant gratification, which she had a tendency to overdo.

Dominique said, "I believe the part about you wanting the kids to have the things you never had, which can't be that much considering the amount of money your family have, but it still doesn't change the fact that you're becoming a common club woman, and if you don't let up, you're out of here," he warned. He had really wanted to say club whore, but thought better of it.

"I won't be missing much, as far as you're concerned," Tashiana hissed, and continued before he could say anything. "I refuse to leave my kids, or my home. I know it upsets you when I go out and stay late, but all I do is dance and have a good time. I want it to be with you, but you never want to go any place," she lied, changing tactics. Tashiana knew Dominique could never make her feel the way the men at the clubs did. For him she held no secrets. However, the men she teased at the clubs would give anything to find out what made her tick.

"I'll try to go out with you more often in the future," Dominique said. He had said that at least a thousand times since she started going out alone.

"I know darling," she said, on her way upstairs to get ready for Harvey Kitchen.

Bishop Harvey Kitchen was the minister of the largest Baptist church in Anchorage, Alaska, and the city's most celebrated Televangelist and widower. Unknown to his congregation, he was also one of the biggest sinners God ever allowed to preach to a congregation in one of his houses of worship. The good bishop was considered the soul of Alaska's religious community. His followers consisted of all races and nationalities. The women in his congregation laid themselves at his feet for both religious guidance and sexual satisfaction. He wore $800.00 suits and $200 shoes. You could catch his sermons every Sunday morning from 7 - 8 a.m. Dominique listened to a couple of his sermons and considered him just another Sunday morning religious pimp, milking the people who were looking for God's help and mercy to change their lives for the better.

Harvey tried to get Tashiana to join his church, but she always told him she couldn't go into God's House pretending to be something she wasn't. She was surprised God hadn't struck him down for being such a phony.

Bishop Kitchen and Tashiana met several weeks earlier at the "Goldminer's Disco Club" in downtown Anchorage. He was supposedly doing some research for an upcoming sermon he was going to give about the evils of hanging out in nightclubs. However, upon seeing Tashiana walk into the club all thoughts of religious research were forgotten. She was so beautiful, Bishop Kitchen experienced a lust so deep he was sure it would land him in hell, but it were a journey he was willing to take if he could get to know her. As soon as she walked into the club, he knew to get next to a woman as beautiful as Tashiana, he would have to be willing to give her the clothes off of his back.

If that's what it takes to get next to her, she can have my church and house as well,
Bishop Kitchen said to himself. He had to have her.

He sat staring at her for an hour before he got up the nerve to go over to her table and ask her for a dance.

"Excuse me beautiful lady, would you give me the pleasure of a dance," Reverend Kitchen asked.

"Sure," Tashiana accepted.

While they were dancing, he asked her name and told her how beautiful she was and what he would do for her, or give her, if she continued seeing him.

"You have got to be the most beautiful woman in the whole state of Alaska, possibly the whole world. I would give you anything your heart desired if you will be my friend," he promised.

When the dance ended the good reverend invited her to share his table. He was everything Tashiana never looked for in a man, short, fat, half bald, and ugly, but there were something about him that was different from the others guys who had hit on her in the clubs. Not being a religious person it took Tashiana a few minutes before recognizing him.

"Excuse me, aren't you the preacher whose sermons are shown

on television every Sunday morning?" she asked.

"Guilty as charge, I'm the one and only Bishop Harvey Kitchen," he confessed.

"Well what bring a man of your stature into this den of sins, located in the bowels of the city?" Tashiana asked.

"I was doing research for a sermon on the evil of frequenting night clubs until I saw you walk in. Now I believe it wasn't the evil of the clubs that led me here it was the chance of meeting with you. God works in mysterious ways," Bishop Kitchen said.

"I don't know about all that reverend, but I'm surprised to find a preacher in a night club drinking cognac," she said.

"My dear beautiful lady, Jesus and his disciples all drank wine. He said it's not a sin unless you abused the spirits and become a drunkard. The only thing I'm drunk with this night is your beauty. Allow me to be your slave for the evening and satisfy your every desire. As a matter of fact allow me to be your slave forever," Bishop Kitchen said.

"My husband may have something to say about me bringing home a slave that is considered the heart and soul of Anchorage's religious community," Tashiana laughed.

"There's my house. How about going home with me and let me be your slave? And I'll make sure you never want for anything as long you live," he promised.

"What about my husband and children? Am I supposed to fall head over heels for you and leave my family? You're a very impressive individual Mr. Kitchen, but I'm not that type of woman. I come to these clubs to satisfy my alter ego that craze the attention of these horny men. However, their attention is all I craze, not sexual satisfaction," Tashiana explained.

Bishop Kitchen was not deterred. He said, "Breaking up your

family is the last thing I would attempt to do. What I'm saying is, I will insure that whatever your husband cannot afford to provide for you I will. Or, whatever is missing in your life I want to fill that void. It doesn't matter if the void is mentally, socially, financially, or sexually, I will always be there for you," he said.

"Look Reverend Kitchen ......

"Call me Harvey, please," he interjected.

"Look Harvey, I know you're supposed to be the next best thing to God and all, but I'm not on the make. So if you don't mind please back off," she said.

Before he could respond, a waitress brought the drinks they ordered to their table and he paid for them with a hundred dollar bill and told her to keep the change, which amounted to an eighty-dollar tip for the lucky girl.

"That tip I just gave to that waitress is nothing compared to what I'm willing to give to you. You are a diamond in the rough and don't know it. Give me the chance to polish and carve you into the lady God intended you to be," he said taking her hand into his.

"Very pretty words for a preacher who makes a living saving people souls. You think God would approve of our union knowing you're taking another man's wife to bed. And you can stop throwing your money in my face. I know you have something other than hundred dollar bills to pay for drinks," Tashiana said.

Still Harvey was not deterred. He said, "Tashiana, for you I'm willing to give my soul to the devil if that's what it takes to get to know you better. I know thousand of women and not one have the effect on me that you have. I don't quite know how to explain it, but if you give me a chance time will make it clear to the both of us. What do you say?" he asked.

"I don't know. Maybe we should take some time to get to know each other better before we start giving our souls to the devil, or forming a union that would be disapproved by God. What would your congregation and the million of people who believe in you say knowing you are going around picking up loose women in nightclubs? I don't know about this Harvey, it's something I have to think about," Tashiana said seriously.

"Take as much time as you like, I'm not planning on going anywhere any time soon. Here is my business card, call me," he handed her the card.

"I'll make it a little easier for you. How about meeting me here tomorrow night," Tashiana said.

"I can't make a habit of being seen in public night clubs, so how about I give you a pass to the private night club I belong to. That is where I counsel my upscale church members, so no one will suspect a thing," he said handing a pass to the "Gentleman's Social Club" to her.

"Alright Harvey, it a date but don't read anything into my meeting you tomorrow. For all I know you may be one of those old bible thumping, women chasing preachers my daddy use to warn me about," she said.

"I assure you I'm not. So, let's enjoy the remainder of the evening shall we?" he asked.

Although Tashiana had caught herself fantasizing about being with another man from time to time, she realized she had not been serious at all until this night. She had been to every club in Anchorage, and met all types of guys. It surprised her that she would be attracted to someone like the good Reverend Harvey Kitchen. She had resisted the temptation of all the hunks that hit on her while cruising the clubs. She even resisted the temptation of cheating on Dominique while hanging with Jessica and her friends, and they were screwing a different guy almost every weekend. Jessica had put her in a couple of awkward situations with men who she had promised them Tashiana would put out. When the guys pressured her, or she found herself losing control of the situation, she left the club and went home. But there was something different about Harvey. She believe he was sincere about his beliefs of how a woman as beautiful as herself should be treated, not so much the amount of money he was willing to spend on, or give her.

She didn't want to appear too easy or anxious so she danced with the majority of the men who asked her. It was well known by the majority of the male patrons of the club that the lovely lady was married, but it wasn't to the reverend she was sitting with.

Watching her dance with other men made him want her even more. He had never felt so insecure around a woman in his life. He was scared to death some tall handsome dude she already knew would come along and take her from right under his nose. After each dance, he had a fresh drink waiting for her. When she decided to accept his invitation to have breakfast with him, there were at least ten drinks left on the table untouched. During breakfast she advised him not to push her to fast. *After all, I'm a married woman and have to protect my reputation*, she said to herself.

She arrived home at 4:15 a.m. Dominique was waiting for her, but didn't say a word when she came in. He just stared as if she was something to be pitied.

"Well, aren't you going to say anything?" she asked, her heart pounding in her chest.

"I had planned on saying a lot, but if I say what I had planned on saying we would only end up fighting as usual. I'll talk to you in the morning after I've calmed down," he said, and started upstairs for bed.

Tashiana followed Dominique upstairs, expecting him to turn on her with each step. He didn't. The prospect of sleeping with another man had her so sexually arouse, she attacked him as soon as they got under the covers. Dominique had no intentions of making love to her, but she was so excited she was not to be denied. It had been a long time since they made love with no holds barred. Afterward, while lying there listening to her gentle breathing, he wondered what had happened at the club, or who she had met at the club, that had gotten her so aroused. There was no doubt in his mind, that a man was involved. He hoped she hadn't made love to that man also.

Because she had gotten home so late, he didn't bother waking her when he got up to cook breakfast for the kids. He knew her lateness should have been a warning sign that her respect for him and their marriage was on the wane. But the only thought going through his mind was the incredible lovemaking of the previous night, or early morning. The anger he felt while waiting for her to get home was also washed from his head by their unhindered passion. However, in his subconscious mind he could not ignore the fact that something, or someone, had caused her excitement.

When Tashiana came downstairs later that morning Dominique asked, "What the hell happened at the club last night to get you so all fired up?"

"If I tell you the truth, you won't get mad will you?" Tashiana asked, with a devilish smile on her face.

"I don't know," he answered, bracing for the worst possible thing she could tell him.

"Well, I don't know if I should tell you," she teased.

"Okay, I promise I won't get mad. So tell me already," Dominique encouraged her, knowing if she said she had been to bed with another man he would probably end up punching her lights out.

"This guy tried to get me to go to a motel with him last night. He's not the first one, but this guy was stupid with his money. He bought me enough drinks to get half the people in the club drunk. He kept telling me how beautiful I am, and what he would give me if he could see me again. So I led him to believe I would see him again. I had him so excited he would've jumped in front of a bull moose if I had asked him to. I waited until the last song of the night to slow dance with him. After the dance it was time to come home to you. That was very exciting to me, being able to make a man do stupid things," Tashiana finished, omitting who the man was and that she had breakfast with him. She knew Dominique would be pissed with her for having anything to do with the Bishop Harvey Kitchen, because to Dominique the televangelist was a Sunday morning pimp, milking the poor religious people for their last hard-earned dime. Tashiana also omitted she was seriously wondering, for the first time, what it would feel like to cheat on him.

"So what the hell is going to happen when you get so excited you can't wait until you get home? Huh? Are you going to screw the bastard you're teasing?" Dominique asked, but felt no jealousy.

"I know how far to go my dear," she assured him.

"Just make sure you do. But this slow dancing shit is out. Understand?"

"Oh, all right. If that's the way you feel about it," Tashiana pretended to pout.

"One other thing, no more of this coming home after four in the morning bullshit," Dominique added.

"I'm sorry about that honey. I guess I lost all tracks of time. It won't happen again. I promise."

"Just make sure it doesn't," Dominique said forgetting several hours ago he had wanted to wring her neck.

Tashiana detected no real anger in his voice. This gave her the confidence to ask, "You don't mind me teasing guys as long as I don't go to bed with them do you?"

"I guess it'll be alright, as long as you know how far to go. And you don't get caught up in your own web," Dominique approved. Beside, he knew she was already teasing men at the clubs, and he was tired of stressing about it all the time.

She got so excited at him agreeing to let her tease the men at the clubs openly it put her in the mood again.

"Where are the kids?" Tashiana whispered, looking around.

"In the basement I think. Why?" Dominique answered.

"Let go upstairs and catch a quickie," she suggested, stroking him to show she was serious. Having been accused of being a male nymphomaniac, he did not disappoint her.

That Saturday evening after dinner, as she was getting ready to go out, Dominique sat in front of the television chastising himself for being stupid enough to allow his wife to openly flirt with other men. Especially with the knowledge that alcohol reduces your resistance level, which meant she would eventually get caught in her own trap. He remembered the ugly women he had woken up with while serving his country. On the other hand, it was exciting to him to think of other men groveling at his wife's feet thinking they could get what already belonged to him, for now anyway.

These liberal feelings he had toward other men hitting on his wife was directly attributed to T. V. Since they had gotten the Cinemax Movie Channel on cable television, he had become addicted to watching the nude, big-breasted women on the screen cheating on their husbands. It made him feel that he was not the only man in the world who couldn't keep his wife at home, being the mother and wife she should be. And if she were being unfaithful, he and Tashiana would sit down and work out their differences, eventually, just as the men and women on television always did. After all, his problem would be the same problem the men on the screen had. The only thing he wondered was, when that time came, would he be able to handle in real life what he knew on screen was make believe. In their on screen lives, the men all had one thing in common. When they found out what was going on behind their backs, they still loved their wives and found it in their hearts to forgive them. Some even joined their wives in their escapades by becoming members of wife swapping clubs.

He watched so many of those type movies he had reached the point where he had started to wonder what it would be like to watch Tashiana make love to another man. Dominique cussed himself for having such unnatural thoughts. The television characters always made him feel if you couldn't have the woman you loved all to yourself, if you tried hard enough, you could learn to live with sharing her. His liberal thoughts were soon to be tested.

Tashiana on the other hand, found these movies to be totally disgusting. Whenever she was home, she would complain so much he would have to change the channel. Although she didn't say it, she did not like the movies because the women on the screen made her feel inadequate in the breast department. All the women they chose to play those roles had breasts twice the size of hers. And to top it off, the majority of them were white.

Later, the movies would make her uncomfortable because she was doing in real life what the women were doing on the screen. Tashiana wished Dominique was as understanding as the husbands on television, but realized those husbands was only make believe while she was playing with real fire. Tashiana figured sooner or later she was going to get burnt, but until that time it was let the good times roll.

While Dominique was wondering what it would be like watching Tashiana with another man, she never told him that their next door neighbors, Raymond and Joleen Simpson, tried to get her to talk to him about wife swapping with them. They were a nice enough looking white couple, but Tashiana thought Dominique would not even consider something so sick. Black men weren't into stuff like that she told them. If for no other reason, she figured, Dominique would reject Joleen because her breasts were even smaller than hers, and Joleen wore glasses so thick they looked like the bottom of coke bottles. Tashiana knew for a fact, she could never go to bed with Raymond because he was no bigger than a broom handle, and had enough acne for several individuals his size.

Several times, while visiting Joleen, she watched while they made love, but never joined in their activities. She had been tempted on a couple of occasions but seeing all that acne on Raymond face relieved her of any desire she may have felt.

Tashiana's little escapade of voyeurism started innocently enough. While taking a day of comp time she had gone over to Joleen's house one day to borrow a couple of eggs, without knowing Raymond was home for lunch. Dominique was at work, the kids were in school, and daycare, and she was bored out of her mind. So she decided to cook a full course mean for a change. After knocking, she looked through the window of the door. There they were on the living room couch getting it on. She knew she should have turned around and left, but the scene inside froze her in place. Joleen was on top of Raymond, riding for all she was worth.

Upon hearing the knock, Joleen looked over. Recognizing who it was, she beckoned for Tashiana to come on in.

Tashiana swallowed the lump in her throat and entered. She could hardly speak when she asked to borrow the eggs. After asking, she turned to go to the refrigerator, but Joleen stopped her.

"Hey, don't leave. Stay and watch. It's a real turn on for us when someone watches while we get it on. Isn't it Ray?" she smiled down at him as she continued to ride him.

"It would be even more of a turn on if you joined us Tashiana. We have wondered for quite some time what it would be like to have you in bed with us," Ray said, his attention focused on her.

"I'm sorry, I interrupted you guys. I gotta go," Tashiana said, feeling both embarrassed and excited at the same time.

"Wait a minute," Joleen said, getting off of Ray in a hurry to stop her from leaving.

Ray's member was now standing erect in full view. Tashiana tried to tear her gaze away from him, but was frozen in place as if hypnotized. It was the first time in her life she had ever seen a white man's thing. It was so red it looked as if he should be in pain.

"Have you ever watched, in person, while a woman pleased her man?" Joleen asked. Tashiana could only shake her head. "Well watch this," Joleen instructed, taking hold of Ray's excited tool and placing it where Tashiana had only read about in true confessions magazines, or watched on porn films when she and some of her girlfriends would get together for a girl's night out.

Tashiana's eyes widened as more and more of Ray disappeared. She kept waiting for Joleen to gag, and throw up all over the place. She soon realized Joleen knew what she was doing. Joleen increased her up and down motion on him until he gave a loud moan and stiffened. Joleen pulled away just far enough for Tashiana to see what the moaning was all about. She felt so nauseous she turned and ran from the house, forgetting why she had gone over there.

Tashiana had been so shaken by the incident it took her close to an hour to calm down enough to finish cooking. No dessert today troops, she said to herself. It wasn't often she was caught in the kitchen cooking full course meals from scratch these days.

Joleen came over a couple of hours later with the two eggs Tashiana had wanted to borrow. Joleen apologized for asking her to stay and watch. Tashiana told her to forget it, because she could've left if she had really wanted to. Joleen tried to convince her that having a man climax where only food and water is suppose to go wasn't bad at all. Tashiana would have none of it. Dominique had been trying to convince her of that since the day they were married.

After that incident, Joleen always told Tashiana when Ray was coming home for lunch. She gave in to their request on a couple of occasions and watched their noontime encounters. It was after these escapades they tried to get her to ask Dominique if he would consider joining them.

Yeah, right, she said, knowing Dominique would never do anything like that.

Tashiana came downstairs looking more beautiful than

Dominique had seen her look in quite sometime.

"Well, how do I look?" she asked, twirling to give him an all around view.

God, I must be crazy for letting such a beautiful woman run loose in the streets. Knowing she's going to go to bed with some man sooner or later, if she hasn't already, he said to himself. To her Dominique said, "Damn, you're beautiful. I don't think I should let you out of the house looking that good. If I were the guy you were teasing, I would follow you out to the parking lot and rape your butt. I don't know. You'd better be careful who you tease," he said seriously.

"What're you doing tonight?"

"There's a couple of movies coming on tonight I wanted to watch."

"Those damn old titty movies again huh?" she said, sounding disappointed. "Don't I have enough to offer?" she asked, standing in a sexy pose.

"Sure, you do baby. Why don't you stay home tonight, and make love to me until the sun comes up tomorrow morning," Dominique suggested.

"I thought you had to work tomorrow," she said.

"I do, but I wouldn't mind going to work tired from making love to my beautiful wife," he answered

Knowing Saturday night was his night to fantasize about being with those big tit white women on the screen she said, "We can do that when I get home."

"Okay, but none of this 4:00 a.m. bullshit," he reminded her.

"Okay, okay, I know. Could you drop me off at Susan house? We're going to hangout together tonight," Tashiana lied. She knew Susan would cover for her if Dominique decided to ask where they had gone that night.

"Sure, but how are you going to get home?"

"If it's not too late, I'll give you a call from Susan's house. Otherwise, I'll just get Susan to give me a ride home," she said.

He dropped her off at the club and hurried back home to the television set, so he wouldn't miss anything. He would get to enjoy both movies because she didn't normally call him until around 2 a.m. to pick her up. It crossed his mind she may be coming home later than 2 a.m. because Susan and her posse was known for closing clubs at 5 a.m., but he dismissed the thought as being paranoid.

Tashiana didn't dare ask Dominique to drop her off at a private club because he would know something fishy was going on. She took a taxi from Susan's house to the club. Upon her arrival she didn't know what to expect, but after showing her pass all her fears were relieved. The club staff treated Tashiana as if she was a VIP who frequented the club on a regular basis. She learned later that all of the Reverend guests were given special treatment. For this second meeting with Harvey Kitchen, Tashiana walked into the club looking like a sex goddess from another planet. She turned the head of every man in the club. Harvey tripped, and almost fell, when he jumped up from the table to come over to meet her. He already had a cognac and coke on the table waiting for her.

"I didn't think you were going to show up," Harvey said.

"I told you I'd be here, didn't I? You think I'm a liar, or something?" Tashiana snapped.

"No, no, please forgive me if that's what it sounded like" he apologized.

Although she was nervous as hell, she didn't want him to know it. She had decided to play the role of a bitch to see how bad he wanted to be with her.

She took a sip of the drink on the table and said, "I can't drink this watered down stuff. If you want to be with me, you've got to do better than this."

"Wait right here. I'll get you a fresh one from the bar."

He hurried to the bar to get the fresh drink. While he was gone she took the time to look around the club. Tashiana had ever been to such an elegant club. The chair cushions were made with soft black leather and the tables were made of mahogany wood. On the walls hung copies of paintings by famous artists like Monet, Van Gogh, Picasso, etc., that she had studied during her short enrollment in college. The place smelled of old money. There was a live band playing music from the Big Band era. Tashiana didn't care for the music but to be a real bitch, while Harvey was at the bar getting the drinks, she accepted a dance with the guy sitting at the table across from theirs. When Harvey returned to the table, he looked like a sick puppy. He sat staring at her on the dance floor.

When she sat down he said, "I guess you couldn't wait to get on the dance floor, huh?"

He said it in such a tone she wanted to make him suffer. There was only one man in the world who could lay claim to her, and that was Dominique, although they were drifting apart. She became angry knowing he was at home watching those damn semi-nude movies, and knowing there was nothing she could do to make him stop. So she took her anger out on Harvey.

"Back off buddy boy, you don't own me, you know. Therefore, I'll dance with whomever I choose to, whenever I want to. If you can't deal with that let's end this little charade right now," Tashiana growled, sounding like a coiled snake ready to strike.

Fearing he was about to blow his chance to be with the most

beautiful woman he had ever been associated with, he became docile. "I'm sorry, Tashiana. I didn't mean to come on like a jealous husband or anything like that. Let's forget everything I have said up to now and start over. What do you say?" he asked pleadingly.

"All right Harvey, but don't forget, I can always go home," she threatened.

Relieved that Tashiana was not going to walk out on him Harvey handed her a menu and told her to order anything she wanted from the menu, including the three hundred dollar bottle of champagne. Just because she had no intention of giving in to his demands didn't mean she should not enjoy herself. Tashiana figured it was a one in a lifetime opportunity to live large so she ordered the most expensive meal on the menu and the three hundred dollar bottle of champagne. Several male members of Reverend Kitchen's club acquaintances asked if they could dance with Tashiana. He told them not to keep her too long because he was counseling her on some very important religious matters that required her full attention.

Despite her early rudeness to Harvey she had a very good time. He catered to her every whim. At 2:30 a.m. they were both pretty drunk, and Harvey was in the mood. So was Tashiana, but she had made up her mind she wouldn't sleep with him that night either. She knew it was going to make him mad when she told him, but if he still wanted to be with her he would wait until she was ready. They were dancing to a slow song. She could feel his tremendous excitement straining against the fabric of her dress.

"Come on, Tashiana, how about it?" he whispered in her ear.

"How about what?" Tashiana asked, pretending ignorance.

Harvey squeezed her tighter, and pressed harder against her.

Tashiana matched his movements. She got so excited she almost changed her mind and gave in, but in the end she stood by her earlier decision.

"You know damn well what I'm talking about. Come on and go home with me. I've never wanted a woman as much as I want you," Harvey pleaded.

"I don't know about tonight. I promised my husband I would be home, no later than 3 a.m., and here it is already 2:30," she informed him.

"Come on, baby. You can't do this to me. I've got to have you. I'll do anything you want me to. Please go home with me tonight, even if it's for only a little while," he continued to beg.

"I'll let you know after the dance," Tashiana answered, giving him a ray of hope.

They continued their shameless pretense of dancing to the beat of the music. She nibbled at Harvey's neck and ears. All of a sudden he groaned and pulled away from her, saying he had to go to the restroom. From the way he walked, she could tell he had become overly excited. Tashiana went to their table and laughed until tears were running down her face. People stared at her as if they were watching a fruitcake coming unglued. Only after seeing Harvey returning from the restroom was she able to compose herself.

"What was that all about" she giggled. It took all the will power she possessed to keep from going into another hysterical fit of laughter.

"You know damn well what happened," Harvey said, embarrassed.

"No, I don't reverend. Why don't you tell me," Tashiana insisted.

He didn't say anything, just moved away from the table far enough for her to see the damp stain at the crotch of his pants. Because he was wearing a dark suit, the stain was not too obvious. A person who didn't know what had happened would not have noticed it. This time she did laugh.

"Hey, that's not funny. See how excited you make me. Come on. Go to my place with me. I won't try to keep you there all night," Harvey said, taking her hands in his.

"I would like to, but like I told you, I promised my husband I wouldn't stay out late tonight. Besides, it appears you have already shot your load," Tashiana said, between giggles.

"The only way to find out for sure is to go home with me," he challenged her.

"Maybe some other time, please take me home. I really do have to be getting home. And you have to be at your church early this morning," she said.

He swore under his breath, but dropped her off a short distance from her house.

"Will I see you next weekend?" he asked hopefully.

"I have your church number. I'll give you a call sometime during the week. Bye, bye for now," Tashiana said, giving him a sisterly peck on the cheek.

When she walked into the house at 3:08 a.m. there sat Dominique in front of the television. On the screen were two women with the biggest set of breasts she had ever seen uncovered. She became angry instantly, but did her best to keep the anger out of her voice. It amazed her how he could watch those damn movies until 3 or 4 a.m. in the morning and still get up in time to go to work.

Tashiana said, "Hi, honey, I'm home. What're you watching?"

"Just a movie," Dominique answered, without even taking his eyes from the screen.

Tashiana laid her purse down and went and sat in his lap. She discovered his member was standing fully erect. She had planned on complaining about the movie so he would change the channel, or turned the television off. Feeling his excited member against her over heated buttocks made her forget her anger.

"Why don't we go upstairs and do the wild thang," Tashiana suggested.

"Good idea," Dominique agreed, clicking off the television.

He carried Tashiana up the stairs and laid her on the bed. Being they were both excited beyond belief, they made love like over eager teenagers experiencing sex for the first time. After they finished, she became angry again.

"Honey, why do you have to watch those damn tittie movies all the time? Don't I excite you anymore?" she asked.

"Sure you excite me. I think it's better to watch the women on the screen where I can't touch them, than going to a club and trying to find out what they look like undressed. Beside, I may run into a teaser like you. Maybe the freaks you tease get off on shit like that, but I wouldn't. Whether I'm looking for anything or not. This way, I get to see women of all nationalities semi-nude. So, by watching them on television, I see what I want to see, and I don't even have to leave the house. But believe me baby none of them can hold a candle next to you" he explained.

"I hear what you're saying, but sometimes when we make love I can't help from thinking you're fantasizing about those big titty white women you be watching on T.V. Like tonight, how long has it been since you got that exited by me saying let's make love?" Tashiana asked.

"You get me excited all the time. It doesn't matter if you are naked or fully clothed. You know that" Dominique defended himself.

She couldn't deny what he said, but she wanted to argue. "How am I supposed to know you're thinking of me instead of those big breasted women on the boob tube? Maybe, I'm a fill in because you can't get to them. Maybe, that's how you compensate for my itty-bitty titties," she said, and continued. "In your mind you put a big set of tits on me, and it's whoopee time."

"I don't know what got your dandruff up, but you're full of it. There isn't a woman in this world that can hold a candle to you. You're my own personal sex goddess. It gets me excited watching them on television sometimes, but in real life you're the only woman I want", he said kissing her.

"Just make sure it remains that way, or I may go a little farther than teasing the men I meet at the clubs," Tashiana warned.

It was Dominique turn to become angry. "What the hell happened tonight that's causing you to be in such a foul mood? Did you finally meet some bastard that made you want to give it up?"

"No, it's not that. It upsets me to know how much you like watching women with breasts bigger than what I have to offer. Not to mention that the majority of them are white. How am I supposed to know you're not thinking about finding yourself one of those big titty white girls to satisfy your curiosity?" Tashiana asked.

"Well, if it upsets you that much, I just won't watch them anymore," he lied. It would take a hell of a lot more than her getting upset to stop him from watching those type movies. He just wouldn't watch them while she was home.

Tashiana figured he was lying but said, "I would appreciate that very much."

Without realizing it at the time, she was looking for an excuse that would allow her to go to bed with Harvey without feeling too guilty. Tashiana realized this upon returning home from visiting a friend several nights later. When she entered the house, there sat Dominique in front of the television watching boobs. They had a shouting match about it before going to bed. She fell asleep thinking what a happy man Harvey was going to be that coming weekend. Dominique had given her the excuse she needed to be unfaithful. And if he found out she was being unfaithful, she would tell him she had warned him what would happen if he didn't give up watching those damn movies. Tashiana tried, to no avail, to convince herself that Dominique had no one to blame for her infidelity but him self. In her heart she knew she wanted the adventure the good Reverend Kitchen could provide. She also knew it was going take sex to get him do what she wanted him to, but what the hell everyone had to give the devil his due to get what they wanted. With mixed emotions Tashiana went through with what she said she would do if Dominique didn't stop watching those movies. She called Harvey several times during the next couple of days saying she needed to see and talk to him, but he couldn't get away from the church until that Friday evening.

Tashiana met him at his private club that Friday night, and after several drinks she said, "Harvey, you've treated me better than any man I have ever known, other than my husband. But, I don't know if I should go to bed with you. How do I know you won't blackmail me by threatening to tell my husband about us if I don't continue seeing you?"

"Tashiana, you can rest assured I would never do anything so juvenile. I want to prove to you just how much I care for you. I'll do anything you want me to. You can call the shots, if that's what you want. But please don't keep me waiting any longer. You're driving me crazy," Harvey said.

"Why the hell should I believe you? Men are all alike, preachers included. You make all kind of promises until you get what you want. Then, it's off to conquer the next woman that looks good to you. I don't think I want to be used like that," Tashiana said looking serious, but smiling inside.

A film of sweat broke out on Harvey's forehead as he thought he saw his chance of being with her slipping away. "I'm not like that at all, Tashiana. I won't tell a soul about the two of us. I'll do anything to be with you. And to show you I mean what I say, you can have everything I own. I'm serious about that. I don't even care that the congregation is starting to talk because it has been reported I was seen making a spectacle of myself while hanging out boozing with you here at the club," he babbled.

"I've never cheated on my husband, and I'm still not sure if I truly want to start now. If I do, I want it to be with someone who cares for me. Not because of my looks. You do care for me, don't you Harvey?" she asked.

"You know I do. And I'm going to prove to you how much," he said, happier than he had imagined he'd be if she finally gave in.

They left the club and went to his house. Compared to Tashiana's home it was a mansion, but being he was a minister it was decorated with modern furniture and the walls were adorned with religious symbols and pictures. The only real luxury he allowed himself was the marble tiled bathroom floor, and showerheads and sink handles made of gold, and his canopied bed.

"Welcome to my humble abode," Harvey said upon opening the

door.

"Humble is an under statement," Tashiana said looking around.

"Everything you see here can be yours, or I can arrange for you have a house just like it if you wish," Harvey said.

"Not on my salary. Beside, you don't even know me yet, and you're saying you'll do all these things for me. I'm starting to get nervous about this whole setup. I'm starting to think you're the stalker type who'll start showing up at my door steps if you don't get your way," Tashiana said seriously.

"You don't have to worry about that. For some reason I know our paths were meant to cross and I'll do anything to see where that path leads. Rest assured my future love, I have only the best in mind for you," Harvey said and took her into his arms.

Harvey was nowhere near as good a lover as Dominique, but it didn't matter because sex was not the reason she started seeing him in the first place. A month after their first sexual encounter Tashiana started using Harvey to fulfill her fantasies of visiting places Dominique had argued about being too expensive to frequent on a regular basis. The Alyeska Ski Resort, and tours of the famous glaciers the state had to offer. Alaska has some of the most beautiful tourist spots in the world and she wanted to see them all. Tashiana knew in time, Dominique would have budgeted all those places in, but she wanted to do everything, and see everything, right then. Not to mention the thrill it gave her to know she could be caught cheating on Dominique every time she and Harvey were together. To cover her tracks for overnight stays with Harvey, she took Dominique's advice and joined a sightseeing club, which sponsored weekend tours once a month, although she only took advantage of the opportunity on two separate occasions. This arrangement was not as exciting as she thought it would be because the chances of her getting caught cheating were no longer in the equation. All she had to do was call Dominique from Harvey's house and tell him she had arrived safely at the appointed place and time. So Tashiana quit the club, and started pushing her luck.

The reason Dominique had suggested she join the tour club was this way he figured he would know where she was at least half the time. Dominique didn't mind her going with the club because they couldn't afford the money it cost to go as a family. Also, during these outings it gave him a chance to be alone, to ponder where their marriage was headed. Dominique came to the conclusion that Tashiana felt their marriage was headed for divorce court, especially after she quit the tour club and stayed gone all the time anyway. He often questioned his logic and his judgment, but he felt their marriage was worth saving. All he had to do was figure out what it would take to get her to stay at home more often. It really annoyed him when she stayed home just long enough to complain about how the kids were dressed, how their hair was combed, or what they should be eating. Tashiana mistook his understanding that husbands and wives needed to be by themselves sometimes, as a sign of weakness. She considered him a first class wimp, who would allow her to continue doing what she wanted to as long as she wanted to. Even the senior Mr. Brown and Mr. Greer was concerned about the rumors of her midnight escapes that was whispered about in the office. They called her in one afternoon and confronted her about it.

Mr. Brown said, "Tashiana, we have endured office rumors about our department supervisors over the years with a grain of salt. With you, I feel like a disappointed father. I have never met such a beautiful, intelligent, young woman like you. And from what I have seen, you have a loving husband who worships the ground you walk on, and is one of the most loving fathers in the world. Your children show nothing but love for their mommy. I'm trying to understand why these rumors about you are floating around this office. Are you having problems at home or here in the office we need to know about?"

"Is my personal life affecting my job performance here at the firm, Mr. Brown?" Tashiana asked.

"No, it isn't. Your contribution to the firm is unquestionable, and we have big plans for you. But in order for us to put you in the position we want to put you in your reputation has to be impeccable," Mr. Greer said.

"What are these plans?" Tashiana asked surprised.

"We want to pay your way through law school, and have you join the firm upon your graduation. We think you would make an excellent lawyer. What do you think of that?" Mr. Brown smiled.

"I'm truly grateful you care that much about me Mr. Brown, but I can't see leaving my children for such an extended period of time. I would happily accept any position within the firm here in Anchorage," Tashiana said.

"Would you at least think about it?" Mr. Brown asked.

"We have all the confidence in the world in you Tashiana, and we hate to see you miss your calling in life. Why don't you think about it for a while? There is no pressure on you to decide right now," Mr. Greer put in.

"I truly appreciate this offer, and I'll give it some serious thought. Meantime, I would like to know what the rumors about me are," Tashiana said.

"Don't worry about them, just give our offer some thought," Mr. Brown said.

"Yes sir, I will," Tashiana assured them.

Tashiana knew the rumors circulating around the office about her were started by Jessica. She didn't care because the firm believed in her. But what she didn't tell Mr. Brown and Mr. Greer was, she was perfectly satisfied with her life the way it was. Not even offering to send her to law school would change that. As with her parents, what the firm said about paying for her to attend law school went in one ear and out the other. She was having too much fun with Harvey's money to let anyone interfere with it. Luckily she never had to officially decline their offer because things came to a head several days after the offer was made.

Tashiana was staying out at least one Friday or Saturday night each weekend without telling Dominique where she was going only saying she would be with friends. She would then call him the following morning to pick her up at different friend's homes that would confirm her story when he called to check her story out. They argued constantly about her running around, but it went in one ear and out the other. Tashiana was having too much fun to stop right then.

Her free reign came to a sudden halt after she left home on a Friday, whereabouts unknown, and didn't return until getting off from work that Monday evening. Dominique was so pissed off, he had her suitcases packed and setting by the door when she arrived home. He was sitting at the dining room table when she walked in. He didn't say a word, just stared at her with the thought of murder running through his mind.

"What's this?" Tashiana asked, pointing at the suitcases.

"What the hell does it look like?" Dominique snapped, and continued, "I figured I'd save you some time. It's obvious you don't want to stay here, any longer. Just kiss the kids good-bye on your way out the fucking door," he said, and went into the living room and turned on the television.

Tashiana stood in the kitchen for a while not quite believing what was happening. She went into the living room and asked, "Are you sure, this is what you want?"

"No, it's not what I want, but I'll be damned if I'm going to let you pull me and the kids down into the gutter with you. If you want to screw every bastard in the state of Alaska, you go right ahead. It won't be while you're living under this roof," he finished.

"And you're not going to try and stop me from leaving?" she asked, somewhat perplexed.

"No, I'm not. Do you really think I'm going to beg you to stay, when I know you're fucking another man? You're the one who should be doing the begging. No my dear, you can get the fuck out, and I don't care if you ever come back."

"Well, I guess I'll have to call a cab," she said.

For some reason, Tashiana thought saying good-bye to Dominique and the kids would be the same as when she was going out for a night on the town. The look of sadness and disappointment in Dominique's eyes made her feel more guilt than she could have ever imagined. Halfway up the stairs she realized she was about to change the lives of her young children forever. How would they cope with life knowing their mom had been thrown out of their lives because she was a no good slut. The same type of women she swore she would shield her girls from, to insure they wouldn't grow up to be like them. The women she didn't want her girls to be like were Jessica and her friends.

As soon as she entered the playroom, and saw her children playing, she knew she was not ready to give up her family. A knot, the size of a watermelon, came into the pit of her stomach. And as they ran to her hollering Mommy, mommy, at the top of their little voices, it was hard to keep from crying. Holding back tears, she told them she had to go away for a while. Their daddy would explain why.

"Is it cause you always gone?" Shantel asked.

"That's a part of it, baby, but I'll be back in a few days. Ok?" Tashiana tried to assure them.

"Ok, I love you mommy," Shantel said, and went back to playing with her toys.

"Me too, love you mommy," little Sheena said.

"I'll see yall in a few days," Tashiana said, and ran from the room before she started to cry. She thanked God she didn't have to face Dominique Jr. and little Zelvina who was asleep. She kissed them good-bye and ran down the stairs.

While she was upstairs Dominique called a cab for her. When Tashiana came back down and went to the phone Dominique said, "I've already called a cab for you. All you have to do is wait until it gets here, if you can wait that long. What did you tell the kids?"

"What the hell do you think I told them?" Tashiana choked back tears. "I told them you would explain why I had to go away for awhile," she answered.

They sat around staring at each other, each waiting for the other to give in. Tashiana thinking it was a bluff to scare her, and Dominique thinking he wouldn't miss her because she was always gone anyway. Ten minutes later the taxi arrived, and he took her suitcases out to the cab for her.

"If you feel there's a chance of us working things out, find me," Tashiana said, as she climbed into the back seat of the cab.

Tashiana knew he had to take a stand sooner or later, or she would continue walking over him. She figured the separation would do them both some good. If nothing else, it would give them time to decide whether their marriage was worth trying to save. After a few days, if they loved each other, they would get back together and try to work things out.

Harvey took this as an omen that they belonged together and tried to get Tashiana to move in with him, but she told him she was not ready to give up her family, regardless of what she had done. The good reverend used God's name in vain because he didn't get what his heart desired, Tashiana as his wife.

Although she wanted Dominique to come and get her, Tashiana tried to mentally prepare herself to walk away from her marriage. She knew it would be difficult to start a new life of her own, but other women had done it and so could she. Having a good job assured she would not suffer financially. However, after several days passed she found herself regretting everything she had done to get thrown out of the house, mostly because of the children. She tried to imagine how she would feel seeing Dominique and her children give their undying love to another woman, and came to the conclusion she didn't want to find out.

Tashiana knew she loved her children, but wondered if she would ever be as caring for them as Dominique was. He was willing to give up his life to ensure they had the things he never had growing up. Therefore, she had no intentions of fighting him for custody of the children if they did get divorced. Another reason she wouldn't fight for custody of the children was because she didn't want to put them in a possible situation of being abused or molested if she happened to choose the wrong man as a mate. Tashiana wondered what would happen to her children if Dominique chose the wrong woman to replace her. How would the woman treat the children? Would the woman try to turn them against her? Would the woman try to get Dominique to keep her away from the house and the children? Would her children grow up hating her for abandoning them? All of a sudden she wasn't too sure about anything anymore, except that she wished Dominique would come to get her. She knew no man would ever love her as much as Dominique did. Even the good Bishop Kitchen said if she were his wife he would keep her locked up in the house away from her loose moral friends. When reality met "what if" a rude awakening was the final result.

Along with this revelation of what could possibly happen if she and Dominique got divorced, she didn't know how well she would be able to handle the ridicule she knew she was going to face on the job, and from her family for abandoning her children.

After coming to the realization that she still loved Dominique and her children, she was anxious to let him know it. She was ready to prove to him that she could change back into the mother and wife she was before hooking up with Jessica and her wild bunch. She had made the mistake of thinking Dominique would confront her before asking her to leave. She vowed not to underestimate him again, if they got back together.

Joleen offered to baby sit the kids for a couple of days for Dominique, if he wanted to go look for Tashiana, and try to work things out. Dominique thanked her for caring. He called the hospital and told his supervisor he had a family crisis at home and needed a week off. His supervisor didn't appreciate the short notice, but granted the week vacation anyway.

Dominique told the children that their mother was not feeling well and needed some time alone to get better. She would be coming back home in a week or so. They were so used to their mother being gone it no longer bothered them when she wasn't around. The two oldest girls said okay without even looking up from their toys.

Tashiana moved in with Jessica, and took a week leave of absent from her job. She didn't want to move in with Jessica, but she was the most willing to give her the temporary lodging that she needed. This move added to her embarrassment, because Tashiana was still pissed at Jessica for making that blatant pass at Dominique at that party. In addition to the incident with Dominique, Jessica made it known to anyone who would listen that she cared only for herself.

Once she had taking up residence with Jessica, Tashiana found it very difficult to deal with her so call friendly advice. Everything she advised after the first night was a repeat of what she had already said. Jessica had walked away from a very bitter marriage, and figured no woman in her right mind would ever re-enter the bonds of matrimony, once she had escaped. Tashiana had heard this before, when they were running around together, but not with the intensity it was being delivered now.

"Don't worry about Dominique girl. All men are alike. Once you say I do, they think it gives them the right to enslave you for the rest of your life. 'You can't go here.' 'You can't go there'. 'You can't do this'. 'You can't do that'. It's about time we as women took control of our own lives. We work just as hard as they do, and can support ourselves. Who the hell needs them anyway?" Jessica spat.

"I guess I do. I've come to the realization that I still love Dominique. And he's so good with the children. I just wish he was more out going, and would stop being such a tight wad. He acts as if he'll be able to take the money to the grave with him.

What bothers me most is leaving my kids. I feel I'm a complete failure as a mother. I swore my children would grow up in a happy home, with both Mom and Dad there to guide them in the right direction. By me screwing around and getting thrown out of the house makes me a piss poor mother, as far as I'm concerned," Tashiana said.

Jessica continued as if she hadn't heard a word Tashiana had said. "After you and Dominique get divorced, you'll get custody of the children, which means he'll have to pay through the nose. Then you can hook up with Harvey on a permanent basis. You know he'll take care of you and the kids. And he'll take you and the kids everywhere you always wanted to take them. That way you'll be doing more things together as a family. Kids don't care who the man is, as long as he treats them good and show he loves them, and wa-la, the bond grows stronger between mother and children. As for Dominique, he'll have some white bitch in his bed and knocked up before you know it. They all do," she assured Tashiana.

"Maybe you're right about the divorce settlement, but as far as Harvey being able to replace their dad is nonsense. No man on this earth will ever love those kids more than Dominique does. Dominique has been more of a mother to them than I've been for the last couple of years. No Jessica, I could never take the kids away from him. I just have to mold him into the man I want him to be. God knows I've tried. Dominique's the only damn man I've met, who doesn't try to satisfy my every whim, even when we were dating. That pisses me off, but at the same time I respect him for sticking with his beliefs. He's setting the example he wants the children to follow. And he would never bring a nasty white bitch into his house, that I know."

He may watch the big white titties on television but that is as close as he is going to get to them, Tashiana thought.

Jessica ignored Tashiana's remark about Dominique not bringing a white woman into his house and said, "He only takes the kids ice skating and skiing on the bunny slope during the winter, camping and fishing during the summer, and hardly anyplace else. How often would he take them out to eat if not for you? How often does he take them on guided tours to learn the history of this great state? Children need to be exposed to things in life so they'll grow up knowing there is life outside of their immediate community," Jessica reasoned.

"Yeah, but the only history I've provided them with since we've been in Alaska, is mommy sleeps around. And daddy has enough balls to throw her out," Tashiana sighed.

"Don't you worry girl. It'll be hard at first, but you'll survive. And things will be so much easier once you remove that yoke, called marriage, from around your neck. Believe me, it was hard living alone at first, now you couldn't get me to marry the richest man in the world to save my life. So what are you going to do once the divorce is final?" Jessica asked.

"If he comes for me, I'm going home and try to be the wife and mother that he expects of me. I've gotten so used to coming and going as I please, it's going to be a hard adjustment to make. For the sake of the kids, I've got to try," Tashiana answered.

"That is dumb thinking, home girl. Once he knows he can kick your ass out and you'll keep coming back, you had better never piss him off in the future. Or, it's out you go," Jessica warned.

"Dominique isn't like that. All he ever wanted is to have a happy family. To ensure the kids grow up knowing the value of life, and money. He's so damned straight laced it pisses me off every time I think about it. Sometimes I wish he would have an affair, just to show he has the same weakness as other men. But no, he has to try and be the perfect father and husband. Hell, how stupid can I get, here I have the type of man girls' dream of marrying when they grow up. What do I do, fuck around on him, and complain because he wants what's best for me, and the kids. I hope I'm not too far-gone to turn my life around, because the streets are in my blood now. I guess I'll have to wait and see what happens when he comes to get me. I'll give him a week. If he doesn't come by then, I guess he's serious about not wanting me back," Tashiana said.

"You are one confused bitch," Jessica shook her head. She couldn't believe any woman in her right mind would want to go back to a man who had thrown her out into the streets, regardless of the reason.

Dominique's supervisor, Allen Taylor, heard why he needed the time off and called three days after Tashiana left to make him a proposal. Dominique went to the office thinking Mr. Taylor was going to ask if he needed childcare assistance while he was at work so they could make some type of arrangement for them. The last thing he wanted from anyone was sympathy, although he would listen to almost anything if it meant getting his life back in order. He knocked on Mr. Taylor's door and entered.

"Hey what's up, Dominique? I heard about what happened between you and the misses. I may be able to help you out of your situation, that's if you two are willing to give your marriage another try," Mr. Taylor said.

"I haven't talk to her yet, but I'm willing to listen to what you have to say," Dominique said.

"Do you know where she is?"

"Yeah, I know where she is. I just haven't taken the time to go and talk to her about our situation yet," Dominique answered.

"When are you going to talk to her?" Mr. Taylor asked surprised.

"How can you help us?" Dominique asked changing the subject.

"There's a job opening for an x-ray technician instructor at Fort Sam Houston in San Antonio, Texas. They want someone from out of state with a military background to fill the position. I don't know why because I didn't bother to ask. This guy I know who use to work here, called from the human resource division there at the academy and ask if I knew anyone who may be interested in the job, so I gave him your name. I told him I hadn't talked to you yet but he said he would keep it on the front burner until he hears from me. I figured if you took the job, and Tashiana agreed to go with you, it would give you guys a fresh start at saving your marriage. So, what do you say?" Mr. Taylor asked.

"I'll have to talk to her about it," Dominique said.

"Look Dominique, you don't have to play this macho shit with me, okay. If you want your woman back go and get her, and make her understand that it's going to take the both of you to work this thing out. At least that's what I would do, and then I would get the hell out of Alaska as fast as I could," Mr. Taylor advised.

"How much time do I have to decide?" Dominique asked.

"I told him I would let him know first thing Monday morning. Will that be a problem?"

"No problem what-so-ever, sir. I'll see you sometime Monday morning regardless of the decision we make," Dominique assured him with hope in his heart that with a change in venue he and Tashiana may be able to work things out.

Dominique called Tashiana the following day and asked her to meet him at what used to be her favorite hangout, The Gold-miner Disco Club, that afternoon so they could talk.

Dominique showed up at the club an hour early so he could have a few under his belt before asking Tashiana if she wanted to move to Texas with him and the kids. He was afraid she may not want to come back, and an alcohol numb brain would make it easier to accept. As he waited for Tashiana to arrive, he looked around the nearly deserted club and wondered how many marriages had been ruined because of establishments like this one. Places where sinful minds, loose morals, and sweating bodies come together to see what happens, or simply to be a part of the in crowd.

Dominique notice the nervous look in Tashiana's eyes and manner when she entered the club. She was still the most beautiful woman in world, as far as Dominique was concerned. However, because of her, he had learned that beauty is only skin-deep. Still, he loved her and wanted her to come back home. He, and the kids, missed her. Dominique hoped she would see his acceptance of the position at Fort Sam Houston in San Antonio, TX as a second chance for their marriage to succeed. A fresh start may be all they needed to make their marriage work. He didn't even want to know the guy's name. He just wanted to pack up, move out, and put that particular episode behind them.

Tashiana walked over to where he was sitting and sat down and said "Hi."

"Hi. How you been?" Dominique asked.

"Okay I guess, how the kids doing."

"They miss you," Dominique informed her.

"I miss them too. So what did you want to talk about?" Tashiana asked.

"I got a job offer at Fort Sam Houston in San Antonio, Texas. It looks like me and the kids will be moving to the lower forty-eight before too long," Dominique said. He was afraid to ask if she wanted to go with them.

"When did you find out about this job? When yall supposed to leave?" Tashiana asked. Her heart was racing because her kids may be leaving the state and she wouldn't be able to see them until her vacation time each year.

"I won't know for sure until Monday," Dominique said.

"I don't want to lose my children Dominique. You have to tell them you can't accept that job. I won't allow you to take my kids to *no* Texas," Tashiana panicked.

"That's why I ask you to meet me here. I wanted to know if you wanted to go with us. I figured if we got a new start some place else we might be able to work things out," Dominique calmed her fears.

"Are you asking me to come back home?" Tashiana asked.

"I guess so. The kids miss you."

"And what about you, do you miss me?" Tashiana asked.

"Yeah, I guess I do. But things can't go back to being the way they were. Otherwise you may as well stay here," Dominique said.

"Don't be silly, I know that. And I can't allow you to just up and take my kids away without me either. I guess we can work things out if we try hard enough. When do you want me back home?" Tashiana smiled relieved she had a chance to make up for her failure as a wife and mother.

"Right now, Joleen is looking after the kids until we get home," Dominique answered.

"Well, less go get our children," Tashiana giggled.

During this happy reunion, Dominique and Tashiana forgot

that she also had a job, a job that paid her more than what he was making. When that realization set in Tashiana asked, "What about my job. What am I suppose to do when we get to Texas?"

"We should have enough severance pay between the both of us to keep us afloat until you find a job with some law firm, or maybe you could start your own legal service. If need be, I'm sure your Mom would help you get started," Dominique said

"You know I'm not going to ask my Mom for anything. Maybe I can get a small business loan. My credit is good and I have already developed a business plan with the help of young Mr. Brown. Even if I don't get the loan, I'm sure my bosses will hook me up with a job with a law office in Texas," she assured him.

"Things look better already," Dominique said.

Three months later Dominique and Tashiana both put in their two- week notices and a short time later Alaska became a distance memory. Brown, Greer, and Brown gave Tashiana a big send off. They also gave her a nice size severance check, and a letter of recommendation to present to Waller and White Law Firm, upon her arrival in San Antonio, TX, which didn't work out.

Now, here she was in San Antonio, screwing around again. Only this time it turned out to be more than she could handle. Tashiana committed the ultimate sin while having an affair. She cared more for her lover than she should have. Not quite love, but as close as you can get.

At the same time, she had fallen in love with Dominique all over again after their arrival in Texas because she finally accepted how much he loved her, and why he dedicated his time to her and the children. As Jessica had been right about her mental state while she lived in Alaska, it also applied there in Texas, she was one confused bitch.

Tashiana appreciated Dominique even more once she realized that Ahmaad was an egotistical jerk. It had taken a while, but his true colors came out once he realized she cared for him almost as much as he loved her. Tashiana in turn became the same type of person he was, conning and selfish. However, she did manage to keep her secret life and home life separate. Now she was caught up in a love triangle in which she had no idea how to get out of. Considering what had happened while they were living in Alaska, Tashiana figured once Dominique found out what she was doing, again, their marriage would be over. A tear rolled down her cheek as she pulled into their garage.

What she didn't know was, Dominique found out about her affair that very weekend, but would wait for her to confess her infidelity before saying anything.

CHAPTER #3

Dominique sat at the bar drinking shot after shot of tequila, thinking Tashiana's death would be the only thing that could keep him from being embarrassed before the world. How could she have given herself to another man, again? The more he drank, the sober he became. He left the bar and drove to a secluded spot on the outskirt of town, to be alone so he could think. On the way Dominique stopped and bought a bottle of rum. If only she had an accident or something before it became common knowledge of what Tashiana had done. In his mind he could see how he could make it happen.

Tashiana would be on her way home after a sordid, steamy hot session of lovemaking. She would be full of herself as she drove along the interstate with the streetlights whizzing by as she sped along. So deep in thought she wouldn't even notice the stars as they blinked and twinkled, the only witnesses to her infidelity. She would be preoccupied because she had a decision to make. An important decision as to whether she wanted to continue with her affair or tell him what was going on and suffer the consequences. He would be waiting along the route she always took coming home from her favorite nightclub. Tashiana had told him she was going to Charlie's, so he had a pretty good idea from which direction she would be coming. Being it would be between 1-3 a.m., traffic would be light making it fairly easy for him to intercept her when she exited I-10 onto the death loop, 1604. He took another gulp from the bottle and headed for his self appointed rendezvous to meet the woman who had been the answer to his most intimate dreams.

Dominique parked on the shoulder of Loop 1604 and waited for Tashiana's car. The new bluish headlights he had recently installed in her car would alert him to her approach. Tashiana had been so happy to have headlights that were different from the average car on the road. Now those same lights would assist in her demise. As he waited, he thought of the sympathy cards, and the condolences he would receive from family, friends, and acquaintances upon losing his loving wife in such a tragic accident. He would endure the accolades Tashiana would receive about what a loving, caring, and honest wife. He would have to bite his lips to maintain his silence on the honest compliment. Dominique decided he would wear the black suit she had bought him for old man Jameson's funeral two years earlier. He would comfort their children, and accept the sympathy of being thrust into the world of single fatherhood. He was use to the routines of the children, so it wouldn't be too big of an adjustment to make.

To cover his crime Dominique used the old model Nissan Tashiana had wrecked the day before. She rear-ended a car that she thought was going to continue through an intersection on the caution light. The lady changed her mind and slammed on her brakes instead. The front end, radiator, and bumper were badly damaged, but the car was drivable. He drove the banged up car around so the neighbors would be able to testify later in court that he drove the car to and from the corner store. Therefore, it would eliminate any suspicion if it came up that he was seen driving the damaged car.

Dominique was roused several times by passing cars, but none with the bluish headlights. He was about to give up and go home when several hundred yards away he saw the headlights of the car he was waiting for. He started his engine, and pulled in behind her after she zoomed past him. Tashiana was too preoccupied to think her life was in danger from the car that had pulled back onto the highway as she passed it. He had to pick one of the known locations where people had died in accidents. A film of sweat broke out on his forehead as he tried to remember what mile marker on Loop 1604 had witnessed the most fatalities. When mile marker 115 flashed by he remembered it was mile marker 123 that had the death curve. Dominique was sure mile marker 123 was where he needed to make his move. Mile marker 123 was located at a deep bend in the road. On either side of the road were trees that had stopped many screening cars as they ran off the road because they fail to slow down while negotiating the curve. Tashiana's exit was 135, so he didn't have to worry about her exiting before the deed was done. At mile marker 122, he made his move.

Dominique checked the highway in front of him, and then his rearview mirror, to insure they were the only cars on the road. Seeing the coast was clear, he step down on the accelerator and closed the distance. When Tashiana slowed to negotiate the curve, he rammed the rear of her vehicle sending her into the dense woods at 50 miles per hour. Dominique watched as the front end of the car got caught by the undergrowth, and was flipped into the air at an odd angle. He knew his mind was playing tricks with the time, but it seemed the car was in the air for an extended period of time before crashing into a tree, windshield first. He watched the glass shatter, and cut into her face and upper torso. Tashiana had tried to cover her face by throwing her arms up, but it was too late. The scream that escaped her lips was silenced by a large piece of glass that sliced through the jugular vein in her neck. The car slid down the tree like butter in a hot skillet held at an angle. He walked over to the car and looked into her dead staring eyes. The impact of the car slamming into the tree at such an odd angle knocked her into the passenger seat. I love you woman, I truly do, he said, before getting into his car and driving off.

Dominique Goodman is that tall, dark, handsome prince charming that all Moms hope their little girls will marry when they grow up. He doesn't run around drinking and gambling. He worships his children and honors his wife. The day he was born the hospital staff should have placed a sign on his crib that read, "Future lover and family man." It is a rare man that possesses the majority of the qualities a woman looks for in a man. Dominique greatest qualities were his dedication to the up brining of his children and the love he has for his wife. He loves them with all his heart and soul therefore he didn't mind sacrificing instant gratification for the sake of their future.

Dominique waved good-bye to his fellow employees, at the end of another day, at good ole' Fort Sam Houston, TX with the conversation he had with Jason Stone and Mark Tillman, earlier that morning, still ringing in his ears.

"Man, if my old lady ever screwed around on me, I would have her out of my life in a heart beat," Dominique said. He could afford to boast because none of his friends in San Antonio knew Tashiana had an affair while they lived in Alaska.

"What about the kids? You know what they say about us black men. Black men are always looking for an excuse to break up with their wives so they won't have to support them and the children, leaving it up to the welfare system to take care of them. That way, we can run around making more babies for the citizens of the state to take care of. Knowing how much pride you have in your family, it's hard for me to picture you saying to hell with everything, and kicking Tashiana out of the house," Jason said.

"Hey, look man, I love Tashiana and the kids, but I don't think I could live with a woman I can't trust," Dominique lied.

"I agree with you Dominique. A man isn't a man if he allows a woman to walk over him," Tillman put in.

"You see these white boys doing whatever it takes so their kids are brought up in a two parent home. Regardless of what their wives have done. Call them stupid, or wimps, if you like, but they're willing to make that sacrifice for their children. I'm sure they go out and mess around too, but all the children see is mom and dad still together. And as long as they can keep up the pretense of being happily married, the kids grow up happy, and in most cases, contribute to society. What do you think about that?" Jason asked.

"To be honest with you Jason, I've never thought about how I would react if Tashiana messed around on me," Dominique lied again and continued. "But I'll tell you one thing, it would definitely be hard for me to deal with. I'm no woman's wimp. I'd rather see her dead than to let the world know she screwed over me. Then again, if we did get divorced, like you said, the first thing most people would say is I didn't give her a chance to prove she could change. The only thing I thought of was my macho ego. What the hell, it's only a hypothetical question anyway, right?" Dominique asked.

"That's what wrong with us. We're always trying to get the

white man's approval to validate whatever it is we're doing. Fuck the white man. If my bitch screwed around on me, and I found out about it, I would go down to the welfare office and tell them they had another black family that needs to be fed." Tillman said.

"You're not married and you don't have kids Tillman, so how the hell do you know what you would do in that situation?" Jason asked.

"I just know that's all," Tillman said.

"You don't know shit Tillman. Yeah Dominique, it's a hypothetical question," Jason shot a glance in Tillman's direction for interrupting before he could answer Dominique. Jason continued, "Still, we as black men have a lot of pressure on us when it comes to keeping the black family intact. We're caught in a no win situation. If we stay in the marriage our black friends will call us wimps, and if we get divorced white people will say we were looking for an excuse to bail out of the marriage anyway. As I see it, we have turned the other cheek to the white man, so we're going to have to be able to deal with our women screwing up like other women. Sometimes we should stick it out for the sake of the kids, if nothing else. I know sometimes divorce is the only solution to a bad marriage," Jason said remembering his own divorce and the three kids he visited every other weekend.

"Feeling guilty for divorcing your old lady, Jason?" Tillman asked.

"I guess you could say that," Jason said not denying he regretted having divorce his wife of fifteen years. He continued, "She had to leave or I would have ended up hurting or killing her and the children. I was a mean son-of-a-bitch when I was drunk," Jason shook his head.

Jason's wife filed for a divorce after an extremely violent

episode. He had come home drunk and angry because he had lost the rent check in a dice game, and he didn't know how he was going to pay the rent. Jason blamed her for his drinking and gambling problems, and commenced to beat her senseless. He was always violent toward her when he drank. He never hurt the kids but she knew it was only a matter of time before the violence spilled over to them. She didn't allow that to happen.

"I know you're right about what people say about us when it comes to keeping the family intact, Jason, but I don't know if I would be able to deal with Tashiana giving herself to another man," Dominique said.

"If anyone can deal with that type situation, it's you good buddy. Of course, I hope you never have to go through anything like that. Besides, any man in his right mind would give anything to have a wife like Tashiana. If there is a lady in this world who has her shit together, it has to be her," Jason said, thinking he was a good judge of character.

"I like Tashiana too Dominique, but there is no such thing as a woman that can't be had if the situation is right. I know. I don't mess with anything but married women. You would be surprise whose wives are screwing around, not that Tashiana is," Tillman added hurriedly.

"Okay lover man," Dominique and Jason both said at the same time. Although Dominique joined Jason in the flippant remark he knew what Tillman said was true.

Well, the ball was in his court, and he didn't have the slightest idea of how he was going to deal with Tashiana's infidelity again.

To his fellow employees, it was just another day at the office. To Dominique, it was one of the most miserable days of his entire life. Although he didn't show any outward signs of his internal

turmoil, he felt as if he would explode at any moment. For the
first time in fourteen years of marriage, he dreaded going home
to his wife. Up until earlier that morning, he was your average,
so-called, happily married man. He had a beautiful wife, four
beautiful children, a home, and money in the bank. He had
enjoyed hearing all the compliments heaped upon them as a family.
He even got secret enjoyment whenever he overheard the guys
talking about what they would give to get a woman like Tashiana
in to bed. And so it had gone until he received a call at work from
Mrs. Laquan Tate, a lady in the community who lived several
street over from him whom he had no dealing with. Not even an
occasional hello, how are you at the local grocery store. He didn't
even know her name prior to the initial phone call.

"Hello, Dominique Goodman?" she asked when he answered
his phone.

"Yes, speaking," he answered.

"This is Mrs. Ahmaad Tate. I called to inform you that your
wife and my husband are having an affair. I know you love your
wife, but you trust her entirely too much," she informed him.

"Is this some kind of sick joke?" Dominique asked, not
wanting to believe what she had said. "Wait a minute Mrs. Tate,"
he continued before she could say anything further," have you
actually seen them together or is this hearsay?"

"No, I haven't seen them together yet, but I'm sure with your
help we could catch them in the act. I know what you must be
thinking right now, but please believe me. It's for the best that
we find out if this rumor is true so we can nip it in the bud. I love
my husband also, but not enough to stand by while he is having
an affair. I'm going to put an end to this rumor, or affair, with or
without your help," she babbled.

"How did you get wind of this affair, if it's true?" he asked becoming angry.

"Mr. and Mrs. Greenway said they saw them coming out of a motel off of Hwy 90 together, this past Saturday night," Laquan answered. The Greenways were her next- door neighbors.

"Well, maybe I should talk to the Greenways before jumping to any conclusions. Have you confronted your husband with this accusation?" he asked.

"Yes, I have. He denied it of course. He then went over to the Greenways house and called them a couple of nosy ass liars. And told them to keep their gossip to themselves," she said.

"Did it ever occur to you that he might be telling the truth, Mrs. Tate?" Dominique asked.

"Yes, it occurred to me he may be telling the truth about it not being your wife, but he was with another woman this past Saturday night. I know Ahmaad is lying and I intend to find out who he was with. Was your wife out on the town this past weekend? It may be a coincidence, but I still would like to know," she said.

"Yes, she was. She met some of her friends over at Lackland AFB to have a few drinks." At that revelation his mind started to race. *She always takes Hwy 90 to Lackland and back, he said to himself.* "Still, that doesn't prove anything," Dominique said to Mrs. Tate.

"All I'm asking of you Dominique is to assist me in putting this rumor to rest before it goes any further."

"I will definitely assist you in doing that, as far as my wife is concerned. That you can be assured of," he said, becoming angrier.

"What time did Tashiana get home? That's her name, isn't it? Mrs. Tate asked without giving him a chance to answer the questions individually

"Yeah, that's her name. She got home around 4:15 a.m., why?"

"That's about the same time Ahmaad got home. Is that the normal time for her to be getting home after a night on the town?" she asked.

"No not normally. But she does stay out rather late sometimes," Dominique answered, gritting his teeth.

"Dominique, I don't want to start any rumors that may not be true, as far as your wife is concerned, but I think we need to meet someplace and have a serious talk."

"I agree. I'll meet you at Denny's, off of I-35, for lunch. Say around 12:30?" he asked.

"That's fine with me. I'll see you there," Laquan agreed and hung up.

After hanging up the phone Dominique remembered a couple of times Tashiana wasn't at the friend's house where she said she was going to be when he called to ask her about something, long forgotten now. Of course she always had a good reason as to why she wasn't where she said she was going to be. He thought about the numerous times she came home complaining of being too tired to make love to him. He had promised her upon their arrival in San Antonio that he would never try to keep her locked up in the house, or away from the friends she would make there whether he liked them or not, as long as she knew how far to go. Now the affair she had while they were living in Alaska came rushing back to him.

Oh God, is this what I have to look forward to every time I find it in my heart to trust this woman? Dominique asked God.

Dominique decided he would not confront Tashiana regardless of what Mrs. Tate told him. He would wait until she went out that weekend and follow her. He wanted to find out for himself if what Mrs. Tate had been told, by the Greenways, was true or not.

Not being able to get any work done, or having any classes scheduled, he arrived at Denny's half an hour early. Dominique was sitting at the table talking to himself when Mrs. Tate walked into the restaurant. He looked up and motioned her over to where he was sitting. She had described to him what she would be wearing.

"Hi. I hate that we're meeting under these circumstances Dominique, but I think we both have a problem that needs our immediate attention," she said, upon reaching the table.

"Same here, you want to know how really blind I've been? I've never notice that you're a very beautiful woman. Please sit down," Dominique smiled.

"Thank you, Mr. Goodman. You're very kind," she said, taking the seat opposite him.

"What would you like to eat? Treat's on me," Dominique offered.

"Thank you, but I didn't come here to eat. I just wanted to talk to you to see what we have to do to put an end to this affair. If they're having an affair," she added hurriedly.

"I realize that Mrs. Tate, but the outcome is going to be the same whether we eat or not. And personally, I do my best thinking on a full stomach," Dominique said, picking up his menu.

"If you insist sir," she smiled. Mrs. Tate knew he was trying to get her to relax.

"I insist," Dominique said handing her a menu.

After ordering, they sat and stared at each other. For the first time, he took a really good look at her. She had beautiful brown eyes that would make the average man believe almost anything she said. Her lips were thin and sensuous, made to be kissed, her breasts just the right size for her figure. He couldn't help from staring at them since she wasn't wearing a bra, and her nipples were threatening to poke a hole through the thin silk fabric of her blouse. She was the type of woman who could make a man forget his problems for a while. If what she was saying was true, he was going to try and find out.

"You want to know something Mrs. Tate? I can't see why a man in his right mind, would want another woman when he has a woman as beautiful as you at home. You're the type of woman million of men dream of marrying. I know if I weren't married, I'd be hitting on you every chance I got. Then again, very few people are satisfied with what they have," he complimented her.

As he was complimenting Mrs. Tate, he remembered how many times women had told him they would give anything to have a dedicated husband like himself. He was sure Tashiana had been told how lucky she was to have a man like him, but some people don't believe anything you tell them. They have to learn the hard way.

"What about you Mr. Goodman? Do you have what you want?" Mrs. Tate asked, in a sexy voice.

"I don't know anymore. If what you say is true, I may need someone to tell my troubles to," Dominique answered truthfully.

"I'm almost one hundred percent sure, I'm right," Mrs. Tate said.

Their food arrived and they ate in silence for a while. Dominique broke the silence half way through the meal.

"I'll tell you what. If I find out what you say about my wife is true, you'll be the first person to know if I have what I want. You won't run and hide will you, Mrs. Tate?" he asked.

"And if I find out what I suspect is true about my husband Mr. Goodman, you won't run and hide from me, will you?" Mrs. Tate asked in return, smiling.

"I'm game for almost anything at this point in my life. Just make sure you know what you want to do when the shit hits the fan, if it hits the fan. So, let's make a plan to catch them in the act. Is your husband planning on going out this weekend?" Dominique asked, getting serious now.

"As far as I know he is. Why?"

"If they don't go out, how are we supposed to catch them together? If he does, don't try to stop him. I, in return, won't say anything to Tashiana. Here, let me give you my home phone number so you can call me after he leaves. I'll take care of everything from there."

"If you catch them together, what're you going to do?" Mrs. Tate asked.

"Don't worry. They won't even know I was there, just you and I. Deal?" he asked, extending his hand.

She placed her hand in his and the contact was magnetic. He tried to convince himself the only reason he felt as he did, was because they both had a problem that needed to be resolved before they could resume normal lives. However, deep down there were no denying that the sexual arousal he was experiencing was caused by the wanting look in her eyes. A look that said if not my husband, I wish I could find a man that will love me for who I am.

"Well, I'll see you Saturday, whether I find out anything or not," Dominique said, pulling his hand free of hers.

Mrs. Tate looked slightly embarrassed as she released his hand, because she to had felt that same magnetic sexual contact he had.

"Okay, until we meet again," she said, in a husky voice. "Oh, what if your wife answers the phone?"

"Tell her your name is Diane. Diane is one of my co-workers who I talk about all the time but she has never met. I'll tell Tashiana I'm expecting a call from her about something that needs to be done at the office. Don't worry, I'm going to get to the bottom of this shit, and neither one of them will be the wiser," Dominique assured her again. As Dominique walked Mrs. Tate to her car he again noticed that she had a fantastic body.

Ahmaad, you are one stupid fool. The last thing you want is for this beautiful lady to start peddling her wares in the streets, he said to himself. At the same time he remembered he had allowed Tashiana, a beautiful lady in her own right, to run loose in the streets in both Anchorage, Alaska and San Antonio. Look what it had gotten him, if the rumor was true. So he was speaking from experience. He waved good-bye as she pulled out of the parking lot, his mind already geared toward what he was going to do that coming Friday night. He had not told Mrs. Tate, later Laquan, Tashiana had already told him she was going out that coming Friday with her friend Janet. He was extra nice to Tashiana that Friday evening. He complimented her on how well she'd been looking these days. Tashiana asked if he was feeling well.

"Why shouldn't I feel alright? I have the most beautiful wife in the world, that love only me, and four of the most charming children God ever put on earth. Yes, why shouldn't I feel good?" Dominique answered.

He noticed the quick change in her expression upon hearing him say that, but he did not comment about it. He had touched a cord in her heart that made her feel temporary guilt. The look passed as quickly as it had appeared.

He laid across the bed watching her. As she continued to

get dress to go out she asked, "Dominique, are you planning on going anywhere tonight? And why are you acting so weird this evening?"

"Am I acting weird? How?" Dominique asked.

"How? You're lying around watching me like a stalker or something. Normally, you would be in the living room watching television," she answered.

"Is there something wrong with a man watching his beautiful wife get dressed to go out?" he asked.

"There is when the husband look like he want to hurt her," Tashiana answered.

"Oh. I didn't realize I was looking like a serial killer. My apology. I'll leave you in peace to finish putting on your face," Dominique said getting up to leave the bedroom.

"You still didn't answer my question. Are you planning on going anyplace tonight?" she asked again.

"No, I'm not planning on going any place. Why? You want me to go with you?" he asked.

"No, it's not that. Besides, you wouldn't have any fun being the only man at a table full of women," Tashiana said. She turned away so he wouldn't see the obvious lie, she had told, written on her face.

"I don't know. It may be fun watching all those guys eat their hearts out with jealousy, watching me with more than one beautiful woman at my side," Dominique prolonged her anxiety.

"Come on, Dominique, you and a table full of women?" she managed a weak laugh.

"Just kidding , baby, I wouldn't want to spoil your fun by having your friends hanging all over me all night," Dominique pretended to laugh along with her.

There was a look of relief on her face upon hearing that. She left the house at nine. At nine fifteen, Mrs. Tate called, and said Ahmaad had just left on his way to Lackland AFB.

"Meet me tomorrow morning at Denny's at ten o'clock. If they see each other tonight, I'll be able to tell you all about it at that time. However, there is one thing you have to promise."

"What's that?" Mrs. Tate asked, cautiously.

"If I do catch them together tonight, you'll say nothing to Ahmaad about it. Not until I find out how long the affair has been going on, and if they're in love with each other. Can you promise me that much?" Dominique asked

"It's a promise. I meant what I said about you being the first person I wanted to know if things between me and Ahmaad don't work out, if you know what I mean," Mrs. Tate said.

The image of her tantalizing body ran through his mind. Just two days earlier he had passed her on the streets and never gave her a second look. It was strange how certain situations change the way one person feels toward another, regardless of how long they have been associated. He knew he still loved Tashiana, but some of the love he felt for her died because of the rumor. She knew better than to get her self in a situation that would cast doubt about her morals again.

As he was getting dressed he kept telling himself, this is going to be a wild goose chase. She wouldn't do this to the kids and me again. Still he had to go through with it. He had to be sure beyond a shadow of a doubt that the woman he loved was not sharing herself with another man, again. He told Shantel to watch her brother and sisters until he got back.

Dominique arrived at the club around ten thirty and sure enough both Tashiana's and Ahmaad's cars were there in the parking lot.

Why would they drive both cars to the club when they could've met some place and rode together? He asked himself. It gave him hope that it was just a coincidence they happened to be at the same club. He parked in one of the far corners of the parking lot, where he could still see both their cars, and settled back for a long wait.

He had been waiting only about forty-five minutes when they came out of the club holding hands. Dominique almost said to hell with his plans when Ahmaad took Tashiana into his arms and kissed her. He got out of his car and moved forward so he could hear what they were saying.

Tashiana's voice came in loud and clear as she said, "Ahmaad, I know I shouldn't keep seeing you. But every time I tell myself that, for some reason, it makes me want to see you even more. This is what it must be like to be strung out on drugs. Anyway, I think Dominique has started to notice something is going on inside of me. God help me but I think I'm falling in love, with you."

Dominique's heart almost fell right out of his chest upon hearing that. Tears stung his eyes. His first reaction was to kill the both of them right there on the spot. But the conning side of him, made him stand fast. Killing them would make everything too easy. They had to suffer as he was suffering.

"It only makes it right," Ahmaad was saying. "I've been in love with you for a long time now. I've been telling you this for quite sometime. So, what're we going to do about it?" he asked.

"I don't know," Tashiana said.

"Let's get out of here," Ahmaad suggested.

"Okay, where to the usual place?" she asked.

"Yeah. Why not? I consider it our home away from home. There at least, you're mine and mine alone for a while," Ahmaad said, and went to his car.

It took all the will power Dominique could muster to keep from going over to where she was and beating her to within an inch of her life, and then taking care of Mr. Tate. Somehow he maintained control of his emotions and fell in behind Tashiana's car at a safe distance. The whole time he was following her, all he could think of was the times she had come home and lie in his arms as if nothing was going on. Of course all the signs had been there, but he had chosen to ignore them. After what he had gone through in Alaska, he should've known better. He sat across the street and watched as they registered and entered their motel room. He had seen enough to last him a lifetime. He stopped by one of the local nightclubs and drank himself into a stupor. When he got home at 3 a.m. Tashiana was already there.

"Where've you been Dominique?" she asked.

Tashiana was truly concerned, because it had been years since the last time Dominique had gone out and stayed so late. Not to mention leaving the kids alone and getting totally blown away.

To Dominique it was nothing more than a front. She was probably scared he had stumbled across her and Ahmaad together by accident.

What the hell do you care where I've been? he thought. To her he said, "I stopped by the Pink Pussycat and had a few. I felt like drinking tonight. Is there anything wrong with that?" he slurred.

"A few, you smell like a brewery."

"Well, I'm not going to stand here all night explaining why I felt like having a drink. I don't question you when you come home drunk as cooter brown," Dominique snapped.

"Well, excuse the hell out of me for caring Mr. Goodman," Tashiana said, sounding hurt.

"I'm sorry, baby. I felt like having a few drinks, okay?" he asked. Dominique was amazed he could maintain control of his emotions after what he had heard, and witnessed earlier that night.

"All right, but I think you better go to bed before you fall on your face," she suggested.

"Yeah, I think I'd better," he said.

As soon as his head touched the pillow he was out like a light. The following morning he had one hell of a hangover. It seemed everything the kids said, or did, was to punish him for getting drunk.

Tashiana was afraid to bring up the subject about the drunken condition he had been in that night, in fear he had somehow found out about her and Ahmaad. She knew him well enough to know that he did not get that drunk just because he felt like it. And she knew he knew she knew him better than that. She had to find out what had caused him to go on a drinking binge.

Pushing her fear aside she asked, "Want to tell me the truth as to why you drank yourself silly last night?"

He tried to think of a good lie. One he was sure she would believe. It was difficult considering the condition he was in. Then out of nowhere it came to him.

"Diane called last night, after you left, and told me they are going to lay off a bunch of people pretty soon. It seems the budget crunch has finally reached Fort Sam Houston. I guess now that Vietnam has been handed over to the commies of the north, they don't need the number of employees they currently have on the federal payroll. Congress has decided that the only way to save money on military installations is to lay off unnecessary personnel. Therefore, the bill authorized every installation commander to terminate all positions they feel are not needed to lower their budget."

What Dominique didn't tell Tashiana was because of the outcry of the federal employees threatened with losing their job the Congressional Bill he mentioned had been watered down to where no one would actually gets fired. When someone retired, or departed the command, those vacant positions would not be filled.

"The bad thing about the whole deal," Dominique continued, "is they're not going by seniority. My job is on the line along with everyone else's. That really pisses me off," Dominique said, sounding convincing. He knew she would believe that because, like everyone associated with Fort Sam Houston, she had heard the rumors that people were going to be laid off because of a personnel draw down.

"You've been working for the government for seven years now. Surely they wouldn't lay you off. It wouldn't be fair," Tashiana complained.

"I don't know for sure. I'll find out more when I get to work on Monday," he stretched the lie even further. And that was the end of it.

Damn, it's so easy to lie when the person you're telling it to believes in you, Dominique said settling into his chair.

At nine-thirty, he told Tashiana he had to stop by his office to check on something he had forgotten to do on Friday. Mrs. Tate was in Denny's parking lot waiting for him when he arrived.

"Have you had breakfast yet?" he asked.

"No, but I don't think I could eat anything anyway. I just want to know if you caught them together or not," she said.

"Let's go inside and have a cup of coffee, or something. Then we can talk," he suggested.

He didn't know how she was going to react to what he had to tell her, so he had to be prepared to control whatever situation arose. A scene at Denny's was the last thing he wanted.

After ordering and receiving coffee, he gave her his full attention and began. "Mrs. Tate ....."

"Laquan, please," she interrupted.

"Okay, Laquan it is. You're not going to like what I have to tell you. After you called last night, I went over to the club, and sure enough they were both there. However, since they were in separate cars, I hoped it was a coincidence they happened to be at the same club. So, I sat in the parking lot and waited to see if they came out together. After about forty-five minutes they came out of the club holding hands." Here, he hesitated to keep his anger from rising to the surface.

"Did you hear anything they said?" Laquan asked, his hesitation a bit too long to satisfy her curiosity.

"Yes unfortunately. After a long heart felt kiss, Tashiana said she couldn't stay away from him. That she thinks she is falling in love with him. Ahmaad on the other hand, said he has been in love with her for some time now." He stopped again, this time because he could see the tears forming in Laquan's eyes.

"Please continue," she requested.

"There isn't much more to tell. I followed them to a motel, and watched as they entered their room," Dominique concluded.

They both toyed with their coffee cups for several moments before either one of them spoke again.

"May, I call you Dominique?" Laquan asked.

"By all means do. So where do we go from here?" Dominique asked.

"Right now, I don't know what I want to do. I need time to think, " she said wringing her hands.

Her voice was so low Dominique barely heard what she said.

He could tell the hurt she was feeling went deeper than what he was feeling, although he hadn't thought it was humanly possible for anyone to feel more cheated than he felt. It bothered him.

"Are you going to be able to face Ahmaad, without letting him know you've found out about his affair?" Dominique asked.

"I would be lying if I said yes, right now. I'm going to do my best not to let on. If I can avoid telling him, can I call you later?" she asked.

"Laquan, you can call me any time you feel you need a friend. And I won't try to take advantage of you because of what you're going through. If a friend is all you need to get you through this, believe me, you have one," Dominique said, forgetting what they had said about letting each other know if they had what they wanted if the rumor about Tashiana and Ahmaad's affair was true.

"You don't know how much hearing you say that means to me, Dominique. You're a very strong man," she said.

"Either strong, or one of the stupidest men to ever walk the face of the earth," he sighed.

"I've got to get out of here Dominique, and go some place so I can be alone, to think about what I want to do," she said, and broke into tears.

Not wanting her outburst to bring attention to them he ushered her out of the restaurant to the parking lot, and told her to wait for him while he paid for the coffee. Upon his return to the parking lot, she was sitting in her car crying uncontrollable. He coaxed her out of her car and into his. She was in no shape to drive any place at the moment.

He drove around while she let the pain and hurt out through her tears. Half an hour later she said she was okay. He drove her back to her car. He had barely been able to hold back his own tears, but one of them had to be strong for the other. When he opened her car door for her, she turned and embraced him.

"With you in my corner, Dominique, I can face anything," Laquan said, and kissed him full on the lips. "I'll call you on Wednesday," she said.

An old saying his father used to say, when Dominique was a boy, came back to him. *Son, there is no greater scorn than a woman's fury.* He knew Ahmaad was in for a very hard time in the near future. As for Tashiana, he would play it by ear. He was so hurt he didn't know how long he could pretend ignorance of her affair. The instinct to beat her to within an inch of her life was still running through his mind on his way home.

So, as not to get caught in a lie, he stopped by his office and picked up some work he truly should have done on Friday, and took it home with him. When he got home, Tashiana noticed the change in his attitude.

"What's wrong Dominique? Was there someone at the office with some more bad news?" she asked, concerned.

"No, I guess I'm worried about what I'm going to do if I'm one of the unfortunate individuals who gets' the ax," he lied.

"Well, don't let it bother you baby. You're one of the best lab instructors Fort Sam Houston's Army Medical Academy has ever had. They can't afford to let you go," Tashiana assured him.

"Still, with Uncle Sam, you never know what to expect," he said, playing the lie to the hilt.

When he came home that Monday evening, she met him at the door. He informed her that his job was safe, although what Diane had said was true. The lay-offs wouldn't come until sometime the following year. Tashiana was genuinely relieved.

I guess you want to be sure I can still support you, if you decide to get rid of Ahmaad, or he decides to dump your ass, Dominique said to himself.

As the days passed, it became a little easier to accept the fact that Tashiana was only human. That maybe, he had taken it for granted she wouldn't mess around again; therefore, he hadn't given her the attention she needed. His next move was to get in good with her best friend, Janet Hardy. If anyone had all the dirt he wanted to know about Tashiana, it would be her.

Janet had a habit of making passes at him whenever Tashiana wasn't around. Dominique figured if he and Janet happened to get something going, and Tashiana found out, she couldn't raise too much hell, because Janet knew about her affair with Ahmaad. If things went as planned, Janet would tell him why he shouldn't feel guilty about taking her to bed. He knew she went to the club there at Fort Sam Houston, every Wednesday evening after work. So, he made a mental note to put his plan into action that coming Wednesday after work.

Laquan called early Wednesday morning to see how things were going between him and Tashiana. He said, fine so far. He asked how she was getting along with Ahmaad. She said it was hard, but she was doing okay. They didn't make any plans to see each other in the near future, but knew they had each other to cling to if their emotions overwhelmed them because of what they were going through.

That Wednesday afternoon, Dominique called Janet and asked if she would like to meet him at the Fort Sam Houston club for a drink pretending he didn't know she could be found there every Wednesday evening. Janet said she would be more than happy to do so. They met at the club later on that evening after work. They talked about everything accept why they were there.

Janet was on her third drink before she asked, "All this time we've known each other, why all of a sudden you ask me to meet you for a drink? Where is Tashiana?"

"Oh, I don't know. I guess it's because I was sitting around the office wondering what it would be like to go out with you. Go out on a real date if you know what I mean. But sitting here now, I don't know if that would be a very good idea, you being Tashiana's best friend and all," he said ignoring the question about Tashiana's whereabouts.

"Hey, come on. I don't tell Tashiana everything I do, you know. And by the same token, she doesn't tell me everything she does," Janet said.

"Are you trying to imply that my darling Tashiana has skeletons in her closet that I don't know about?" Dominique asked.

"I didn't say that," Janet said.

"I didn't say you did. It was the way you smiled after saying Tashiana doesn't tell you everything she does," he explained.

"I always smile when I talk to you, Dominique. You should know that by now," Janet wrinkled her nose at him.

"Can't argue with that, but let talk about us," Dominique suggested.

Tashiana's name was not mentioned the remainder of the evening. Before he left the club, they had made plans to meet on Friday, there at the club but later in the evening. The dogs come out at night, don't they?

He had intended to keep their date, but at the time he was making plans to be with Janet, he didn't know Laquan was going to call that Thursday asking him to meet her on Friday. There was never any doubt who he would rather be with. That Friday evening, it was his turn to ask Tashiana if she was going anyplace that night.

"No, I'm not going anywhere tonight. Tracy, *her music-loving friend*, is coming over to record some records, and gossip most of the night away. Are you?"

"I thought I would go by the club at Fort Sam Houston for a while and have a few," Dominique answered, smiling inwardly.

"I hope you're not going to be in the same shape you were in last weekend," she said critically.

"You don't have to worry about that. It'll be a long time before anything happens to make me that stupid again," he said.

"Alright. Be careful," she advised.

Dominique and Laquan, met at a small bar called the "Crow's Nest" off of Austin Hwy. He had several drinks before she arrived. He smiled when she walked in the club, because it was easy to tell going to nightclubs was something new to her, or it had been a long time since she last frequented one. She looked like a fish out of water. He got up and went to her before she got too uncomfortable. Her face flooded with relief when she saw him headed her way.

"Hi. Were you expecting a ghost or something? You looked like you were ready to take off," Dominique said, making her smile.

"No, it's been so long since I've been to a night club. And never with anyone other than Ahmaad," she confessed.

"Well, you have nothing to worry about while you're with me. I'll gladly lay my life on the line to protect your honor," he bowed.

"Let's hope that won't be necessary," Laquan laughed, allowing herself to be guided over to his table.

Dominique was anxious to get her on the dance floor, but the music being played was not the type of music he liked to dance to.

He held out until the DJ played a song he liked. He took her hands into his and asked her to dance.

"Oh God, it's been so long since I last danced. I don't know if I still remember how," she hesitated.

"Sure you do," Dominique said. "It's like riding a bicycle, once you learn you never forget. An old clique I know, but I bet I'm right." He was right she was an excellent dancer. Two songs later they sat down.

Once they were seated, Laquan said, "I must confess Dominique, the only reason I wanted to meet you tonight was to get an update on how things are going with you at home. Sorry," she apologized.

"You don't owe me an apology. I was wondering how things were going with you and Ahmaad as well. As for me, everything is going as well as can be expected, considering. It was real hard the first couple days, but I finally realized I've been taking Tashiana for granted. Very seldom taking her out to dinner without the kids in tow, or buying her flowers. Always trying to save every penny I get my hands on. I guess I'm partly to blame for what's going on. Not totally, but I should've known how she felt," Dominique updated her on what was going through his mind.

"Well I guess I'm being taken for granted, because Ahmaad never takes me anyplace anymore, except to those boring office parties where he has to give the appearance that he is a happily married man. And he never buys me flowers either," she grumbled.

"Well, you have a friend now who'll not only buy you flowers, but would consider it an honor to take you anyplace you so desire," he offered.

"Do you really mean that? What about Tashiana, and not

showing her the attention she deserves?" Laquan asked.

"Let me worry about Tashiana," Dominique said.

"Why are you willing to risk your reputation by messing around with me?" she asked.

"You're a very beautiful lady. I could take you to Hugh Hefner's Playboy mansion and still have to beat the dogs off you. You're that beautiful."

"Thank you, very much, Mr. Goodman. I admire a man with good taste," Laquan laughed. "But seriously, I know you're kidding about taking me anywhere I want to go. You're kidding aren't you?"

"I'm not kidding. But let's keep the hot spots here in the state of Texas," Dominique said.

"I may take you up on that promise. I don't plan on running all over the state of Texas, but you can take me to lunch or dancing any time you feel like it," she said.

"I hope you're serious about that," Dominique smiled.

As the drinks started to take their toll on her, she opened up more than she had intended to.

"Dominique, if I ask you a question, would you think I was too forward?" she asked in an awkward voice.

"I don't know. Why don't you ask me first?"

"Okay, here goes. If I ask you to take me to bed, would you?" she asked, embarrassed.

Dominique thought about it for a few seconds before he answered, and then said, "If your reason for going to bed with me is to get back at Ahmaad, the answer is no. I admit, at first I wanted to go out and screw every woman who came along. But after thinking about it for a while, I realized it wouldn't solve my problem, nor would it be fair to the women I would be with. All

I would be doing is taking out my revenge against Tashiana by mistreating them. So, I guess my answer is, as long as you were going to bed with me because you wanted to, not under any other circumstances."

"To be honest with you, Ahmaad is not the reason at all. I've watched you, off and on, for some time now. You're one of the most considerate men in our community, not to mention you're also handsome. Most men as handsome as you are are in love with themselves. Also, since Charlene told me about you comforting her when her marriage was on the rocks, I've wanted to meet you on a personal basis. So, I guess this mess with Ahmaad and Tashiana has afforded me the perfect opportunity. And after talking to you the second time at Denny's, I must admit, your confidence and strength impress me. I feel I could lose myself in your arms because I know no matter what comes up, you'll be able to handle it. Just thinking of what it must feel like to have you hold me in your arms makes me tingle all over. Right now, I want you more than I've ever wanted a man in my life. And believe me, Ahmaad has nothing to do with it," she finished.

The song "One In A Million" started playing at that moment by the club DJ, as if her confession to him made the request for them. He stood and led her onto the dance floor without asking if she wanted to dance. As he took her into his arms, his only thought was of her. Her soft body seemed to melt, and cover his as if she was a part of his natural skin. He imagined her nipples being so hard he could feel them pressing into his chest. Being somewhat out of practice they grinded into each other ever so slowly. They didn't even bother trying to keep to the beat of the music. Her breathing became slightly erratic as he nibbled at her neck and ears. They could hear the pounding of their hearts as their passion rose.

When the song ended she asked, "Am I truly one in a million Dominique?"

"We'll soon find out," he answered huskily.

They checked into one of the local Motel 6 motels a short distance up the street from the club. Dominique knew if he wasn't careful, this fling with Laquan could shape up to be a continuous relationship. He didn't know if he was ready for that. Still, he could hardly control himself as he again took her into his arms. He kissed her ever so gently at first then he increased the pressure as her pelvis area ground against him.

Suddenly she pulled herself from his grasp and said, "God, I want you so much, but this is wrong. I don't think I'm ready for this. Please, forgive me for leading you on."

Dominique wasn't angry with her he actually understood what she was going through. He had to treat her with kid gloves. "Look Laquan, I don't want you to do anything you don't want to do. If you don't want to go through with this, believe me, I understand. As I told you at the club, I want you to be sure this is what you want before I take you to bed. Why don't we put this little rendezvous on hold until you're sure it's something you want to be a part of. I'm willing to wait until you make up your mind, regardless of your final decision. If you decide you truly want to be with me, give me a call on Monday. If you want to confront your husband and try to work things out, I'm for that also. Me myself, I have to find out what's so exciting about having an affair. I wanted that affair to be with you. Why? Because I feel you're the only woman in this world who can hold a candle next to Tashiana. You're sensitive, warm, and very beautiful. As you told me, most women as beautiful as you, are in love with themselves.

Let's get out of here," he finished, and headed for the door.

"Could you hold me for a little while, and make me feel wanted?" Laquan whispered.

Dominique sat on the bed and drew her down beside him. She sat like an obedient child. He stroked her hair and said, "You're one of the most beautiful women in the world. I would give anything for you to be mine, even if it's for one night. Your eyes are like whirlpools, sucking in the heart of every man who dares to look into them. You have lips the average man only dreams of ever getting a chance to kiss. Breasts made to be fondled, stroked and kissed. A body, men have died for in days of old, and will again in the future. I want you more than I have ever wanted a woman in my life, but you have to want me in return", Dominique said.

Laquan laid back drawing him down with her. "Please, Dominique, tell me everything is going to be alright. Tell me, I'm not making a mistake by going to bed with you. Tell me, you're not going to use me to satisfy your curiosity and then toss me aside like an old used up whore. I never thought I would meet another man I would be willing to go to hell and back for. God help me, I want you to," she said, raising her lips to meet his.

She had gotten used to Ahmaad's wham bam thank you ma' am type sex, which creeps into every marriage after a while if you're not willing to experiment. Dominique took her to heights she had never known existed. She swore over and over she never knew sex could be so good.

After showering, and getting dressed, Laquan stepped into his arms and said, "After tonight, I don't think things will ever be the same between Ahmaad and me. I never knew sex could be so good. Please don't tell me this is the end for us. Tell me you want to see me again."

"I told you pretty lady I truly believe I could learn to care for you very much. Can I see you again Wednesday night?" he asked, kissing her.

"Yes," she said happily. "What time?"

"About seven o'clock, same place," Dominique said.

"I'll be there," Laquan promised.

And so was the beginning of who could screw around the most in the Goodman's household. Dominique knew two wrongs didn't make a right, and the ones who stood to lose the most were the kids, but his ego took control of his senses and assured him it would make him more of a man to beat Tashiana at her own game. A game in which he had been drawn into reluctantly, a game that no one ever wins, a game he should never have allowed to continue in the first place. But now that he had crossed that line where he no longer had righteousness or morality on his side, he would see where this unsound logic would take him. Dominique knew he would have to make up a lie to tell Janet why he was unable to meet her at the club, but he would cross that bridge when he came to it.

Dominique arrived home around 1 a.m. Surprisingly, he felt no guilt as far as Tashiana was concerned. However, he felt a tingle of guilt when he thought about how the kids would react if they found out what he was doing. Tashiana and Tracy were still recording when he got home. So, he left them in the living room and went into the den to watch television. Tashiana woke him at 3 a.m. and told him to go to bed. She and Tracy had just finished recording. Tashiana never asked him where he had gone, assuming he had gone to the club at Fort Sam Houston as he had said he would.

Early Monday morning, he received a call at his office, it from Janet. "You son-of-a-bitch, I waited for your ass until the damn club closed. What happened to you?" Janet asked.

"Sorry, about that Janet. I tried to call you at home to let you know I wouldn't be able to keep our date, but was told you had already left for the club. Beside, I think I would feel too guilty about taking you to bed. You being Tashiana's best friend and all," Dominique apologized.

He said that just to get himself off the hook although he knew Janet wouldn't say anything to Tashiana about him not being at the club, because she didn't want to blow her chance of being with him, eventually.

"Believe me, Dominique, you'd have nothing to feel guilty about, if you knew what is going on behind your back," Janet said, her anger getting the better of her.

"Oh, and what is going on behind my back that's so terrible, I wouldn't mind risking my marriage and family?" Dominique dared her to tell him.

"I don't know for sure, but there's a rumor going around that Tashiana is having an affair, with someone in the same neighborhood where you live," Janet answered.

He could tell by the tone of her voice, she knew who it was. "And who's that?" he asked.

"I honestly don't know," she insisted.

"You must have some idea, who it is, since yall go out together all the time. Normally, there is a name that goes with a rumor," Dominique said.

"I've heard a name, but I don't want to continue a rumor I don't know anything about," she said.

"Come on Janet tell me who it's supposed to be. I can tell by the way you talk, you know who he is," Dominique pressured her.

"Nope sorry, I don't."

"Okay, when can I see you, for sure this time?" Dominique said letting her off of the hook.

"Look Mr. Goodman, I'm not accustomed to being stood up. If you stand me up again, you'll never hear the last of it," Janet warned.

"It won't happen again. I promise," he assured her.

"How about tomorrow night, say seven at the club?"

"That's fine with me," Dominique agreed.

He was glad she had chosen Tuesday, because that Wednesday night was reserved for Laquan.

Dominique decided to start putting a little pressure on Tashiana by asking indirect questions about where she goes, and with whom. And what she did when she got there.

While watching television that evening Dominique said, "I don't know what this world is coming to."

"What on earth are you talking about?" Tashiana asked.

"Some of the guys, at the office, are spreading rumors that your best friend, Janet, is sneaking around with a married man. Said she meets him over at Lackland sometimes, and from there they go to one of the sleazy motels off of Hwy 90. You're her closest friend, is this rumor true?" he asked. He enjoyed the wide-eyed expression the question brought to Tashiana's face.

"I don't know whether it's true or not. She doesn't tell me everything she does you know," Tashiana answered defensively.

"You don't have to get upset. I thought since you two are such good friends, maybe she would confide in you," Dominique said.

"Just because we go out together, doesn't mean I know everything she does. It's not Janet you are concerned about anyway, is it?" Tashiana asked.

"Since you put it that way, I guess you're right," he confessed.

"Well, you don't have anything to worry about. Even if she is, I've learned my lesson about having affairs. Besides, I haven't met anyone that appeals to me here in San Antonio. So you can stop your snooping," she called herself assuring him.

Baby, you're one hell of a good liar, Dominique thought. To her he said, "You can't blame a man for checking up on his investment every once in a while, especially, when her best friend is supposedly screwing half the men in the state. You know what they say, monkey see, monkey do," he quipped.

"Well, I'm not a damn monkey," Tashiana snorted, and stormed out of the room.

Dominique smiled, knowing he had hit the nerve he had been searching for in her guilty heart. From that day forward, he spent the majority of his waking moments scheming on how to make life miserable for her and Ahmaad.

Ahmaad's office was located on the other side of the installation from where Dominique worked. Ahmaad was in charge of the Security Inspections Office on Fort Sam Houston. Their paths had crossed twice since Dominique had been in San Antonio. The first time was at the party where Tashiana met him, and second time was during a Physical Security Inspection two months earlier. Neither of them knew they were members of the same homeowner's association, and lived in the same neighborhood.

Dominique stopped by Ahmaad's office the following day, after the little episode with Tashiana, pretending he needed a copy of the updated physical security manual for an upcoming security class he had to give at the academy.

"Come on in, and have a seat, Mr. Goodman. What can I do for you?" Ahmaad asked.

"I'm looking for a copy of the new Physical Security Manual, the updated edition. Normally, we're the first office at the Academy to receive them, but for some reason we didn't get one this time around. I hope you can help me," Dominique said.

He had an unbelievable urge to beat the shit out of Ahmaad. He doesn't know where he got the power to restrain himself, but he gave an academy award performance.

"Let me see if I have an extra copy lying around here some place. I didn't know x-ray instructors needed security manuals, "Ahmaad said.

He looked for a give away sign that Dominique was there for a reason other than to borrow a security manual.

"Normally we don't, but after your last security inspection we feel we need one. I guess you've forgotten the Unsatisfactory rating you gave the x-ray lab the last time you were there," Dominique reminded him.

"That was a couple of months ago, wasn't it?" he asked.

"Yeah, it was. I just inherited the physical security duties for the lab. I want to know what the security requirements are, so we don't get dinged the next time you come around," Dominique said.

"I see. Well, let me check for you."

While Ahmaad was away from his desk, Dominique noticed he had a picture of Laquan and Ahmaad Jr. on it.

"Laquan, you're more beautiful in person," Dominique said to the picture.

"I'm sorry Mr. Goodman. I don't have an extra copy I can let you have, but you can borrow mine as long as you return it after you're finish with it," Ahmaad offered, upon returning to his desk.

"No, that won't be necessary. Thanks anyway. Maybe they have one in the military library that I can check out for a day, or two. Didn't I see you at the club over at Lackland a couple of weekends ago?" Dominique asked.

Although the question caught Ahmaad by surprise, he didn't miss a beat. "No, I don't believe so. I haven't been to the club at Lackland, AFB in months," Ahmaad lied.

"Maybe Tashiana mentioned your name for some reason. You know my wife, don't you?" Dominique asked.

"Tashiana? I can't say I have met her officially, unless it was at a party or some function here on Fort Sam," Ahmaad answered, becoming a bit nervous.

"Maybe, it's not you. I guess it must be another Tate she mentioned. Well, thanks anyway, for taking the time to try and help me out. I'll be seeing you around," Dominique said, extending his hand.

Now, I want to see if Tashiana has the balls to tell me I mentioned she and Ahmaad might know each other, he thought. He left Ahmaad's office with a smile on his face. Dominique figured Ahmaad would call Tashiana right after he left the office.

As Dominique predicted, Ahmaad wasted no time in calling Tashiana to see if she knew what was going on. He wasn't stupid. He knew Dominique had come to his office for some ulterior motive.

"Tashiana, have you told Dominique that you know me personally?" Ahmaad asked.

"Ahmaad, be serious. What makes you ask such a silly question?" she asked.

"Dominique just left my office, but before he left, he asked if I knew you. When I said no, I don't know you. He said, you must've mentioned my name to him for some reason. He sounded strange. It's as if he knows something is going on between us, but can't quite figure out what, or what to do about it," Ahmaad explained.

Her heart skipped a beat. "Are you sure?" she asked. Tashiana remembered the conversation they had about Janet sleeping around. It all made sense now.

"Hell yes, I'm sure. You think Janet, or one of your other friends said something to him about us?"

"No, I don't think so, especially Janet. She is too involved with Charlene's husband to tell anything on anyone else. And he doesn't know my other friends that well. Maybe he heard someone in his office say something about seeing us together, without knowing he was around. He did tell me he heard some of the guys in his office talking about Janet sleeping around. Since we go out together all the time, he wanted to know if I was doing the same. Of course I told him he had nothing to worry about. How the hell your name came into the picture I don't know, unless he knows something," Tashiana said, nervously.

"I don't know either. Is our date still on for this weekend?" Ahmaad asked. It would take more than Dominique possibly finding out about them to keep him away from the woman he loved.

"Sure it is," she answered, without any hesitation. "If anything comes up between now and then, I'll give you a call there at the office."

"Okay darling. You know no matter what happens, I'll always love you," he said before hanging up.

Yeah, I know. However, I can't afford to love you that much in return. I have got to let you go, Tashiana said to the dead line.

As promised, Dominique met Janet that Tuesday at the club on Fort Sam Houston. "Hi. Dominique. I was beginning to think you weren't going to show up. I would hate to be stood up again," she said.

"I'm only ten minutes late, Janet. What type of men are you used to dealing with?" he asked annoyed.

"Men who show up before I do," Janet answered.

"I'll keep that in mind from now on," Dominique said, taking her hands into his. "Please forgive an over worked, under paid, slave," he pretended to beg.

"Okay this time, but if I were you, I wouldn't make it a habit," Janet laughed.

They made small talk for a while, before the conversation got around to them going to bed. "So, when do we get together for that real date you were talking about the last time we met here?" Janet asked.

"I still think it would be a mistake to take you to bed. You keep saying, I'd have nothing to feel guilty about, but you won't tell me why," Dominique answered.

"Don't ask me a lot of questions about Tashiana, just believe what I'm saying," she said.

"I don't know about that. I never condemn a person without knowing the facts," Dominique insisted.

Janet breathed deeply and said, "I wish I could tell you what I know, but it would not be fair to Tashiana, or the guy she's seeing. Please don't make me the bad guy."

"Okay, for now. But after I get through making you feel, as no other man has ever made you feel, you'll tell me everything I want to know," Dominique said with confidence.

"My, aren't we sure of ourselves. Is that a promise you think you can live up to?" Janet swooned.

"If I can't do it, it can't be done," Dominique bragged.

"God, I do love a man with confidence in his abilities. So,

when do you want to prove your prowess to me, Mr. Goodman? Tashiana is always bragging about how good you are in bed. I've wanted to find out for myself for some time now," Janet confessed.

Dominique found it somewhat comforting to know he could, at least, still satisfy Tashiana in bed.

"I can't say right now, but soon," he said, busting her bubble.

A look of disappointment crossed her face. "Come on, Dominique. You get me all worked up talking about how you're going to make me feel, and then turn around and say you don't know when. One thing you should know about me, Mr. Goodman, I don't play games," Janet snorted.

Who does this bitch think she is? he asked himself. To her Dominique said, "Look Janet, I don't know what type of men you are used to dealing with, but don't make the mistake of putting me in that category. No woman dictates policy to me. I want to take you to bed, but it'll be on my terms, not yours. And if you can't accept that, let's keep things as they are, friends and nothing more," he said, staring her down.

She hadn't expected this type of attitude from Dominique, because she knew it took a lot, a lot more than what she said to make him angry.

Janet stared at him for a moment and said, "I didn't know this side of you existed. You have always seemed so docile. What's wrong Dominique? Do you already know something about what Tashiana is doing, and you're trying to get me to confirm it?" she asked.

He had expected her to catch on, sooner or later, that he wasn't completely in the dark about Tashiana's affair. Therefore, he was prepared for the question. "The only thing I know is what you told me, which happens to be nothing. This is the side that say, if I'm going to risk my family, it has to be in a situation in which I have control. That's all," he explained.

"I guess I can understand that. I still wish you would make it as soon as possible," Janet said.

"Tell you what, I'll call you at your office tomorrow and set a date. One I'll not back out of. How about that? Can you wait that long?" Dominique teased.

"I'll be waiting for your call," Janet assured him.

They had a few more drinks before calling it a night. He started to leave right after she pissed him off, by acting like a spoiled little bitch, but realized that in order for his plan to work, he had to play the role he had started to the end, regardless of the outcome.

On Wednesday, he met Laquan at the "Cove." She didn't even want a drink. She wanted to go straight to a motel.

While lying in his arms, Laquan said, "When I'm with you, nothing matters. It would be so easy to fall in love with you. I know you don't want to hear this yet, but I think in time, we could love each other. Once I showed you what we have, was meant to be."

"What do you mean about meant to be?" Dominique asked.

"I believe everything happens for a reason, even bad things. This incident happened to bring us together. It's faith," she explained.

"Aren't you forgetting a couple of people?" Dominique asked.

"No, I'm not. We stay married for now, but when the time is right, we'll break the news to them together. Oh, this is so exciting," she squealed. "Who knows, I may become Mrs. Dominique Goodman in a year or so," she said.

Dominique hadn't expected her to say anything like that so soon, but it was nothing he couldn't handle. "Let's not get carried away with these fantasies just yet, my dear. We'll have to see how things develop between us as time goes by. You have a special place in my heart already, but we shouldn't rush into anything. This is only the second time we have been together. You may come to think of me as being a first rate asshole," he said.

"You make me feel like a little girl again," she said.

That night when she got home, Ahmaad noticed the change in Laquan's attitude. She was happier than he had seen her in the past three years of their marriage.

"Laquan, what're you so happy about?" He asked.

"I don't know. I guess it's the wine I drank while I was at Sarah's," she lied.

Ahmaad knew it wasn't the wine, because she had started to drink rather heavily as of late. He decided she must have let Sarah talk her into smoking a little pot with them. It was common knowledge Sarah and the majority of her friends were potheads. They got giggly after smoking it. He let it go for the time being because it was bedtime. Not once did it cross his mine that she may be having an affair with the husband of the woman he was so madly in love with.

That morning, after breakfast, Ahmaad asked her again, "What were you so happy about last night?"

"I told you, it must've been the wine I drank at Sarah's," Laquan insisted.

"I don't believe that shit, for one second. She probably talked you into smoking a little grass with them. Everyone knows she's nothing but a pothead. I haven't seen you that happy, in quite a while."

"I may have gotten a contact from being in the room with them, but I didn't smoke it outright. Would you be terribly upset with me if I did?" she asked, enjoying the game she was playing.

"Hell no, not if it's going to have you in such a good mood all the time," Ahmaad said.

"Well, maybe next time I'm over at Sarah's, I'll take a couple of hits," Laquan giggled.

"It's about time you stop being so damn straight laced, and have a little fun," he encouraged her.

"I guess you're right, Ahmaad," she agreed. All the time thinking of how alive she felt when she was in Dominique's arms. *I guess you're right*, she repeated to no one in particular.

Several days later, Dominique and several of his fellow employees, decided to eat lunch at one of the local Chinese restaurants. Sitting at one of the table way back in a corner, were Ahmaad and Mrs. Greenway. It didn't dawn on Dominique they might have something going on. Since they were board members of the neighborhood homeowner's association it was common for them, male and female, to have lunch together. That was, until he noticed Ahmaad had his shoe off, and his foot under Mrs. Greenway's dress, under the table.

Damn, now I know why Mrs. Greenway was so eager to squeal on Ahmaad. She is screwing the bastard herself. Maybe I should be talking to her, instead of Janet. I wonder what type of man the bastard is, Dominique wondered.

The answer to his question as to what type of man Ahmaad Tate were was answered by one of his fellow lunching companion. Greg Farley, the eldest of the group, and white, answered his question. He had stared in Ahmaad's, and Mrs. Greenway's, direction since they entered the restaurant.

Finally Greg said, "See that son-of a-bitch sitting over there with Grace?" he asked pointing in their direction. Everyone nodded. "That bastard had an affair with my wife, a few years ago. I started to kill him, but some friends talked me out of it. I should've killed the both of them," he said angrily.

"There has to be, at least, a ten year age difference in your wife's age and his," Dominique pointed out.

"Twelve to be exact. He was 28 and she was 40 at the time," Greg said, and continued. "That's how he got to her. Always telling her how young she looked. Had her head so screwed up she was giving him money to take her out with. Can you believe that shit?" he asked.

"Why didn't you divorce her?" Dominique asked.

"Believe it or not, I still love Vera. Besides, I'm convinced all women mess around. So why go through all the bother of finding out that your next love is a whore also," Greg said.

It had never crossed Dominique's mind to keep an eye on their bank account. Surely, Tashiana was not that obsessed with the man. It was better to be safe than sorry. He would check their account as soon as he got a chance, and he would keep an eye on it from then on. Checking on their bank account was something he hadn't done for quite some time. He didn't like the hassle of writing checks. So he left it up to Tashiana to deal with the day-to-day check writing, and paying the bills, as well as balancing the checkbook against the monthly bank statement. He got the amount of money he was going to need for the week from her. If he ran out before the end of the week, she always had money in her purse. Now he had something to think about.

Dominique asked Greg, "Is money the only reason Ahmaad gets involved with married women?"

"I don't know about every woman he messes with, just Vera. Why do you ask?" Greg asked.

"Just curious, that's all. If there are women out there with money to throw away, hell, I might be interested in getting some of it myself," Dominique laughed.

"I don't know for sure, but I hear Grace is giving him anything he asks for. The son-of-a-bitch love to play on the vanity of older women. He'll get what's coming to him one day. If not by his wife, some woman is going to fuck him good. Mark my word" Greg said.

He shook his head remembering what a dope he had been. Ahmaad was the bulk of the conversation throughout the meal.

Well, two can play that game. I'm sure Mrs. Tate won't mind spending a little of your hard earned cash to have a good time with yours truly Mr. Tate, Dominique said to himself.

Ahmaad, and Mrs. Greenway, were still playing their little game as if they were the only ones in the place when Dominique and his companions left the restaurant.

Dominique had never known a man who asked women for money to take them out. If he found out that Tashiana had given Ahmaad one cent of his money she would have hell to pay. As for Ahmaad Tate, he would learn a lesson he would never forget if he lived to be a thousand years old, because the worst thing that can happen to a cheater is to be cheated on by the woman he thought he had complete control over. Before Dominique left the restaurant he started planning subtle ways to get Laquan to start paying for their intimate encounters. He was sure it wouldn't be too difficult, because of what Ahmaad was putting her through.

That evening while Tashiana was preparing dinner, he went through her checkbook looking for discrepancies, such as checks written to places out of the ordinary, or for large amounts of cash that couldn't be accounted for. Nothing out of the ordinary jumped out at him, however they didn't have as much money in the bank he felt they should've had. He couldn't think of anything they had purchased that would cause their account to be as low as it was. He swore if he found out she had given that bastard one red cent of his money, he would divorce her in a heart beat. It was bad enough she was giving him her affection.

He was so determined to find Ahmaad's fingerprints in her checkbook he didn't notice Tashiana watching him go through her checkbook. It made her nervous because he hadn't done that in well over two years. She was very aware of Ahmaad's reputation for getting women to pay his way. It shamed her to know she had been one of his victims. But surely that was not the reason Dominique was checking up on her, she hoped. She would ask him after putting the kids to bed.

During dinner, she tried to detect any unusual behavior he might display. There was none. As usual, he joked with her and the kids throughout the meal. It gave her hope that he wanted to see how much money they had in the bank because he wanted to buy something.

After the kids had taken their baths and gone to bed she snuggled up to him on the sofa and asked, "Why were you going through my checkbook? You haven't done that since our heads been above water."

Without any hesitation Dominique said, "I'm thinking about buying a boat, and wanted to know where we stood, financially. I'm sorry if you thought I was checking up on you," he apologized.

"That's okay. It's just that normally you would've asked me how much money we had in the bank," Tashiana accepted his explanation.

"You were busy cooking, and I didn't want to bother you. So, what do you think? If we had our own boat we could go fishing anyplace we choose," he said.

"Baby, we don't have enough money saved to buy a boat, right now. I mean, we could, but I would hate to use most of our savings to get it. We're living comfortably right now. Let's not spoil it by getting something we don't really need," she pleaded seriously.

"Hell, what is money for if not to spend?" he asked. He became angry, for not having the guts to tell her why he felt they didn't have the amount of money in their saving account he thought they should have.

"Don't be mad baby. I just don't want to spend most of our savings, that's all," Tashiana said cautiously, because Dominique were the last person in the world who Tashiana thought she would hear say money was made "just" to be spent.

"Alright this time, but as soon as we can afford it, without taking too much from the family, I'm going to get the boat, with or without your approval," he snapped.

"I promise. I'll even help you, as soon as we can afford it," she promised.

To see how Tashiana would react to being accused of mishandling their account Dominique asked, "Tashiana, why are we almost fucking broke?"

"What do you mean, almost broke?" she asked, nervously.

"Don't play games with me, Tashiana. The last time I asked you how much money we had in the bank you said around $9,000.00. Now we only have $6,000.00. When you put money in the bank, your account is supposed to grow, not decline. And we haven't purchased anything of any significance lately. Talk to me Tashiana," he demanded.

"It's obvious you have forgotten how expensive it is to raise four kids these days. Shantel is in junior high school now, and is a member of the honor society. It's important to her that she keeps up with the latest fashions, that's not cheap. And then there is Dominique Jr., who is involved in every little league sport being played. When was the last time you counted how many uniforms he has in his closet? Or how many balls, gloves, bats, and other sport equipment he has lying around? Sheena, our cheerleading daughter, needs a new uniform every time I turn around. Plus she has to supply snacks for the whole team at least twice a week, year round. And then there is Zelvina, who needs new clothes every month, because she outgrows them as fast as we buy them. All of that is not cheap you know. Don't forget you have to keep your bar stocked, so you and your buddies can get shit faced whenever they come over to watch ball games, also year round. Not to mention the mortgage payments every month, and the property taxes every year. The lawn sprinkler system, you had to have this past summer. Should I continue?" she asked, hoping she had sounded convincing.

"You left out the money you blow partying with your friends, or should I say friend?" he asked sarcastic.

"And what the hell is that suppose to mean?" she asked, really nervous now.

"What I said. The way you talk we stopped working a year ago. What happens to our paychecks every payday? Don't tell me we don't make enough money between the two of us to pay our monthly expenses, put a few dollars in the bank, and still have a little left over to spend on the kids. I may not be a math major, but I do know something is wrong here," he said becoming angry for real.

"Maybe you should keep the checkbook, if you think you can do a better job," Tashiana said, threw the checkbook into his lap and stormed out of the room.

He heard the door to the bedroom slam shut. He went to the refrigerator and brought back a six-pack. It was going to be a long night. Tashiana had been complaining about how much money was being spent to keep the kids in their extra curricular activities as of late, but his mind was set against any rational explanations.

Tashiana lie across the bed, and cussed herself for being stupid enough to let Ahmaad talk her into spending her money early in the affair. He had called it borrowing, and had repaid her twice the amount she spent on him, however it didn't ease the guilt she felt for being that weak. Tashiana wished she had put the money Ahmaad repaid her back in the bank instead of spending it on the house, or the kids. She knew Dominique was bound to check to see how much money was in the account sooner or later, especially if he wanted to buy something expensive. He would know that something was wrong, but she figured she would be able to explain where the money had gone. She had failed miserably, she thought. Now she had to change her game plan. She should've known something was wrong because when he got home from work he did something he had never done before, shown impatience with his son.

Dominique Jr. gave him a note from school, informing them he had forgotten to turn in a book report. Tashiana paid very little attention to the incident because at the time she thought Dominique was being the typical over reacting father.

"What the hell has gotten into you, boy? We try to give you damn kids everything you want and you can't remember to do your damn schoolwork," he said. Dominique Jr. burst into tears.

"Come here, son. I'm sorry I raised my voice at you. You've never failed to turn in your homework before, what's wrong?" he asked. Dominique hugged his son to stop the tears, because it was not really him he was angry at.

"I'm sorry, Daddy. I forgot to take it to school with me when I left this morning. That's all," he said, between sobs.

"Alright, alright, just make sure you don't forget your homework from now on," Dominique said, feeling guilty.

"I will Daddy. I promise," he sniffed.

"That's my boy. You go ahead and get ready for supper. And remember, dad loves you."

"Okay, I love you to Daddy."

Tashiana had intended to ask Dominique why he had scolded the child so severely for forgetting to take his homework to school with him, but after their discussion about their bank account, she figured she already knew the answer.

That night, Dominique had the most bizarre dream of his entire life. He dreamed he awoke, to find Tashiana gone from their bed. He got out of bed and cautiously went to the den. Why he was tiptoeing he hadn't the slightest idea. Something deep in his subconscious, told him it was the thing to do. As he approached the den he could hear loud breathing coming from somewhere inside. His whole body stiffened, as he stooped, and peeked through the keyhole.

There she was, lying on the floor next to his easy chair, totally naked. At her feet, gently nibbling at her toes was Ahmaad. Her head was thrown back. She had such a look of ecstasy on her face he got involuntarily excited. It had been years since he had seen that look in her eyes. It was a real turn on.

As Ahmaad slowly worked his way up her thighs, she looked in his direction and extended her index finger, motioning for him to join them. He almost fell when he jerked away from the keyhole. Dominique was sure she had made the gesture without any real intentions toward him.

Dominique's heart beat a thousand times per second as he forced himself to peek through the keyhole, again. This time, as the scene inside came into focused, both Tashiana and Ahmaad were motioning for him to join them. He again moved away from the keyhole. He was drenched with perspiration. It was the sexiest scene he had ever seen in his life. It was as if he was watching an X-rated movie, starring Tashiana.

Dominique's fantasizing days while they were living in Alaska came rushing into his mind. He had no recollection of sitting down. But as he sat there beside the door, debating whether to join them, or get his gun and blow them both away, the door opened. There stood Tashiana in all her glory. She looked like a sex goddess from the cover of one of the science fiction magazines you see on magazine racks in department stores.

His first reaction was to reach out and take her into his arms, but something in the back of his mind said, *Wake up man. This is your wife. You caught her with another man, and all you want to do is screw her also?* No matter how hard he tried to get angry, there was no anger in his heart. At that moment, he had never wanted her more.

She reached her hand out to him and said, "Please baby, join us. I could never be happy unless you share this experience with me. I love you so much."

He stood, and took her into his arms. Ahmaad appeared behind her.

"I know how you must feel, Dominique, but Tashiana said she

couldn't enjoy this encounter unless you joined us. I tried to tell her it wouldn't work, but she insisted. So come on, she says she's more than enough woman for the both of us."

Dominique tried again to get angry, but there was still no hatred in his heart toward either of them. Ahmaad and Tashiana, each took a hand, and led him into the den. She laid him in the same spot she had been lying a short time earlier.

"Dominique, I just want you to lay back and watch. I'm going to show you the things I have wanted to do to you, but was afraid."

She turned to Ahmaad and laid him beside Dominique. She then blazed a trail of hot kisses from his toes to his head. As she started back down, Dominique could see Ahmaad shutter from the pleasure he was experiencing. He watched with fascination as Ahmaad trembled as if he was having a seizure. So engrossed was he in what was going on, Dominique didn't realize Tashiana was slowly manipulating him at the same time.

When his passion reached the boiling point, he found himself pushing Ahmaad out of the way, to take his place. Dominique visibly stiffened as she let go of Ahmaad and turned her total attention toward him. She told him relax so she could prolong his pleasure.

"Not yet. Lay back and relax. I'm going to take you to heights you've never experienced before. I want you to know that no matter what I do with another man, I'm yours and yours alone. There's no one else in this world who could ever take your place in my heart."

Hearing this, Dominique turned to point out to her that she had started out sexing Ahmaad instead of him. Ahmaad was nowhere to be found.

"Where the hell did Ahmaad go?" he asked perplexed.

"Where did Ahmaad who go darling?" she asked.

"Don't play dumb with me, Tashiana. I'm talking about the bastard you were in here with earlier," he snapped.

"Why Dominique, we're the only ones here. Do you actually think I would do something like that without your approval?" Tashiana asked demurely.

"You don't have to lie to me, because I must admit, it was a real turn on watching how you could bring a man so much pleasure," he admitted.

"Would it bother you to see me turn the both of you on, at the same time?" she asked.

Dominique didn't know how he formed his lips to say it, but he said, "Yes. Bring the bastard on back, and let's see who is the better man."

Ahmaad reappeared as ready as he was before he disappeared.

"I don't care how good you think you are mister, I'm going to show you that no man can satisfy my wife better than I can," Dominique said.

"I hate to tell you this good buddy, but when it comes to satisfying beautiful women, you don't stand a chance," Ahmaad grinned.

"We shall see you egotistical bastard," Dominique said, and took Tashiana into his arms.

While Dominique was kissing and caressing her breasts, Ahmaad was caressing and kissing her long slender legs and thighs.

"I can't stand too much more of this," Tashiana moaned. "One of you, please make love to me. I need to feel the love of a man."

"Who, which one of us do you want to make love to you?" Dominique asked loudly.

"You darling, you," Tashiana responded.

Dominique pushed Ahmaad aside and took his wife. He made love to her as if there were no tomorrow. When he reached his peak it was almost unbearable. He grabbed a hand full of her hair and pulled her backward to keep her from pulling away from him. Dominique awoke just in time to feel the wet stickiness soiling his underwear. It had been years since he last had a stimulating sexual dream. He felt both ashamed and angry at the same time.

CHAPTER #4

Tashiana left the bed at 4 a.m. and went into the living room and sat down. Dominique had come home drunk at 2 a.m. and was in a nasty mood. He demanded degrading sexual acts, which left her sore and the muscles in her jaw cramping from over exertion. Afterward, he rolled over and fell asleep without a second thought about her protest of the way he handled her. He always told her it was the duty of the wife to satisfy the needs of her husband, regardless of how bizarre the request may have been, otherwise he would have to seek his satisfaction outside the home. Tashiana had protested in the past, but only mildly because she didn't mind experimenting once in a while herself. Tonight was beyond experimenting it was cruel, and she couldn't let the cruelty go unpunished. If she did, who knew where it would end.

Tashiana went into the kitchen and got the new package of razorblades from the drawer. They were originally purchased to scrap the rust and mildew from around the shower knobs and sink handles. Now they, one anyway, were going to be used to perform a home procedure that would leave one domineering husband balls less. Never again would he use and abuse her or any other woman. She could still hear his maniacal laughter as he called her, his own personal little sex toy. Once the deed was done, she knew she would have to get out of the house fast because he would try to kill her. Tashiana put a few necessities she would need for a short time in a bag and sat it by the front door. Before going into the bedroom to complete the *de-balling* of her husband she rehearsed what she would tell the police and judge, upon the investigation and later the trial, for the mutilation of her husband.

With tears in her eyes Tashiana would explain what happened on the night in question. She would tell how she was in bed sound asleep when her husband entered the bedroom at 2 a.m., and without even taking the time to wake her he jammed his finger into her backside and started to abuse her, while uttering another woman's name. When she resisted he threatened her with bodily harm and eviction from her home. For the next hour he made her perform degrading sex acts on him until she gagged and her mouth cramped and ached. When he performed shotgun sex with her he didn't even bother to lubricate him self or her. The pain was unbelievable. She tried to get out of his grasp but he held her firmly until he was finished. She had been in so much pain she could hardly move, but she managed to drag herself to the bathroom, run water in the tub, and soak her aching body. After bathing and getting back into bed he awoke and started assaulting her again.

It was at this time I remembered I had bought some razorblades to scrape lime and rust from the bathroom faucet in the nightstand. I beg him to stop but he wouldn't. Even after I reached into the nightstand and threatened to *de-nut* him with the razorblade, he still persisted. When he grabbed me by the throat and started choking me I panic. I remember kneeing him in the groin, and when he rolled over I jump on top of him and started cutting. I didn't realize it was his genitals I was cutting until it came off into my hands. I seen the blood, and heard his screams, but the fear of what he was going to do me for refusing to submit to his degrading sexual request drove me temporarily insane. While he was in the bathroom, I threw a few things into a bag and ran from the house in my nightgown. My neighbors can testify as to the state of mind I was in that night.

With her courage in tow, and a story she was sure any jury in their right mind would believe, Tashiana went into the bedroom and looked down at her sleeping husband. You will never treat me, or any other woman, like a whore ever again she said to Dominique's sleeping frame. With this, she reached down and gently took his limp member into her hands. Tashiana was half way out the door before the screams began. With bag in hand she knocked on the door of a neighbor, and fell into their arms when they opened the door. In a state of hysteria, she told them how Dominique had come home drunk and out of his mind. How he sexually attack her, and she had done everything within her power to fight him off. She had cut him with a razorblade, but she didn't know where. Could they please call the police? When she heard the wailing of the sirens, an inner smile crossed her lips knowing she, nor any other woman, would ever have to endure his sick advances ever again.

Dominique showered, dressed, and left for work before anyone got up that morning. Still mad at himself because of the dream, he called Janet and asked if she could meet him for lunch. Why the hell should Tashiana have all the fun?

"Is it just for lunch, or are you ready to prove to me you can make me feel as you promised?" she asked.

"I'm going to show you what a real man is like. Just meet me at Wyatt's restaurant off of 410 West, in fifteen minutes."

"I'll be there, lover. Just make sure you are," she said.

This is a, really, dumb idea, Dominique thought heading out the door.

Twenty minutes later he pulled in next to Janet in Wyatt's parking lot. She acted like a little kid about to ride on a merry-go-round for the first time.

"Oh God, I've waited a long time for this moment," she said.

"Hey, I hope you haven't wet your pants yet. Leave that to me," Dominique said. "Do you want to eat first, or what?"

"You're the only thing I want to eat right now," Janet said.

"I hope you know what you are doing," he warned her.

"No, I hope you know what you're doing. Every man who have been here couldn't help but to come back for more," she warned running her hands over her body.

They got a room at the nearest motel.

"I want you to know, I'm not going to bed with you because of anything Tashiana has done. It's because I think you're one hell of a good-looking guy, and you're nice as hell," Janet said once they were inside the room.

"Look, I'm not here to talk about Tashiana. Let me show you why I'm here," Dominique said.

Dominique had told her once he got her into bed, she would tell him everything he wanted to know. He was about to find out if he could deliver on that promise. When Janet started to undress he stopped her.

"I want the pleasure of undressing you myself. If you don't mined," he said.

"Be my guest," Janet said, spreading her arms.

Dominique approached her slowly, not wanting her to think he was overly anxious. He kissed her ever so gently on the lips, ears and neck. Unzipping her dress, which zipped down the front, he kissed her shoulders and arms as he slowly peeled it off inch by inch. He kissed the exposed portions of her breasts, not covered by her bra. Her passion rose with each gentle kiss, her breathing became erratic. He followed the course of her dress as it slid down to expose her mid section and panties. As he kissed her stomach and the top portion of her panties she pressed herself into his face. When the dress slid down around her ankles, he kissed each long slender leg.

"Hey lover, how about if I lay down on the bed? I don't think I can take too much more of this standing up," Janet said, shaking like a bowl of Jell-O.

Dominique laid her on the bed and continued his teasing kisses. Whenever she tried to kiss him in return, he told her to just lay back and enjoy what was happening to her. He unhooked her bra and let her breasts fall free. Janet shuddered as he manipulated one breast and then the other. He toyed with her breasts as if they were ripe, sweet melons, kneading and squeezing the soft flesh.

"Oh my God I don't believe this. I'm getting off just by your handling of my breasts," Janet moaned.

"Am I living up to my promise, so far?" Dominique asked his ego inflated ten-fold.

"Just don't stop what you're doing," was her reply.

Dominique resumed kissing and nibbling at her breasts until she let out a loud moan, and her whole body stiffened. He still hadn't touched the center of her being. He left her breasts, and started downward. He removed her panties, and kissed the inside of her thighs.

Damn, this is one hot number, he said, enjoying the pleasure he was giving her. When he touched her sacred spot, she nearly jumped off the bed.

God, why in heaven's name does Tashiana have to sleep with Ahmaad, when she has a lover like you at home? Janet asked herself aloud. After realizing what she had said, she looked at him and said, "I'm sorry, Dominique. I didn't mean to say that."

"We didn't come here to talk about Tashiana or Ahmaad, remember?" he asked, and continued the exploration of her trembling body.

When Janet could endure his probing no longer she said," Now it's my turn. Lay back and enjoy."

Janet returned the favor as she undressed him. When she performed the act he could never talk Tashiana into doing, he became putty in her hands. When she was satisfied with his readiness it was time for the real thing.

"Now I want to feel you," Janet said, rolling onto her back.

"How long has Ahmaad and Tashiana been seeing each other?" Dominique asked.

"I thought we weren't here to talk about Tashiana", Janet reminded him, raising her buttock to meet his thrust. "And why didn't I detect any surprise reaction when I said who she was sleeping with? You know don't you?"

"I do now, but we won't mention her again after you answer that one little question," Dominique promised.

"Okay, what question?" Janet asked impatiently.

"How long have they been seeing each other?"

"Two years, as far as I know. Now come on. You know you're driving me up the wall wanting you," she said more impatiently than before.

When he fulfilled her wish she moaned. "Ah yes. Make love to me Dominique. Do it as if there is no tomorrow." Janet wrapped her legs around his hips, to insure he fulfilled his promise.

"Slow down a little. Let's enjoy this moment to its fullest," Dominique said working his magic.

As Dominique passion rose he increased his speed. Janet matched his movement. When they reached their peak, she screamed so loud he was sure if anyone had been walking by the room at that moment, they would have called the police and reported someone in the room was being murdered. When their passion subsided, Dominique kissed her on the cheek and she began to cry.

"What the hell's wrong with you?" Dominique asked.

"My whole life I've been looking for a man who could make me feel the way you just did," she said but did not elaborate.

"Meaning?" Dominique asked.

"I mean someone who would take the time to ensure I had as much fun as he did. Believe it or not, this is the first time in my life I've reached a true orgasm. I never knew what I was missing," Janet said and started sniffing again.

Dominique wondered if the tears were because she felt guilty because she had made love to her best friend's husband, or was it truly because he was that good of a lover. He had to know.

"Are you sure you're not crying because you just finished making love to your best friend's husband?" he asked.

"No, I'm crying because it was the best sex I have ever had in my life. Also because it's probably the last time you're going to want to be with me," she sniffed.

"Only, if that's what you want," he assured her.

"Please don't lie to me Dominique. After today, I'm going to try to get you into bed every chance I get, even if I have to get on my knees and beg you."

"That won't be necessary, Janet. I meant it when I said this doesn't have to be the last encounter between us. I'll give you a call later on this week. Right now, we'd better get back to work. I, for one, am already late." Dominique said taking hold of her hands and pulling her off the bed. "I hope you don't have a jealous lover, other than your husband, out there who is keeping tabs on you. I would hate to have to jack some guy up over a woman not my wife," he smiled.

"What're you trying to say? If Tashiana is messing around on you, I must be messing around on Jerry. Of course you're right. Up to now it has been Rick, but from here forward it will be only you," she confessed.

"Hey, look Janet, I won't be running the streets as much as you and Tashiana, so I'll see you whenever I can," he said, wanting her to know he wouldn't be at her beck and call.

"I know that silly, but I want to see you whenever I can," she agreed.

"In the meantime don't change your routine, nor try to convince Tashiana she should change hers," he said.

"I know that Dominique. I'll keep my regular schedule until I hear from you, okay?" she asked.

"Ok," Dominique said.

After they finished showering and getting dressed, he held her in his arms. "You're more woman than I thought you were. I hope you're not lying about us getting together again."

"I never knew sex could be this good. I would walk through hell and high water to be with you again," Janet assured him.

On that note, his life changed for the worst. He had entered deeper into that world he deplored, the world of lying, cheating, and deceit. Although he knew it was a stupid excuse, he blamed Tashiana for his infidelity.

"Where the hell have you been, Dominique? I had to cover for you. You knew you had a one o'clock class today," Jason reminded him upon his return to the academy.

"Had a hot date that didn't want to let me go," Dominique answered with a smile. "Beside, you were supposed to cover for me if I didn't make it back in time anyway, and you know it."

"Hey no problem, but unless she has a friend, you had better meet her on your own time," Jason joked. "Who is she anyway? Is it anyone I know?" he asked.

"Yeah, you know her," Dominique answered and walked away.

Dominique called Laquan that Tuesday afternoon and told her he wouldn't be able to meet her on Wednesday as they had planned. That something came up that required his presence at home. He wasn't in the mood for back-to-back cheating. He had to call the shots if he was to maintain control of the game he was playing. She was disappointed, but said she understood.

If you knew the real reason, you probably wouldn't want to see me for a while, he said.

That evening when Dominique got home, dinner was on the table. For the first time in a long while, they ate in silence. Dominique because he didn't like the world he had entered, and Tashiana because she felt guilty for continuing her affair. While Tashiana was washing the dinner dishes, Dominique came up behind her and grabbed her around the waist.

"Hey, I'm sorry about last night. I guess I got upset because it seems we never have enough money to get the things I want. I know if we could afford it, you wouldn't mind. Apology accepted?" he asked.

Tashiana giggled, "Yes, I accept your apology, but let's not go through that again. From now on, I'll keep you up to date on our financial situation. That way, you'll know if we have the money to get whatever it is you're planning on getting okay?"

"Okay, you got it love," he promised.

He got himself a beer, and went into the living room where the kids were watching television, and plopped down on the sofa. *Two can play this game, my dear. I'm still going to find out if you gave that SOB any of my money*, Dominique thought.

"Hey, what are you guys watching?" he asked Shantel.

"Nothing," she answered.

"What do you mean nothing? What's on the T.V.?" he asked.

"Oh, we're watching a Charlie Brown special," she laughed.

"Okay, I'll watch it with you guys, but after it finishes it is bedtime," he informed them.

He laid low the remainder of the week. However, he couldn't resist the urge to make Tashiana feel guilty while she was getting dress to go out with Janet that Friday evening. He asked Tashiana, "Who is Janet seeing?"

"I don't know, why?"

"I was just wondering. I heard she's fooling around with Charlene's husband, Rick. Where are you guys going tonight, to Lackland?" he asked.

Dominique asked the question to see if anything in her face would give her away. Sure enough a surprised expression escaped her before she could bring herself under control.

"I don't know anything about it. You're the first one I've heard say anything about her and Rick. And no, we're not going to Lackland. We're going to check out that new club on W. W. White Road. It's supposed to be the hottest club in town, right now. You want to go with us?" she asked seriously. Tashiana truly hoped he would say yes, because she didn't feel like dealing with Ahmaad that evening.

"Naw, I'll pass. I asked about Janet, because I don't know anything about her extra curricular activities. She might be a freak. Or she may be trying to get you to run off to Alaska, or some other God forsaken place with her, so you two can be the female version of Butch Cassidy and the Sundance Kid," he pretended joked.

Tashiana stiffened upon hearing the state mentioned. "Why are you so interested in Janet, all of a sudden?"

"If asking you about your friends, and where you two go, bothers you that much, I guess I should mind my own business," Dominique snapped.

"Are you trying to start an argument?" Tashiana asked, looking at him suspiciously.

"No, I'm not trying to start anything. When a man stops caring where his wife goes, and who with, they may as well divorce and go their separate ways. Don't you think?" Dominique asked.

"You're acting awfully damn strange, tonight. If you want me to stay home, say so. Don't beat around the damn bush," Tashiana said angrily.

"Hey, sorry about that, you and Janet go ahead and have a good time. Forget I even brought the subject up," Dominique said as he walked out of the room.

Tashiana knew something was wrong. She suspected he had, either heard something about her and Ahmaad, or had run across them by accident while they were together, and hadn't said anything about it yet. Tashiana figured he was giving her enough rope to hang herself. She had to find out, somehow, because the suspense had started to wear on her nerves. Especially since he went out every weekend that she did. Tashiana was afraid one of these weekends he was going to walk up on her and Ahmaad at some club and start kicking butts.

When Janet arrived and the formalities were over, Tashiana said, "Guess what, Janet. Mr. Goodman thinks we're on our way to meet our boyfriends. Tell him what we do when we go out together."

"Oh, Dominique, don't be silly. When two girls go out together, we sit around and laugh at all the guys trying to pick us up. Besides, I've already found the man of all my sexiest dreams", Janet said.

"I bet. I know how you women are, you sit around pointing out the guys with the biggest bulge in their pants," he laughed.

"Out of here with you, Dominique Goodman," Janet said, giving him a playful push.

"Are you going anywhere tonight Dominique?" Tashiana asked.

"I may go by the club at Fort Sam later on, but I'll be home early. I guess I'll see you around, three in the morning," he said his voice filled with sarcasm.

"I'll be home before three. I'll probably be back before you get home," Tashiana said.

"Okay, I'll see you then, my dear."

As they were leaving, Janet turned to Dominique and said, "Don't do anything we wouldn't do, Dominique."

"Who me, I wouldn't know what to do with another woman, if she was naked and laid herself in my lap," he responded.

"I doubt that," Janet said in such a sexy voice, Tashiana looked at her with jealousy written all over her face.

"Let's go Janet, or we'll be too late to get a good table," Tashiana said firmly.

"I was only kidding, Tashi. Why are you so uptight tonight?" Janet asked seriously.

"I'm sorry, Janet. I had a rough day at the office."

"Well, a few drinks will take care of that," Janet assured her.

On their way to the club, Tashiana kept thinking of the way Janet had joked with Dominique. As if they were sharing a secret in which she wasn't a part of. She became angry thinking about it, but didn't want Janet to know she was angry.

"Has Dominique asked you anything about me, and Ahmaad?" Tashiana asked.

"No, why do you ask? Does he know about you and Ahmaad?"

"Call it a woman's intuition if you like, but he knows something is going on between me and another man. Are you sure he hasn't said anything that would lead you to believe he suspects me of messing around," she pressured Janet.

"If he does, you'll be the first to know. Are you sure it's not your guilt catching up to you?" Janet smiled.

"The guilt is getting worse, but that's not it. All of a sudden he's become interested in where I go, with whom, and what time I get home. I tell you Janet, someone has either pulled his coattail, or he has started doing the same thing that I am. The funny thing about the whole situation is, I'm jealous as hell. Can you believe that? Here I am, been having an affair for two years, may even be in love with the guy, and still have the audacity to be jealous of what Dominique does. Am I selfish or what?" Tashiana finished.

"Girl, you have a good man. I don't blame you for being jealous. If I were you, I would drop Ahmaad's ass so fast it would leave his head spinning," Janet advised.

"I've tried so many times. For some reason I can't. I know I've got to let him go, if I want my marriage to remain intact. I hope I can do it before it's too late."

"Hope doesn't have shit to do with it Tashiana. You've got to decide what you want, and go for it. I'll tell you one thing, there's a lot of women out there who would love for you to dump a good man like Dominique. Hell, you would even have to get pissed at me for hitting on him," Janet took a chance at saying.

"I know you're right. I would hate to lose him. Know what I mean?"
Tashiana said.

"Amen to that, girl. Amen to that," Janet said tingling all over, remembering how good Dominique had made her feel several days earlier.

Tashiana and Janet met Ahmaad and Rick at the club at Lackland. Throughout the evening, Tashiana's mind was elsewhere. She toyed with her drinks, and barely heard anything said to her.

"What's wrong with you, Tashiana?" Ahmaad asked. "We've been here for an hour and you haven't wanted to dance once. You're toying with your drinks, and haven't heard a word I've said all night. What gives?" he asked annoyed.

"I don't feel like partying tonight, that's all," she answered.

"You're upset because Dominique keeps giving impressions that he knows something is going on between us, right?" Ahmaad asked.

"I guess so," Tashiana agreed.

"Well, don't worry about it. If he knew anything he would've confronted you, or me, about it by now, don't you think?" Ahmaad asked.

"Maybe you're right. It still doesn't make these guilty feelings I'm experiencing right now go away," Tashiana said. Neither could she shake the feeling that Dominique was someplace, with another woman, even as she spoke.

"Do you want to go home?" Ahmaad asked. In her present state of mind, they were having a very boring evening, and Ahmaad didn't want any parts of it.

"No, maybe I'll get over this feeling in a little while," Tashiana said.

"Well, I know one thing, if he does anything to hurt you, I'll mess him up," Ahmaad said.

Tashiana didn't even bother to reply. She knew Ahmaad was talking a lot of smack he had no intentions of backing up. She managed to overcome her guilty feelings but could not get over the premonition she felt about Dominique being with another woman, but she did manage to put up a good front.

Meanwhile across town, Dominique and Laquan, were having one hell of a good time.

"God Dominique, I can't remember the last time I had so much fun. Being with you makes me feel like a new woman. I could spend the rest of my life with you, if it means having fun like this" Laquan said.

They decided to check out one of San Antonio's newest nightclub, called "The Love Nest." It was small and in a secluded location. It was not the type of club Tashiana and her friends frequented.

"I wish things was that simple," he responded.

"It's that simple if you don't think about Ahmaad and Tashiana, all the time. They've been having fun together for a long time now. I think it's time that we had some fun of our own, for a change," Laquan said and kissed him.

"Sure, you're right. Come here woman. Me Tarzan, you Jane," Dominique laughed.

Tashiana told Ahmaad she had a headache, and didn't feel

like having sex that night. He got pissed, and told her she was becoming a frigid old woman. She told him to fuck off and die. If he didn't want to see her anymore it would be fine with her. Ahmaad apologized, and they went their separate ways.

Dominique and Laquan checked into a motel. He went through the same routine with her he had gone through with Janet. She didn't cry, but said it was the best sex she had ever had in her life and that it proved they were meant to be together.

"If I tell you something, promise not to laugh at me," Laquan said seriously.

"I promise, and cross my heart and hope to die," Dominique laughed.

"Well, here goes. Ever since that first night we went to bed, I don't want Ahmaad to touch me anymore. You're the best lover a woman could ever hope for. Not only that, it's so easy to talk to you. And you make me feel like I'm the most important woman in your life, when we're together. I said I wasn't going to say this, but I think I'm starting to fall in love with you already. I know we've only been intimate for a short period of time, but it seems like I've known you all of my life," Laquan said.

"How the hell could I laugh at something like that? I must be honest with you Laquan. I enjoy being with you, but let's keep the love talk under wraps for a while. I don't know if I'm capable of loving two women, at the same time," he confessed, and continued. "I do still have feelings for my wife you know."

"I don't expect you to feel the same as I do right now, but in time I'm going to make you want me more than you do Tashiana. And that Mr. Goodman, is a promise", she said.

Dominique knew that wasn't possible, but didn't want to hurt her feelings, so he left it at that, without making any further comment.

Tashiana was home waiting for him. It was a strange feeling for her because she had never had to wonder where he was, or what time he would get home. She wondered if he would be drunk, or have another woman's perfume on his clothes. Whenever she came home late, and found him still up waiting for her, she always told him if it was him staying out late all the time she would not lose any sleep over him. Now here she was scared to death, that he had found another woman to spend his time with. It was 3:30 a.m. when he finally stumbled through the door. She didn't say a word, just stared at him.

"How long have you been home? I'm going to bed. You coming?" he asked, heading for the bedroom.

She followed. While he was getting undressed she asked, "Where did you go tonight?"

"Oh, I thought I would try that new club I heard about off Perrin Beitel, "The Love Nest" is the name of it. You and Janet should check it out," he answered.

"I guess you had a good time, judging from what time it is," Tashiana said in a huff.

"Don't tell me you're pissed, because I came home around the same time you normally get home. Why are you giving me the third degree act, baby?" he asked.

"It's not like you to be out all night, leaving the kids home by themselves," she said trying to make him feel guilty.

This pissed Dominique off instantly, because he had never used the kids being home alone as an excuse to question her. On more than one occasion when he attended business functions that lasted until late in the evenings she would already be gone when he got home.

"Oh, I guess I'm the only one who's supposed to give a damn about these kids," he said, and continued before she could answer. "How many nights have I lain awake wondering when you'd get home, or if you were coming home at all? Don't play this concerned mother bullshit with me Tashiana. Beside, Shantel is old enough to look after the other kids. If you want to dog me out for coming home late do it, but don't you dare put the kids into this," Dominique said.

"I never would stay out as late as I do, if I knew you weren't home, whether you want to believe that or not," she said. Tashiana knew the kids being home alone would've not made any difference since her involvement with Ahmaad. But she wasn't about to admit that to him.

"Hell, I ain't gonna stand here all night defending myself because I decided to have a good time for a change."

"Who, did you go with?" Tashiana asked.

"Me, myself, and I," he answered.

"You don't have to be a wise-ass about it," she hissed.

"Ask me no questions, and I'll tell you no lie," he quipped and got into bed.

"I hope you don't think ...."

"I'm going to sleep now. If you want to continue this conversation in the morning, I'll be happy to do so. Right now, I'm tired, and need to get some rest," he said with finality.

Tashiana got into bed and covered her head. But she lay awake listening to his snoring and prayed.

"Please God, I know I've said this before, but don't punish me for being weak of the flesh. I believe in you, and I love my family more than I do myself. I'll do anything to keep it intact. I swear to you, God, Ahmaad is history, a fling of the past. Please don't let me lose Dominique," she prayed. Then she wondered if God was tired of her false prayers, and that was why she couldn't let Ahmaad go.

For the first time since they had been married, she cried herself to sleep. For the first time since they had been married, she felt she might lose him. In Alaska, she could sense that he still loved her and would do anything to keep their marriage intact, but she didn't sense he felt that way this time. She awoke the following morning, with Dominique serving her breakfast in bed.

"I'm sorry I came home in such a foul mood last night baby. This is a peace offering. What do you say?" he asked.

Tashiana was so moved by the jester, she almost broke into tears. "God, I love you," was all she managed to say.

Things went fairly well between them for a while after that night, although they were headed on a collision course because of their infidelities. Dominique realized he still loved Tashiana very much, but things would never be the same between them again.

The affair Tashiana had while they lived in Alaska hurt him deeply, but there were never any doubt whether he would be able to live with her infidelity. He understood how easy it was to go astray. Although not an official organization, the sisterhood of Independent Women was very good at convincing new arrivals that women independence was the way of life there in the state of the northern lights. Men, husband included, were secondary to their careers. Tashiana bought into their rhetoric hook and line, but fortunately for her she avoided the sinker.

Dominique had plenty of opportunities to play the field. Women of the sisterhood, married and single, independent and dependent, offered themselves to him often. Of course he was attempted to indulge himself in the hot female flesh that was offered, but he believed in the vows of matrimony. The other reasons were he didn't want to put his kids on that roller coaster ride called divorce. He came close to joining Tashiana in that world of sexual deceit with a German co-worker at the clinic where he worked.

Greta Hilmrich was a 24 year-old single beauty from Munich. The only draw back for Dominique was she was white. His fellow male co-workers told him he had to be crazy, or a racist, not to accept her offer after they found out she had tried to seduce him and he had turned her down. Most of them catered to her every request. Dominique's reason for not sleeping with Greta was two-fold. The obvious reason was he was a married man and didn't want to jeopardize his marriage, even though he wasn't sure whether his marriage was going to work out at the time. The second reason was mental. Growing up in Arkansas during the 1950s and 1960s it was ingrained in the minds of black boys and men from the cradle to the grave that it was taboo for a black man to even think of sleeping with white women. To prove to him the white men were serious about what they said, his parents saved newspaper articles from black newspapers sent to them over the years by his uncle who lived in Chicago. The newspaper article was always accompanied by a photograph showing black men hung from trees, abused and brutalized. The reporter made sure the reader knew the men were killed because white women had accused them of rape. In some cases the white women admitted to having sexual relation with their black counterparts willingly, and they still killed them. The south was not the place for interracial relationships.

When he left the south that belief system stayed with him. So whenever Dominique saw an interracial couple together the memories of the horror stories he read, and was told by his parents and older neighbors about black men being hung, shot, and burned to death, resurfaced. He would catch himself saying the black man had better be careful because white women always yelled rape when their reputation were on the line. He carried this racist baggage with him well into his 40's. If not for those two forces controlling his mind, Dominique probably would have succumbed to the desires that Greta stirred in him.

Greta asked Dominique to help her pick up a table she had purchased from a friend one day after work. They picked the table up and he helped her carry it into her apartment. When he started to leave she offered him a drink to thank him for helping her with the table. He didn't see any harm in a friendly drink. Beside, he wasn't in a hurry to get home, and he didn't have to pick the kids up from daycare for another hour or so. They made small talk about the weather and some of the things that went on at the clinic, including stories about the horny men who were always chasing after her. A couple of drinks later, the conversation turned serious.

"You want to know something, Dominique?" she asked.

"The way you asked that question, I'm not sure whether I do or not," he answered.

"You know I don't date any of the guys at the clinic. The reason I don't is going to blow you away. I know you're married, and are dedicated to your children and all, but you're the only man at the clinic I want to sleep with. I figured if you seen that I don't sleep around it would make it easier for me to seduce you. Crazy, huh?" she confessed.

"I can't say you're crazy. Hell, to be honest with you I don't know what to think. Why me?" he asked.

"I like the strong silent type. My mum always told me you

guys are the best lovers," she said licking her lips.

"That may be true, and it may not be true. To be perfectly honest with you, I have had moments of fantasizing about ripping your clothes off and making wild passionate love to you. But it passes when I think of the consequences our union may cause. You're a beautiful woman, and have all the parts to match. I don't know what to say," he again confessed, and was immediately sorry for the confession because he knew it was going to give her hope that he would sleep with her.

"Say you want me, and I'm yours. I'll make your fantasies come true. Right here right now," Greta offered herself while getting out of her chair and sitting next to him on the sofa.

Dominique felt the stirring in is loins, but when he looked into her deep blue eyes he was overwhelmed with the memories of how many black men had died because of white beauties like her. He said, "I have to think about this."

"I've overheard you tell a couple of the guys at the clinic about your apprehension of sleeping with white women. I believed you said it's because of what happened to black men in the south who were foolish enough to let them selves be seduce by horny white women. I'm not a southern belle, and I would never do anything to hurt you. Believe me, Dominique. No one will ever know that we made love," she said taking his hands and placing them on her breasts.

His hands trembled as he squeezed the soft warm flesh of her buxom. He didn't know if the trembling was because of his internal fear of sleeping with a white woman, or he was feeling guilty for groping a woman not his wife. He pulled his hands away and said, "Damn, I don't know if I want to do this."

Without a word, Greta pulled her sweater over her head,

removed her bra, and threw the garments on the floor. She placed his hands on her naked breast and said, "Please Dominique, don't make me beg."

He drew her to him and said, "Greta, although I want you more than anything in the world right now, I can't do this. I'm not in the right frame of mind. I have to feel I'm the one doing the seducing, and I don't feel that way."

"What're you saying?" she asked.

"I have to be the one who initiate the seduction, otherwise I'll feel used," he lied.

"I said you could do the things you fantasized about doing to me. I didn't mean to be too aggressive it's just that I want you to make love to me," she pressed herself tighter against him.

"I would like to, but not today," he said easing him self from her grasp.

Sensing he was serious, she put her sweater back on and said, "I'm not giving up on you. I want to help you get over that stereotypical bullshit about what happens to black men who sleeps with white women. We're not all evil."

"That not the only reason," he said.

Greta took his hands in her and said, "I know. Even with all the rumors about your wife cheating on you, you still love her. You're one in a million. If you change your mind about wanting to be with me, I'll be waiting." She kissed him ever so gently on the lips and escorted him to the door.

Dominique thought about that incident every once in a while after he found out about Tashiana's affair in San Antonio. He wished he had screwed Greta's brains out so he could have told Tashiana not only did he watch the big white tittes on T.V. he played with them in real life while she was running around doing her thing. Unfortunately, he blew the opportunity because he was a faithful husband. He wondered what hold Ahmaad had on Tashiana that kept her going back to him. It had to be more than just having fun, and not having to worry about making a commitment.

After the checkbook incident with Tashiana, Dominique believed Tashiana had given Ahmaad money so he got Laquan to start paying for their nights on the town every once in awhile, including the motel rooms. He reflected back over how he had accomplished that feat. The conversation with Greg Farley, about Ahmaad getting married women to pay for their nights on the town was his motivation.

Dominique called Laquan and said, "I didn't get a chance to go by the bank before it closed today. I only have ten dollars to my name. I wouldn't even think of taking you out with only ten lousy dollars in my pockets. I guess you'll have to take a rain check for tonight."

"Hey, don't worry about it. You have spent your money on me, so it's only right that I spend my money on you. How much do you think we'll need?" Laquan asked. It made her proud to be looked upon as a liberated woman for a change.

"I would say, at least a hundred dollars. Can you come up with that much without Ahmaad becoming suspicious?" he asked.

"That's no problem. I have two hundred dollars I was going to go shopping with tomorrow that he doesn't know about. As far as Ahmaad is concerned, as long as we don't starve, and I keep him dressed, and with a little money in his pockets, I can tell him anything. Especially, since he is the one who does most of the spending anyway, through me of course. So all I have to do is tell him to slow down on the spending, and he won't suspect a thing," she assured him.

"I don't know if I'm going to enjoy this night. I've never had a woman spend her money on me before," Dominique teased.

"Don't worry about it. What mines, is yours. And I do mean everything, Dominique," she said.

It was that easy.

While Dominique, and Tashiana, was busy playing their little games, their two oldest children, Shantel and Sheena, spent many nights talking about their parent escapades.

Shantel said, "I wonder if dad has gotten wise to mom running around with another man. Or, have they joined the wife swapping society of the shameless?"

"What makes you think dad has joined the society of the shameless?" Sheena asked.

"Have you forgotten, this is how mom got started, since when does dad like nightclubs so much, he stays until they close? I hope they don't end up in divorce court," Shantel sighed.

"Don't be silly, Shantel. Mom and dad love each other too much to be getting a divorce," Sheena said.

"I hope so, for our sakes," Shantel responded.

"If dad has started seeing another woman, I wonder if we know her," Sheena said.

"I hope not. It'd be so embarrassing to find out dad, or mom, is messing around with the mother, or father, of one of the kids in our class. I think I would have to run away from home. I don't think I could bear living with parents like Sherry's. Her parents don't care who knows they sleep around," Shantel shuttered.

Sherry's parents were none other than Charlene and Rick Tillman.

"Mom and Dad have more class than that, Shantel. What

they're doing isn't right, but at least they keep it out of the public's eye."

"Yeah it's out of the public's view for now, but for how much longer? In case you haven't noticed, mom and dad aren't getting along too well these days. They pretend everything is okay in front of us, but it's obvious they're having serious problems. Maybe we can help them to be lovey-dovey again somehow," Shantel smiled at her younger sister.

"I hope so. What do you have in mind?" Sheena asked.

"I don't know yet, but I'll think of something," Shantel said.

Whatever they would have eventually come up with might have worked, but they never got the chance to put a plan into action. Things fell apart a short time after their conversation.

Dominique had predicted long ago, that things in the Tate's household would become very unsettling. Not only was Laquan going out every other weekend, she started buying expensive dresses. Although Ahmaad didn't like her spending that much money on clothes, he had to admit, the dresses made her one of the best looking ladies in the community. Her defense for buying the clothes was that she wanted to look good for him. That she was tired of being the most under dressed woman at all of his social functions and homeowners association meetings, which wasn't that many. However, after buying a baby blue, hip hugging, low cut neckline evening gown for $250.00, Ahmaad finally blew a fuse.

"What function do we attend that requires you to wear a damn $250.00 dress?" he snapped. "I don't like this shit at all, Laquan. The only type of woman who wants to look as good as you've been looking the past few months, is a woman who is getting dressed up for her lover. Do you have a lover, my dear?" Ahmaad asked sarcastically.

"That's not fair, Ahmaad. I've never accused you of having a lover because you look your best, when you go out on the town. Why should things be different for me?" Laquan asked, forcing tears. "I'm not a whore. I'm not a whore," she repeated, knowing her tears always disarmed him.

"Look, I'm sorry if that's the way you took it. I didn't mean to insinuate you're a whore, or any other such nonsense. It's just that, you've been looking so damn good lately. I guess I'm jealous. Can you forgive a jealous fool?" Ahmaad asked, trying to kiss her.

Laquan wasn't about to let Ahmaad off the hook that easy. Not after what he had insinuated, because he was still involved in an affair that he had lost control of. Whore was what he called women who cheated on their husbands.

"If I was jealous of how well you dressed every day you go to work, and when you go out, I guess we would be divorced by now. Don't you think?" It was her turn to be sarcastic.

"Laquan, don't be a bitch about this. I said I was sorry for what you thought I implied. You know damn well I have to present a well-groomed appearance in my position. What's eating at you, anyway? I can't say a damn thing lately without you jumping down my throat," Ahmaad said.

"You call all women who cheat on their husbands whores. But when you accuse me of cheating on you I'm suppose to believe that what you say have a different meaning? Come on Ahmaad, be man enough to tell me what you meant when you ask if I have a lover," Laquan challenged him.

"I didn't mean anything by it. It was just a figure of speech for Christ sakes. Hell, I don't even know any women who are cheating on their husbands," Ahmaad lied.

"That hasn't stopped you from labeling women who you

thought had loose morals in the past. If you think I'm screwing around on you say so. Don't beat around the damn bush," Laquan said.

"I didn't mean it the way you're making it sound. As usual you're blowing what I asked out of proportion. Any man in his right mind would question his wife when she starts dressing as you do. Not to mention you have started leaving the kid with babysitters while you party at nightclubs. What am I suppose to think?" Ahmaad asked.

"I don't go out that often. Why don't you stay home and baby-sit when I go out. You sure as hell don't take me with you when you go out. When I do ask you to take me with you, you always say you're meeting with rowdy friends too crazy for me to be around. How am I supposed to know you're not meeting your girlfriend and that's why you never want me to go with you?" Laquan asked.

"Here we go with this girlfriend shit again. Look, I'm sorry I made a snide ass remark about you dressing for a lover, ok? So let forget it," Ahmaad said, sorry he brought the subject up.

"I guess I've been a little bitchy lately. I'm sorry. My damn job is starting to get to me," she lied. "I've been working for Mr. Kruger, and that damn agency for eight years, and he hasn't even thought about giving me a supervisory position. He has given me pay raises sure, but no supervisory position and that's what I want. I want to be recognized for the job I'm doing. Well, tomorrow I'm going to tell him to either move me up to the front office, or I quit. Tomorrow is Brenda's last day on the job, and I want her supervisory position. I told you about her. She's the one who always come to me for advice when thing don't go right in her department. Beside, I've made sure I know her job backward, and forward," she finished. Laquan had constantly talked about Brenda Morgan, the claims department supervisor, coming to her whenever something went wrong.

"If you quit, where are you going to find another job?" Ahmaad asked.

For the first time, Ahmaad realized how much he depended on Laquan's paycheck to supplement his own. He needed the money, if he was to maintain his image. He no longer had the three or four women he would normally have paying his way since Tashiana entered his life. He was barely able to keep up his well off image around the office, with only Mrs. Greenway giving him money.

"I don't know. I was thinking of trying to find a job on Fort Sam Houston. I'm sure they have something just waiting for an ambitious, smart, and energetic young woman like myself," she answered.

"I don't know about that, Laquan. You know because of budget cuts on military installations around the country they are cutting back on quite a few jobs that used to be open at Fort Sam. I think you should stay with the agency you're working with, for a while longer. At least where you work you don't have to worry about being laid off every time some a-hole says we need to save a little money," he tried to convince her.

"I'll see what Mr. Kruger has to say tomorrow. If I quit the job it shouldn't matter anyway. You make enough money to take care of the three of us," Laquan stated flatly. To herself she thought, *but I don't think you'll be able to continue wining and dining Mrs. Goodman.*

"If you continue buying $250.00 dresses, I don't make enough," he said, not afraid to let her know he was still mad about the purchase of the dress.

"Hell Ahmaad, you spend more money in one week than I do in a whole month," she said, becoming truly angry. Because she knew the money Ahmaad spent when he went out on the town was spent on Tashiana. "Where does all your money go? Men who spend as much money as you do have to have a woman on the side. Do you have a woman on the side Ahmaad?" she asked seriously.

The tone of the question caught him by surprise. It took him a few seconds to get his thoughts together. "I spend the majority of my money trying to generate more business. Not giving it to some floozy on the street," he defended himself. "Are we going over this cheating shit again? Give it a rest Laquan."

"Who said it's a floozy? She may be more intelligent and beautiful than I am. Maybe you have to keep her dressed in beautiful clothes, or she would dump your ass. I don't know. I don't be with you enough to say," Laquan said, staring him down.

"Why in the hell would I want another woman? I can hardly keep you dressed these days. Let's get off this subject of who's cheating, because it doesn't make any sense. Damn, I'll never complain about you buying a dress ever again if this is what I have to go through. There's not a woman in the world that can make me spend my money on them, knowing I have a beautiful wife and kid at home," Ahmaad said.

Ahmaad had been giving Tashiana any amount of money she asked for, if he could afford it, for over a year. To make himself feel good about it, he pretended he was repaying her the money she had spent on him earlier in the relationship. Ahmaad remembered the time he had caught pure hell trying to explain how he misplaced, or lost, an entire paycheck when Tashiana had demanded it. Tashiana told him she would never see him again if he didn't give it to her. She gave the check back to him the following day, saying she just wanted to see how much he valued their relationship.

"If you don't want to talk about who may be screwing around on whom, don't bring it up," Laquan admonished.

"Oh, forget it. I can't say a damn thing without you twisting everything around to suit yourself," he said. Ahmaad stormed out of the house, and made a beeline to the "Ebb & Flow," the local little dive around the corner from their house.

Ahmaad sat staring into his beer wondering what had happened over the past few months that had caused such a radical change in Laquan's attitude. She was more confrontational than at any time since their marriage. He may have been more concerned about her attitude if he wasn't holding on to the hope that he and Tashiana would be together some day soon. He was sure Dominique knew about the affair and would confront Tashiana any day now, and would divorce her. Tashiana would then become his wife after he got rid of Laquan.

After Ahmaad left the house, Laquan tried on her new dress, and admired how beautiful she looked in the full view mirror. She ran her hands across her breasts, down her sides, and over every mound and curve she possessed.

I know you're going to like me in this dress, Dominique, she said to her reflection.

Lately, Dominique was all she could think about. It didn't matter she was now paying half the tab for their nights out on the town. She kept telling herself that spending the money on Dominique was worth every penny, because she loved him, and eventually he would love her as well. He would then start taking care of her, which would make the sacrifice worthwhile.

Laquan had been tempted on several occasions to tell Ahmaad

she was in love with another man, but wouldn't tell him who it was until Dominique said it was okay. However, deep in her heart, she knew he never would. Unless she somehow got him to love her so much, that nothing else mattered. Or, maybe she could arrange it so they could get caught together by, either Ahmaad or Tashiana, assuring their marriages would end in divorce, but knew if she did something like that, he would probably never talk to her again let alone fall in love with her. She was reaching her wits end, and had no earthly idea how to hold on to the man she loved if he decided to end the affair.

I love you so much Mr. Goodman it hurts. If only you loved me half as much as I do you, everything would be so beautiful, she said to an invisible Dominique.

Although Dominique had been fooling around with Laquan and Janet for six months, he felt no love for either of them. However, he did feel sorry for what Laquan had been through during her marriage to Ahmaad. The only difference in the two affairs was he was seeing Laquan more than he was Janet. The last time he was with Janet, she had been in a foul mood. He didn't know how much longer he could put up with her possessive attitude.

While lying in bed after making love, she asked, "Dominique, are you seeing another woman, other than me?"

"Me seeing another woman, are you serious?" he laughed. "I'm stressed to the limit trying to deal with what Tashiana is doing, and trying to keep you happy. Why did you ask me that, anyway?"

"Because, Tashiana said you're gone quite a bit as of late, and I know you're not with me, especially on weekends."

"Did she bother to tell you most of the time I'm not at home I'm at the office working? And as far as the weekend goes, I think I owe myself the time to unwind after a long week of work the same as everybody else?" he explained.

"Yeah, Tashiana told me that's what you say, but where do you go when you're not at the office? And where do you go to unwind? Those are the questions I'd like to hear you explain," she said.

"Look, Janet, I don't ask you where the hell you go, or how you spend your time. Hell, Tashiana doesn't keep tabs that close of where I go and what I do once I get there. So lay off if you want to keep seeing me. We're not married you know," Dominique said harshly.

"I know. Believe it or not, in these few short months we have been seeing one another, I have managed to fall for you, and I mean hard. I have reached the point where I rather be with you than with Jerry. Hell, I'm even starting to get jealous when I see you and Tashiana together. Isn't that a bleep? I keep telling myself that she doesn't deserve you because of what she's doing to you, and the kids. The bad thing about the whole situation is, you've never even told me that you like me, let alone having feelings for me," Janet said sadly.

"When we started this affair, we agreed it would be with no strings attached. I also told you I didn't think I could love a woman other than Tashiana. I do like you. I like you a lot. And I like being with you, but let's not rush anything," Dominique said.

"I'm sorry. No matter how many times I tell myself I'm crazy for falling for you, it doesn't help. It has gotten to the point where I'm making up all kinds of excuses to keep Jeffery from touching me when we go to bed at night. Believe me Dominique, you're a hard act to follow. If I can't get you to love me, can I at least, see you more often?" she asked.

The whole time Janet was talking Dominique was asking

himself, *what have I gotten myself into? Two damn women, other than my wife, are saying they love me. And so help me God, I don't give a rat's ass about either one of them. No, that's not completely true, but it's nothing even similar to love. I've got to put an end to these affairs before these women find out about each other. Something is telling me this game I'm playing will be coming to an end soon.*

After she finished talking he said, "I'm flattered, but I don't know if we should continue seeing one another at all. We're already seeing each other more than we probably should be, and it's putting a financial burden on my wallet. If I continue spending money at the rate that I am, Tashiana is going to start asking questions. I manage to trim a little money off my pay check before I deposit it, but I can't afford to go any deeper than that without her becoming suspicious."

Janet didn't believe him because she knew Tashiana was the one who balance their checkbook and would know instantly how much of his paycheck was deposited. However, she ignored his weak excuse and said, "Hell Dominique, if it's money that's keeping you from seeing me more often, I can fix that. You know Jeffery and I don't have any kids, so we have money to burn. You can have as much of it as you want, or need. Then you can see me more often. So, what do you think?" she asked.

Not expecting this turn of events, he had to collect himself. Finally Dominique asked, "And what is Jeffery going to say, while you're spending your money on me?"

"We have separate bank accounts. He doesn't balance my checkbook and I don't balance his. But for the hell of it, I ask him for money sometimes to remind him he still has a wife," she laughed.

"I appreciate the offer, but I have to decline. I would feel I owe you more than I'd be willing to give you in return. Sorry. Besides, how would I explain to Tashiana how I could go to these clubs and not spend any money?" Dominique asked.

"I thought it was worth a try. I still want to see you more if possible," Janet said.

"I'm not going to make any promises, but let's wait and see what happens in the future," Dominique said.

After Dominique and Janet departed company, and he was on his way back to his office, he got the fright and shock of his life. He glanced in his rearview mirror and several cars back was Tashiana. He barely missed hitting the car in front of him, who had slowed to let traffic from the access road onto the expressway. Dominique's car airconditioning system was on full blast, but there was a small film of sweat forming on his forehead.

Damn, I wonder if she followed me to the motel. I knew I was getting too careless he scolded himself.

To see if she was really following him, he took the next exit and turned right onto the first street he came to. Sure enough, she took the same exit and turned right on the same street. Becoming nervous, he began cussing Janet under his breath.

Damn you Janet, you set me up. I wondered how long it would take before you felt guilty enough to confess. Well, no matter what happens, I'll never speak to you again. What can I say to the kids to make them believe it's their mother's fault that I am being unfaithful? It's your own fault this shit is happening, he shouted at Tashiana in the rearview mirror. *I'll change direction one more time and if she follows me, I'll pull over and have it out with her right now,* Dominique decided.

A short distance further up the street he turned left onto a cross street, and pulled over a couple of hundred feet down the street to wait for her. Tashiana kept going straight, lost in her own depressing world. Dominique turned around and fell in behind her at a safe distance. Several blocks down the street, she pulled into the parking lot of a small motel. He slowed almost to a stop, to make sure his eyes had not deceived him. He had to make doubly sure it was Tashiana, hoping all the time he had somehow mistook another woman to be her. After seeing her get out of the car there was no doubt.

He made a U-turn, and pulled up to the curve across the street near the motel and got out. He ran to the corner of the motel office building and peeked around. He was just in time to see her and Ahmaad break their embrace, and enter the motel room. The fear he felt when he thought he had been caught cheating on her was now replaced with anger.

For the second time, because of her, tears stung his eyes. This time the tears rose to the level of over flowing and running down his face. He refused to let them flow. The betrayal of his loved one caused the blood in his veins to run icy cold. His heart was so grief stricken, he could hardly move. He wanted to go over and kick the door in and beat the hell out of the both of them, "again."

Suddenly, an annoying, voice in his head said. "You wouldn't be justified in doing that, Dominique. You had your chance to put an end to their affair six months ago, and without any guilty feelings whatsoever. Everyone, in their right mind, would have understood you beating the hell out of them when you caught them together that first time, but not now, not after allowing the affair to continue for this length of time. Also, how would you justify beating the crap out of them now that you're doing the same thing? At least she only has one lover. How many do you have

Dominique my boy?"

"That doesn't matter," Dominique tried to convince the voice.

"Oh, but it does, Dominique, my boy. What happens when Ahmaad goes home half beaten to death for continuing an affair you should have put an end to six months ago? Do you think Laquan is just going to cuss and scream, and let it go at that? Come on Dominique, my boy, wise up. She'll cuss and scream all right, but eventually she is going to say those magic words. What are they, Dominique, my boy? You say them," the voice taunted.

"I don't care, because I'm in love with Dominique," Dominique said, grinding his teeth.

"Very good, Dominique, my boy," the voice congratulated him. "Now, allow me to complete the scenario for you. Damn, this would make a good movie," the voice laughed and continued. "The gossip around the neighborhood would go something like this. Did you hear about Dominique Goodman and his wife, Tashiana, and Ahmaad Tate and his wife, Laquan? It seems Dominique followed Tashiana to a club over at Lackland, Air Force Base about six months ago, and discovered she and Ahmaad were having an affair, but didn't say anything to either one of them.

Instead, he went to Ahmaad's wife and told her what was going on. And to get back at Ahmaad and Tashiana for what they were doing, what did Dominique and Laquan does? They started having an affair of their own. I guess he didn't mind Tashiana having an affair, as long as he didn't see her and Ahmaad together. Now there's a rumor going around that Dominique and Ahmaad is going to switch wives and act as if nothing ever happened. I sure feel sorry for those poor kids. Can you imagine how they must feel about their parents right now, especially Dominique's fourteen year old? I hope it doesn't mess them up for the rest of their lives.

And let's not forget Janet. What happens if she decides to put her two cents in, Dominique, my boy?" the voice asked in a fatherly tone. When Dominique didn't answer, the voice continued. "When you're hot, you're hot. When you're not, you're not. You're definitely not hot right now, my boy. They'll say you got greedy, playing both Laquan and Janet for fools. Because you know for yourself, you don't really care for either one of them, which is only going to piss the both of them off that much more.

Just think Dominique my boy, you're going to shatter the hearts of a lot of people, simply because you can no longer stand for Tashiana to continue doing what you should have put an end to six months ago, especially since you're doing the same thing she is. So what chew gon do, Dominique, my boy? Do you need help making up your mind?" the voice asked with a deep-throated laugh.

"No," Dominique said. "I started this pay back game, and I'm going to see it through no matter what."

With the mental argument finished with the voice of reason in his head, he went back to his car and got a pen and some paper. He wrote a note to leave stuck to the door of their motel room. So that Tashiana would not recognize his handwriting, he wrote the note left-handed. As he approached the door to the motel room, he felt sick to his stomach. After placing the note on the door, he turned to leave, but the dream he had that night long ago came rushing into his mind.

"*No, don't be stupid,*" he scolded himself. Still, he could not force himself to leave.

Suddenly that pesky, repetitive, little voice was back with him again saying. "Go ahead Dominique, my boy, take a peek. Maybe your dream will come true. Maybe they already know you're out here, and they're waiting for you to join them. Go on Dominique, my boy. You know what they're getting ready to do," the voice insisted.

Dominique shook his head, and turned again to leave, but again stopped. Feeling powerless to stop himself, he kneeled on one knee at the keyhole and was grateful that he couldn't see them, or what was going on inside. He let out a sigh of relief and left.

Upon returning to his office Dominique call Tashiana's office, knowing she wouldn't be back anytime soon, and left a message for her to call him when she got back. Dominique wanted to see how long her little rendezvous with Ahmaad lasted. He also wanted to see if he could detect any guilt in her voice when he talked to her, after she had just finished cheating on him. And to see if he could keep the pain he was feeling in his heart, from coming out of his mouth.

"Ahmaad, there's a note on the door," Tashiana pointed.

"It's probably from someone working in the manager's office. I can't imagine why," Ahmaad said, taking the note off the door.

Tashiana watched as the expression on Ahmaad's face change from annoyance to bewilderment.

"What does it say?" she asked.

"Here, you read it," he handed her the note.

Tashiana read it aloud. "To Ahmaad and Tashiana, enjoy yourselves while you can, because you have been found out." When she finished reading the note, she started shaking all over.

"Who do you think wrote it?" she asked.

"I'll be damned if I know. I haven't told anyone about us, and no one knew I was going to meet you here today. What about you?" he asked.

"Don't be stupid, Ahmaad. I haven't said anything to anyone

either. But hell, hell, someone knows we were here," Tashiana said.

"Do you think it could've been Dominique?" Ahmaad asked.

"I doubt it, but it does looks like a man's handwriting," she answered.

"Do you recognize it?" Ahmaad asked.

"You've got to be kidding. A five year old can write better than this. Who ever it is has us by the gonads, and sound like he's getting ready to squeeze. What're you going to do?" she asked, panicking now.

"I don't know. Do you think Dominique found out about us and is ready to make his move?" Ahmaad asked.

"I don't believe so, but we can't rule anyone out at this point. I believe if Dominique knew we were in that room, excuse the expression, he would have kicked some ass. Yours and mine," she said nervously.

"Maybe he would maybe he wouldn't. Whoever it is, I hope they realize it would be a waste of time to try to blackmail us. What would you do if Dominique did find out about us and wanted a divorce?" Ahmaad asked.

"I do know one thing. I wouldn't marry you," Tashiana answered.

"Why in hell not?" Ahmaad croaked sounding hurt.

"Every time I looked at you, I would blame you for breaking up my family. Because of you, I was stupid enough to lose the only man I've ever truly loved. Because of you, I could never trust myself, or another man, ever again. I couldn't live like that. I'd rather live with, and by, myself," Tashiana finished.

"You're upset and don't realize what you are saying, that's all. I love you. I know it'd be pretty rough going at first, but I love you enough to weather the storm," he assured her.

"I asked Shantel how she would feel if I divorced her father and married another man. You want to know what she had to say when I asked her that? She said if I divorced her father because we couldn't get along with one another anymore, or no longer loved each other, she could understand that, but if I divorced him because I messed around and fell in love with another man she would never forgive me. And if I got custody of her, she would run away every chance she got, to her father of course. I may have waited too long to save my marriage and family, but one thing is for sure. I'll never see you again. You'll never know how much it hurts me to say those words, and mean them. I know I've said we were finished a hundred times in the past, but this time I really mean it," Tashiana said. Tears ran down her cheeks.

"Tashiana, you know how kids are. They can adapt to anything. Once they see how happy I can make you, and them, they'll change their minds about me. Please, don't say we are finished," Ahmaad begged. He realized, this time, she really meant what she said.

"I'm sorry I have to hurt you like this, but I have to choose between you and my family. I wish you all the luck in the world. I hope Laquan can find a way to make you happy. Good-bye Ahmaad," she said. Tashiana kissed him on the cheek, and left him standing in the motel parking lot mumbling.

God, I know I've been lying to you for some time now, but please don't let it be too late to save my family, Tashiana prayed, the tears now flowing freely. *Please don't let Dominique find out about the money. If for no other reason, he would divorce me for that.*

"When this is over, I'll still be waiting for you, Tashiana. I'll never stop loving you," Ahmaad shouted after her.

Tashiana threw caution to the wind, and walked up and down both sides of the streets, to see if their tormentor was anywhere in sight. Seeing no one in the vicinity, and no one approaching her, she went back to work.

Ten minutes after arriving back at her office, Dominique called, "Hello, baby. I got your message. I was just about to call you. To what do I owe for this unexpected call?" Tashiana asked, trying to sound cheerful.

"I called to see if you wanted to take the kids out for dinner this evening. My treat," Dominique offered, fighting back the anger trying to gain control of him.

"I don't really feel like going any place tonight. We'll see when I get home. Okay?" she said through her guilt.

Dominique could tell by the tremble in her voice she, and Ahmaad, had found the note he had left on the door of their motel room. "What's wrong, baby?" he asked, feeling slightly guilty for what he was putting her through, and for not putting an end to her affair six months earlier. Most of the guilt he felt was for taking the wimpy way out, instead of putting his foot down after finding out about the affair. "You don't sound too good. Are you alright?" he asked.

"Yes, I'm fine," Tashiana lied. "I must be coming down with something."

"Are you sure?" Dominique asked,

"Yes, I'm sure. I'll be okay," she sniffed as if she had a runny nose.

Dominique started to prolong her agony by asking where she had gone for lunch, but didn't have the heart to put her through anymore of his self-centered torture, not that she didn't deserve it, but mainly because he felt himself losing control of his emotions as he toyed with her.

"Are you going to be able to finish the day?" Dominique asked instead.

"I only have a few more hours before I get off, I can make it."

"Okay, I'll see you when I get home. Love you," he said.

"I love you too," Tashiana said, choking back tears. After hanging up she rushed to the bathroom and cried her heart out.

"Whoever said revenge is sweet, didn't know what the hell they were talking about, or have never been in love," Dominique sighed after hanging up.

CHAPTER #5

She sat in front of the television set watching an old movie starring Harry Belafonte and Dorothy Dandridge. Oh how she envied the black glamorous women on the silver screen. They had everything they ever wanted at their fingertips. How often did she catch herself daydreaming of what it must feel like to be rich and famous like Tina Turner, Diana Ross, or the legendary Lena Horne! She would see herself attending huge galas where only the people of substance could attend. She wore thousand dollar dresses, men bowed at her feet and kissed her hand, maids waited on her hand and foot, limos waited to take her to her destinations, and she sipped champagne for breakfast. She imagine having it all, but when fantasy was replaced with reality her thousand dollar dresses turn into Wal-Mart specials. The men bowing at her feet and kissing her hands became the building and construction workers she pass to and from work each day, who whistles and heehaws at anything in a skirt. She herself became the maid for her family. The limos turns into station wagons used to transport snotty nosed kids and groceries. The champagne turns into a six-pack of Old E from the corner store. *Why did I settle for a mediocre life with a man I knew wouldn't be able to fulfill my dreams?* Tashiana asked herself. So, when Dominique entered the room with a beer in hand the argument began.

"Drinking beer again? Don't you get tired of drinking the same old crap every night? You know how much money we could save if you stopped drinking beer and booze? Probably enough to take the kids to Disney World, or some other place that would be special to them," she started.

"I work hard all day. I deserve to be able to sit back with a beer in hand and relax. What's bugging you anyway?" he asked.

"What's bugging me you ask? I'll tell you what's bugging me. I watch these women on television with everything their hearts desire and I ask myself, why didn't I marry a man who could give me all those things instead of a broken down old jock?"

"Who the hell are you calling a broken down old jock. I have a career as an x-ray technician. The job insures you and kids have clothes on your backs, food on the table, and enough money to keep yourselves entertained. What more do you want? Maybe you should have pursued that law degree. Maybe by now you would be that big fancy lawyer your momma wanted you to be," Dominique sneered.

"Don't think I haven't thought about that? I don't know what the hell I was thinking to give up my dream because of you. I may have married a millionaire. Instead I sit here with a mediocre man who makes a living taking pictures of peoples bones," Tashiana said.

"Really. There are a lot of women out there who would love to be with this mediocre x-ray technician. Whenever you get ready to hit the road let me know," he said and continued. "If I remember correctly, you had a second chance to go for the gold when you worked for that law firm in Alaska, but you were to busy running the streets with your whoring friends."

"I might have changed my mind and went back to school if you hadn't knocked me up before I could even think straight. You know I couldn't run off to a damn law school and leave the kids for that length of time. And for your information I wasn't whoring around. I screwed up, I know that, but I still deserve the finer things in life," she said.

"We have money in the bank," he reminded her.

"The money in bank you're so proud to point out to anyone who will listen isn't enough to get a fingernail repaired outside of our bargain hunting world. Why don't you invent a new radical way of taking x-rays or something, so you can make some real money for a change? I want to go on cruises, and I want to be able to go shopping without getting sticker shock. I want a big fancy house with a swimming pool, tennis court, and a guesthouse where our families can stay when they come to visit. I want a big fireplace where we could sit in front of it, on a shag carpet, and drink champagne. I'm tired of this mediocre existence," she finished.

"You watch entirely too much television. You have a few good years left in you. Get that law degree, defend a rich asshole, get him off, and you'll live the rest of your life on easy street. I'll even sacrifice my career and stay at home and take care of the house and kids," Dominique said toasting her with his can of beer.

"You're pathetic, you know that don't you?" Tashiana asked, and got up and left room.

"If you had listen to me and took your strong willed ass back to school like I told you to do my dear, you may be living that dream by now. But like they say, that's water under the bridge," he said, and toasted her disappearing frame as she closed the door to the bedroom.

For the remainder of the afternoon, Dominique could only think of his wife. Where had he gone wrong he asked himself? He thought he had done everything in his power, to make Tashiana happy since their move to San Antonio, Texas. With tears in his eyes, he reminisced of days gone by. He remembered the good times they had shared together over the years, as well as the heartaches and mental anguished they caused each other. Through it all, they had survived. However, the final chapter to their story was yet to be written. The promises they made of loving only each other forever during their courtship and early marriage flashed through his mind as if it were yesterday. It took him back to that period of innocence when they believed all their dreams were carved in stone.

Eighteen year old, Dominique Goodman, and his best friend, Oscar Felton, stood outside of their high school gym, in Lakeview, Arkansas, in the winter of 1969 watching the cheerleaders as they entered.

"You want know something, Oscar? Tashiana is the most beautiful babe in the whole world. I sure wish she were my girl. From what I hear her parents don't want her associating with nappy headed, low life athletes," Dominique said.

Tashiana was, affectionately called Miss Thang by the girls in their class, because she had long straight black hair and she dressed immaculate. It was easy to see that she came from a family of means. In Dominique's circle of male friends she was called Old Iron pants because she refused to date athletes, or any other boy her parents considered beneath her. They all agreed that her parents had fitted her with a chastity belt to keep her from being deflowered by the dogs that were always chasing her.

"Hey, groin face you're the most popular athlete in the whole damn state. You can have any girl you want, including Miss Thang," Oscar assured him.

"Oh yeah? That's what you think. I asked her if I could take her to a movie sometime. She said I had to ask her parents first, at least a week in advance. Then she tells me they don't trust boys when it comes to her dating, so they probably wouldn't approve of it. And even if they did approve, she wasn't sure if she wanted to go out with Lakeview's super star athlete because I would think I could do anything to her I wanted to. She stressed the point that if her parents don't like me, I'm shit out of luck. So, as you can see, my friend, my all star status doesn't mean a thing to her," Dominique said.

"Can't you see that's her way of scaring off the dogs? I'm sure her parents wouldn't mine her going out with you. After all, you're the school's star basketball player. Girls are dying to go out with you, and you run around acting as if you're just your average jock on campus," Oscar said.

"Until I start making some money at this game, I am just another jock on campus, a jock that wants a date with the most beautiful babe in the world, but is too afraid to ask her parents. What if they don't like me?"

"How could they not like you, my friend? With your reputation, I would trust you with my sister if you two were stranded on a deserted island, in the middle of the Pacific Ocean, for three months. If asking her parents is what it takes to get a date with her, by all means ask them. What do you have to lose?" Oscar encouraged him.

"I don't know. I guess it's worth a try. They can only say yes, or no."

"Hey, that's what I'm talking about,'" Oscar grinned.

Dominique made up his mind to ask Tashiana's parents if he could take their daughter out, if she would go out with him, but it took a while before he actually got up the nerve to do so.

After basketball practice that evening, and her cheerleading practice, he caught up with her half way to her house. They both lived a short distance from school in adjoining neighborhoods.

"Hi Tashiana, may I carry your books for you?" he asked.

"I live right up the road, you know. I'm capable of carrying my own books thank you," she snapped.

"I know where you live, girl. We're almost next-door neighbors. What's eating you anyway? I was only trying to be nice to you. If that's the way you act when someone tries to be nice to you, forget I even asked," he said.

"I'm sorry," Tashiana said, stopping him in his tracks. "It's just that you're the only guy the girls on the cheerleading team talks about. I don't want anyone to get the wrong idea, and think I'm one of your bimbos," she attempted to explain.

"For your information, Miss Hamilton, I don't have any bimbos. What do they say about me?" he asked smiling.

"That you can have any girl in the school you want. What a dream come true it would be to have you all too themselves. Especially the ones who have been out with C. V. White's super star basketball player," she sneered.

"Not one of the girls I have been out on a date with can say I got out of line with them," Dominique said defensively.

"Oh? Are you still a virgin, Mr. Goodman?" Tashiana asked.

"Look, I didn't ask to carry your books so you could insult me. All you had to say was no. I'll check you later," Dominique said, and sprinted for home.

Dominique tried to figure out why Tashiana was so hostile toward him, but he couldn't. All of the parents in the community respected him. Although he was the most idolized young man in the community, he never once treated anyone with anything other than respect. His coach, Mr. George Coleman, taught Dominique over the years, that if he went around treating people less than how he wanted to be treated himself he would end up alone in the end. Dominique never forgot their father and son talks, especially the first one, because he had been acting as if he was the king turd all during practice that evening.

It was after he embarrassed one of his teammates so badly, the boy ran from the gym in tears. Dominique laughed along with everyone else.

Coach Coleman said, "Dominique, I want to see you after practice."

Dominique knew he was in for a long lecture.

After everyone had left the gym, Coach Coleman sat him down in the bleachers and began the lesson Dominique would carry throughout his life.

"Dominique, you're the best damn athlete C.V. White High School has ever known. Maybe the best damn athlete the state of Arkansas has ever known. It would break the hearts of a lot of people to see you get a big head, and blow your future by thinking you already have it made," Coach Coleman said.

"Coach, I know it was wrong to laugh like I did, but you have to admit that Mohawk is nothing but a wimp," Dominique said. Mohawk was the teammate he had embarrassed.

"Believe it or not, your major sports are full of guys who were wimps at one time or another. However, with the help of family and friends, they are now making thousands of dollars at their chosen professions. The one thing I want you to never forget is, even the greatest athlete in the world needs a friend sometimes. Without those athletes who are not as gifted as you are, you would be just another jock running around the campus thinking he is Mr. Big. And there's always the possibility of a career ending injury. Where would you be then? Without a friend in the world willing to stick by you, while you're cussing the world because you feel it isn't fair."

"Coach, I hope you know what you're saying is scaring the hell out of me," Dominique confessed.

"Good, Dominique. I hope you never lose that fear. If you do, you're on your way out, without a friend in the world. Remember, when a jock strap is used up we throw it away. I want you to be in the public's eye long after your playing days are over. The only way a black man can do that in America, is to show the world he has class."

"You got it, coach," Dominique said.

The following day at school, Oscar told Dominique that Mohawk had quit the basketball team.

"Why?" Dominique asked.

"After the way you made him look like a fool yesterday, wouldn't you`?" Oscar laughed.

Dominique thought about what Coach Coleman had said about wimps making it big in sports and felt bad because he was responsible for a fellow teammate giving up a dream because he was not as good as he was. During lunch, Dominique sat beside Mohawk in the school cafeteria.

"Hey, Mohawk, what's this I hear about you quitting the team?"

"I don't have what it takes to play the game, man. Let's face it; I can't beat anyone on our team, or anyone on any other team for that matter. We've played six games so far, and out of those six games, I've played a total of six minutes. That averages out to one minute per game, and four of those minutes were in the first game of the season. And after you made me look like a total fool yesterday, let's face it man, I'm no athlete," Mohawk said.

"Tell you what. I'll work with you every day after practice, if you stick it out. Don't ever give anyone the satisfaction of thinking you're a quitter. I may not make you a super star, but I guarantee you'll improve enough to get more playing time. Hell, you're not the first person to fall for one of my moves," Dominique said smiling, and playfully punching Mohawk on the shoulder.

Mohawk smiled in return, and asked, "Guaranteed?" He knew he couldn't find a better teacher if he searched high and low, except for Coach Coleman. But Coach Coleman didn't have the time.

"Guaranteed," Dominique assured him.

"I'll see you at practice this evening," Mohawk grinned.

True to his word, after practice that evening Dominique worked with Mohawk for an extra hour, and each day afterward for the remainder of the season. Dominique even chose Mohawk to be on his team during pick-up games at the playground. At first it was very frustrating because he was so much better than Mohawk. However, as time passed, Mohawk improved dramatically. During the Christmas break tournament Mohawk became a starter. He was still no super star, but he was a major contributor defensively. Dominique had no way of knowing it at the time, but Mohawk would go on to become one of the best defensive players to ever play college basketball. Sports Illustrated documented Mohawk's defensive prowess in one of their articles on college hopefuls, and the NBA. Dominique took pride in knowing he contributed to Mohawk's defensive ability on the basketball court.

Dominique had very little contact with Tashiana over the Christmas break because of out of town tournaments. Cheerleaders did not accompany the team on road trips at Lakeview. He made a promise to himself that the first week back at school he would ask her for a date. If she said no he would leave it at that. He was not about to beg a girl to go out with him if she didn't want to. He kept the promise he made to himself.

The first week back at school after the Christmas holidays, Dominique asked Tashiana if she would like to go to a movie with him. He thought she would still be hostile toward him, but to his surprise she wasn't. He figured it was because she had gotten everything she wanted for Christmas.

Dominique caught up to her on her way home after school. "Hi. Want me to carry your books for you?" he asked.

"Sure, why not. So how was your Christmas and New Year?" she asked.

"Same old thing, clothes for Christmas and apple cider to bring in the New Year. "What about you? Did you get everything you ask Santa to bring you for Christmas?" he asked.

"Santa's bag couldn't hold everything I wanted for Christmas, but I got some good stuff," Tashiana answered.

"What was your favorite gift of all the stuff you got?" Dominique inquired.

"My own stereo system, it has an eight track tape player, a turntable, and a reel to reel recorder/player system. It didn't come with any tapes or records, because my mom and dad didn't know what to get. But my mom took me shopping later and I got all of the new sounds from Motown," she beamed.

"Must be nice? I bet they didn't let you get any of that boogie woogie music like what Little Richard and Ray Charles plays," Dominique predicted.

"Momma said I could get any kind of music I want. I don't like that music. Believe it or not, my mom and dad are forward thinking people. They're not hypocrites like most of those old fuddy duddy suppose to be Christians at the church," she said.

"I know what you mean. How would you like to go to a movie with me Friday night?" he asked.

"Are you sure you want to go out with Miss Thang, Old Iron pants herself?" Tashiana asked in return, repeating the names she had been labeled with by the boys she would have nothing to do with.

"No, I want to go out with Tashiana Hamilton. The other two girls can stay at home or find their own date. What'd you say?" Dominique laughed, with his fingers crossed behind his back.

"Sure. I guess I'll be safe as long as there are a bunch of people around," she laughed. "But, I told you what you have to do before I can even think about going out with you."

"You would be safe if we were the last two people on earth. The only reason I'm asking you is because I've notice you don't get asked out that often. Why is that?" he pretended not to know, at the same time ignoring the reminder he had to get permission from her parents in order to take her out.

"You should know why that is. I don't associate with scumbags and dumb jocks. You guys have a bad habit of thinking with the head in your pants instead of with the one on your shoulders."

"Well, you don't have to worry about that with me, because you have about as much sex appeal as Frankenstein's bride," he countered.

"That's a low blow Mr. Goodman, but it doesn't matter, because I don't believe you have the guts to come within three miles of my house, anyway," she dared him.

"Oh yeah, I'll be at your house Thursday evening, around seven," Dominique said.

"Well, Mr. Goodman, I can hardly wait for Thursday to come. I hope you don't get a case of amnesia, between now and then."

Dominique had sounded brave while talking to her, but on Thursday as he approached her house, he was as nervous as a death row inmate taking that final walk to meet his maker. Tashiana's father was a sergeant with the Lakeview Police Department, and her mother was the most respected lawyer in Lakeview, a really intimidating pair of people. The horror tales he had heard, from guys who supposedly asked Tashiana parents if they could take her out, was enough to scare the average, well-intended fellow off. The ones with bad intentions didn't dare go near her house. Dominique hoped he could convince them he had nothing but good intentions toward their daughter. He knocked on the door, Mr. Hamilton answered.

"Come on in, son. Tashi told us you would be dropping by to see her this evening. To what does our daughter owe for this visit?" Mr. Hamilton asked.

"I came over to meet you and Mrs. Hamilton, and to ask for your permission to take Tashiana to a movie tomorrow night. If that's okay with you sir," he added hurriedly.

"We'll see. Have a seat," Mr. Hamilton offered. "I'll let Tashi know you're here."

While he was waiting for Tashiana, Dominique couldn't help from thinking about the 357 Caliber Pistol, Mr. Hamilton had strapped at his side. He hadn't expected him to still be in uniform.

I bet that baby could blow a hole in you the doctor couldn't patch up, he was thinking, when Tashiana's mother walked into the room.

"Hi, Dominique," she smiled.

"Hello, ma'am," he returned the courtesy.

"I sure have been hearing a lot about you young man. Have you decided which college you want to attend? I hear you have scholarship offers from as far away as UCLA."

"Yes, ma'am, I have. I'm waiting to see which college my family and Coach Coleman think I should attend before deciding where to go. I'll make my decision based on their recommendation," Dominique explained.

"It makes me feel good to hear a young man put his faith in his family and coach. I'm sure they have your best interest in mind," Mrs. Hamilton assured him.

"Yes ma'am. I believe so," Dominique said.

Tashiana walked into the room with a big smile on her face, and said, "Hi Dominique, I didn't think you were going to show up."

"I told you I would be here this evening," he said.

It made Tashiana feel good to know he thought enough of her to face her parents. "Mom, would it be okay if Dominique and I went into the game room and shoot some pool?"

"Sure, honey. Just be careful on your dad's table. You know how much he loves that thing," Mrs. Hamilton cautioned.

"Yes, Mom, we'll be careful," Tashiana assured her leading Dominique into the game room. After he racked the balls, and she had broke she said, "You want to know something, Mr. High School Super Star?"

"What's that?" Dominique asked.

"You surprise me by the way you act. The other guys on the basketball team walk around acting as if they're king of the world, but not Dominique Goodman. If I didn't know better, I'd think you were an average run of the mill jock, running around campus just trying to graduate. Not the super jock, that has offers from major colleges all over the country," she complimented him.

He laughed and asked, "Does that bother you?"

"No, I think it's great. I'm glad to see you handle yourself so well. With that type of attitude, if it remains that way, you should go a long way in life. At least that's what my parents keep saying."

"I certainly hope so. Thank you for that vote of confidence in me. Do you think your parents are going to let you go out with me tomorrow night?" he asked.

Tashiana hesitated before answering. "I'm sure they won't mind, as long as you don't ask for my hand in marriage, right away. My Mom couldn't wait to meet you. Said I should've caught your attention a long time ago. I told her I had, but I don't trust super stars," she laughed, and continued. "Dad, on the other hand, he'll probably let me go as long as Mom approves. He says you quiet types have to be watched, because you guys are sneaky. Are you sneaky, Dominique?" she smiled.

"Yeah, I'm the sneakiest guy in the whole world. My only reason for trying to get in good with your parents is so I can kidnap you, and take you back to my home planet, Lovetron. It's just east of the moon. What else do you want to know about me?" he asked. Now it was his turn to laugh. Tashiana laughed along with him.

Mr. Hamilton came into the game room. He had changed into civilian clothing. "How good are you at pool, Dominique?" he asked.

"Not too bad," Tashiana answered for him.

"Everyone beats up on you, Tashi, well Dominique? Are you as good a pool player as you are at basketball?" Mr. Hamilton asked.

"I don't like to brag sir, but I've held my own against some of the best pool players in the community."

"Let's see. Rack'em," Mr. Hamilton said.

It was true. Dominique was one of the best pool players in his circle, but he was no match for Mr. Hamilton this night. Mr. Hamilton had mastered his table. Twice Dominique didn't even get to shoot. Dominique did come close to beating him in the last game, but blew the shot on the eight ball. After beating Dominique, five straight games Mr. Hamilton said he had had enough.

"You're pretty good Dominique, but you have to be damn good to beat the best," he bragged.

"I guess you're right, sir. However, I don't like losing at any game. In time sir, I'm going to give you a run for your money," Dominique said seriously.

"Dominique, let me ask you a question. Why's it you call me Mr. Hamilton when everyone else in the community calls me Officer Hamilton?" he asked.

"Well the way I look at it Mr. Hamilton, men were called Mr. as a form of respect long before they started attaching labels to themselves. I feel labels are attached to a person's position rather than to the man himself. So if it is okay with you sir, I've rather show you the respect I feel you deserve as a man and not as a profession," Dominique answered.

"That's one of the most profound reasons I've ever heard in my life, as to why a man should be called Mr. instead of being referred to because of his title. What you said makes a lot of sense. So I guess it'll be okay for you to call me Mr. Hamilton," he laughed. They moved into the living room and sat down.

"I think I could learn to like you Dominique. Have you decided on which college you want to attend upon your graduation?" Mr. Hamilton asked.

"Not yet sir, I'm waiting to see which college my folks, and

Coach Coleman, think I should attend," Dominique repeated what he had told Mrs. Hamilton earlier.

"Not trying to influence you in any way, but if I were you I would jump at the chance to attend UCLA, or Kentucky, those are big time schools. If you do well at either one of those schools, you're a shoo-in for the NBA, NFL, or the Major Leagues. I should know. I attended UCLA myself," Mr. Hamilton informed Dominique.

"I believe you, sir, but I still want to wait and see what my folks have to say," Dominique said.

"I can understand that," he agreed. Then asked suspiciously, "You're not failing any of your subjects in school are you?"

"Daddy, Dominique is on the honor roll for Christ's sake. And he has already passed his college entrance exams," Tashiana interjected.

"I'm making sure he has his bases covered, that's all," Mr. Hamilton said apologetically.

"I assure you sir, my education comes first. I appreciate the concern you're showing on my behalf," Dominique said.

Although he knew Mr. Hamilton was trying to find some fault with him, Dominique still felt they could become friends, of some sort, if given the time. Of course he was wrong.

"That's perfectly okay, son, because we know you're going to put Lakeview on the sport map. Now for the reason you came over here. I naturally assume you've already asked Tashi, if she would like to go to a movie with you tomorrow night?" Mr. Hamilton asked.

"Yes, sir, I have, and she accepted. Providing you and Mrs. Hamilton approve," Dominique added.

"Is this true, Tashi?" Mr. Hamilton asked, turning to face her.

"Yes daddy. I think Dominique is the nicest boy in the whole school," she said.

Dominique was very embarrassed by what she said. He had never been praise by a girl, in front of her parents.

"Well, I've already talked to your mother about it, and she said it's okay with her if it's okay with me. I guess it'll be okay, as long as you two behave yourselves. But how are you going to take her anywhere when to don't own a car. I assume you have a driver's license," Mr. Hamilton said.

"Yes sir, I do have a driver's license. And I have already asked my dad if I can use one of his cars to take Tashiana out if you and Mrs. Hamilton approves," Dominique informed him.

"Okay, but like I said, you'd better behave yourself young man or you may end up playing basketball for the county jail," Mr. Hamilton threatened.

"Believe me, sir, I have no intention of trying anything. I have too much respect for her, and you all, to try anything that stupid," he assured Mr. Hamilton.

"Alright, permission granted. But remember what I said son, no hanky panky," Mr. Hamilton warned.

Having finished saying what he wanted to say, Mr. and Mrs. Hamilton left the room, so Dominique and Tashiana could be alone.

"So, how do you like my parents? Especially, my dad," she laughed.

"To be honest with you, your dad scared the you know what out of me," he whispered.

"Well, don't be afraid of him. His bark is worse than his bite," Tashiana assured him.

"That's easy for you to say, you're his daughter. Hey look, it's getting late. I'd better get going. I'll see you tomorrow at school."

"Okay, I'll walk you to the door, Mr. Superstar," she said, doing a curtsy.

"Cut that out. It is bad enough you embarrass me to death in front of your parents. Oh, I think Dominique is the nicest boy in the whole school," he mimicked her. Dominique tried to sound upset, but he loved every minute of it, now that her parents were not around. He said good night to Mr. and Mrs. Hamilton before he left.

If I'd known it was going be this easy, I would've ask her parents to let me take her out a long time ago, Dominique said to himself. He felt pretty good. At last, he had a date with the most beautiful babe in the world. Dominique felt blessed.

The following day at school after being told that her parents had approved of his taking Tashiana out Oscar asked, "What did I tell you? You should listen to me more often."

"Personally, I think it was a lucky guess on your part," Dominique laughed.

"Lucky guess, lucky guess? I know about women my friend. I started to ask her out myself, but I know how hung up on her you are. I didn't want to hurt your feelings," Oscar said.

They both laughed at this because it was well known throughout the community that Oscar wasn't Officer Hamilton's favorite teen.

When Dominique, and Oscar, entered the school cafeteria at lunch, they spotted Tashiana and a couple of her cheerleading friends at one of the cafeteria tables.

"Let's go over and sit with them," Oscar suggested.

"Why not, me and Tashiana do have a date tonight," Dominique agreed. They walked over to where the girls were sitting.

"Hi, Tashiana, Loraine, Mary Lou, would you ladies mind if we sat with y'all?" Dominique asked.

Loraine was the first to speak. "Not at all, Dominique, you can share my table anytime," she said batting her eyes at him.

"Why, thank you," Dominique said, and slid in beside Tashiana. Oscar sat beside Mary Lou. Although Dominique got the majority of the attention, Oscar was happy to be sitting at the same table with the girls.

"I hear you're taking Tashiana to the movies tonight," Mary Lou giggled.

"Yes, I am. Why?" Dominique asked.

"Oh, no reason," she continued to giggle.

"I think she may be a little jealous," Tashiana teased.

"I'm not," Mary Lou protested.

"Don't feel bad Mary Lou, I'll take you out," Oscar volunteered.

"No thank you, "Oscar the Octopus". I've heard about you," Mary Lou declined.

"You must be mistaken. I'm always a gentleman when escorting a lady," Oscar pleaded his case.

"Yeah, about as much a gentleman as a vampire after the sun goes down," she countered. Everyone at the table laughed, including Oscar.

They talked about their teachers, and who was messing with whom the remainder of the meal.

"I'll see you later Tashiana. I'm going out to the playground and shoot around before the bell rings," Dominique said when he got up to leave.

Once he and Oscar were outside, Dominique busted out laughing. "Oscar, the Octopus?" Dominique asked.

"Bad rap, good buddy. Marlene Sawyer branded me with that

title, after our date last weekend. She's nothing but a damn tease. I thought she wanted to get it on, after all the talk she did about how good she is in bed. She even let me undo her bra, and play with those big gorgeous boobs of hers. When it came time to put up or shut up, she told me to get lost. The next day she told her friends I was all over her, like an eight-armed octopus. Hell, I'd do the same thing again, if she let me," Oscar explained.

"You'll get no argument from me. I've always wondered what those big knockers look like, uncovered," Dominique said.

"Believe me man they're a sight for sore eyes. If you weren't such a damn gentleman with these girls, you would've seen half the tits, and ass, of all the girls in our class," Oscar said.

"Yeah, but that's not my style," Dominique said, but wondered if what Oscar said was true. He dismissed the thought because he had a reputation to uphold.

That evening, he showed up early for his date with Tashiana, so he could challenge Mr. Hamilton to a game of pool, before they left for the movies. To his surprise, he walked away with a victory. He felt he had won the biggest challenge of his life. It didn't matter the score was seven to one, counting their last encounter.

"You got lucky, young man. Don't think it's going to happen too often," Mr. Hamilton advised him.

"As they say in the game of life, sir, luck also counts," Dominique boasted.

"I'll show you what counts," Mr. Hamilton said as he racked the balls.

It would be quite a while before Dominique beat Mr. Hamilton again. It was obvious Mr. Hamilton took every challenge he faced very seriously. It was also obvious that Mr. Hamilton didn't like smart young men who had a mind of their own, which Dominique didn't recognize until later.

Tashiana came bounding into the poolroom and announced that she was ready to go. Mr. Hamilton looked as if he was letting her associate with a known rapist.

"Like I said yesterday young buck, don't try anything with my daughter," Mr. Hamilton reminded Dominique.

"I won't sir, you can believe me," Dominique said.

Mr. Hamilton grunted something unintelligently and then said, "don't keep her out too late."

"Yes sir, I won't," Dominique said heading for the door.

Getting into the car Tashiana asked, "Was it hard getting your father to let you borrow his favorite car?" She was talking about his fathers' 65 Mustang.

"Not really. He knows I'm a careful driver."

"I hope so", she said. "But don't worry, I don't scare easily. By the way, you never did tell me what movie we're going to see."

"It's called, The Creature from Hell. You're not afraid of scary movies are you?" he asked making a monster face.

"Me afraid, I'm not afraid of anything, or anyone," she answered.

"We'll see. You're a regular Attila the Hun, huh?" he asked.

Tashiana didn't answer.

As it turned out, he had chosen the perfect movie. She didn't take her head off of his shoulder the whole time the creature was doing his thing. Her half eaten box of popcorn and watery soda was left on the floor beside the seats where they had sat for the theater employees to clean up.

On their way home, Dominique said, "If I hadn't seen it with my own eyes, I wouldn't have believed it. You're the only girl who didn't jump throughout the whole movie. Man, you're the first girl I've met that isn't afraid of anything. I don't know what I would've done if you hadn't been there for me to hold on to," he laughed.

"Very funny Dominique, you jumped a few times yourself," Tashiana pouted.

"I wasn't jumping. That was you almost knocking me out of my seat, every time you jumped," he laughed again.

"Well, the creature was scary. Even you have to admit that," Tashiana said.

"Okay, I admit it. Next time, I'll take you to watch a love story, if that's not too scary for you too?" Dominique teased.

"It'll be scary only if you try to play the starring role."

"And what is that suppose to mean?" Dominique asked, with raised eyebrows.

"Meaning, I won't be your starring lady," she quipped.

"Fine with me, you're probably a lousy actress anyway," he said.

"You'll never find out," Tashiana said, sticking her tongue out at him.

"Maybe, maybe not, but I can honestly say I've enjoyed being with you tonight. You're a very special girl," Dominique turned serious.

"I like being with you too, but don't get any funny ideas," Tashiana warned.

"Why are you always so defensive, when we talk? You act as if I'm a convicted rapist, or something," Dominique said, tired of her defensive attitude.

"I guess it's because when I'm around you, I find it hard to control myself. Sometimes I want to throw my arms around you and never let go. I've never felt this way about anyone before, so it scares me. God knows, I don't want you to think I'm a push over," Tashiana confessed.

"Never happen, Tashiana. To me you're a very special girl who I want to see again, and again. We'll go as slow as you want to, and I'll never try to take advantage of what you just told me, or force you to do anything you don't want to do. I respect you too much to try something like that. Besides, your father would kill me, if he even thought I was trying to get you to do something like that before we're married. Not that I'm asking you to marry me, or anything. Just that, like I said, I want to see you again and again," he stammered.

"I'm glad to hear you say that Dominique, because I'm looking forward to meeting the person inside of the superstar. That is, if my mother and father allow us to continue dating on a regular basis," Tashiana said.

"You'll get to know me through and through. I'm sure your parents won't mind. It seems they already like me a little," he said hopeful.

When Dominique pulled up in front of Tashiana's house, he opened the car door for her. They walked to the front door of her house holding hands.

"May I kiss you good night or is that asking too much?" he asked.

"I guess, that'll be okay," she smiled.

It was only a brotherly kiss on the cheek, but to Dominique, it was a kiss from one of God's own angels. It was only eleven o'clock, but he went straight home. Normally he would have gone to the Red Barn, where all of his friends hung out until two, or three in the morning. He didn't want to part with the warmth surrounding his heart, by having to answer a lot of questions from the guys about why he hadn't tried to get into Tashiana's pants. Those questions would come soon enough, like the following day at the school playground. Oscar, as always, was the first to ask how far he had gotten with Miss Thang.

"It was nice," Dominique said, not elaborating.

"That's all, just nice?" Oscar asked unbelieving.

"What did you expect me to say? That I got in her pants. Well, I didn't. I didn't even try," Dominique admitted.

"You didn't even try!" Oscar exclaimed, as if it was impossible to go out on a date with a girl and not try anything. He continued, "You go out with the foxiest chick in the whole damn school, and all you can say is you didn't even try? Either, you can't get it up, or you're a faggot who hasn't come out of the closet yet. Which is it?" Oscar asked laughing.

"Neither. With Tashiana, I'm looking for more than just a one-night stand. The girl has class. I mean real class. Something you wouldn't know anything about, considering the type of girls you date," Dominique said.

"She has a beautiful body," Oscar continued, as if Dominique hadn't spoken. "If you screw around and wait too long before making your move, someone is going to snatch her from right under your nose," Oscar warned.

"Oscar, I've only taken her out one time. It's not like we're engaged, or anything," Dominique reminded him.

"That's what I mean, good buddy. So, why not go for the gusto. I'm just looking out for your interest, that's all," he said.

"Yeah, thanks," Dominique said.

He didn't dare tell Oscar what Tashiana said about having trouble controlling herself whenever she was around him, because Oscar would never let him live it down.

Tashiana showed up at the playground later in the day. Dominique couldn't help from showing off in front of his girl. Not that it required much more effort.

After playing his last game, he walked with her on their way home. "Did you mean what you said last night?" Dominique asked.

"Yes, I did. I hope you didn't tell your friends," Tashiana said embarrassed.

"I wouldn't do anything like that. It's none of their business what you tell me. Besides, I know my friends," he laughed.

"Good. There's something else you should know, before we become too fond of each other," she said.

"What's that?" Dominique asked her hesitation too long.

"I don't quite know how to say it," Tashiana began.

"Just, let it all hang out," Dominique encouraged her.

"It's not quite that simple. Anyway, here goes. My mom likes you very much, but I don't know about my dad. I get the impression he doesn't like you for some reason, and he won't tell me, or mom, why. They have plans for me they don't want anyone to interfere with," Tashiana explained.

Before she could continue, Dominique said, "What you're trying to say is, your dad doesn't want you getting involved with someone like me. A boy who is not going to amount to anything if he doesn't make it big in professional basketball, and that's a chance they're not willing to take. Am I right?" Dominique asked.

"I would say you hit the nail on the head, but with your intelligence, I'm sure you can convince them you only have my best interest at heart, and that you're going to be a star no matter what you end up becoming. What they're concerned about is I may fall in love with you and you'll make me change my mind about becoming a lawyer. They said most guys wouldn't be willing to wait until I finish law school. They said you might try to get me to marry you so you can keep me at home bare foot, pregnant, and in the kitchen. Not that you're like that. They're also concerned about what kind of life you would be able to provide for me if you don't make it in professional sports," Tashiana finished.

"Who the hell said anything about getting married, for Christ's sake? Look Tashiana, even if I don't make it in professional sports, I'll have a college education," Dominique said. This was the first time anyone, other than Coach Coleman, had voiced the fact that some un-for-seen incident may prevent him from reaching his dream.

"Please, Dominique, I didn't mean to make you mad. I just want you to know what you're up against if you want to keep seeing me. Mom is going to ask you a lot of questions, the next time you come over. Think you can handle yourself under pressure?" she asked.

"I may not be able to convince them my intentions toward you are honorable, but I'll give it my best shot," Dominique said.

Dominique couldn't shake the feeling that he had been betrayed, by the girl he wanted more than anything in the world. He believed Tashiana wanted him to prove to her that he wanted to keep seeing her and were using her parents to wrangle this verbal confession out of him.

"I guess, I can't ask for anything more than that of my superstar. When are you coming over to the house?" Tashiana asked.

"I'll be over tomorrow afternoon, sometime after church. Will your father be home to interrogate me?" Dominique dreaded the thought.

"No, he started working swing shifts last night. Three in the afternoon, until eleven at night," she informed him.

"Okay, I'll see you tomorrow," he said.

He was grateful that her father, at least, wouldn't be home during the interrogation. They walked in silence, until they reached her house.

"Do you really think you'll be able to convince my parents to let you continue to see me?" Tashiana sounded doubtful.

"Sure, I can. I convinced you, didn't I?" Dominique smiled.

Tashiana didn't answer. He squeezed her hand and was off and running. That night Dominique asked his father what he would do, if he were in his shoes.

"How much do you care for this girl?" his father asked.

"I care for her a lot Dad," Dominique confessed.

"Well, if you feel that strongly about her, by all means, talk to her parents. They can only say no. But let me caution you against showing Tashiana that you're willing to do anything to be with her. Eventually she, and most of the other girls in this town, will peg you as a wimp and a sucker. Go ahead and ask her parents if you can date her. If they say yes, let her know from jump-street, that you'll be calling the shots from then on. Otherwise, she'll walk all over you," Dominique's father advised.

"Thanks, Dad," Dominique said.

This relationship is already over, he was thinking, if that was the only advice his father could give him. Dead before they even had a chance to breathe life into it.

He lay awake that night thinking of everything that could possibly happen to prevent him from reaching his dream of being a superstar in the NBA. Drugs never, a busted knee, maybe. A messed up foot, possibly. Academics, no way could grades hold him back.

Before falling asleep, he rationalized with himself. *I'll bet every professional athlete has worried about getting hurt, or something happening to them, that would prevent them from reaching their dream at some point in their lives. It didn't stop them, and it won't stop me. If I truly want to be a professional basketball player the only person who can stop me is me, and if Mr. and Mrs. Hamilton don't want me to see their daughter anymore, it won't be the end of the world. At least, I'll be able to see her at school.*

However, Dominique realized it wouldn't be enough, just seeing Tashiana at school. He was determined to convince her parents he had no intention of changing anyone's mind, about anything, especially about Tashiana becoming a lawyer. Convinced he could do it, he slept the sleep of babes.

The following day at the basketball court after church, he was too nervous to say much to anyone. To make matters worse Tashiana didn't show up to watch him play. He could hardly wait for the confrontation with Mrs. Hamilton to be over and done with. That evening, as he approached Tashiana's house, he conditioned his mind as he did before a game. He felt calm. That sense of urgency to get the confrontation over with vanished. He felt he was ready to take on the world. Dominique also knew he couldn't go into the Hamilton's house and act as if he owned it.

Dominique rang the doorbell, and Tashiana answered the door. "Hi, Dominique, come on in," she said. She was happy to see he hadn't backed out of the confrontation with her mom.

"Who's that, Tashi?" Mrs. Hamilton asked from the kitchen.

"It's Dominique. Can we go into the game room, and shoot some pool?" she asked.

"Sure, baby. I'll be in there in a little bit. I want to talk to Dominique alone, if you don't mind," Mrs. Hamilton announced.

"No ma'am. We'll be in the game room." As soon as they entered the game room, Tashiana asked, "What're you going to tell her?"

"I'm going to tell the truth. That no matter what happens I'll be able to support the woman I love, even if that means I have to clean every toilet in the world, foreign and domestic. And they don't have to worry about me trying to keep you from graduating from law school," Dominique answered.

Tashiana laughed and said. "I don't think you'll have to stoop that low, as having to clean toilets for a living."

"I know, but it does make me sound determined to make it in life. Don't you think?" Dominique asked.

"Yeah, but let's not overdo it," she cautioned him.

"Don't worry, I won't."

They had not finished the first game when Mrs. Hamilton entered the room.

"Would you mind leaving us alone, for a few minutes, Tashi?" Mrs. Hamilton asked.

"No ma'am. If you need me, I'll be in the living room," Tashiana informed her.

"Thank you, baby," Mrs. Hamilton said as Tashiana left the room.

The way Tashiana looked at him before leaving the room gave Dominique the impression that this wasn't the first time she had charmed a young man to the point he thought he was ready to face her parents. He wondered how many had dared, but fail to achieve their goal.

After Tashiana left the room Mrs. Hamilton turned to him and asked. "How's your family?"

"They're doing fine, ma'am," Dominique answered.

After a slight pause she continued. "I don't know what Tashi has told you, but we have big plans for that girl. She's going to be a lawyer like her mom, come back here to Lakeview, Arkansas, and eventually own one of the biggest law firms in the south," Mrs. Hamilton explained.

"That'd be a good thing for her, and Arkansas. Who knows, she may end up being my agent in the future," Dominique said.

"That's one of the things I wanted to talk to you about. What are your plans, if something happened, God forbid, that would keep you from reaching your goal of becoming a professional basketball player?" Mrs. Hamilton asked sincerely.

"Believe me, Mrs. Hamilton, my eyes have been opened to that possibility for some time now. Coach Coleman has planted it in my mind that I have to look beyond professional sports to live a full life. So, I'm going to major in business management. That way, no matter what happens, I'll be able to make a living for myself, and who ever happens to be unlucky enough to marry this jock," Dominique answered. By the expression on her face, he could tell Mrs. Hamilton liked what she had heard so far.

"My next question is could you love a woman who has career goals, the same as you do?" she asked.

"Having never been in love before, I don't know how to answer that question truthfully, ma' am. However, I suppose if I truly cared for her, and our relationship, it wouldn't pose too much of a problem. Nothing, I'm sure, we couldn't work out." Dominique said pleased with his answer.

"Would it bother you to have to wait until Tashiana finished college, before getting too involved?" Mrs. Hamilton asked.

"No ma'am. The woman I eventually marry will have to have a college education. This way, I'll be able to confide in her whenever I need advice from someone other than a business partner," Dominique answered.

"You have everything planned I see," Mrs. Hamilton said. She was impressed with his answers.

"Yes, ma'am, I do. I just hope nothing happens to change those plans," Dominique said.

"Okay young man, you've come up with all the right answers so far, one final question. Why should Mr. Hamilton, and I, allow you to continue seeing Tashi?" Mrs. Hamilton asked placing her hands on her hips.

He had practiced answering that particular question all day, but he hesitated before answering so as to give the impression he was giving it some serious thought. "Well, for one thing ma'am, I would never interfere with her desire to make something of herself. Second, you would never have to worry about me trying to take advantage of her when we go out on dates. I have too much respect for her, and you and Mr. Hamilton, to try anything stupid," Dominique answered truthfully.

Mrs. Hamilton hesitated a long time before saying anything further. He had started to wonder if his answers were too cut and dried. He thought she was seriously contemplating asking him to leave her house and never return.

Where were you when I was growing up? Mrs. Hamilton asked herself aloud remembering the arguments she and Mr. Hamilton had before he finally gave in and supported her having a career. Mr. Hamilton had been so against the idea of her working they had come close to getting a divorce.

"Ma'am?" Dominique asked confused.

"Oh nothing, I was just thinking out loud to myself. You're a very impressive young man, I must admit. But how do I know you're not just another smooth talking jock, trying to get his way with my daughter?" Mrs. Hamilton asked.

"I guess the only way for you to find that out ma'am, is to allow me to date your daughter. If she ever tells you, or her dad, that I did anything to try and change her beliefs, or tried to get her to go against the plans you all have for her, by all means ma'am never let me set foot in your house again," Dominique answered.

"I admire your confidence, Dominique. Still, I have to discuss this with Tashi's dad before making a final decision. He was looking forward to talking to you himself, but he's working swing shift and had to be at work at three o'clock this afternoon. I'm sure he wants to talk to you himself, before a final decision is made. For some reason he doesn't think you're trustworthy, but I'm sure you'll be able to change his mind. You certainly impress me," Mrs. Hamilton informed him.

"Yes ma'am, I understand," Dominique said.

"You can stay a while longer, and finish your game if you like. I have some business to attend to in my study," Mrs. Hamilton walked out of the game room with a smile on her face.

"Thank you, ma' am," Dominique smiled in return.

Tashiana came back into the game room and asked what he had said to her mother, because she was grinning from ear to ear. As he told her what had been asked and how he had answered the questions, the smile on her face got wider and wider.

After being filled in, she said, "I don't think you'll have any problems with dad. Normally, if mom says something is cool he goes along with her judgment. Looks like we're going to be seeing a lot of each other in the future," Tashiana smiled.

"Don't count your chickens before their hatch, "Dominique warned her. "She didn't say I could date you yet. All she said was, she would discuss it with your dad," he reminded her.

"What did I just finish saying? Mom was grinning from ear to ear. That means she was very impressed with you. That's a sure sign that everything is a go," Tashiana assured him.

"I hope so, for your sake. Someone have to keep the dogs off of you," Dominique joked.

"Yeah, and someone have to keep the female dogs off of you. God knows they're always in heat," Tashiana countered.

They both laughed having stated their objective to protect each other from the predatory classmates they knew so well. That was the beginning of a lifetime commitment.

Dominique was so happy, he felt lightheaded when he left her house because Mrs. Hamilton said, "I guess we're going be seeing a lot of you around here after tonight."

"I hope so ma'am," Dominique replied.

Because of Tashiana's aspirations to become a lawyer, Dominique started referring to her as *Miss Lawyer* on occasions. And as she had predicted, her father went along with her mother's wishes. The only thing Mr. Hamilton had to say was if Dominique tried anything with his daughter, he would have to answer to him.

Tell me something I don't already know, Dominique mumbled to himself after Tashiana told him what her father had said.

On their next date Dominique asked Tashiana, "Miss Lawyer, how many guys have tried to convince your parents they were worthy of your affection?"

"Oh, I don't know. At least a dozen," she laughed.

"Come on, be serious. A grouchy lady like yourself would be lucky to have more than one guy brave enough to hit on her, let alone brave enough to ask your parents for permission to see you on a regular basis. Really, how many?" Dominique asked.

"To be totally honest with you Mr. Know-it-all, a total of two. You and a boy named Robert Tye. He graduated from Miller's High School. He's attending Howard University to become, of all things, a chemist. He wants to work in an FBI Lab some day. I thought he was a nice enough guy, but mom and dad said he was a real creep after he said he wouldn't allow his wife to work. They told him they would never allow me to date a male chauvinist pig," she laughed. "They said they didn't want him near me as long as they both lived. The poor boy was sweating like crazy after they finished with him. He never even attempted to talk to me again after that."

"Well, at least you're batting five hundred," Dominique said.

"How many moms have you charmed into letting you have your way with their beloved daughters?" Tashiana asked pretending to be jealous.

"Believe it or not, Miss Lawyer, you're the only girl I've ever wanted to go out with more than once. So it hasn't been necessary for me to beg for any girl's affection as I did for yours," Dominique said, taking her into his arms.

Tashiana's face lit up as if someone had flicked on a light from somewhere deep within her. Her eyes twinkled like the North Star on a clear beautiful night. Her breathing became labored as Dominique pressed her tight against his trembling body. Tashiana tilted her head upward to meet his forthcoming kiss. As their lips met, hers were far sweeter than anything he had ever imagined. His father had told him there were no sweeter juices than those of the woman you loved. He didn't know if he was in love or not, but it was the greatest sensation he had ever experienced. Had they not been oxygen-breathing mortals, he didn't think the kiss would've ever ended. They could hardly catch their breath so intense was the kiss. Tashiana was visibly shaking after he released her.

"My goodness, does it get any better than this?" she asked.

"If it does, I don' think I'm going to survive," Dominique replied

They kissed a few more times before calling it a night. On dates after that one, it took all the will power they had to keep from going all the way. They somehow restrained themselves, to the satisfaction of her parents.

Dominique's team won the Arkansas state basketball championship, and he chose to attend USC. However, the biggest thrill of the year for him was when Tashiana accepted his engagement ring. They were to get married upon her completion of her first four years of college, but before she entered law school. During the remainder of the school year they were inseparable. They had eyes for only one another.

Oscar chose to attend Lakeview Junior College there in Lakeview. That way he would be home to help his dad run their flower shop during the first two years of college before moving on to the University of Arkansas.

Mohawk received a partial scholarship from Georgia tech., with the understanding that if he became a starter, it would be upgraded to a full scholarship, which he did halfway through the season during his freshmen year. However, Mohawk never was good enough to play in the NBA. He went on to become a high school basketball coach/history teacher there in Georgia after several tryouts with NBA teams.

Several days before his scheduled graduation Dominique received a letter that would change his and Tashiana's lives forever, his draft notice from good Ole' Uncle Sam. The day after receiving his draft notice Dominique went to talk to Coach Coleman.

"Come on in and have a seat Dominique. What's on your mind? Worried about your upcoming visit to USC?" Coach asked.

"I have a decision to make and I don't know which will be the right choice," Dominique said handing him the draft notice.

"Is this what I think it is?" Coach asked.

"I've been drafted Coach. What should I do?"

"Well, you have two options. One, you can go out to the college and enroll early so you can apply for a deferment until you finish school, and be considered a draft dodger, or two, I can talk to Coach Meyers and see if he's willing to hold your scholarship open until you complete your service obligation. If he's willing to do that, I'll help you get back on track when you get out," Coach advised him.

"Which way do you think I should go?" Dominique asked wanting a straight answer.

"The decision is not mines to make. What you have to decide is whether you want to live with the label of being called a draft dodger, or you can do your two years and carry on with you life. Think about it for a couple of days and let me know what you decide," Coach again evaded the question.

"If it were you who were drafted Coach, what would you do?" Dominique persisted.

Coach Coleman leaned forward in his chair and said, "I think like the white boys do. They don't give a damn about this war, or this country, if there's nothing in it for them. I would say to hell with the military and finish school. However, I have the luxury of being able to say that because I'm too old to be drafted. You have a bright future ahead of you regardless of the decision you make. I hear if you're good enough to make the All Army Basketball Team, you don't have to worry about going to Vietnam. I know you're good enough. You're better than most of the guys I played with, and against, while I was in college. Let them know you have a basketball scholarship waiting for you after your two years are up. I'm told they're always on the lookout for talented athletes. Like I said, think about it for a couple of days and let me know what you decide," Coach said, getting up from his chair and patting Dominique on the back.

"What 're you going to do, Dominique?" Tashiana asked, that evening as they sat on the porch.

"Hell, I don't know. I have two options. One, I can go ahead and get my two years in the Army out of the way, or two, I can delay my draft until after I finish college. Which do you think I should do?" Dominique asked.

"If you don't go ahead and serve your two years, people are going to call you a draft dodger. So you can go head and serve your two years in the service and make people happy. Or you can go ahead and finish college and say to hell with the people who are going to call you a draft dodger. At least that way if anything happens to you while you're serving in the army, hopefully not Vietnam, you'll have a college education to fall back on," Tashiana advised.

"I had a talk with Coach Coleman about me getting drafted and he assured me I should be able to get another scholarship upon my discharge from the service if I choose to go that route," Dominique said.

"That's if nothing happens to you while you're in the army," Tashiana insisted.

Why are you so sure something is going to happen to me?"
Dominique asked becoming angry.

"I'm not saying anything is going to happen to you, just that
you should be prepared for any situation that might come up,
that's all. They're sending bright young black men like yourself
to Vietnam you know. And from what I hear, Charlie doesn't give
a crap if you have a college scholarship waiting for you when you
get back home," Tashiana tried to reason with him.

"So you think I should ahead and finish college before going
into the army. Say to hell with all the a-holes who are going to
be calling me a draft dodger for the rest of my life. Is that what
you're saying?" Dominique asked.

"No, that's not what I'm saying. What I'm trying to get
across to you is, its up to you to do whatever you think is best for
you. But you should keep everything in its proper perspective,"
Tashiana advised further.

"I want to go ahead and finish college before going in, because
it sound like the right thing to do, but on the flipside I don't want
anyone running up in my face calling me a draft dodger. Besides,
nothing is going to happen to me while I'm in the service whether
I go to Vietnam or not. I can always finish college when I get out
of the army. I'm only serving two years. No matter what happens,
I'll get a college education. The only way I won't get a college
education is if I'm dead, and then it wouldn't matter anyway, now
would it?" Dominique asked trying to convince himself he would
be making the right decision if he went ahead and served his tour
of duty.

"Regardless of what you decide to do, I'm with you one
hundred percent. You don't have to rush into a decision right
away, anyway. You have thirty days to make up your mind. And

like I said, I'm with you all the way. The only thing I'm going to demand is that you spend all thirty days with me," Tashiana said, hugging him.

"Miss Lawyer, there is nothing in this world that could keep me away from you," Dominique hugged her in return.

It was the shortest thirty days of his life. Having Tashiana there to comfort him was more than he could've hoped for. Dominique decided to go ahead and serve his two years, get out, and continue his dream of playing basketball in the NBA. He also convinced Tashiana that his being in the army was no different than them going to different colleges, which they were going to do anyway.

Coach Coleman told Dominique, although he thought he was making a mistake by going ahead and serving his tour of duty before going to college, he supported him all the way. He would be waiting to help him get through college when he returned home from the war. Dominique's family, on the other hand, was very upset with his decision.

"Dammit boy, why the hell do you want to do something that damn stupid? You don't see these white boys with scholarships running down to the recruiter's office to join up. You should get your education first and then worry about Uncle Sam," Dominique's father advised.

"I know what you're saying is true, but I want to get this army stuff over with so I won't have to worry about it when I get to college," Dominique tried to reason.

Dominique's mother said, "Son, don't you know that black kids like yourself is dying every day in that crazy war. If you go ahead and go to college the war may be over by the time you graduate. I don't want to lose you."

"Why does everyone keep telling me that something terrible is going happen to me if I go ahead and serve my time in the army?" Dominique asked.

"No one said anything is going to happen to you boy, but kids are getting their asses blown off every day in this stinking war, and I don't want you to be one of them," his dad said.

"I might be making the wrong decision, but it's the one I'm making. With you guys in my corner I'll be alright," he assured them.

His parents tried to get Dominique to change his mind every day until the day he left for boot camp. Although they didn't like his decision they realized he had to live his own life.

Dominique smiled to himself as he remembered the sad parting he and Tashiana shared the day he went off to serve his country. They knew the world as they knew it would never be the same. They took comfort in knowing their love for one another would never change. The day he left was a sad day indeed.

"I'll write you every day we're apart," he promised, while they were sitting at the bus station waiting for the bus that would take him to the induction station in Memphis, Tennessee.
And I'll write you every day too," Tashiana promised, with tears rolling down her cheeks.

"Do you get the feeling God is testing our love?" Dominique asked.

"It doesn't matter what test I have to pass, I'll always love you," Tashiana answered.

"And I'll always love you," Dominique assured her.

They held on to each other for as long as possible. Not until the bus driver threatened to leave him, did he let go of her. Dominique always blamed himself for neither of them reaching their dreams, as well as for the sad times they experienced early in their relationship.

As promised, they wrote one another almost daily. It was her support that helped him through the rigorous training and constant verbal abuse he had to endure during his basic combat training. And later, it was Tashiana's undying support that helped him through the disappointment of knowing he would never play professional basketball during his lifetime.

While in high school, Dominique had taken several first aid courses. Because of that knowledge, they chose to put him in the medical field upon his graduation from basic training. He didn't mind, because being in the medical field reduced his chances of going to Vietnam considerably, not to mention his commander at his basic training unit was a big basketball fan at all levels and knew he had signed to play at USC. Dominique didn't know if the captain in his basic training unit had anything to do with it, but he ended up being assigned to the 158th Medical Evacuation Hospital in Thailand. It was where they sent wounded soldiers from Vietnam to be patched up, recuperated, and sent back to the jungle to start the process all over again. Dominique felt bad sending his fellow comrades back to the front when they should have been sending them home, because psychologically most of them were screwed up in the head and needed psychological help for them to be normal human beings again. Listening to them talk about not knowing if they would be able to stop killing people once they return to the states concerned him.

While stationed in Thailand, he quickly became the star of the post basketball team. It had been arranged for him to go to the all Army tryouts in San Francisco, CA, during their next recruiting phase. But during a pick up game one afternoon, he severely injured his right knee and was transferred back to the states for surgery. After three major surgeries and a couple of months of rehabilitation at Walter Reed Hospital in Washington, D.C. he was given a medical discharge.

Only eleven months of active service, and Dominique's dreams had been shot to hell. Although he realized it could've happened while he was in college, it was no consolation. He was a very hard person to live with. After the medication of the first operation wore off, he wrote Tashiana at Hampton University where she was attending school. Since it was meant to be a one-way conversation he did not put a return address on the envelope. Dominique told her what had happened to him, and explained his present feeling regarding their future together.

"Dear Tashiana:

Maybe I should've listened to what you were trying to tell me, about finishing college

before worrying about saving my brittle pride. Now that it's too late, and I know I'll

never reach my dream, I realize that you were right. I hope you, at least, will achieve

the dream you have set for yourself.

Since my dream has been shattered, I guess the best thing for me to do is step aside

and let you do your thing. I'll never feel I'm doing my share to help support you or our

family when we decide to have children. Let's face it. I don't know what's best for me,

so how in the hell am I suppose to know what is best for the both of us? I guess what I'm trying to say is, I want the best for you. Right now I feel I would only get in the way and ruin your life, as I've ruined my own. I love you, but I don't think under the present circumstances, I would be of very much help or encouragement to you. I'm going to go to college, but I have no idea what I want to do. Maybe I can become a registered nurse or something. God knows that's all I've been since I've been in the army. If I sound bitter, it's because I am. And the part that hurts the most is I brought it all on myself. All my life, I've tried to maintain a stupid all American image. Deciding to go ahead and serve my tour of duty to my country was no different. It would look good on my record. Everyone would say, although Dominique is a superstar, he still took the time to help win the war in Vietnam. Well, everyone has to face reality sooner or later. My reality came sooner.

Maybe I'll write you again soon, after I get over this babbling stage. Whatever you do Tashiana, don't you drop out of college because of what has happened to me. Maybe our love wasn't meant to be. Well, to make a long story short, I love you but I'm forced to say good-bye. I hope you get everything you deserve out of this stinking, unfair, messed up world, he finished, trying his best to keep the tears rolling down his face from wetting the paper he was writing on.

Dominique wrote Tashiana again several days later, but it was a short, unemotional letter. Two months after his last letter to Tashiana, he was medically discharged, and given a 30% disability rating, which meant he was authorized to go to any army medical facility for treatment, if needed. He also received a monthly check for the disability, but it was nothing to write home to momma about.

Since he didn't have the courage to face his family, or the people in his community, he wrote and told his family he would keep them advised of his whereabouts and progress by mail.

The last thing he needed in his life right now was pity. As far
as Tashiana was concerned, he didn't know how he would react
to seeing the pity for him in her eyes when she came home
from college to visit her parents, so he figured he made the right
decision not to go home after his discharge from the hospital. He
had no intention of seeing her again until she had met the man of
her dreams and they were happily married. Life is so simple when
you're young and think your plans will always work out the way
you plan them.

Prior to being discharged from the hospital at Walter Reed, he
had made arrangements to attend Arizona State University, using
the Army's GI Bill. Dominique chose Arizona State University
because he felt he could lose himself in the white crowd and not
have to explain his disappointments and failures to anyone there.
He wrote and told his parents he had been accepted at ASU, but
didn't know if he wanted to attend that particular college. He told
them he had also been accepted at Howard University there in
D.C. He would let them know which college he decided to attend,
after he got his life back on track. Until that time, they need not
bother trying to contact him because he would be out of touch with
everyone.

Although Dominique felt bad for not corresponding with his
family he could not bring himself to do so until a year had passed.
He finally wrote to his parents to let them know that he was okay,
and was attending Arizona State University studying to become
an X-ray Technician. In her first letter to him his mother begged
him to come home as soon as possible. Tashiana had dropped out
of school because of him, saying if she couldn't live her life with
him, her life was already over. Her decision had caused such a
rift between her and her family they were threatening to disown

her. Officer Hamilton even blamed them for what she did because he was their son. She said the confrontation between his dad and Officer Hamilton wasn't pretty.

Officer Hamilton pulled up in front of their house in his patrol car a couple of weeks after Tashiana quit school and returned home. He got out of the car and looked around as if he was about to commit a murder and didn't want any witnesses. Dominique's mother answered the door upon hearing the knock.

"Hello, Officer Hamilton. Come on in and have a seat. What can we do for you?" she asked.

"Is Joe home? I wanted to talk to him about something," Officer Hamilton said calmly.

"Yeah, I'm home. What do you need to talk to me about?" Dominique's dad asked entering the living room.

"I wanted to talk to you about Dominique. I need to know where he is. As you have probably heard, Tashi dropped out of school because of what happened to Dominique. Now she refuses to go back to school until she talks to him. So, I would appreciate it if you would tell me how she can get in contact with him," Officer Hamilton informed him.

"I wish I could help you Officer Hamilton, but the truth is we haven't heard from Dominique since he was discharge from the hospital. The last letter we got from him he was still at Walter Reed. He said he hadn't figured out what to do with his life, and until that time he would be out of touch with the world. But as soon as he got himself together, he would let us know where he is and what he's doing. We're just as anxious as to hear from him as Tashiana is," Dominique's dad informed him.

"What're saying Joe? Your boy is so fucked up in the head because of what happened to him he has isolated himself from his family and the world?" Officer Hamilton asked suspiciously.

"I guess you can say that. Why don't you call Walter Reed Hospital and find out where he went after he was discharged from the hospital," Dominique's Dad suggested.

"That was the first thing I did when Tashi started talking this nonsense about quitting school if she couldn't marry Dominique. You people make it sound as if Dominique vanished from the face of the earth. Since he's not a criminal, no other law enforcement agency will assist me in finding him. So, it's back to my original question, do you know how to get in touch with your son," he made it sound as if they were lying to him about Dominique's where about.

Dominique's dad was not about to be intimidated by Officer Hamilton. He said, "My answer is still no. I don't know how to get in contact with him, and since he's not a criminal with the law I could give a shit less. When he's ready, he'll get in contact with us," Dominique's dad said, becoming angry at the tone of Officer Hamilton's line of questioning.

"When he decides to bring his ass back home, I'm sure he's going to break some type of law. When you hear from Dominique tell him to call Tashi and tell her to get her butt back in school. Otherwise, he'd better watch his step if he decide to come back home," Officer Hamilton smiled.

"Why don't you go and threaten to lock your daughter up. Maybe that'll scare her into going back to school. What'd you think?" Dominique's dad asked sarcastically.

"Don't be a wiseass Joe. What's in store for your boy could just as easily be applied to you," Office Hamilton again threatened Dominique's dad.

"If I hear from him, we'll let Tashiana know right away. Maybe if you tried talking to the girl instead of threatening her all the time she might listen to reason," Dominique's dad advised him.

"You run your household, and I'll run mines. Be sure to let me know when you hear from your cowardly son," Officer Hamilton said walking toward the door.

"Will do, officer," Dominique's dad said showing him out the door.

Dominique felt bad for Tashiana when he heard the news. He knew how much it meant to her, and her family, that she became a lawyer. Still, he couldn't bring himself to write, or call her, although he wanted to tell her she was making a mistake by dropping out of school. She should take her butt back to college and get her degree. He also hesitated calling her because he knew her parents blamed him for her dropping out of school. *Oh well,* he thought to himself.

After much pleading in every letter he received from his mom, he reluctantly gave her the number to the pay phone in the dorm hallway outside his room, with the understanding that he very seldom heard it ring. So, if whoever answered the phone didn't let him know he had a call he wouldn't know about it. He also asked his mom not to give the phone number to anyone else, including Tashiana. He knew it was wishful thinking, because Tashiana was going to be the first person his mom gave the number to, and she would give it to anyone else she wanted to give it to. Two weeks later while studying for an exam, he was told he had a phone call.

"Hello," he answered the phone thinking it was his mom. She was the only person who had called him so far.

"Hello, Dominique. Guess who this is? Tashiana said in a strained voice.

Dominique almost hung up and ran back to his room to drown

himself in sorrow, as he had done since the accident. Instead he said, "My mom wasn't suppose to give this number to anyone, including you. Why did you call?" he asked, realizing that was the stupidest question he'd ever asked anyone in his life.

"Dominique, I know what you must be going through. But believe me, I love you more now than I ever did. Simply because you were willing to give me up to some else, so I could reach a stupid dream my mom and dad wanted me to pursue. Let me help you through your disappointment and pain," she pleaded, sounding as if she was about to cry.

He was surprised to realize how cold the accident had left him. All he felt at that moment was that she was invading his private world, where no one was allowed. Still, it was good to hear her voice again. But the bitterness and self-pity had a strong hold on his emotions as he said, "Look Tashiana, I've already ruined my life. Why do you insist I ruin yours too? My Mom told me you dropped out of school because of me. You want to tell me what possessed you to do such a stupid thing?" he asked too harshly.

Tashiana was now truly on the verge of tears as she responded. "It had nothing to do with you. I just used you as an excuse to drop out of school." Dominique tried to protest, but she continued before he could interrupt. "I guess I wasn't meant to be a lawyer. So I'm studying to be the next best thing. I'm attending Lakeview Junior College here at home to become a legal assistant. Mom and Dad support me fully. And after I graduate, I'll be working for my mom. I'm sure you could find a job here as an X-ray technician at the hospital," she suggested, having been told by his mother what he was studying to become.

Dominique knew she was lying about her parents supporting her to become a legal assistant but let it pass without commenting on it. He said, "I could never be happy there in Lakeview. I have to find my fortune and fame someplace else. Maybe here in Arizona," Dominique said, letting her know he had no intention of coming back to Lakeview to stay. He could feel the block of ice he had built around his heart start to melt somewhat as they talked. The last thing he wanted was to hurt Tashiana more than she had already been hurt.

"Don't you love me anymore?" Tashiana asked, and broke into tears.

For several moments, Dominique was speechless. When he found his voice, he said, "Tashiana, please stop crying. Of course I still love you. I love you more than I do myself. It's just that I don't know what to say or do. I'll never be able to give you the things I promised, or take you to the places we talked about visiting someday. And I don't know if could live with myself knowing it was because of me that you gave up your dream. God, it seems so long ago that we were carefree youngsters who had our lives all planned out, thinking nothing would happen to interfere with those dreams," Dominique said feeling sorry for himself.

"Surely things can't be that bad. I told you before you left you left I would stick by you no matter what life threw in our paths. Let me help you through this temporary set back," she said, dismissing his promises of riches and fame.

"Give me a few days to think about it. Believe me baby, this is hard for me to say, but I need time to think about whether I should burden you with my wasted dreams. I'm the hardest person in the world to live with right now. So please, give me the time I need to get my act together before I have to deal with the both of us," he begged.

"Is there another woman?" Tashiana asked sounding defeated.

"No, Tashiana, there isn't another woman in my life," he assured her. "I need the time to think about us. I want to do what is best for you. Hey, I've got a test tomorrow. I gotta go. I'll call you in a couple of days," he said. Here was the only love of his life, and he needed time to figure out if he still wanted to be with her or not. He was convinced the injury had driven him insane.

"Dominique Goodman, I want to know where we stand before you hang up," she demanded.

He wanted to say I love you and can't wait until I get home so we can get married. Instead he said, "I'll be bale to answer that question in a couple of days. I have to go now. I don't want to hurt you any more than I've l already hurt you, but I need the time to think things through. Just give me a couple of days to get myself together. Okay?" Dominique asked.

"Okay Dominique, but please call me and let me know what you decide in a couple of days," she agreed, stressing a couple of days.

"I will. I promise," he said and hung up.

Now where do I go from here? Dominique asked no one, after he had hung up.

Dominique had convinced himself he would never be able to face Tashiana again, because he would never be able to give her the things he had promised. At the same time he knew in his heart it was stupid to think he wouldn't have to deal with her until after she was happily married. *Welcome to the real world, Dominique Goodman*, he scolded himself. Instead of going home as a future superstar, engaged to marry Lakeview's future lawyer, he would be going home to a place of busted dreams of how things should have been.

During the next couple of days, Dominique realized there was no way of getting around dealing with Tashiana and her parents. And because their daughter would never be what they wanted her to be, he knew they would do anything within their power to keep them apart, by Mr. Hamilton anyway. Instead of calling Tashiana, he called Mrs. Hamilton.

"Hello, this is the Hamilton's residence," she answered, not expecting a call from the man who held such a hold on their daughter she would defy their wishes.

"Mrs. Hamilton, this is Dominique. I called your office and they told me you had taken the day off. I wanted to tell you I'm sorry for what Tashiana has chosen to do, supposedly because of me. I love your daughter more than you can imagine. If there is anything I can do to get her to go back to school and become the lawyer you have always wanted her to be, believe me, ma'am, I will," he said, his mouth as dry as desert sand.

"I have my doubts about you, Dominique. The first time you run across a situation which you have no control, you want to run and hide. Do you really think the people around here are going to love you any less because you won't end up being a superstar in the NBA? I've always pictured you as being stronger than that for some reason. Tashi has defied our wishes she loves you so much. If you can't see that, then I hope you never speak to her again as long as you live. That would really satisfy Mr. Hamilton, because he never wanted you to date Tashi in the first place. He trusted my judgment. Now she's suffering because she think you no longer loves her, and it tears my heart to pieces to think I believed in you to the point I could hardly wait for you to become my son-in-law. All it would've taken was a simple phone call telling her that although your dreams were no longer attainable, there was no reason for her to abandon hers. If you love Tashi, that's what you'll tell her the next time you talk to her. Convince her it's not too late for her to reach her dream," she said. It was more of a plea, than advice.

Dominique had expected a lot more anger, and hostility, toward him. To his surprise, he detected very little anger in her voice. Disappointment yes, but outright hostility no.

"Mrs. Hamilton, I do love Tashiana, but for stupid some reason, I thought things would be different since my dreams were shot to hell. I'll never be able to give her the things I promised, or take her around the world on our honeymoon. After my mom told me what she had done, I was afraid you and Mr. Hamilton wouldn't let me talk to, or see her again. I'm sorry I'm not the man you thought I was," Dominique said in such a hurt voice Mrs. Hamilton felt sorry for him.

"Tashi gets out of school at five. She's the one you should be telling this to, not me. Remember one thing, Dominique, if you don't call her and explain what was going on in your mind, you can rest assured I'll never forgive you for ruining my daughter's life," she smiled through the phone. He could see the smile as clear as if she was there in the dorm with him.

Mrs. Hamilton sounded as if she could find it in her heart to forgive him someday, as long as Tashiana went back to school and became a lawyer. Dominique knew Tashiana's parents wouldn't be satisfied with just her happiness.

"Yes ma'am. You can be sure of that," he said, happier than he had been in a long time. Still, he had a hard time convincing himself that by making that call, he would be doing the right thing. He had hurt her once. What was the guarantee it wouldn't happen again? But call he did. That evening, as he dialed her number, his hands were sweating. His throat was bone dry. At 5:15 p.m.,

Tashiana answered the phone.

"Hello….. hello, Dominique, is that you?" Tashiana asked, before he could answer.

"Yes, Tashiana, it's me."

"I didn't believe mom when she told me you had called her today to explain why you never got in contact with me," Tashiana said happily. She continued before he could say anything further. "But thank God you did. Have you decided what you want to do with your life?" she asked.

"Yes, I have. I want to live the rest of my life with you, if you'll have a lowly X-ray Technician who will have to learn to keep a budget, and will probably not be able to take you to Hawaii on our honeymoon," Dominique informed her.

"I would love you if you were nothing but a bum on the streets," she said, her heart soaring through the heavens.

"I have a little over a year before I graduate. I can't even think of marrying you before then," he informed her, so she wouldn't think he was about to jump up and run home to her right away.

"I was willing to wait four years, in case you 've forgotten, turkey," she reminded him.

"No Tashiana, I haven't forgotten a thing. Especially how beautiful you looked the day I took my proud butt off to war. How I convinced your mother and father I was the best thing since sliced bread. How I convinced everyone I would be the superstar they all expected me to become. How I convinced myself I was Superman, incapable of getting hurt. How I convinced my mother and father of the wealth that was coming their way, but most of all, I remember the promises I made to you. No Tashiana, I haven't forgotten a thing," he said feeling he had let the whole world down. He wiped a tear threatening to run down his face. "No Tashiana, I haven't forgotten a thing," he repeated.

He sounded so defeated she wanted to reach out and hold him. "Dominique, please don't put yourself down like that. You had no idea this was going to happen to you. It could've happened just as easily in college as it did in Thailand. Maybe we were meant to live simple lives as husband and wife. You could be Freddie the Freeloader and I would still love you. I could never love you more than I do right now, even if you could give me the world on a silver platter. So, lets talk about our future plans, not what was not meant to be," Tashiana consoled him.

It was Mr. Hamilton's day off. He sat and watched as his daughter's face change from being the happiest girl in the world, to one of sincere concern. He couldn't sit back any longer without saying something to the boy who he felt had ruined his daughter's life. Mr. Hamilton went into the bedroom, picked up the extension phone and said, "Look here you low life bastard. Whatever you said to Tashi, you had better straighten out before you hang up. You two have been talking only five minutes, and she's ready to start bawling like a damn baby."

"Mr. Hamilton . . . . .," Dominique attempted to explain what was being said, but Mr. Hamilton continued

"I knew you were bad news the first day I laid eyes on you, superstar my ass. If Tashi had listened to me, she wouldn't be going through this crap right now." *'Wait a minute, Tashi,'* he heard her dad say before continuing. "You may have ruined our hopes of her being a lawyer, but I'll be damn if you're going to ruin her life as well," Mr. Hamilton swore.

"Mr. Hamilton, if Tashiana tells me she feel the same as you do, I'll never bother her again. But I have to hear it from her, not you," Dominique sad maintaining his composure.

I see you haven't lost any of the cockiness you displayed before going off to war and getting yourself messed up, without firing a shot I might add," he sneered.

"Sir, if you're finished, may I please talk to Tashiana alone?" Dominique asked, trying to keep the anger he felt out of his voice. He felt guilty enough without having to deal with an asshole like Mr. Hamilton.

Tashiana came back on the phone and said, "I love you, Dominique. No matter what anyone says. I'm sorry daddy, but I love him."

Upon hearing this, there was an unmistakable click as Mr. Hamilton hung up the phone.

About damn time, Dominique said to himself

"So what about us Dominique," Tashiana said, taking his mind off her father.

"I still love you, always have always will, and if you still want me, I'll be the best husband possible, how about that?" Dominique asked.

"You haven't asked me to marry you yet. Or should I say again?" she laughed and cried at the same time.

"Miss Hamilton, would you please be the wife of a broken down young jock, who never got a chance to prove to the world just how good he really was?" Dominique asked.

"Yes, Mr. Goodman. I would be more than happy to be your wife. So, when do you propose to me again in person?" she asked, all giggles now.

"Spring break is coming up in a couple of months, so I guess I'll see you then. And I'll be counting the days," he assured her.

"So will I lover boy," Tashiana responded.

"I hope I can straighten out this mess I've caused with your parents," Dominique sighed.

"You did it once. I'm sure you can do it again," Tashiana said sounding sure of his diplomatic ability.

"I hope so. I'll call you tomorrow. If your mother believed what I said, maybe she'll talk to your father on my behalf. What do you think?" Dominique asked hopefully.

"I don't know. I've never seen him this upset about anything before, but it couldn't hurt. Let me and mom work on him, and I'll let you know how things are going when you call tomorrow," she suggested.

"Okay, until then. I hope I'm able to sleep tonight. I haven't been this happy in a very long time," he confessed to his love.

"Tell me about it," Tashiana laughed. "Sleep in peace, my love. My love and thoughts will be with you always," she said as if she was auditioning for a movie role.

"And mine with you. I love more than life itself lady. Until tomorrow," he said and hung up.

Damn, all this suffering alone for nothing. All I had to do was call her, and I would've had someone other than mama and daddy supporting me. Well, I Guess it's better late than never to know the woman you love still loves you, Dominique thought. He felt the weight of the world was lifted from his shoulders. He fantasized about what it was going to be like when he and Tashiana got together again.

Dominique pictured Tashiana standing in her doorway staring down the street that would bring him to her house. Seeing him approach, she rushes out of the door and down the road to meet him. She is more beautiful than he remembered. Her hair now fixed in a more mature style, her ebony skin still smooth and flawless. Before he reaches her, he sees the tears of joy in her beautiful brown eyes. The smile on Tashiana's face is the most beautiful smile he'd ever seen in his short life. She's the most beautiful woman God ever created. As he takes her into his arms, he never felt more loved than he did at that moment. When he kisses her lips, they are sweeter than any sugar or honey on the face of this earth. This is going be the longest couple of months of my life, Dominique said, after the fantasy completed its course in his mind.

Since the injury to is knee, Dominique had withdrawn inward. He wanted no one to enter his private world, or personal hell. One look at the expression on his face was enough to tell the friendliest of people to keep their distance. Because he had no close friends to share his happiness with after his conversation with Tashiana, the students and faculty members who had notice his sour demeanor whenever he was on campus wondered what he was up to. They had never seen such a happy smile on his face for more than five minutes at any one time. Even the slight limp, caused by the injury and subsequent operations, all but disappeared.

Mr. Hamilton's feelings toward Dominique changed after the grandchildren came along, but Dominique didn't care one way or the other. He had allowed nothing, or no one, regardless of who it was or what it was, to keep him away from Tashiana again.

He called Tashiana almost every night until it was time for him to go home for Spring Break. The day prior to leaving for home, he called Tashiana and sensed that something was bothering her.

"What's wrong honey? You sound as if you're worried about something," Dominique said.

"It's dad. He's still pissed at you because I no longer want to be a lawyer. He said, you'd never set foot in his house again as long as he lives, and if at all possible after he dies he's going to haunt you for the rest of your rotten life. It doesn't matter what I, or mom, say to him. He refuses to change his mind. He considers you a traitor to our family. I'm sorry. I didn't mean to ramble on like that. I just wanted you to know what you're up against when you get home tomorrow," Tashiana finished.

"That's okay, babe. No apology needed. Well, the only thing I have to say about that is, he'll have to kill me, because only death will keep me from seeing you tomorrow. You can tell your dad to get ready to do his thing, because after I finish saying hello to my family, I'll be on my way to your house. I won't start anything, but I'm not going to run away either," Dominique said.

She laughed and said, "I was remembering what you always said about Dad's service pistol whenever you saw him in uniform. Man, I bet that baby would blow a hole in you big enough to drive a truck through. I hope he never gets mad at me. You remember saying that?" she asked, still laughing.

"Yeah, I remember, and I was serious. Still am, but things have changed slightly, since I know a lot more about guns now than I did then," Dominique answered.

Tashiana didn't like the way he had answered the question. "You don't own a gun do you, Dominique?" Tashiana asked suspiciously.

"No, I don't own a gun. I was in the army for eleven months you know, and it's the army's policy to train soldiers in the use of their weapons. Just in case they have to defend themselves against the enemy. They do teach soldiers things like that you know," Dominique said.

"You know what I meant," she said apologetically.

"Yeah, I know exactly what you meant. Don't worry, there ain't going to be a shootout on your front lawn," he assured her.

"I didn't mean it like that, and you know it."

"Okay, lets drop it. Are you going to meet me at the bus station tomorrow? I'm sure my mom and dad would be happy to let you ride along with them," Dominique said.

"I don't know, but I'll try," Tashiana said, embarrassed because her father had already told her there were no way in hell he was going allow her to meet Dominique at the bus station, or any other place.

"You're no longer daddy's little girl, Tashiana. He shouldn't be dictating what you do any longer. As long as you conduct yourself as a responsible adult, what can he say?" he asked, trying to persuade Tashiana to defy her father's demand. He knew it was a losing proposition because he could tell by the sound of her voice her father had won this round, and she wouldn't be at the bus station to meet him.

"You know the rules here in this house as well as I do. As long as I live under their roof, I abide by their rules," Tashiana reminded him.

"I know baby. It sure would be a thrill for me to step off of that bus and see you standing there as pretty as a fresh picked flower," Dominique said.

"If I can, I'll be there waiting for you. Otherwise, I'll see you when you come over to the house. What time does your bus arrive here in Lakeview?" she asked as if she would try and meet him at the station.

"I should be home no later than 3 p.m. tomorrow afternoon," he informed her.

"Well, until we meet again, stranger," Tashiana pretended to kiss him through the phone.

After he hung up, he reflected back to Mr. Hamilton's attitude toward him before he left for basic training. For the first time, he could see the fake smiles and forced jokes as clear as day. Well not Mr. Hamilton or anyone else was going to keep him from seeing his high school sweetheart and future wife.

The next day, as the bus pulled into the station, his heart was beating like a jackhammer in anticipation of Tashiana being there. She was nowhere to be found.

I guess her dad got his way this time, he said to himself as he stepped off the bus, not surprised she wasn't there.

It had been two years since Dominique had been home. He was happy to see his parents again. His mom laughed and cried at the same time, she was so happy he had decided to come home for his spring break. His parents were happy to see he had only a slight limp. They had expected much worse, especially after the way he had carried on about the injury. They assured him it didn't matter to them that he wouldn't be a star in the NBA. They were happy he still had his health, and was in the process of getting a college education. His parents assured him he would do just fine.

That evening, as Dominique was getting dressed to go over to Tashiana's, his father warned him to be careful because Officer Hamilton had been telling everyone in the neighborhood that he would kill him before he allowed him to continue ruining his daughter's life. Dominique told his father the same thing he had told both Tashiana and Mr. Hamilton, only death would keep him from seeing her.

Dominique had hoped Mr. Hamilton wouldn't be at home when he arrived, but he knew the law of average was not in his favor. He knew Mr. Hamilton had forbidden Tashiana from leaving the house knowing Dominique would be home that afternoon. As he approached Tashiana's house, he felt as if he was about to confront he devil himself. Dominique kept telling himself the worst thing Mr. Hamilton could do was kill him and eat him, but with any luck he would give him a fatal case of indigestion. With this in mind he knocked on the door.

"What the hell do you want?" Mr. Hamilton asked when he answered the door.

Damn, why did he have to be in uniform? Dominique asked himself. He was tempted to turn around and leave, because Mr. Hamilton looked bigger and more dangerous than he remembered. Dominique knew he couldn't allow Mr. Hamilton to intimidate him. He had to make a stand, or it would be twice as hard to see Tashiana the next time he came over to visit her. He gathered his courage and confronted Mr. Hamilton head on.

"I came over to talk to Tashiana Mr. Hamilton," Dominique said not backing down.

"Look son, you have caused this family enough heartache and disappointment to last a lifetime. So why don't you just leave Tashi alone, so we can help her make something of herself," Mr. Hamilton said, making it obvious he was annoyed at Dominique's presence.

"Mr. Hamilton, I can understand you being upset because of what Tashiana has done. I told her not to worry about me. That she should enroll back in school and I would come to visit her there. I also told her to become the lawyer you and Mrs. Hamilton have always wanted her to be. It was Tashiana's own decision to quit school, not mine. However, I can assure you of one thing, Mr. Hamilton. If I can talk Tashiana into going back to school I will. As I told you and Mrs. Hamilton a long time ago, sir, I'll be the last person on this earth to try and stop her from getting an education," Dominique said, staring him eye to eye. Dominique could tell by the expression on Mr. Hamilton face he didn't quite know what to make of what he had said.

After a slight hesitation, Mr. Hamilton said with authority, "You're right. You made that same bullshit statement before you left here, but look what has happened since then. You have gotten yourself screwed up and have no future worth looking forward to, and Tashi has quit college. What is she doing now, attending a small ass community college to become a fucking legal assistant? No, I don't want you near her," he said, menacingly.

This left Dominique with only one alternative. He had to lay his cards on the table, and let them fall where they may. Mr. Hamilton had to know he was going to see her one way or another, with or without his approval. So Dominique said, "Mr. Hamilton, you know as well as I do we're going to see each other somehow, with or without your consent. I hoped we could handle this situation like men. If I have to sit outside your house and wait for her to come out, I will. It doesn't really matter to me," Dominique tried to reason with him.

Mr. Hamilton almost choked on his words as he said, "If I see you hanging around outside of my house, I'm going to blow your damn head clean off, and I'll swear to God I thought you were a burglar. And if I see you talking to Tashi anywhere, I'm going to haul your ass in for harassing my daughter, and I'll make the charge stick. So why don't you go home to your mother and father. You're welcome there, not here." To place emphasis on what he had said, Mr. Hamilton placed his hand on his service revolver.

The move pissed Dominique off. He took a deep breath and said, "Mr. Hamilton, you do not scare me. If God intends for me to die trying to see the woman I love, she is a woman you know, so be it. You may as well go ahead and shoot me right now, because I'll be damned if I'm going to lose her again."

"You are either very brave or plain stupid. Either way, there's no way you're going to set foot in my house," Mr. Hamilton said, blocking the door's entrance way as if Dominique was trying to enter the house.

Dominique was about to use every four-letter word in his vocabulary, when a small voice in his subconscious mind suggested he try a little more diplomacy. "Mr. Hamilton, I can only imagine how you must feel. I'll make a deal with you, sir. If you allow me to come in and talk to Tashiana this one time, I promise I'll never attempt to set foot in your house ever again. But if that's not satisfactory with you sir, I would be just as happy to talk to her out here," Dominique said.

Mr. Hamilton relaxed a little and asked, "How do I know this isn't another one of your con job? You're a very impressive bullshitter you know. No, I don't buy it for one second," he said, but with none of venom he spat at the beginning of the confrontation.

"Very well sir. I guess that leaves us with only one alternative. You can shoot me now, or shoot me later. It's up to you, because I'm not leaving Lakeview without seeing her. I thought it would be better if I talked to her here at your house so you and Mrs. Hamilton would know what we were talking about," Dominique said with finality.

Mr. Hamilton realized what Dominique said was true. There was no way he could keep them apart for any length of time without locking her in a closet until Dominique left Lakeview. Lakeview was too small a community to do anything that drastic. Everyone in the community would be gossiping about him and his family for the next fifty years. Beside, he had gone through a similar incident with Mrs. Hamilton mother. He persisted until he got what he wanted, and he was sure Dominique would do the same. Still, his instinct was to tell Dominique to go to hell and leave them alone.

Reluctantly Mr. Hamilton said, "I suppose you're right. I want you to understand one thing you smart-ass bastard. Whether I allow you to see Tashi or not, it won't change how I feel about you. I hope Tashi realizes you're nothing but bad news before it's too late. Come on in. I want to hear what lies you're going to tell her anyway," he stepped aside allowing Dominique to enter. The tension between them was so thick, Dominique felt as if he was walking in quicksand, and was sinking deeper and deeper in the muck with every step.

As he entered the living room, Tashiana jumped up from the sofa, but did not move toward him.

So much for her rushing into my arms, Dominique said to himself, remembering his fantasy. However, everything else was right on target. Tashiana was the most beautiful woman in the whole world. It took all the will power he had to keep from running to where she was standing, and take her into his arms. The look on Mrs. Hamilton's face told him that was not a good idea.

"Good evening Mrs. Hamilton. How have you been?" Dominique asked.

"I've been doing fine, how about you?" Mrs. Hamilton asked from where she was sitting.

"Not very well, I'm afraid. But I've manage," Dominique answered.

"That's too bad. Maybe Tashi can help you get back on the road to good health and prosperity," Mrs. Hamilton smiled.

"Thank you very much ma'am. If anyone can get me back on track its Tashiana," Dominique smiled in return.

At last, he turned his attention to Tashiana. "Hi Tashiana, how have you been?" Dominique asked awkwardly.

"As well as can be expected under the current circumstances I guess. It's so good to see you again. God, we have to talk," Tashiana said, taking hold of his hand and drawing him down on the sofa.

"I think you two would have more privacy if you went into my study," Mrs. Hamilton smiled at the both of them. It made Mrs. Hamilton feel good to see her daughter happy again.

"They can stay right here, so I can hear everything Dominique has to say," Mr. Hamilton snorted, as if he was a jealous old bull.

"Dad, you promised you wouldn't do this if he was able to convince you to let him see me," Tashiana reminded her father.

"Hmp ….." was his reply.

As soon as the door to the study was closed behind them, Tashiana was in his arms. "I thought I would never see you again," she said, holding on to him as if he about to leave again.

"I'm sorry for what I put you through. God knows I am. I'm ready to do whatever it takes to make it up to you. Nothing will ever separate us again," Dominique promised kissing her.

"The injury you suffered must have been awful," Tashiana said with a painful expression on her face.

He grimaced every time someone mentioned an injury, whether it was his own or someone else's. He hadn't told anyone about the thoughts that went through his head at the time of the injury, or describe the pain he felt. And he had never told anyone about the deep depression he felt while he was laid up at Walter Reed Hospital.

"Yeah, it was pretty bad. Lets sit down and I'll tell you about it." After they were seated, he told her what happened. "It was a routine drive to the basket. I've made that move a thousand times. Anyway, when I came down, I landed on one of the guy's foot. Instead of twisting an ankle, as usual, I somehow landed where my knee twisted instead. It was the loudest pop I've ever heard in my life. I knew right away it was serious. The pain was so intense all I could see was a white light. Beside, cussing like a salty marine, the only other thing I could think of was how disappointed everyone was going to be in me. How I would never be able to give you the things I had promised. How I would be a cripple for the rest of my life. I had never known fear like that before. After the first operation they told me my knee was damaged to the point it would never be the same, that my basketball playing days at a high level was probably over. Of course I didn't believe them. After a couple of days they told me they had to go back in because they found something in my x-rays they had missed during the first operation. When they finished this time there no doubt in their minds that I was finished as a top rated athlete. They told me I would be able to run and jump, but the knee wouldn't hold up very long. They suggested I get use to the idea that my dream of playing basketball in the NBA was over. So, instead of facing the situation like a man, I ran and hid. I cried myself to sleep quite a few nights worrying about what everyone was going to say when I came hobbling home like a crippled old man. When I got to school, I enclosed myself in a cocoon and wouldn't let anyone into my depressed world. Other than going to the gym, and an occasional movie, I stayed locked in my room studying. Sorry baby," Dominique finished.

There were tears in Tashiana eyes as she said, "You'll never have to run and hide from anyone or anything ever again. We have each other now. Nothing's ever going to separate us again," she said, the tears now rolling down her cheeks.

"At least because of the injury, I'm a much stronger person. I now know I'm capable of dealing with any situation which may arise in my life in the future. And whether your dad believes it or not, I'm going to tell him the exact same thing," Dominique said.

"I don't think it's going to change the way he feels about you," Tashiana sighed.

"We'll see in a few moments when I again ask for your hand in marriage," Dominique smiled, holding her tighter.

"I have to admit Mr. Goodman, when you make up your mind about wanting something, you go all out," she said, pleased Dominique was his old self again.

"That's the only way to be, otherwise people will not take you seriously. Now, if you would accompany me, I have to talk to your parents," Dominique said, leading the way into the living room.

"Mr. Hamilton, Mrs. Hamilton, may I speak to the two of you for a second?" he asked.

"Sure Dominique, what do you want to talk to us about?" Mrs. Hamilton asked.

"I want to do everything right where Tashiana is concerned. So, I figured it's only fitting that I again ask you for your daughter's hand in marriage along with your blessing," Dominique said, with fingers crossed behind his back.

"Well, you're wasting your time if you think I'm going to give my daughter's hand in marriage, to a broken down jock, who'll probably never amount to anything. Give it my blessing, you gotta be kidding," Mr. Hamilton said, not believing Dominique had the balls to ask such a question, not after what he had put his family through.

"Don't listen to him. He's nothing but a bullheaded old goat that's afraid to let go of his baby girl. If marrying you is what it takes to make Tashi happy, and get back in school, you have my approval and blessing," Mrs. Hamilton said. But she left no doubt her blessing depended on whether Tashiana went back to school, or not.

Dominique was not about to be the fall guy in this matter. They already knew Tashiana had changed her mind about becoming a lawyer, and it no longer had anything to do with him. She told him that since she had told them she didn't want to be a lawyer they had been on her case twenty-four seven.

"Mrs. Hamilton, I'm going to try my best to get Tashiana to go back to school. I know her becoming a lawyer has been your plan since the day she was born. But if she changed her mind, what am I suppose to do? And will you hold it against me if she doesn't change her mind and go back to school?" Dominique asked, letting Mrs. Hamilton know he had gotten her message loud and clear.

"Lets put it this way Dominique. It was because of you she dropped out of college in the first place. So, as I see it, it's up to you to get her to change her mind and go back. She loves you so much, she would do anything you ask her to," Mrs. Hamilton said as if Tashiana wasn't even in the room.

"I'll do whatever I can, ma'am," Dominique assured Tashiana's parents.

"You'd better convince her to take her butt back to school or you'll have to deal with me for the rest of your natural life," Mr. Hamilton warned, finally realizing what his wife was attempting to do.

While they were talking, Tashiana was sitting on the sofa

fuming. After they finished talking she took hold of Dominique hand and asked to be excused.

Once back in the study she said, "They can't make me be something I don't want to be. Lets hurry and get married so I can move out of this house," Tashiana pleaded. She continued angrily. "Ever since I quit school they've been on my back day and night. It doesn't matter what I want to do with my life, it has to be what they want. Well, I'm fed up with it. If we got married, I could move to Arizona with you and finish my legal assistant course at ASU along with you," she pleaded.

"Hey, calm down. They only want what they think is best for you. You know that. The same as I do. The difference is, I want you to do whatever makes you happy," Dominique calmed her.

"I know, but I don't want to be a damn lawyer. I'll tell them again, for the thousandth time. I don't want to be a lawyer, and if they don't like it, tough. But as usual, they probably won't listen. Neither will they listen when I tell them I'm going to marry you, whether I go back to college or not. I don't care what they have to say about it," Tashiana said, sounding tired of the same old argument about her future and school.

"What can I say? Maybe, in time they'll accept your decision. I guess it's hard for parents to accept the fact that their children grow up and make decisions for themselves. As you have supported me, I'll support you in any decision you make, now and always. But we can't get married until I finish college, and have a place for us to live," Dominique said, kissing her on the cheek.

"We don't have to be married for me to attend ASU," she suggested.

"I know, but we would end up playing house, and that would only make things worse between us and your parents. I don't want to start our lives together like that," Dominique explained.

"I guess you're right, but don't you leave me hanging again, Mr. Goodman. Or the next time you come back home, no one will know where I am," Tashiana laughed.

"There's nothing, or no one, on this earth who could make me even think about letting you get away from me again," Dominique assured her. However, Dominique was soon to learn differently.

Tashiana's parents eventually gave in to her wishes after seeing how much she and Dominique loved each other during his summer vacation between semesters, but they still blamed Dominique for her not becoming a lawyer. He returned to school feeling as though he was on top of the world. Although his dream of becoming a superstar in the NBA had been shattered by the injury, he still had the people he loved the most in his corner pulling for him.

CHAPTER #6

The week before his scheduled graduation, Dominique went home to tell Tashiana it wasn't a good idea for her to attend his graduation, because he was breaking off their engagement. He didn't want to embarrass her by introducing her to his fellow graduates as a friend from back home, instead of the future Mrs. Goodman.

It was hard to believe after everything they had gone through to be together, a woman he had known only a few months could step into the picture and screw everything up. And screw everything up was exactly what Jewel Blackwood had done. Dominique knew backing out of the marriage was going to hurt Tashiana more than he could imagine, but he was not willing to deceive her into thinking nothing had changed. His first thought was to take the coward's way out by calling her on the phone and telling her the wedding was off, but decided she deserved better. Dominique knew it would be better if he took responsibility for his actions. He hoped he would be able to make her understand that what happened between him and Jewel was not planned, it just happened. He had to make her understand that he had no intention of ever cheating on her, but unforeseen circumstances cause him to fall into the clutches of Jewel's lustful arms.

Even if she buys this crap, what the hell is she suppose to say. I understand, and wish you the best of luck with your new whore,

Dominique scolded himself. Using a worn out phase, Dominique knew Tashiana was not going to be a happy camper. Prior to breaking the engagement, he asked his mom if he could talk to her about his relationship with Tashiana.

"What's wrong this time, son? Officer Hamilton on your backs again about this wedding?" she asked thinking she had heard it all before.

"No ma'am. It's a lot more complicated than that I'm afraid," Dominique said but didn't elaborate.

"Well, are you going to tell me what makes it complicated, or am I suppose to guess?" she asked.

"Mom, I've met another girl at school and I rather be with her than Tashiana. We didn't plan on falling for each other, but we did. Now, I don't think I want to get married," he explained.

"What the hell do you mean you don't want to get married? That child gave up her life ambition to be with you. What's so damn special about that girl at your school?" his mom asked.

"It's hard to explain, Mom. I've never met a girl like her. She's intelligent, funny, and very mysterious, and she makes me feel special," he said.

"If you ask me, I think you're in lust, not love. How long have you known this gal?" she asked.

"Only about four months, but it seems like I've known her all my life," he answered.

"You have known Tashiana all your life. Do you realize how much breaking off your engagement is going to hurt that poor girl? God help you, son. What're you going to do if a month from now you find out the only thing between you and that other gal is lust? Beg Tashiana to take you back? When are you going to tell her?" she asked.

"Tomorrow, I guess," he answered.

"You know Officer Hamilton is going to be after your butt for doing this to his daughter. If I were you, I would wait until it was time to leave before dumping her. God, I feel so sorry for Tashiana. She's such a sweet girl," Dominique's mom said and left the room.

Dominique thought about getting his dad's opinion about the planned break-up, but knew the only thing his dad was going to say is he should keep the both of them. In the old days every man had a woman on the side, Dominique's dad always told him. So, Dominique called Tashiana and invited her to a picnic the following day.

Tashiana was happy as she slid in beside Dominique and they were headed for the countryside. In one week, Dominique would graduate and start his career. She was determined to convince him that they should get married right after his graduation and start a family if their own. She realized September was not that far off, but May was closer.

"What time is your graduation next Sunday?" Tashiana asked.

"You've asked me that for the last three weeks. You know the ceremony is at 3pm Sunday. I wanted to talk to you about that," he said.

"Let wait until we get to the picnic sight. I don't want to spoil the moment. Me and my future husband cruising down a beautiful country road looking for that one special spot where we'll be out of the view of the world, which will give us the privacy to do whatever we want," she winked knowingly at him.

"Ok," he said, thankful for the delay in having to burst her bubble.

Dominique wondered what a city slicker like Jewel would have to say about speeding down a country road lined with an array of different trees like these. He was sure her physic powers would help her to come up with something original, because she was good at stuff like that. Finding the most seclude spot he could, he and Tashiana spread their blanket and laid out the food. Knowing what he was about to do, he had no appetite.

Tashiana noticed Dominique's agitated state and lack of an appetite, but shrugged it off as his being nervous about his upcoming graduation and the talk about their upcoming marriage. Her mom told her men always got nervous and agitated when big events occur in their lives. That is why they need a good woman at their side to keep them balanced. Seeing he wasn't going to eat anything further she asked Dominique to go for a walk with her.

"You seem to be preoccupied, Dominique. What's wrong?" Tashiana asked.

"Uh, uh, there's something I have to tell you, and you're not going to like it. But I don't know where to start," he began.

"This sounds serious. Why don't you start at the beginning," she suggested.

You know I love you, but something has come up that may delay our wedding. I may take a job in Thailand for a year. The pay is good, and I'll be able to save a lot of money," Dominique lied, losing his nerve to tell her the truth.

"When did you decide this? " she asked.

"I was talking to an army recruiter on campus a few days ago and he was telling me about the great jobs the army have for civilians overseas. I figured you could go back to school while I'm in Thailand and we can get married when I get back. What do you think?" Dominique asked hoping she wouldn't see through his lie.

"Dominique, is there something you're not telling me? For

some reason I don't believe this Thailand shit. If you're getting cold feet about marrying me, tell me. I refuse to sit around wondering if you've changed your mind about us. Wait a minute. You said you wouldn't work for the government if they were the last organization in this world, and paid you a million dollars a year. You want to tell me what the hell is really going on?" Tashiana challenged him to tell the truth.

"I changed my mind, okay," Dominique said avoiding her eyes.

"You changed your mind about working for the military, or you changed your mind about wanting to marry me?" she asked.

"I'm confused right now. I don't know what I want to do. I want to marry you, but what kind of life can I offer you. Maybe your mom and dad are right. Maybe you should go back to school and become the lawyer they want you to be," he said reaching for straws.

"If I didn't know better, I would say you're breaking our engagement. You've got to have a better reason than money to dump me. After everything I've given up for you, you owe me the truth, Dominique. I smell the stench of another girl in your lame excuse for why you no longer want to marry me," she said. Tashiana grab hold of Dominique's arm forcing him to look her in the eye.

Dominique cleared his throat and attempted one last lie. "There's no girl in this world who can keep me from marrying you. It's just that I want to save some money before we get married."

"You said we would be together if you had to clean toilets, and I said that was okay by me. Come on Dominique give me a reason I can believe. You have a girlfriend at that college don't you?" she asked the tears starting to fall.

"Its not that. I want to make sure we have something before,

before, before . . . I'm sorry Tashiana. I didn't plan on getting involved with anyone else, it just happened," he confessed.

"Oh Dominique, how could you. I love you with all my heart and soul. I was willing to give up everything in my life for you. I even alienated myself from my family because I love you so much. Now you tell me it was for nothing. What's the winches name?" she asked between sniffles.

"Does it matter?" Dominique asked. He could never understand why people always wanted to know the name of the people who made them miserable.

"Yes, it matters to me. Since she's not here for me to scratch her eyes out, at least I'll have a name to hate. I'll have a name to remind you why we're not together if she decide to dump you, and you come running back to Lakeview asking me to take you back. Yes, it matters to me," she hissed.

"Her name is Jewel Blackwood. She's from California," he informed her.

"I guess us country girls aren't sophisticated enough for you anymore, is that it?" she asked, her tears turning to anger.

"I told you it just happened. It has nothing to do with where she's from. I'm sorry," he apologized for the umpteenth time.

"I've been fighting with my dad about you for how many years now? He's been telling me since we started going together that you would dump me the first chance you got. I told him hell would freeze over before you would leave me. The devil must be freezing his butt off along about now. Maybe that's why he sent one of his little sexpots to screw up my world. Take me home please. I'll try to convince daddy not to bother you, but you know how he is," she said running to the car.

They drove home in silence. When he stopped in front of

Tashiana's house to let her out she said, "I'll always love you Dominique, but you've really hurt me. I hope you never have to feel the pain I'm feeling right now. It feels as if someone ripped my heart from my body and left my bones for the dogs. Remember, Dominique, you only find one true love in a lifetime. You're mine's, let's hope Jewel, or whatever her name is, is yours. I wish you luck," she said and kissed him as she got out of the car.

"Are you going to be alright?" Dominique asked.

"No," she said and ran into the house in tears.

Dominique knew he would have to face Mr. Hamilton somewhere down the line, because he wasn't going to let anyone hurt his little girl without having a say so in the matter. Especially since it was Dominique. The bold assed young boy who had the balls to come into his home and make demands on his family. Until that time Mr. Hamilton, Dominique said on his way home to say good-bye to his family and retrieve his bag before heading back to school. Unknown to Dominique "until that time" came a lot sooner than he thought it would.

Officer Hamilton couldn't help but notice that his precious little girl was crying when she ran past him into her room. He was on his way to work. He went and knocked on her door. "Tashi, open the door," he demanded. Tashiana opened the door with tears streaming down her face. "What happened?" he asked entering her room.

"It's Dominique, Dad. He met a girl at college and now he don't want to marry me," she said throwing herself into his arms, crying hysterically.

Mr. Hamilton was both happy and angry at the same time. Happy because he would be rid of that nuisance asshole and Tashiana would be free to go back to college and become the lawyer they always wanted her to be, angry because Dominique continued to dictate the mood of his household. "When did he tell you this?"

"Just now," she sobbed.

"Listen to me, baby girl. You're better off without that loser. I know it hurts right now, but in time you'll get over him and find your true love," Mr. Hamilton comforted his daughter.

"Dominique is my true love, dad. I don't think I could ever love another boy as long as I live," she cried.

Mr. Hamilton didn't say anything for a while. He held his little girl in his arms until the sobs subsided. After her sobs turned to sniffles he said, "Tashi, me and your mom is going to help you through this. Let him go. I promise you everything is going to work out for the best for you. You believe me don't you?" he asked kissing her on the forehead.

"I know dad. It's just that I never thought Dominique would do this to me. Not after what you put him through to be with me. I guess you know more about boys than I do," she sniffed.

"Of course I do. I've been around a lot longer than you have. Plus I deal with the scum of the earth on a daily basis. You get to the point where you can spot the rotten apples before they spoil the other apples around them. I take no joy in telling you that I told you so. Dry your eyes, and go tell your mom what happened. I have to go to work," he said with Dominique on his mind.

"Ok dad. Dad, please don't do anything to Dominique. I still care about him," she said knowing her dad was pissed for what Dominique was putting her through.

"He's probably on his way back to school anyway," Officer Hamilton said heading for his patrol car. He drove straight to the Goodman's house to see if he could catch up with Dominique before he left. Upon his arrival he was informed that Dominique was being dropped off at the bus station even as they spoke.

Officer Hamilton thought Dominique would be reluctant to get into his patrol car to talk to him, considering he was the cause of Tashiana's present state of mind. Then again, he knew Dominique was not an average young man. Dominique was sitting outside the terminal drinking a soda when Officer Hamilton drove up. He rolled down the car window, leaned over and said, "Dominique can I have a word with you."

Dominique walked up to the car and said, "Mr. Hamilton, I know what I did to Tashiana is wrong. But I didn't plan for this to happen."

"What time do your bus leave?" Officer Hamilton asked.

"I have about forty minutes before it leaves, Dominique answered.

"That's enough time. Get in. Let's go for a short ride," Officer Hamilton said.

Dominique knew Mr. Hamilton was pissed and was going to read him the riot act, but he had faced him in every other situation where Tashiana was concern, this time would be no different. He got in the patrol car and they drove off.

Officer Hamilton drove behind some old abandon buildings a short distance from the bus station. He parked the car and turned to Dominique. "You're one of the cockiest bastards I've ever known. You know I'm pissed at you for what you're doing to Tashi, and still you get into my patrol car as if nothing has happened. As I said before boy, you got balls. But you know what? I'm going to bring you down a notch," he said taking out his gun and placing it between Dominique's eyes.

Dominique didn't panic. He looked Mr. Hamilton in the

eyes and said, "Mr. Hamilton, you know if you pull that trigger everyone in Lakeview is going to know it were you who killed me. And although I've hurt Tashiana she would never forgive you for doing it. I know she doesn't hate me that much, not yet anyway. And what about Mrs. Hamilton? How long will she visit you in prison before moving on with her life? Mr. Hamilton, please believe me. I had no intentions of hurting Tashiana, it just happened. I cannot marry your daughter knowing I care more for another girl. Would you rather I string her alone, or be honest with her so she can have a chance to be happy with someone else?" Dominique asked.

"You think you can talk your way out of any situation, don't you? Well, for your information Mr. Goodman, I'm not going to shoot you. What I am going to do is this," Officer Hamilton caught Dominique upside his head with butt of the pistol. Again and again the butt of the pistol careened off his head. Satisfied with the beating he had administered to Dominique Officer Hamilton sat with a satisfied smirk on his face.

Dominique sat in the passenger seat bleeding from the mouth and nose. Still defiant he said, " Mr. Hamilton, I'll take this ass whupping for what I did to Tashiana, but if you ever touch me again you had better kill me."

Although he still wanted to kill Dominique, Mr. Hamilton couldn't help but to be impressed with Dominique's will and determination to do what he felt was right as far as Tashiana was concerned. He said, "God, boy you don't know how bad I want to blow your brains all over these streets, but I have to give credit where credit is due. You did the right thing by telling Tashi what was going on, but if you ever come around trying to get her back, should your winch dump you, I'll kill you. That is as close as it gets to a thank you for not leading my daughter on." He gave Dominique a towel to wipe the blood from his face and dropped him off at the bus station.

Dominique watched as Mr. Hamilton drove away. If it were anyone other than Tashiana involved in this scenario he would have been planning his revenge. *Mr. Hamilton, you're lucky I care about the happiness of your daughter*, he thought as the car tuned the corner. The military instilled a mean streak in him he hadn't known existed. He was serious about what he said to Mr. Hamilton. If he ever laid hands on him again, one of them would die.

Dominique was serious when he told Tashiana there was no woman who could ever make him doubt his love for her. That was before he met Jewel Blackwood during his final spring semester at ASU. Jewel wasn't the most beautiful girl in the world, but her sex appeal was equal by none, including Tashiana. The first time they met was at the campus library when they reached for the same book.

"Go ahead and take it. I've already passed the test on x-ray film development. I just wanted to refresh my memory since I start my practicum next week," Dominique offered.

"Thank you. My test is in two hours. You sure you don't mind?" Jewel asked, laying on the charm.

"Not at all," Dominique assured her.

The whole time they were deciding who should take the book he couldn't keep his eyes off her.

"I know you've probably heard this a thousand times, but you have the most beautiful eyes I've ever seen in my life," Dominique complimented her.

"Yes, I have, but it still makes me feel good to hear it from a handsome guy like yourself. I believe they are affectionately referred to as bedroom eyes," Jewel smile broadened.

Feeling somewhat embarrassed Dominique said, "Yeah, I know, but that's not quite what I meant. I didn't mean to give you the impression that I was trying to hit on you!"

"I wouldn't mind one bit, if you did. My name is Jewel Blackwood. I've wanted to meet you for some time now, but something has always caused me to put our meeting on hold until now. Is it true you had scholarship offers from USC and UCLA to play basketball, but ended up getting hurt in Thailand while you were in the Army? Or something like that?" Jewel asked.

"Yeah, something like that," he answered. "My name is Dominique Goodman. How did you find out about it? I haven't talked to very many people about that part of my life," he said, surprised she knew what had happened to him.

"I guess I talked to the right person. I work as a helper here in the library in the evening, and love talking to Mrs. Hartfield. Sorry if I stuck my nose in your personal business. Mrs. Hartfield felt that you needed a female friend to keep you company sometimes, since you're alone every time she sees you." It was Jewel turn to apologize.

Mrs. Hartfield was Dominique favorite person at the school. He had confided in her whenever he felt the need to talk to someone to keep from going crazy. He met her a couple months after arriving at on campus. Dominique was determined to prove the doctors wrong about his not being able to play basketball on the same level as he did before the injury, so he lived in the gym.

Mrs. Hartfield's exercise class worked out in the gym three

times a week. Dominique always laughed at them until one day while going through his paces on the court his knee gave out and he went crashing to the floor. It was their turn to laugh at him. He hobbled over to the bleachers and sat down.

While sitting there dejected, Mrs. Hartfield came over and put a hand on his shoulder and said, "I've watched you push yourself week after week young man. When are you going to accept your fate and move on with your life?"

Dominique looked at the little white lady in amazement. Who was she to tell him it was time to give up on his dream. "Excuse me ma'am," he said.

"I can tell you were a fine athlete before the knee injury. Have you considered that God caused your knee injury because He wants to use you in a way other than sports?" Mrs. Hartfield asked.

"To be honest with you ma'am, I've cussed God ever since the day it happened. How could he give me all this talent and ability to play basketball just to take it away like that?" Dominique asked himself more than to Mrs. Hartfield.

"Look at this," Mrs. Hartfield said rolling up her right sleeve and showing him a long white scar almost the length of her arm. "I was the top high school female tennis player in the nation when I started my career at the University of North Carolina. Everyone knew I would be ready to start my quest for Wimbledon by my sophomore year. While playing in a doubles match my partner and I attempted to return the same shot. I hit the ball and she hit me, broke my arm right at the elbow. When I was told my tennis playing days were over I must've cried for a month straight. Then, after my elbow healed enough for me to endure the pain, I set out to prove them all wrong.

Like you, I stayed in the gym lifting weights, running wind

sprints and swinging the ratchet. Well, one wrong swing and it was back to the operating room. After that surgery I couldn't even grip a tennis ratchet for six months. They honored my scholarship and I became a librarian. It's not the most glamorous job in the world, but I wouldn't trade it for any other. I guess what I'm trying to say is stop beating yourself up and find out what else you're good at and go for it. They haven't figured out how to make a knee brace that restore a knee to its original strength," she said while examining the latest knee brace he had purchased on his quest to return to his previous greatness.

"I know what you're saying is probably true, but I have to be satisfied with myself. I have to feel I've tried my best to get back to where I was before the injury. I want to be sure it is physical and not mental," Dominique said.

"You come to the library and see me whenever you need someone to talk to," Mrs. Hartfield gave his shoulder an understanding squeeze and left the gym.

It was during these talks he told her his life story, including the university visits and scholarship offers. He wasn't angry Mrs. Hartfield had shared his life story with Jewel, but he felt she should have at least told him she had.

"That's all right, now. However, a month or so earlier, I would've chewed your head off, and spit it in the gutter," he laughed, enjoying the attention Jewel was giving him.

"What changed your attitude?" Jewel asked.

"I guess it was learning that my family and friends still love me as much now, as they did before the injury. I said what the hell, be happy," Dominique explained.

"What's her name?" Jewel asked.

"What's whose name? My mother's?" he asked, perplexed.

"No, the girl you called almost every night before you went home. The same girl that sent you back to school happy," Jewel said, giving him a knowing smile

"You are inquisitive, aren't you, and a spy to boot. Her name is Tashiana Hamilton. Why?" Dominique asked.

"Like I to know the name of my competition," Jewel said.

"Is that a fact?" Dominique asked wondering what she was up to.

"That's fact, Mr. Goodman," Jewel said and walked back to the table where she was studying with friends.

Ordinarily, Dominique didn't like bold, pushy girls, but there was something about Jewel that made him want to get to know her better. And it wasn't just her sexy eyes. As she walked back to her table, Dominique noticed the excessive swaying of her well-rounded buttocks, and perfectly shaped, long slender legs. Most of all, there was an air of confidence that surrounded Jewel. The kind of confidence that make the instinct bred in men to conquer women kicked in. He resisted the urge to follow her to her table to prolong the conversation. As he was leaving the library, he hesitated beside the table she was sitting at, as if to say something, but continued on. She gave him a knowing wink and a smile as he walked away.

They met again several days later at a party, at the local Hilton Hotel. Seeing the amount of food laid out, buffet style, and the booze at the bar, it looked like the whole student body on campus chipped in for the party.

"So, we meet again inquisitive lady," Dominique smiled.

"So, we do. Only this time, there's no librarian to save you," Jewel said, giving him one of the sexiest smiles on record in his memory bank.

"Oh? I wasn't aware I had to be saved from anything, or

anyone. I guess I owe Mrs. Hartfield a big 'ole thank you the next time I see her. The only thing I can't figure out is why would I want to be saved from a girl as pretty as you are?" Dominique pretended to be shocked.

"Stick around and you may get a chance to find out. I, in return, might find out why you're so secretive about yourself," Jewel said.

"I guess it's, or was, because my whole life was laid out before me, and because of one missed step, I wasn't able to live up to my part of the bargain. I was treated like a god. So, I don't talk about it. I don't want anyone feeling sorry for me because of the injury. I also feel, felt, like I had let everyone who believed in me down. I guess faith has a way of testing your courage, to see what you're made of. It's still a painful memory, but since going home everything is fine now," he explained. It made him feel better to be able to talk about his injury.

"What's her name, again?" Jewel asked.

"What's whose name?" Dominique asked.

"Your girlfriend silly, who else would I be asking you about?" Jewel answered.

"Why, does it really matter?" Dominique asked, annoyed at being asked for Tashiana's name again.

"No not really. But like I said at the library, I like to know the name of my competition. It adds a little spice to the chase. Don't you think so?" she winked.

"I wouldn't know", Dominique answered, becoming wary. Jewel seemed like the type of female who got her kicks from living on the edge.

"Don't let me scare you off, Dominique. I won't call her in the middle of the night and ask, guess who is in bed with me? It's just that you can tell a lot about a person by their name. Come on, what's your future wife's name?" Jewel pressed him.

"If it's that important to you, her name is Tashiana Hamilton," Dominique conceded again.

"Tashiana Hamilton. Tashiana Hamilton," she repeated, looking through him as if he no longer existed. Her eyes changed colors as those of an angry animal. "What's her sign?" Jewel asked, focusing on him once again.

"She's a Virgo. Why? So you can read her horoscope or something" he asked.

"I see you don't put much faith in the stars. You must be a Capricorn, right?" Jewel asked excitedly.

"Yes, I am." Dominique stated flatly beginning to get bored with her antics.

"Don't you see?" Jewel asked, as if what she was trying to get across to him was as plain as the nose on his face.

"All I see are you bugging out. Have you been smoking grass or something?" Dominique asked seriously.

Jewel let out a heart felt laugh and said, "No, I don't do drugs. I get high by figuring out what makes people tick. For instant, I know you take everything you do seriously, and you can't stand to be around those who don't. You're very much in love with Tashiana, and have no intensions of cheating on her. But, since you're a good lover, you would accept a dare to prove your masculinity. You're a warm hearted, caring person who can get nasty if you have to. Also, you're like a guard dog when someone messes with anything you have laid claim to. Am I right, so far?" Jewel asked, confident what she had said was right on target.

"I would say that you're fairly accurate. Except for that part about me screwing any woman who doubts my masculinity," Dominique corrected her.

Jewel only smiled and said, "Tashiana, on the other hand, is a very strong-willed woman who sticks by her decisions, come hell or high water. Like you, whatever she decides to do, she will stick with it until she gets the desired results. She, nor you, realizes it yet, but she's going to be an outspoken person. Not loud, but she's going to question almost everything said or done where her interests are concerned. She is also very possessive. You're going to have to be able to explain your whereabouts at all times. Otherwise, she is going to think you were with another woman. This is still the age of the "free love society" you know. And everyone knows how us college girls are these days," she laughed.

"I know, but I think you're wrong about Tashiana being overly jealous," Dominique defended his girl. "I have known her a little bit longer than you have."

"Oh? Don't call her this weekend and see what she has to say Monday night when you call. Do you dare?" Jewel challenged.

"If it means I get to spend the weekend with you, I'll give it some thought. Or, for no other reason than to prove you wrong," Dominique said, thinking if she was willing to put out, why not take advantage of the situation. *Hell, I'm not married yet*, he thought.

"I left one thing our, Dominique. Want to hear it?" Jewel smiled, as if she was hiding a secret.

"Sure, why not? It can't be that bad," Dominique said.

"You don't care too much for women like me. You consider us too outspoken, too argumentative, and too forward. Correct me if I'm wrong," Jewel challenged.

"It's true. I don't care too much for women like the ones you just described, but it's nothing I can't handle," Dominique assured her.

"Prove it to me," Jewel dared him again.

That weekend he was introduced to sex games he had only read about in nudie magazines. They spent the entire weekend in bed at the hotel. They only got out of bed long enough to get something to eat. Dominique expected her to be a freak in bed, but he never imagined her being as good as she was. At the end of their little encounter, he was totally exhausted, but happy. When he called Tashiana that Monday night, she was pissed.

"Where were you all weekend?" Tashiana asked, trying to control her anger.

"Me and a couple of the guys in my dorm went camping. We didn't get back until after midnight. I wasn't about to wake your parents at 1:30 in the morning. Where did you think I was?" Dominique asked trying to sound disappointed that she didn't trust him.

"I didn't know what to think. Unless you've forgotten, you didn't say anything about going camping the last time we talked," Tashiana reminded him.

"That was because I didn't know I was going. It was a last minute, lets go deal. Next time, I'll tell them they have to wait until I report my intentions to you," Dominique said.

"You don't have to be a wise-ass about it. If you don't want me to worry about you, fine, I won't," Tashiana snapped.

"Sorry, I thought you were checking up on me. So, what did you do this weekend?" Dominique asked, trying to change the subject because he was starting to feel a little guilty. "I trust you, Dominique. It's just that I love you so much, and I want to hear your voice every day of the week. You can't blame a girl for missing her man, now can you?" Tashiana asked, not ready to change the topic.

"I guess not. I'll keep you informed of my plans in the future. That's if it's not a last minute decision type thing. Okay?" Dominique asked, feeling guiltier as they talked.

"You don't have to report your every move to me. Just let me know when you're going to be away from the campus for the weekend so I won't be worried whether you're alright or not. Is that asking too much?" Tashiana asked.

"No baby, you're not asking too much of me. I promise I'll let you know where I'm going to be in the future. Especially if my plans take me away from the campus for the weekend," Dominique assured her.

They talked an hour longer before Tashiana finally hung up, still not convinced that Dominique was telling the truth about where he had been that weekend.

After replacing the receiver back in its cradle, he frowned and said to himself, that was a lucky guess Jewel. But lucky or not, he was impressed with her ability to predict how Tashiana would react to him not calling her that weekend. He also had to admit to himself that he was attracted to her like a bee is to honey. He didn't like the feeling. He avoided her for as long as he could.

Several days later Jewel cornered him coming out of the campus snack shop. "Why have you been avoiding me Dominique?" she asked, with serious look on her face.

He hesitated before answering. He didn't know whether to tell the truth, or try and convince her he had been busy. He hadn't said a word yet, and already he could feel his hormones raging. He chose to tell the truth.

I have avoided you because I knew when I looked into those eyes of yours I wouldn't be able to resist wanting to take you to bed again. By the way, you were right about Tashiana being pissed because I didn't call her this past weekend," Dominique confessed.

"I'm very seldom wrong," Jewel said nonchalantly, but not in a bragging tone. "I also have a confession to make," she continued. "I dig the hell out of you too, and I want to be with you every chance I get."

"Hey, look Jewel, as much as I want to be with you, I can't afford it. There's too much at stake. I'm going to marry Tashiana after I graduate, and no one will stop me. It wouldn't be fair to you to make you think otherwise," Dominique cautioned her.

"I'm not trying to take you away from Tashiana. I like being with you, that's all. It'll be a relationship with no strings attached. What do you say?" Jewel asked, placing her hands in his.

"No strings attached, huh?" he asked.

"No strings attached," she repeated.

Against his better judgment, he gave in. Try as he might, he couldn't stop himself from looking into those hot, sexy, bedroom eyes. He felt his desire to resist her dwindle to nothing during the course of the conversation.

"I know I'm making a mistake. But I have to admit I'm attracted to you more than I want to be. Do you really think we can have a sexual relationship without one of us becoming attached to the other?" Dominique asked, squeezing her hands.

"To be honest with you, I don't know. Not even the stars can predict tales of the heart, but I'm willing to take that chance, if you are. If you feel yourself falling for me, you can always tell me where to get off," Jewel offered her companionship.

"And if you catch yourself falling for me, you can tell me where to get off also," Dominique offered in return.

"Yeah, we'll see," she laughed.

"I'm about to get involved with a girl I don't know anything about. Other than she can read minds, and can tell me what I'm going to do a hundred years from now. So what about it? You know all about me. Tell me your story," Dominique said.

"I have to warn you. I'm not from your average run-of-the-mill family. My dad started his own religious cult in the 1940s after graduating from the University of California. They called themselves God's Reefer Children. Believe it or not, they worshipped marijuana. The police didn't mess with them because they said their religion was based on the same beliefs of the Navajo Indians who used marijuana during their religious ceremonies. Needless to say, it pissed the Indians off to have their religious ceremonies disgraced by a bunch of black and white weed smoking potheads. Anyway, when my dad got high he saw all kind of weird shit.

He said while he was in a trance God told him when the world is going to end, and how. And what he needed to do to save his followers. He said he met my mom in a dream six months before she joined his cult. She said it was so unreal because he knew everything about her although they had never met. He told her she was from Louisiana, had two brothers and three sisters, which she was the oldest and expected to set the example for her siblings too follow. She was a junior at UC Berkeley with a GPA of 3.022. Actually, her GPA was 3.032, but she was so impressed with him it didn't matter he was slightly off on the GPA. My dad also told her she never wanted to get married and have children, but would marry him and have one child because they were soul mates. So, here I am. The product of potheads who believes God has given them the right to stay high on the wacky weeds," Jewel finished.

"Does he still have followers?" Dominique asked.

"He did when I left home, but not as many as in the past," she answered.

"So, when is the world going to end? And how is he going to save you out here in Arizona?" Dominique wanted to know.

"My dad said God told him the world was going to end August 12, 1990, on his 73rd birthday," she said.

"And how is he going to save you and his followers?" Dominique persisted.

"A spaceship of course. It's going to pick him up first, and then pickup whomever he point out to be saved. If you don't want to go to hell kid, you'd better stick with me," Jewel said with a wink.

Dominique laughed and asked, "How did you become, what do they call them, a psychic?"

"It started when I was about four years old. It scared the crap out of me at first because it was freaky. I knew what my mom and dad were going to say before they said it, and I would blurt out the answer before they asked. They thought it was cute at first, but later they tried to guard their thoughts. I really had to watch myself when visitors came around because I would blurt out when the person was lying about something. My dad finally realized he had passed his psychic gift on to me. They put me in private schools and hired other psychics to tutor me in the art of voyeurism. I put up with their unrealistic expectation until I graduated from high school, and then got the hell out of there. Now here I am at ASU. End of story," she finished.

"Not quite. Where did you get those sexy ass eyes?" Dominique asked.

"Their just like my mom's," she answered.

"God bless her," he laughed.

That evening, it was back to the hotel for more games of sex and fun. Jewel had a friend working the front desk of the hotel in the evening, and he always gave them a key to an unoccupied room. She was better than the first time they were together. During this encounter, and all following encounters, they gave themselves to each other fully and freely, heart and soul.

Later that night after talking to Tashiana, while lying in his dorm bed unable to sleep, Dominique wondered if it was possible to continue having such fantastic sex with Jewel, without getting somewhat attached to her, or her to him.

I don't have that long before graduation. Surely I can control my emotions for that short length of time, Dominique deceived himself

As Jewel and Dominique became more involved, Dominique had to lie to Tashiana on several occasions as to why he had not called her, or why he was very seldom in the dorm anymore when she called him. He told her he needed all the study time he could get because the university helped the top five graduates get jobs upon graduation and he wanted to be one of the five who got hired. The sooner he got a job and an apartment after graduation the sooner they could get married and start a life of their own.

Tashiana agreed with what he was doing, but said she wanted to hear his voice every day to reassure herself that he was thinking of her. Therefore, they had one hell of an argument after one supposedly fishing trip which he had failed to tell her about. The conversation came to an abrupt halt when Tashiana hung up on him. They made up the following day by Dominique promising he would try and come home that coming weekend, although he knew he wouldn't. He called her on Thursday and told her he wasn't coming home because he was offered a chance to take real pictures, X-rays, at the hospital that coming weekend. If he didn't show he was serious about the job there was no way they would hire him upon his graduation. Tashiana was upset, but she knew that was how the system worked. Dominique really did want to go home, but he couldn't tear himself away from Jewel.

Toward the end of the semester, he started to wonder if he would be able to break off the relationship with Jewel come graduation day. He was no longer sure who he wanted to be with more, although Jewel had an advantage because she was there with him, while Tashiana was back in Lakeview, Arkansas.

Dominique forced himself to go home a couple of weeks before his scheduled graduation to be with Tashiana. He knew it was the only way he would know for sure who he wanted to be with. The moment he took Tashiana in his arms at the bus station he knew Jewel was the odd girl out. What he and Tashiana had was true love for each other, not just lust. He would make it official upon his return to school.

Dominique ended their relationship a couple of days before graduation. The split had to be complete before Tashiana arrived that weekend. He picked Jewel up at her dorm, and they drove out into the desert under a clear sky filled with stars. The night was so still, the only sounds they could hear was the sound of their own shallow breathing. They sat and stared at the moon and stars, which looked close enough to reach out and touch   He didn't know how long they sat there before Jewel broke the silence.

"Dominique, remember when we first started seeing each other and I said if you found yourself falling for me, you could always tell me where to get off?" she asked, knowing what he had planned.

"How could I forget?" Dominique answered.

"Well, I meant it at the time. But I didn't think I would fall for you as I have. It tears me up inside to know what we have is going to be over after tonight. When is Tashiana supposed to get here?" Jewel asked, wiping away a tear.

"She will be here Saturday afternoon. I never thought any woman could make me doubt my love for Tashiana. Yet here I am holding you in my arms wondering if maybe we were brought together by fate for some crazy test. To see if what we have going was meant to be. But in my heart, I know its Tashiana who I want to marry. I know that's a mean thing to say, but it's the truth. Especially, since you mean more to me than just a woman who has shown me the greatest time of my life. Damn, I wish I didn't have to choose between the two of you, but I know I can't have my cake and eat it too," Dominique said.

"Leave the star gazing to me," Jewel tried to make light of the situation. "Regardless of who you choose between the two of us, I'll always love you. God, if anyone had told me I would be saying this to a guy I've being going with for only four months, I would've told them they were crazy. I should've seen what was coming, but like I said, no one can predict the mystery of the heart. Just hold me every chance you get until she gets here. Okay?" Jewel asked.

"Wouldn't miss the chance for the world," Dominique promised.

Because they were finished with finals, they sat there in the desert until sunrise the following morning. He kept his promise by being with her up to the time he left the campus to pick Tashiana up at the airport. As planned, Tashiana arrived that Saturday evening prior to his graduation on Sunday.

While they were registering for their room the hotel clerk, Jewel's friend, asked, "Where's Jewel?"

"I don't know. Why?" Dominique answered. He gave the

clerk such a deathly look he didn't reply. The clerk shrugged his shoulders and said nothing more.

After entering their room, Tashiana asked who Jewel was. Dominique told her Jewel was a girl on campus that the clerk liked. He had introduced them at a party some students had given at the hotel one night. Now the clerk acts as if it is his job to keep tabs on her. She didn't mention Jewel again.

He was happy she was there to share his accomplishment. When he picked her up at the airport her presence reaffirmed that Tashiana was his one, and only, true love. While helping her get settled, he told her he had to go on campus to tie up some loose ends. He would be back shortly. She wanted to go with him, but he told her he would give her the grand tour of the school after the graduation commencements. He caught found Jewel in the campus snack shop.

"Did she show up?" Jewel asked.

"Yeah she did," Dominique answered.

"Well, what's the verdict?" she asked, refusing to believe he had been serious when he told her he was going to marry Tashiana.

"I'm sorry Jewel, but I love Tashiana too much to let her go. We weren't supposed to get this attached to each other in the first place. I'm sorry I have to hurt you like this," Dominique apologized.

"You don't owe me an apology. It was my stupid idea, in case you have forgotten. It doesn't ease the pain I feel in my heart, but still it was my idea," Jewel said and started crying. "Please leave, Dominique, before I make a complete idiot of myself."

His heart went out to her. He wanted to take her in his arms and promise her he would never let her go, but he knew as well as she did, that their love was never meant to last. They were two lovers existing on borrowed time, but they loved each other as much as their hearts would allow before the flame that had sustained them was snuffed out forever.

Knowing this didn't ease the guilt he felt for having to leave her that way.

"Maybe another place, another time, things would have been different for us," Dominique said using a clique he heard at a movie. He walked away close to tears.

When he returned to the hotel, Tashiana noticed that something was different about him. He looked sad for some reason.

"What's wrong with you, Dominique? You look as if you lost your best friend," Tashiana observed.

"In a way, I guess I did," Dominique said.

"Well, can't you guys stay in touch by phone or mail?" Tashiana asked, not having the foggiest idea his friend was a woman.

"I guess so. He's on his way to the Army. They wouldn't even let him stay an extra day so he could walk the stage with his classmates," Dominique lied, just in case Tashiana wanted to meet this friend that he was so close to.

"Don't you worry about a thing, I'll be your best friend from now on. How come you never talked about him before?" Tashiana asked, wrapping her arms around his waist.

"He was just a gym buddy. I guess I feel this way because he may end up getting messed up in the Army like I did, if he don't end up getting killed in Vietnam," Dominique extended the lie.

"Well, let's hope for the best for him," Tashiana said.

He never saw Jewel in person again after his graduation. However, she became one of America's top stargazers, and after getting established in that profession, her picture appeared in all of the major stargazer's magazines. He wrote a couple times asking her how she was doing, but she never answered his letters. He guessed she didn't have time for an under paid X- ray technician. Or she could never forget, nor forgive him for hurting her. He had to admit, she was hell in the sack.

The excuse Dominique used of having to study, which was partially true, to convince Tashiana he couldn't come home on weekends actually paid off. He graduated first in his class of future x-ray techs. For this achievement it was arranged for him to start work at the state sponsored Arizona State Memorial Hospital, in the x-ray clinic. The hospital was located near the university.

Dominique told no one that the hospital had advanced him enough money to get an apartment, and to buy food until he started getting paid on a regular basis. He found a nice little one bedroom furnished apartment for him and Tashiana to stay until they could afford something bigger. She didn't know he planned to keep her there with him as his wife. After the ceremony he showed her around the campus and introduced her to Mrs. Hartfield.

"Tashiana I want you to meet the lady that saved my life. When I got here I was determined to make a new knee or die trying. She made me realize that everything God put us through He does it for a reason," he said.

"He's so dramatic, but it's true. I felt so sorry for him. Everyday I would check to make sure he was okay, because he was pushing him self beyond human endurance. You have yourself a special man there young lady. He's going to make you a fine husband," she said.

Tashiana thanked her and he finish showing her around campus. At the end of the tour he told her he had a surprise for her. When they pulled into the apartment complex she asked why they were there. He told her to come on she would see. He opens the door and welcomed her to his apartment.

"How long have you had this apartment?" Tashiana asked.

"I got it a couple of day ago. I wanted to surprise you," Dominique said.

"Well, you surprised me alright, now what?" she asked.

"What do you mean now what?" Dominique asked.

"Mom and dad is going to have a baby when they find out you have plans for us to live in sin," Tashiana laughed.

"I have no such plans. We've both graduated, so why don't you call your parents, and I'll call mines, and invite them to the wedding next Sunday," he said hugging her.

She broke the embrace and asked, " Are you serious? I told mom I was going to have a big church wedding at home." Tashiana was happy at the prospect of marrying Dominique sooner than anticipated, but she stood there looking at him in disbelief.

"Well, what do you say?" Dominique asked. Seeing her hesitation he added, "If you want to go home and think about it for a couple of days, that's okay to. Well, say something," he encouraged her.

"Mom and dad are going to freak out! What the heck, lets do this," she said nervously.

Dominique's parents were not able to attend his graduation so he called and told them the good news. They were happy for him, and readily accepted the invitation, but wondered if he was rushing things. Tashiana had to beg and beg her parents before they reluctantly agreed to attend the wedding.

Mrs. Hamilton knew right away that Tashiana had some bad news to tell them by the way she asked if her dad was home. "I know you Tashi. Whenever you whisper on the phone its bad news. So what's the problem?" she asked.

"Uh, uh, I don't' quite know how to tell you this mom," Tashiana hesitated.

"Well, tell me for Christ's sake," her mom said.

"Okay. I'm calling to invite you and dad to our wedding," Tashiana said not adding next weekend.

"We're already invited to your wedding. It's scheduled for September. What're you trying to tell me?" her mom asked.

Tashiana swallowed hard and said, "Dominique has a job here at the Arizona State University Hospital, and he already has an apartment. He asked me to marry him next weekend and I accepted."

"You did what?" Mrs. Hamilton croaked, as if she had been sucker punched by a heavy weight fighter.

"Me, and Dominique is getting married next Sunday and we want you and daddy to be here," Tashiana said, trying to sound brave.

"Girl, you must be out of your damn mind. Did you really think your dad and I would be a part of your little charade of a marriage! You tell Dominique the wedding is off, because we have been planning your wedding here in Lakeview for years. No, you tell Dominique we forbid you to elope with him," Mrs. Hamilton sputtered.

"Mom, whether you and dad like it or not, I have to live my own life. And I'm going to marry Dominique next weekend whether you guys are here or not," Tashiana said with such venom Mrs. Hamilton was lost for words. "Mom, are you okay?" Tashiana asked when her mom didn't say anything.

"No, I'm not alright. And neither will your dad be all right when I tell him that Dominique has gotten you to agree to elope. I have a headache. Call me tomorrow and we will see what we can work out," Mrs. Hamilton said and hung up.

Having been denied the fancy wedding they had put money aside for, Mr. and Mrs. Hamilton had nothing but contempt for Dominique. Mrs. Hamilton was true to her word. When Tashiana refused Dominique's pleas to go back to school and become the lawyer they wanted her to be, Mrs. Hamilton joined her husband in the Dominique hating club.

Dominique and Tashiana had a small, simple ceremony at the University campus Chapel. They managed to get through the weekend without their parents killing each other. Heaven knew there were no love lost between the Goodman and the Hamilton.

Mr. Hamilton's parting advice to Tashiana was she would regret the day she married a broken down bum. He said if Dominique ever mistreated her, she could always come back home. He then gave her the $10,000 they had set aside for the wedding she never had. Dominique didn't want to accept the money, but Mr. Hamilton made it perfectly clear that it was not for him. Dominique thank God he never had to ask the Hamilton's, or his parents, for money during their marriage.

Dominique and Tashiana were the happiest young couple in the world. So happy, Tashiana became pregnant three weeks after they were married. And the others came so fast, approximately two years a part, she resigned herself to thinking she would never be anything other than a housewife for the rest of her life. They both agreed that she should get her tubes tied after the fourth child. That way she would be able to start a career if she wanted to.

If it had been up to Mr. and Mrs. Hamilton, Dominique and Tashiana would have had one child. They paid their first granddaughter, Shantel, a visit several days after she was born. They were so proud to be grandparents. Mrs. Hamilton held the baby as if she was a fragile piece of china.

"She doesn't look anything like Dominique, does she," Mrs. Hamilton said to her husband showing him the child.

"That's because our side of the family has the stronger genes," Mr. Hamilton said.

"Mom, Dad, the baby is only a few days old. She doesn't look like anyone yet," Tashiana said seeing the annoyed look on Dominique's face.

"With any luck she'll look like her mom. I would hate for any girl to have to go through life looking like me," Dominique joked. Tashiana thought it was funny but her parents blew the joke off.

"You're going to the lawyer your mommy should have been, aren't you?" Grandma Hamilton said wiggling her nose at the baby.

"Our children will choose what they want to be when they grow up," Tashiana advised her mom.

"Children, what do you mean children? You're planning on having more than one child?" Mrs. Hamilton asked.

"Yes mom, we are," Tashiana said.

"How are you going to raise more than one child on Dominique's measly salary?" Mr. Hamilton asked his daughter ignoring Dominique.

"There are eight of us, and my dad managed to provide for us," Dominique said.

"Yeah, barely, I've seen your home. How many vacations have you and your family taken in the last ten years?" Mr. Hamilton asked.

"We value the love of each other Mr. Hamilton. Vacations and material things are secondary," Dominique defended his Dad.

"That easy to say when you don't have the money to go

anywhere. What I'm trying to get you to see Tashi is, the more kids you have the less you'll be able to do for them. One kid is plenty," Mr. Hamilton said.

"If I were you baby, I'd get my tubes tied right now. What kind of college education are you going to be able to provide for the children?" Mrs. Hamilton asked.

"All of our children will get a college education, if that's what they want," Dominique interjected.

"On the salary of an x-ray technician, you've got to be kidding? Tashiana is going to have to work just to help you keep food on the table. God knows I don't want my grandchildren living in poverty. And I want them to grow up and be somebody," Mrs. Hamilton said.

"My dad did okay, and so will I," Dominique said starting to get hot under the collar.

Heaven forbid!" Mrs. Hamilton said and continued. "You're an x-ray technician and your daddy is a farmer. My grandchildren are going to be professional people, if I have anything too say about it," Mrs. Hamilton spat.

"Mrs. Hamilton, I'll never try to keep you and Mr. Hamilton from being involved in your grandchildren lives, but Tashiana and me are the parents, and as such, we'll the decisions about their future. What they want to be when they grow up will be up to them," Dominique reiterated what Tashiana had already said earlier.

Mr. Hamilton said, "Since you two are talking about children, plural, you should want all the help you can get because you're not going to be able to send them to a very good school with the amount of money you two will be able to make. You have been too proud to listen to anyone in the past, Dominique. Maybe it's time for you to start listening to people that's smarter than you have to say for a change, time to start listening to people who have been around the block a couple of times."

"We'll manage Dad. Lot of people has more than one child and they're doing fine," Tashiana said not wanting the conversation to get out of hand.

"And that's why so many black families are living in poverty. Living like rats in those run down shacks they call home, never having enough of nothing for their kids. My grandchild, or grandchildren, won't live from hand to mouth with without a future to look forward to," Mr. Hamilton swore.

With gritted teeth Dominique said, "I thank the both of you for your concern for your granddaughter, and future grandchild or children, and the offer to help raise them. But as the man of my house, raising my kids, I'll raise them as I see fit. However, if I ever find myself in such a bind that the only way out is to come to you and your wife for help, I'll sacrifice my pride and do it. Understand though, the only way I'll ever ask anyone for help is if it's a life or death situation. Other than that, we'll manage."

"In that case there's still hope we will have a say in the raising of our grandchildren," Mrs. Hamilton smiled.

Dominique's mouth opened and closed several times, but he said to hell with the argument and let her have the last word.

Dominique's parents came to visit the child and were just happy that it was healthy and had all its fingers and toes. And said knew Tashiana and Dominique was going to be good parents.

Because Dominique was a Disabled Veteran, he applied for a position with the U.S. Government, and was told the only position available was at Elmendorf Air Force Base Hospital, in Anchorage, Alaska. At the time he accepted the job in Alaska he didn't know the impact the move would have on their marriage, and their lives. When Tashiana told her parents where they were moving to they almost blew a heart gasket.

"Why the hell does Dominique have to go all the way to Alaska to get a decent job? How are we going to see the grandchildren? We can't drive up there," Mrs. Hamilton said.

"Mom, you and dad can afford to fly up and see the kids whenever you want to and you know it," Tashiana reminded her.

"The children is going to stay sick up there in that cold weather. You're not Eskimos you know," Mrs. Hamilton reminded her.

"What the hell is going on with those damn kids now?" Tashiana heard her dad asked her mother. "Going to move where!" He boomed after being told of their plans. He got on the phone. "Tashiana, why the hell are you allowing Dominique to drag you and the kids to that frozen ass state where only Eskimos want to live? Tell him to go and see what it's like and you and the kids will come up later. I don't want you dragging the kids around in all that ice and snow looking for a place to live."

"Dad, Dominique's new boss have already found a house for us. When we leave here, we'll be moving right into our new home. Will you two be excited for me for once in your life, please."

"We'll come and visit whenever we get a chance," Mr. Hamilton said and handed the phone to his wife.

Mrs. Hamilton had heard what Tashiana said to her dad and said, "We are happy for you Tashi, but we worry that if anything happens you're going to be so far away. Well, you two have did alright so far with your marriage and the children, I guess it's time we started trusting that you know what you're doing. I still wished you wouldn't move so far away."

"Mom that's why they built telephones. So we can stay in

touch," Tashiana smiled through the phone at her mom.

"Remember, you can always call us if anything goes wrong. I love you and the children too much not to worry about you, you know that," her mom said.

On that note they moved from Arizona to Alaska, and as they say the rest is history. After three years of fun and heartaches on the frozen tundra of Alaska they packed their bags and moved to San Antonio, Texas, hoping to forget the mistrust and deceit associated with Tashiana's affair. A knock at the door brought Dominique back to the present.

At least you never had to live with the knowledge of what happened between Jewel Blackwood and me, Dominique said to an invisible Tashiana, as he got up to answer the door.

CHAPTER #7

Dominique sat listening to Tashiana spilling her guts about how sorry she was for hurting him because of her affair with Ahmaad. And for again abusing the trust he had in her. He didn't believe a word she said. He felt she hadn't given a damn about his feelings since she started screwing around in Alaska. The alligator tears, she was shedding was for herself. She had been caught and was afraid she may lose her family and that no good bastard she had been laying up with every chance she got. The longer she talked the madder he got.

When he could stand her babbling no longer he said, "You haven't given a shit about me since you hooked up with those whores in Alaska. And because I came running to ask you to come back home after your affair there, you felt you could do whatever the hell you wanted to when we got to San Antonio. You see me as a weak assed wimp who doesn't have the balls to demand respect. Therefore, I deserve none."

"Dominique, why are you bringing up Alaska? You promised not to throw that in my face when we got into an argument," Tashiana said.

"You promised not to screw around again. Which do you think is worse? My breaking a promise not to remind you that you screwed around on me before, or you breaking your promise not to screw around again knowing how it would affect me and the kids? I'll say promise number two was the more important of the two promises that was made, and broken. Wouldn't you agree?" he asked.

"I do respect you, Dominique. I know you feel I don't because of the affair, but you're wrong. You're the glue that holds this family together, and gives the kids that foundation they need to make it in life. I know I haven't kept my part of the deal, but I swear if you give me just one more chance I'll be the mother and wife you and the children deserves," she pleaded.

"Give you one more chance, huh? Give you one more chance to find a different lover that you can hideout with for another two or three years, before getting caught again. Give me one good reason why I should risk having my heart torn from my chest again?" he asked gritting his teeth.

"I love you and the children, and I swear to God I'll never mess with another man as long as I live," Tashiana said trying to sound convincing.

"If that's the best reason you can come up with this marriage is doomed. Because if I remember correctly, that's the same bullshit you said before we moved here," Dominique said sarcastically.

"I have grown up since Alaska. I finally realized what we have as a family I'll never have with anyone else. I wanted to end the affair a year ago, but I was afraid you were going to find out and throw me out of the house, so I figured I might need someone to fall back on. I'm sorry, Dominique. I'm truly sorry," she said starting to cry again.

"How bad do you want this marriage to work?" he asked, ready to drop a bomb on her about her friend Janet and her lover's wife.

"I'll do whatever it takes to make things up to you," she said. Upon hearing the question whether she wanted to work things out it gave her hope that he may be willing to stay in the marriage.

"I want you to forgive me for sleeping with Janet and Laquan. You see, while you were out doing your thing I was doing my thing." Seeing the shocked look on her face, he continued. "I found out about your affair six months ago. Instead of confronting you, I wanted to see how long it would take you to confess your infidelity. In the meantime, I comforted Laquan because of what Ahmaad was putting her through, and Janet comforted me for what you were putting me through. So, what do you say, deal?" he finished.

"You slept with Janet! You slept with Janet! I don't believe you. Janet may be a horny bitch, but I don't believe she would stab me in the back like that. She wouldn't dare sleep with you after all the secrets we've kept for each other. As far as Laquan is concern, I don't know anything about her, other than the lies Ahmaad told me about her. You're kidding to make me jealous, right?" she asked.

"I'm afraid not. I've never said anything to you bout Janet hitting on me whenever you weren't around because I wasn't attracted to her. The only reason I took her to bed was to get her to tell me who you were sleeping with. She told me all your business," Dominique said rubbing her friend's deceit in her face.

"You sound like you're really enjoying telling me this crap. Why?" she asked becoming angry. She was angrier with Janet than Dominique, because she thought her and Janet had a special bond that nothing could break. As for Laquan was concerned, Tashiana suspected Dominique was seeing someone and felt she could deal with it.

"Why? If we're going to work things out between us, we have to start with a clean slate. Are you willing to do that?" Dominique asked.

"I don't believe you actually slept with my best friend. I can deal with you sleeping with Laquan a lot easier than with you sleeping with Janet. I know it sounds hypocritical coming from me, but if you slept with my best friend it shows that you have no respect for me either. I can't believe you slept with her. That bitch!" Tashiana screamed.

"I agree. You're not the one to be preaching to me about respect. I've shown you nothing but respect since the day you defied your parents and married me. The only reason I didn't sleep with Jessica while we were living in Alaska was because I felt it would be disrespecting you. But now that I know respect is not high on your moral list, I said to hell with it and did what I thought I had to do to find out who your lover was," Dominique said, refusing to apologize for what he had done.

"I know about Jessica hitting on you. I threatened to kick her ass if she didn't leave you alone. Sleeping with Janet is something totally different. I told her things I've told no one on the face of this fucking earth. I would've gone to hell and back to maintain the friendship I thought we had. Now, you stand there proud of yourself knowing what you've done with Janet hurts me to the core of my being. If your purpose for sleeping with Janet was to hurt me, you succeeded. That bitch!" Tashiana said, feeling betrayed by her best friend.

"So, where do we go from here?" Dominique asked.

"I don't know. I think we both need some time to figure out what we want to do about this marriage. I love you, and never intentionally set out to hurt you, but you knew what sleeping with Janet would do to me. Yes, we need some time from each other to decide where we want go from here. I'm going to call my mom and let her know I'm coming to visit her for a few days. You'll be okay with the kids for a few days won't you?" she asked, choking back another round of tears.

"Yeah, of course I will. This won't be the first time I've been left alone to look after the kids by my self. Tell your mom and dad the truth about how we reached this crisis in our marriage. I don't want your dad calling me again talking about what a damn loser I am. When are you planning to leave?" he asked.

"Tomorrow, I gotta get out of here," she said and left the den.

"If you don't want anyone to hurt you, I would suggest you don't hurt him or her," Dominique said after her disappearing frame. He had been tempted to tell her about Jewel, but figure telling her about sleeping with Janet was punishment enough for this go round.

On her way to the airport the following day Tashiana decided she had to pay Janet a visit before leaving for her mom's. She had to know why her so-called-best-friend had committed the ultimate no-no of a friendship. Tashiana never knew she was capable of harboring a hate so intense she didn't care is she ended up in jail or dead. Janet was about to feel the brunt of her rage. Tashiana checked to make sure the small .32 caliber pistol she purchased from a corner thug was loaded. She placed it back into her purse before knocking on the door.

"Hey Tashi girl, what bring you my way?" she asked, opening the door and inviting her friend in.

"Where's Jeffery?" Tashiana asked looking around to make sure they were alone.

"He left with one of his drinking buddies. He probably won't be back until sometime late this evening," Janet informed her. "So, what brings you into my neck of the woods?"

"I needed to talk to you about something Dominique told me. Something that's hard for me to believe," Tashiana informed her.

Janet could tell by the tone of Tashiana's voice that this was not going to be a pleasant visit. "What on earth are you talking about?" Janet tried to sound nonchalant. She needed time to formulate a story Tashiana might believe as to why she slept with her man.

"I told Dominique about my affair with Ahmaad last night, and asked for his forgiveness. After listening to me pour my heart out about how sorry I was for what I had done, he calmly told me that he knew about the affair six months ago because you told him about me and Ahmaad after you had finished fucking him. Tell me he only said that to get back at me," Tashiana said in a deathly tone.

"Girl, you know I'd never sleep with your man. We've been girlfriends too long for me to do some shit like that. Why do you think he picked me to lie on?" Janet asked. Because Tashiana had asked if it was true as appose to saying it was true, Janet thought she might be able to talk her way out of the situation.

"That 's the question which kept me awake all night. It wasn't enough that he told me about sleeping with Laquan, he had to bring you into the equation. Why would he do that?" Tashiana asked herself instead of Janet.

"Dominique slept with Ahmaad's wife?" Janet asked with a twinge of jealousy in her voice, which did not go unnoticed by Tashiana.

"You sound upset hearing that Dominique was sleeping with Laquan. Why is that Janet?" Tashiana asked her anger starting to reach the boiling point.

"I was reacting to what you must be going through. You poured your heart out to Dominique because you want to save your marriage and he tells you he's sleeping with two women. I was feeling your pain Tashi, that's all," Janet talked fast.

"You remember that night we were getting ready to go out and Dominique said he wouldn't know what to do with a naked woman if she offered herself to him, and you said you doubted it. You knew the way you said it pissed me off, but you chose to ignore my feelings. And to top it off, after telling you I may lose Dominique if I didn't drop Ahmaad you said I would have to worry about you hitting on him. Don't think I haven't noticed how you throw yourself at him whenever you think I'm not looking. I just thought you had better sense than to mess with him," Tashiana said.

"Tashiana, listen to yourself. You're making things up to take some of blame off of yourself for Dominique going astray. You know me and Dominique has been kidding each other like that for years. Are you going to confront Laquan about this allegation?" Janet asked trying to get the conversation off of her.

Tashiana reached into her purse and pulled out the gun. "We both know one thing for sure Janet, Dominique is not a liar. He'd never say he slept with you if he didn't. And here I was thinking you were my friend. How could you do this to me after all we've been through together? The secrets we've shared. I would've given my life to keep anyone from hurting you. And this is the thanks I get for trusting you," Tashiana said with a tear running down her cheek.

Janet knew no matter how much she denied the allegation now it wouldn't make any difference because Tashiana was convinced she had slept with Dominique. Holding her hands out in front of her as if to deflect the bullets that was soon to fly she said, "

Tashi, let me explain what happened. When Dominique came to me asking about your affair, I swear he already knew. All I did was confirm what he suspected all along. I had no intentions of sleeping with him, but he said he needed someone to help him get through the pain and disappointment he was feeling because of your affair. I know it was wrong, but I never tried to break you guys up. Come on, Tashi, out the gun down," she pleaded.

"You know what my family means to me. And you chose to put my marriage in jeopardy almost guaranteeing I would lose my kids. I don't know whether to shoot your bitch ass right now, or tell Jeffery what has been going on and see what happens," Tashiana said. She alternated target spots on Janet's body as she talked.

"For God's sake Tashi, put the gun down. That's a good idea, lets tell Jeffery what happened and see what he has to say about it. If we both end up divorced, we'll be even," she said.

"Even!" Tashiana screamed. "You screw my husband, and I tell your husband about it, and you want to call that even. You have no children to lose Janet," Tashiana said shooting Janet in the left arm.

Janet fell back onto the floor screaming in pain. "Tashi, wait. Don't do this. I'm sorry for hurting you. I swear, I'll never do anything like this again," she pleaded for her life.

"I know you won't, darling sweet friend," Tashiana said shooting Janet in the right arm.

Now delirious with the pain, Janet no longer cared because she knew she was going to die. "Go ahead and kill me you crazy bitch. I never told Dominique he should leave you, but I should've. You don't deserve a good man like Dominique."

"You want to know something Janet? You're right. I don't deserve a good man like Dominique, that's why I thank God he's willing to work things out. As for you, I'm sure Jeffery will give you the send off that you deserve," Tashiana said aiming center mass.

Janet tried one last attempt to save her life. "Tashi, it doesn't matter what happens to me. The important thing is that you and Dominique will remain a family. And regardless of what you think, I still love you. You're the best friend a girl could ever have.
"

"And you're the best friend I ever had, but your lust was stronger than our friendship. I love you Janet, but this is how it has to be," Tashiana said as the bullet exploded into Janet's chest blowing her heart to pieces. Tashiana looked at her watch and was pleased to see she had plenty of time before her plane departed for Arkansas.

That evening before Dominique arrived home, Tashiana called the children together to explain what was going on between their father and her. The guilt, and shame of having the affair with Ahmaad was now ten-fold, as she watched the pained expressions on her children faces.

"Mom, does this mean you and dad are going to get a divorce?" Shantel, their oldest child asked.

"I don't know baby. We haven't discussed the matter yet. I've wanted to tell your dad what was going on for a long time now, but I could never find the courage to do so. I guess I was afraid he wouldn't love me anymore," Tashiana confessed to her children.

"Could you blame dad, if he stopped loving you? Mom, can I be honest with you?" Shantel asked.

"Sure, baby. Say whatever is on your mind," Tashiana encouraged her.

"Well, Sheena and I have been talking about your affair for a long time," Shantel began.

Tashiana's eyes widened in disbelief! Before Shantel could continue she asked, "How did you know I was having an affair?" If it was that obvious to the kids, surely Dominique knew as well. Why hadn't he said anything? What was he waiting for to confront her? She only had questions, and no answers.

"Come on, Mom," Shantel sighed, as if what she was saying should be obvious to her mom. "Do you think we're that young and dumb? It takes you two hours to get made up and dressed, before going out. Everyone knew it wasn't to look good for daddy. You stay gone most of the night every time you go out, and you say you never spend any money. Who goes places with friends as much as you do, and never spend any money? No girlfriend is that generous mom.

I have also notice on several occasions you left home with make-up on, but didn't have any on when you got back. What truly concerned mother leaves her children alone almost every weekend and not have something going on. In case you haven't noticed mom, dad has started keeping the same hours as you do on weekends. We think he knows something is going on with you but he is waiting for you to mess up or something. Sometimes I feel like you and dad are depending on me, and Sheena, to raise Jr. and Zelvina," Shantel voice quivered. She took a deep breath and continued. "Are we going to be split up like other kids whose parents decide to sleep around?" At this point Shantel broke into tears.

Tashiana looked from one face to the next, they were all crying. She felt as if she was a complete failure as a mother and a wife. She knew Dominique Jr. and Zelvina were crying because their sisters were crying, but it didn't lessen the pain. Without realizing it, she too was crying. The tears rolled down her cheeks into her lap.

"What can I do, or say, to make things right?" Tashiana asked, more to herself than to them. She expected no answer. "I'm sorry for putting you kids through this mess. If God give me another chance, I swear, I'll be a good mom and wife. I'll not disappoint you all again. Can you find it in your hearts to forgive me for what I've done to hurt you and your dad?" Tashiana sniffed. She was thankful that they had been shielded from what happened while they were living in Alaska, otherwise they probably would have brought up that episode also. All heads nodded yes, except for Shantel. She had a look of utter disgust on her face.

"Dad loves you more than he does himself," Shantel said, twisting the guilt into her mother's heart as if it was a jaded knife. "I have sat in my room many nights listening to Dad cuss and almost cry, because he doesn't know what to do to keep you at home. You really don't think Dad is so stupid he doesn't know you're sleeping with someone else do you? Let's hope he feels your marriage is worth saving. Who is this creep anyway? Are you still seeing him, and do you love him?" she almost spat the words at her mother.

"I'd rather not say. Does it matter? I'm never going to see him again," Tashiana answered.

"Yes, mom, it does matter, to me. I don't want the man's son or daughter coming up to me, asking if I know about the affair you two are having," Shantel explained.

"You don't have to worry about that because his kid is only five years old. But if you must know, it was Mr. Tate," Tashiana admitted.

"You mean, the Mr. Tate that lives a couple of blocks down the street from us?" Sheena asked, in disbelief.

"Yes," Tashiana answered, and lowered her head no longer able to face her children.

"Mom, if you left Daddy for that playboy, I would never speak to you again as long as I lived," Sheena said, with such conviction, it jerked Tashiana's head erect.

"Why is that?" Tashiana asked, stunned.

"Mom, the man has slept with nearly every married woman in this neighborhood. And to make matters worse, he's a gigolo. Everyone in the neighborhood knows what he is. I hope you weren't as stupid as some of these other women who gave him money. Oh Mom, I don't think I can ever show my face in public again," Shantel moaned, and ran from the room.

"I don't understand why you and Shantel are reacting this way," Tashiana said to Sheena, who looked as if she too was about to run from the room as well.

"I guess you haven't heard the latest rumor concerning Mr. Tate. He's into fifteen year olds now," Sheena informed her mother.

"What're you kids talking about?" Tashiana asked dumbfounded.

"Lisa Green, Mom. Mr. Tate is sleeping with her, as well as sleeping with her mother. I'm surprised you don't know this Mom. He's your boyfriend, or was your boyfriend. All in all Mom, Mr. Tate's a complete jerk," Sheena concluded.

Wiping tears from their eyes, Zelvina and Dominique sat fascinated by the knowledge of their older siblings.

"How do you know so much about Mr. Tate?" Tashiana asked becoming angry. Not at Sheena, but her own stupidity. Sure she heard the rumors about Mrs. Green and her daughter Lisa, as well as about all the other women he was supposedly sleeping with. Ahmaad convinced her that all the rumors she was hearing about him sleeping with other women was nothing than just that, rumors. How could she be so stupid to believe his every denial about the other women he was supposedly sleeping with?

"It's no big secret, Mom. Lisa tells everyone at school about it. She even said she's in love with him, and he love's her. If you don't mind Mom, I'm going to hide myself in my room for a month. It's sure going to be hard to face my classmates from now on knowing my Mom was slept with a no good S.O.B. like Mr. Tate," Sheena said and walked out leaving her mom with Zelvina and Jr.

Tashiana told them to go to their rooms while she cooked dinner. While preparing the evening meal, Tashiana couldn't help but wonder if her marriage was over. The last argument she and Dominique had made her believe he was having an affair also, and that was why he hadn't confronted her. If the kids knew she was having an affair, surely Dominique knew.

The week before her confession, Tashiana had gotten annoyed with Ahmaad for calling Dominique an idiot for not knowing she was having an affair and went home early. Dominique was not home yet and the kids were asleep. She paced back and forth waiting for him to get home because she was itching for a fight. She didn't care what time he got home she would be waiting up for him.

Unknowing that Tashiana was waiting for him Dominique walked through the door at 3 a.m. with a big grin on his face. "You just getting home, man what a night?" Dominique said.

"I hope you had fun. So, where did you go?" Tashiana asked, ignoring his remark about her just getting home. He could plainly see she was wearing a nightgown.

"No where special," Dominique answered.

"You must've gone somewhere special to say *"man what a night."* Maybe it was with someone special," Tashiana pressed Dominique for an answer.

"I'll be damned. You're jealous aren't you? Since when did you start caring what I do when I go out, or whether I'm having an affair or not for that matter. You're always going out and staying until around this time in the morning. So what kept you out until 3 a.m., another man?" Dominique asked.

"This isn't about me. Why is it you only go out on nights I go out? Is it so you won't have to feel guilty about doing whatever it is you're doing?" Tashiana asked. She wanted to ask if he was trying to catch her having an affair but was afraid he may say yes, or that he already knew.

"I go out on the same nights that you do so you can't complain about me going out too much. To put your mind at ease, when I go out on the same nights as you do it's not to try and catch you doing anything wrong, if that's your concern," Dominique answered sensing the question that wasn't asked.

"You can follow me anytime you like. I don't have anything to hide," Tashiana lied.

"And you can follow me anytime you like. So, did I answer your question?" Dominique asked.

"No, I asked you where you went tonight," she said.

"I went to the *Totally Guys Lounge*," he answered.

"That's in Austin. That's where the white high society bitches hang out. And they're always looking for some black stud to satisfy their horny asses. How often do you go there?" Tashiana asked. She didn't stop to think that she had never mention to

Dominique that she knew about the club, or that she had been to it herself. "And you have to be with someone to get in. Who is she?"

"How do you know about the *Totally Guys Lounge?* Tonight was my first time going there. I had to pretend I was with one of the ladies hanging around outside the club trying to get in. Since you know the procedure and all, who took you to the lounge? And don't tell me you hung around outside until some guy took pity on you and pretended to be your date. I know you would never do that. You act like those high society ladies you mentioned, although you're not white," Dominique said.

"I've never been to the club myself, but Janet has. She told me about those white broads giving it up to any black man who ask them for it. But she never told me anything about them hanging around outside the club trying to get men to escort them in" Tashiana said without any hesitation.

"Well I guess I was lucky tonight because there were a couple of them hanging around. For your information the ladies that were hanging around outside the club were black, and they didn't offer me anything. Am I to assumed that the black ladies who goes there isn't on the make. I guess not, the lady I escorted in was gone before I could even get a table. Believe me, the place is overrated," Dominique said heading for bed.

"There must be something to it. You stayed until it closed," she quipped.

"Cute. Hey, you didn't tell me where you went to night. Was it over at Lackland AFB? Isn't that where married women meet their lovers, and from there they spend the next couple of hours making wild passionate love in some cheap motel?" he asked playing on her guilt

"For your information Mr. Smarty Pants, we went to that little hole in the wall called the Cove. It's not at all what I thought it would be. I know I would never catch you with another woman in a place like that," Tashiana said looking him in the face to see if she could detect any guilt.

Dominique smiled to himself because Janet had told him that Ahmaad told Tashiana there was a rumor he was meeting a woman there at the Cove. He said, "If I was having an affair, that is exactly the type place you would find me. It's small, not crowded, and it has pool tables. Hey, it's me."

"So what're you saying?" Tashiana asked.

"I guess it means, since I wasn't there I'm not having an affair," Dominique quipped and got into bed.

"If you're messing around I'm going to find out," Tashiana said.

"Yeah. And I'm sure you already have someone to help you catch me, right," Dominique said.

"You think you're so smart don't you?" Tashiana asked.

"Baby, when you catch me messing around and call yourself chastising me, make sure you don't have any skeletons in your closet," Dominique said.

"Is that supposed to mean you think I'm having affair?" Tashiana asked.

"No, it means if you're going to accuse me of doing something make sure you aren't doing the same thing that's all I'm saying," Dominique said.

"We'll see who has the last word on this topic," Tashiana said.

"Yeah we will," Dominique said and turned over in went to sleep.

After Dominique had fallen asleep Tashiana checked his shirt for the scent of a woman's perfume or lipstick, she found neither.

Knowing he was probably messing around the same as she was, and the possibility of a divorce being real, she realized she didn't want to lose him. A fear she had never known possessed her. She knew the charade they were living had to end, and it had to end soon. *What would I do, if the shoe were on the other foot? Would I be willing to forgive him a second time?* Tashiana asked herself. Her mind was still searching for an easier way out of her predicament when she dozed off to sleep.

At dinner that evening, Dominique knew by the way Tashiana and the children were acting, that Tashiana was ready to throw her cards into the winds of the hurricane and hoped they wouldn't all be blown away. He had seen that look before, but not quite as intense. No one said a word throughout the meal. It was more like a wake, than a meal. In Alaska, she wasn't sure if she wanted to be married to Dominique any longer, but now she knew her family was the most important thing in her life. After the kids went to bed, and she making sure they were asleep, Tashiana asked Dominique if she could talk to him in the den. He told her to go ahead, he would be there shortly.

A couple of stiff shots of bourbon and a fresh one in hand, Dominique went into the den wondering if he would still want to be married once the fallout ended. He sat on the sofa beside her and waited for her to start the conversation. Her mouth opened and closed several times but nothing came out. Tears were had welled up in her eyes. Watching the expression on her face made Dominique both angry and sad at the same time, angry because she had betrayed him, sad because she was about to bear her inner soul.

The naked realization of what she had done, and of what he had allowed to continue, finally hit him with full force in the face. The pain tore at the most sensitive part of his grieving heart. He too, was temporarily speechless. He had never experienced both these emotions at the same time. Dominique had thought he would be able to discuss the situation rationally knowing what he did about the affair.

With his voice close to breaking he asked, "How long has this affair been going on, Tashiana?"

Now the tears did come. She didn't even ask how he knew that was what she wanted to talk to him about. Didn't say anything about the kids saying they knew she was having an affair why didn't he. And if the did, why didn't he say anything about it. She said, "I'm sorry Dominique. Yesterday was the last time we're going to see each other," she managed to say between sobs. How long, Tashiana?" he shouted.

"A little bit over two years," she answered in a small weak voice, confirming what he already knew.

Still, it didn't lessen the blow to his ego. That empty feeling he had felt in his stomach the night he followed her to the club, and the day he saw and Ahmaad together at the motel returned. His anger pushed itself to the forefront, extinguishing all other emotions.

"How many more men are out there laughing behind my back because they have taken my wife to bed"? Dominique sneered, but did not give her a chance to answer. "I know I should've said something to you about those nights you weren't where you said you were going to be, all those nights you came home complaining of being too tired for me to touch you when we went to bed. I guess you were tired, since you'd already been screwed. My love and trust in you thrown out the goddamned window. Who is it? And do you love the son-of a-bitch?" he hissed, hoping she had come to realize she didn't love Ahmaad, because if she did, he was partly to blame. He had heard her tell Ahmaad she wasn't sure. Maybe he had given her the time she needed to make up her mind. He cussed himself for allowing the affair to continue

"At one point in the relationship, I thought I did. Whether you believe me or not, it's you who I love," Tashiana answered.

Dominique didn't realize he had been holding his breath anticipating her to say she loved Ahmaad. Now that she said she didn't he let it out and continued his assault on her morals. "Oh, I see what you mean. You love me, but he's the one who gets you off in the sack. Hey, that's great to know, baby," he said, trying to hurt her as much as she had hurt him, short of confessing his own infidelity. "God help me," he moaned, stood up, and walked over to the fireplace and stared at the ashes he should've cleaned out after the last time it was used.

She had expected him to be hurt when he found out about the affair, but the pained expression on his face was much greater than she could've imagined possible. She wanted so much to go to him and say something that would ease the pain that was so obvious in his face. She could see the tears in his eyes trying to burst forth, but they were being held back by his shattered ego. She wanted so much to go to him, to reassure him that no matter what she had done, she still loved him, and only him, more than he could ever imagine, and would never hurt him again. But the expression on his face kept her at bay.

All of a sudden, Dominique's expression changed completely. The muscles in his face relaxed, and the tone of his voice returned to normal. It was so eerie it frightened Tashiana momentarily. He had been so angry he almost told her he had known about the affair for six months now. That the only reason he hadn't said anything about it was because he didn't think their marriage was worth saving. He knew if he told her that she would automatically assume he was having an affair himself. He was gone just as much as she was lately

"When we got married," Dominique began, "we made a promise to each other that no matter how angry we got at each other, we would discuss our problems in a civilized manner. God knows this marriage has had its trials and tribulations! I love you, Tashiana, with all my heart and soul, but I don't know if I'll ever be able to trust you again. I don't know if I want to live like that. Every time you leave the house, I'm going to be wondering who you're going to see this time. And what do I tell the children is wrong with us when they see us walking around the house acting like strangers toward each other? All their lives we have taught them that when you love someone, and they do something wrong, you should have the capacity in your heart to forgive them. Well, I don't know if I'll be able to practice what I preach this time. They're the ones who are going to suffer the most because of this you know," Dominique said, shaking his head.

"Dominique, I know I wouldn't do anything to hurt the kids. Besides, I've already told them about what I've done. I told them I was going to tell you about the affair and ask for your forgiveness," Tashiana informed him.

Dominique continued as if he hadn't heard a word she said. "Why's it, when parents decide to forsake everything for a cheap thrill, it's always the kids who ends up getting hurt the most?" he asked facing her.

"Why are you bringing the kids in to this?" Tashiana asked knowing he was talking about getting a divorce.

"I have turned down every woman who has ever offered herself to me." It was true up until he found out about her affair there in San Antonio. "Why? I love you and thought you would never betray me again. Not to mention the respect we have manage to earn since moving here to San Antonio. No woman could ever replace what I thought we had," he said and turned away. He didn't want her to see he was crying.

Dominique thought that since he already knew about the affair, it would not hurt as much when she got around to confessing. He had never been more wrong.

Tashiana's heart was breaking into so many pieces, she wondered if she would ever be able to put it together again. She knew Dominique had to be totally devastated, because she had never seen him cry over anything in his life. He believed it was a weakness no man in his right mind should ever let anyone see, especially his woman. But there he was balling like a baby. And she felt there was nothing she could do, or say, to ease the pain. She felt the only thing that would ease the pain for him was a swift, painless death on her part.

Dominique had always been so strong Tashiana convinced herself that nothing could penetrate his coat of armor. Not even her infidelity. In Alaska, although hurt and angry, he had taken her affair in stride and never looked back. Now she wished with all her heart and soul she could turn back the hands of time. But all she could do was go to him. Try to convince him that no man could ever replace him in her heart. Explain to him how Ahmaad had caught her at a weak moment, when she was unsure how much he loved her, and had held that first encounter over her head ever since. *[Tashiana would have felt more confident in saying that if she didn't know in her heart it was the same lie she had been telling herself for at least a year.]* How she had planned to lay her cards on the table as soon as she built up the courage to do so. And how she hoped he would somehow understand and eventually forgive her for her sin again.

Tashiana felt she had only one shot left to save her marriage. She somehow found the courage to go to him. With tears running down her face she said, "Dominique, I wouldn't blame you if you killed me for what I've done to you and the family. No matter what you decide to do, I want you to know, I do love you. If you can find it in your heart to forgive me this one last time, you'll never have to worry about this happening again. And if you decide you want to sleep with another woman, I'll understand. As long as the kids didn't find out about it. I don't think their young mind could stand the shock of the both of us screwing up," she said in one breath.

Even through the hurt and pain, he still loved her. Dominique grabbed Tashiana by the shoulders and asked, "Why? In God's name, how could you bring this shame and disgrace down on your family again?"

"Alright, Dominique, I'll tell you, but please let me finish before you say anything," Tashiana began, releasing herself from his grasp. "Do you remember the night at the Anderson's party? When I saw you and Charlene coming down the stairs holding hands and whispering as if you two were sharing a secret you wanted no one else to hear?" Of course he remembered. "I found out later nothing happened between the two of you, but at the time I thought you had just finished making love to her. I knew it would've been a stupid for you to do with me there at the party, but I couldn't convince myself nothing happened. You hear these stories all the time about how married couples go to parties and one manages to make out with someone at the party without the other one knowing anything about it. I guess my imagination got the better of me.

That was the same night I met Ahmaad. He was at the party also. After our little argument about Charlene and you took off to talk politics with Greg, he showed up on the scene and made me feel wanted. I tried to tell you how lonely I felt but you were too busy having fun and talking politics. I felt you didn't want me around. I didn't even know Ahmaad was married, and lived several streets down from us, until I saw him and Laquan together weeks later grocery shopping. I had seen her on several occasions at the grocery store and in her yard, but never with Ahmaad.

Anyway, I felt as though you didn't love me as much as I thought you should've, so we made a date for the following weekend. I have lied to myself that ever since then Ahmaad has been holding that night over my head, telling me if I didn't continue seeing him, he would tell you everything. However, about six months ago, I realized that wasn't what kept me going back to him. It was the fun we had together. No kids to worry about. Not having to worry about how much money we had spent that night, because he was footing the bills. It was almost like being single again. What went wrong? I finally came to my senses and realized I had everything I ever wanted in my life right here at home, with you and the children. A man who loved me, and four beautiful children who think their mom is the greatest in the world.

I have wanted to tell you this for a long time. I just couldn't find the courage. I was afraid you would kick me out of the house, like you did when we lived in Alaska, only this time you would never let me see the kids again. Or you would let me stay for the sake of the kids, but you would never forgive, or love me again. I know what I did was wrong, but, oh God, please forgive me," she finished, sobbing uncontrollably.

Dominique waited until she regained her composure, and said, "There's still one matter that has to be cleared up, and you have to tell me the truth. How much of our money did you spend on Ahmaad, or give that gigolo? Everyone knows his reputation. And from my calculation, we came up a few dollars short in our bank account." When she hesitated too long in answering he again asked, "How much, Tashiana?" This time he held her at arms length.

Tashiana took a deep breath, sat down and said, "All total, I would say about $4000.00. It wasn't all at once though. Ahmaad kept saying he needed money for this and that. He said he was shame to ask me for money, but Laquan had a drug habit and spent all their money on drugs. He said Ahmaad Jr. would starve if not for him. However, he would pay back the money as soon as he got Laquan to enter a drug treatment facility, or divorce her. It took close to a year before I realized I was being had. I guess it took that long for me to realize I was being had because he was spending most of the money I supposedly loaned him on me. So in essence, I was paying him to take me out.

This past year however, I've gotten back the money I gave him, and more. I had planned on taking as much of Ahmaad's money as I could get from him, but I didn't have the heart to hurt Laquan and her child. They had done nothing to me, and by this time he would do anything I told him to. I even called his house when I knew he was supposed to take Laquan someplace, demanding that he meet me someplace instead. Was it jealousy? Not really. At first it was for the hell of it. Then it was because I felt I might have to fall back on him once you found out about the affair. I guess I was afraid to let him go. I had planned to put the money back into our bank account, but I kept spending it on the kids and the house. I guess I was having too much fun to think straight. I knew as long as I didn't give you any reason to think anything was wrong financially, I would be safe. Or, as long as you saw me spending the money on the children, and the house, you'd have no reason to check up on me. It worked until you decided you wanted a boat. It was then I finally realized this double life I was leading had to end. So, yesterday it ended for good. This you can be sure of. I'm truly sorry, Dominique. I don't know what else to say," Tashiana defended her actions.

"You've said quite enough for one night," he said.

"What happens now?" Tashiana asked.

"I don't know baby. Right now I'm too torn up inside to even think straight. We'll have to wait until tomorrow and see how things are between us," Dominique answered.

"There's not much more I can say, or do," she said and started crying again.

Dominique started to tell her he didn't really want a damn boat. He just wanted to find out if she had given any of his money to Ahmaad because he knew about the affair, but he didn't dare. They sat in silence until they decided it was bedtime.

That night was the first time since they had been married that Dominique felt any regrets about having marrying Tashiana. He did not sleep at all. Every time he closed his eyes, there stood Ahmaad, beside his bed, saying, *I'm still going to get her from you if I can. She may love you, but she'll never be convinced you can ever love her again.*

Dominique knew what the image said was partly true. If he didn't show Tashiana that he was capable of forgiving her, over time, she would probably feel it was best that they go their separate ways. As far as Ahmaad trying to get her away from him, that was Ahmaad's problem. Dominique decision whether to stay in the marriage took his children into consideration as it had in Alaska. He didn't want his children going through the emotional roller coaster ride divorce causes. Dominique knew it was going to be harder to accept Tashiana's infidelity this time because it was her second time around, but he would try his best to weather the storm. He had to show his children he was willing to practice what he preached. Show them that there was still forgiveness left in the world. Show them that divorce was not the only way out. Show them that if two people were willing to work things out to save their marriage it was better for everyone involved.

The following morning when it was time to get up, he hoped he didn't look as bad as he felt. The lack of sleep, along with what Tashiana had confessed, had taken its toll on him. And she was sleeping as if nothing had happened. His anger rising, he shook her awake. "Tashiana, I'm going to try and live with this, but I can't make any promises. But at least I'm willing to try. If you can prove to me that you're capable of being faithful, and that you love me, who knows, in time I may be able to get over this. I never thought in a million years that losing you, or you sleeping with another man, again, would affect me the way it has," Dominique confessed.

"If it's any comfort to you, you haven't lost me to anyone," Tashiana said. She wanted to throw herself into his arms but knew then wasn't the time, because the pain of her infidelity could still be seen in his face.

"So, what happens when good 'ole Ahmaad decides he doesn't want to give you up this easily, and keeps showing up when I'm not around? I know what'll happen if I see the bastard even looking in your direction. Damn, I feel so stupid, and inadequate. Not to mention my ego has been shot to hell. You want to know the worst part about the whole thing? You're still the only woman in this whole damn world that I want. It won't be easy, but I'll get through this some how," Dominique said.

"Why is still wanting me the worst thing about the whole deal?" Tashiana asked, feeling he didn't really want her.

"I didn't mean it the way it sounded. What I meant is, the average man would be asking you for a divorce. And here I am can't stand the thought of living without you. It makes me feel I don't have any balls."

"Well, if you ask me, it takes more balls to forgive the person you love than it does to divorce them, and kick them out on the streets," Tashiana theorized.

"Really? How would you know?" Dominique quipped.

"I don't really, but I imagine it does," she said.

"At least the kids won't have to deal with living in a broken home," Dominique said.

"Are the kids the only reason you're willing to give our marriage another try?" Tashiana asked.

"It's not the only reason, but they play a part in my decision. Are you saying you didn't take into consideration how a divorce would affect the kids?" he asked.

"Of course I did. I just want to be sure you're not staying strictly for the sake of the children."

"What if I did say that was the only reason I was staying. Would you divorce me?" he asked becoming angry.

"I'm not trying to start an argument Dominique. I love you and want you to love me in return, not just for the sake of the children," Tashiana answered.

"I meant what I said. I'm willing to give our marriage another chance because I still love you. However, don't expect me to forget what you did right away. You have to give me time to deal with this shit on my own terms. So that I don't bring it up every time we get in an argument, I need time to deal with it," Dominique said.

"I know that. As long as you're willing to give us a try, I'll do my part to help you through it. I promise," Tashiana assured him.

Dominique let it go at that, because he was serious about making things work out between them if he could. He knew there would be a barrier between them, for a long time to come.

It was several days before he made love to Tashiana, and it wasn't the same. Some of the old magic was gone. He wondered if it would ever be the same. His ego laid in wait just waiting for Tashiana to do, or say, something out of the ordinary, so it could take over the controls of his emotions. Once was shame on her. Twice was shame on him. And he had too much pride to let himself be reduced to a blubbering idiot again.

Tashiana thanked almighty God for a second chance to prove her love for her husband, and to dedicate herself to her family. She was truly thankful, but Ahmaad had more control over her than even she realized. The love between her and Dominique was about to be tested beyond the affair. To her dismay, she came to the realization that she loved Ahmaad after all. Not enough to leave her family, but enough to take one final chance on meeting him for a proper good-bye. The way they had split wasn't how their relationship should've ended. At least, Ahmaad convinced her it wasn't. That Monday, following Tashiana's confession, Dominique went to Ahmaad office to warn him to stay away from Tashiana, because he knew about the affair and didn't want to have to hurt him. When he entered the office Ahmaad stood up to greet him.

"Good morning, Mr. Goodman. What can I do for you this bright sunny morning?" he asked extending his hand.

Dominique ignored his hand. "Cut the crap, Ahmaad. This is not a social call. Tashiana told me about your little escapades. I'm here to warn you. If I catch you two together, or even in the same room, someone is going to get hurt. And it won't be me," he warned.

"I don't know what you're talking about," Ahmaad said defensively. The panic in his eyes betrayed his calm demeanor.

"Look, Ahmaad, I didn't come here for any bullshit. If you don't believe she spilled her guts, we can call her right now at her office and ask her. I'm sure you know her number," Dominique said, picking up the phone and handing it to him.

"Okay, okay. We did have something going until a couple of days ago. She told me to screw off, because she still loves you and her kids. And she didn't want to lose that. You can kick my ass, or whatever, but I do care for her. However, she's made her choice, and I intend to honor her decision. You're the luckiest man in the world to have a wife like Tashiana. I don't blame you for holding on to her. I know it won't do any good to apologize for what happened, but I assure you what we had is over," Ahmaad said calling himself reassuring Dominique.

"For both of our sakes, I hope you mean what you said." Dominique said and turned to leave.

Ahmaad stopped him in his tracks saying, "Remember one thing, Mr. Goodman. If you ever decide you can no longer live with her, I'll be waiting in the wing."

"What about your wife and son? Are you going to throw them

out on the streets?" Dominique reminded him that he had a family of his own.

"I have everything planned, Mr. Goodman. You just remember what I said," Ahmaad said in a cocky tone.

Dominique couldn't remember the last time he had been in a fight. Before he realized what he was doing, he had turned back around and grabbed Ahmaad by the collar and pulled him half way across his desk. "Let me tell you one more time, asshole, how serious I am. If I see you and Tashiana together, your ass is mine. Get my drift?" he asked, pushing him down into his chair. Ahmaad nodded.

After leaving Ahmaad's office Dominique went to work. As soon as he walked into the lab Greg Farley said, "Damn Dominique, you look terrible buddy. What's wrong?"

"Remember when we went to that Chinese place several months back and Ahmaad and Mrs. Greenway were there? You told me your wife had an affair with him. How long did it take for you to trust her again?" Dominique asked.

"Why?" Farley asked in return.

"As much as I hate to admit this, I found out Tashiana has been having an affair with the son-of-a-bitch also. I'm so pissed I don't know what to do," Dominique confessed.

"To be honest Dominique, I still don't trust Vera. I don't get pissed as often when I think about what she did, but I don't know if I'll ever fully trust her again. Man, I thought Tashiana would be the last woman in this world to fall for an asshole like Ahmaad. So what're you going to do?" Farley asked.

"I don't know. If I divorce her, the kids will suffer. If I don't, I'll suffer because I don't know if I can ever forgive her. How do you cope with Vera on a daily basis?" Dominique asked omitting he had already told Tashiana he was going to stay in the marriage.

"Just like a junkie on crack, I deal with it one day at a time," Farley laughed.

"I'll give it some time before making a final decision. Man this shit hurts," Dominique sigh.

"I know what you mean, but that old saying about time healing all is somewhat true. You learn to cope with the hurt," Farley said happy someone else knew his pain.

"Time has its' work cut out for it if it can heal my pain," Dominique said.

He sat down at his desk and called Tashiana. He wanted to let her know he had been over to see Ahmaad, and that they had a very unfriendly conversation. She wasn't in. He was told she had called in sick.

She can't be with that asshole Ahmaad, he said, thinking maybe Ahmaad was only one of a number of guys she had strung out around the city. And she was in the process of getting rid of those too. He called home and was relieved when she answered the phone.

"Hello, this is the Goodman's residence," she answered sounding depressed.

"Hi, Tashiana, it me. I called to let you know I paid a visit to your ex-boyfriend's office. We had a nice unfriendly chat, and I think we came to an understanding that he is to leave you alone," Dominique informed her.

"You didn't have to do that, you know. I told you it was over," she said.

"Yes I did. You're not angry because I paid that bastard a visit are you?" Dominique asked.

"Of course not. I just don't want you to suffer anymore than you have already, that's all." What she thought was that he had gone over to Ahmaad office and beat the hell out him.

"I figured it was better that I go ahead and talk to him while I'm still numb from the blow. You don't have to worry, I didn't best the shit out of him or anything like that, although it was the first thing that crossed my mind. As far as I'm concerned, he's not worth me getting in trouble over," Dominique relieved her anxiety.

"What did he have to say?" Tashiana asked trying to sound disinterested. But she was curious, because he had always bragged about what he was going to say to Dominique once he found out about them.

"Nothing much, just that you made your choice of who you wanted to be with and he's willing to live with it. Why? Were you expecting him to put up a fight, or something? Or maybe, you thought he was going to tell me something you forgot to tell me, "Dominique said.

"Dominique, please don't go there. I feel bad enough as it is. Please," she asked.

"Sorry. Why didn't you tell me you weren't going to work this morning? I called your office, and they said you called in sick. Are you okay?" he asked.

"I just didn't feel like going to work this morning, that's all," she said.

"Okay, I'll see you when I get home this evening," Dominique said, not caring that she was probably in pain because of the humiliation she had to endure because of the affair.

"Okay darling. I'll see you then," she said and hung up.

What she didn't have the heart to tell him was, if she went to work, Ahmaad was going to call her, and she didn't know if she would be able to resist seeing him. She cared Ahmaad, a great deal more than she cared to admit. As soon as Dominique hung up, she instinctively started to call Ahmaad at his office.

What the hell is wrong with me? she asked herself.

That small, annoying, subconscious little voice from long ago returned to harass her. "Don't play stupid Tashi. You know exactly why you started to call your lover boy. You're still hung up on Ahmaad and don't want Dominique to know it. You don't want Dominique to know that you want both of them. Dominique is solid as a rock, but Ahmaad makes you feel like you're the only woman alive because he caters to your every desire," the voice teased.

"I won't listen to you. I ignored you once, and I can do it again, "Tashiana admonished the voice.

"Yes, you did Tashi, but look where it got you. You were almost the star of divorce court. Dominique is going to watch everything you do, and everywhere you go, from now on. You may be able to ignore me, but will you be able to ignore Dominique, if he ever walks in on you and Ahmaad doing the nasty? You know he's going to follow you when you go out from now on. What'll you say that you're sorry again? Are you really stupid enough to believe he will forgive you, again? Come on Tashi, wise up. Dominique is the better man," her subconscious voice said seriously.

Tashiana covered her ears, and ran into the bedroom, and cried because she knew what the voice said was true. Still, it took all the will power she could muster to keep from calling Ahmaad.

God, please help me, she cried. Again, God had nothing to do with what she ended up doing.

CHAPTER #8

Dominique sat in his den cleaning his guns. He wasn't a big gun advocate. He bought the 357 Magnum pistol, and 12-gauge shotgun to protect his home from possible intruders. Tashiana had been afraid it was too dangerous to have guns in the house because of the children. Any parent will tell you, you can't hide anything from a child she always said. He knew that to, that was why he purchased a gun case with a lock. And he kept it out of reach of the children by placing it them on the top shelf of his bedroom closet. It wasn't the kids Tashiana should have been afraid for.

While putting a thin coat of oil on the moving parts of the shotgun he wondered if it was the appropriate weapon for the job he had planned. It would definitely cause more damage to the body, but it would be messy. Then there was the possibility that someone might accidentally see the bulge underneath his coat if he happened to pass someone on his way to the designated crime site. On the other hand, the 357 Magnum pistol would be easier to conceal, and would allow him to walk among the people without the pistol being detected. There were no doubt regardless of which weapon he chose, either one would serve his purpose.

He laid the shotgun down and picked up the pistol. He loved the feel of it. He had watched dozens of western movies and heard the cowboys say the gun had just the right weight and balance when they found the one they wanted. He had never paid attention to those words until now. The gun felt like an extension of his arm when he aimed it at imaginary targets above the fireplace. Each moving part had been carefully oiled, and he had applied a thin coat to the exterior to make it shiny. The cold blue steel matched the hatred he felt in his heart toward Tashiana's lover. He placed the pistol in his waistband and left the den. It was time to end the life of that would be home wrecker.

Dominique followed Ahmaad several times when he got off from work to see if he was screwing around with anyone else beside Tashiana. He had picked the right day, Tuesday, to follow him, because Ahmaad met Mrs. Greenway's daughter, Lisa, at a sleazy little motel on Austin Highway. As it turned out, Tuesday was their designated meeting day. He estimated the girl's age to be about 16. After each encounter with Lisa Ahmaad went to a little hole in the wall for a drink before going home. Before separating during their last encounter Lisa had told Ahmaad she wouldn't be able to meet him until 9 p.m. next Tuesday. He had laughed and said since she was the only woman in his life he would be willing to wait forever, as long as she showed up. Dominique was happy to hear this because the darkness would provide the cover he needed when the time came to take Ahmaad out. *I'm going to enjoy taking you out when the time comes, Dominique* said during that last surveillance job he pulled on Ahmaad before it was time to complete his mission.

Dominique parked a block away from the motel. He had given himself plenty of time to pick the spot he would grab Ahmaad after Lisa departed. She always left first, and he would linger around to ensure no one would make the connection that they were together. Ahmaad showed up at 8:45, he had paid for the room on his way home after work earlier that evening. With a big smile on his face he went inside to wait for Lisa. True to her word, Lisa rolled into the parking lot as close to nine as you can get. Having called and told Lisa what room he was in, she knocked on the door and fail into his arms as soon as he opened the door. Dominique sat in the shadows and waited for them to complete their business.

While he was waiting for Ahmaad and Lisa to finish satisfying their lust, he wondered how many times Ahmaad had gotten a room ready for Tashiana and himself. Janet told him of one conversation Tashiana and Ahmaad had in her presence.

"How much longer do you think you're going to be able to cheat on Dominique before he finds out about us?" Ahmaad asked.

"Don't worry about it. I have everything under control. He's a wimp. I can do anything I want to. He's so in love with me, he wouldn't do anything to hurt his darling sweet wife. The mother of his children," she laughed.

"Yeah. That's what you say. Men get crazy when another man is messing with their stuff," Ahmaad said.

"What? Are you afraid Dominique's going to whip your ass if he find out we're sleeping together?" she asked.

"I haven't had my ass whipped since I left home. I want to know how you feel about Dominique, because if he finds out about us I may have to take him out. Know what I mean?" Ahmaad asked.

"Right. I know exactly what you mean. You talk a lot of crap when Dominique ain't around," Tashiana said, using the one word that irritated the hell out of him.

"There you go with that ain't shit again. I'm serious. Just say the word and I'll go to you house and tell him you love me, and wants a divorce," he boasted.

"After I divorce Dominique and marry you, are you going to

let me go out alone? Or give me the freedom to hang with my girlfriends?" Tashiana asked seriously.

"Hell no. You'll have to quit your job and stay home with the kids. I'll want to know where you are at all times. Hell, you're cheating on Dominique why shouldn't I believe you wouldn't cheat on me?" Ahmaad asked.

"See what I mean. Why in the hell would I want someone as controlling as you, when I have my own loving little wimp at home who let me do whatever I want. And he doesn't get pissed when I say ain't," she teased.

"Keep messing with me and I'll tell him anyway, and whatever happens will be on your head," he threatened.

"Yeah, right. You don't have the balls to do that. Anyway, if you tell him I would deny it. I would then stand by and watch while he whipped your butt," Tashiana laughed, knowing this always made him angry.

"In time Tashiana. In time, I'm going make you eat those words, and I'm going to mess Dominique up. You just wait and see. I'm this close to doing it already," Ahmaad said, leaving a small gap between his thumb and index fingers.

Thinking about what Ahmaad boasted about what he would to him when he found out about their affair infuriated Dominique. He was tempted to go and kick in the motel room door and do both him and Lisa, but she wouldn't feel the burnt of his rage this night. He hoped Ahmaad had himself a ball because Lisa was the last piece of flesh he would ever taste in this lifetime. He was still deep in thought when he heard the door to their room open.

"Ahmaad, you make me feel like a real woman," Lisa said hugging him.

"You are a woman. Don't let anyone tell you you're not," he

said, grabbing her behind and kissing her.

"When are you going to divorce Laquan and marry me?" she asked pouting.

"You know we have to wait until you finish high school. You don't want me going to jail do you?" he asked.

"No, because I love you and wouldn't know what to do without you," she answered. She turned and left Ahmaad standing in the doorway.

Ahmaad went back into the room to wait for Lisa to get some distance between them before making his departure. With rage flowing through his veins Dominique knocked on the door and told Ahmaad he was the motel manager and needed to talk to him.

"What do you want?" Ahmaad asked, opening the door. He eyes widened when he saw who it was and tried to close the door, but he was too slow.

"You think you can just walk into a woman life and destroy her family whenever you get ready, huh?" Dominique asked sticking the guns between Ahmaad's eyes, while pushing him back into the room. "Have a seat lover boy. I want to ask you a few questions before you meet your maker," Dominique said, forcing Ahmaad to sit on the bed.

"What the hell is wrong with you man? I thought you said as long as I didn't mess with Tashiana again everything was cool?" Ahmaad said.

"That's what I said, before Tashiana told me how you always boasted about how you would f-me up if I found out about your affair and started something. Well guess what a-hole, I'm starting something. Lets see what you're going to do about it," Dominique challenged him.

"Not as long as you have that gun in your hand. You think I'm crazy?" he asked.

Yep, sure do. The day you started screwing my wife told the world that you're crazy. You see Ahmaad not every man who allows his wife the freedom to go to clubs alone isn't turning her out for predators like you to take advantage of. And now you're into, 'what?' 16-17 year olds? I figured it's time to rid the world of a piece scum like you," Dominique said.

"Wait man. Wait man. I tried to get Tashiana to end the affair a year ago, but she kept saying you were going to kick her out on the streets and needed me to help her out when you did. I respect you man. You have one of the most beautiful, and respected families in San Antonio," Ahmaad talked fast. Dominique lowered the gun while he talked.

"I'll be damned. You screw my wife, get her to spend my money on you, and then have the balls to say you respect me. If that's what you call respect, then I respect you so much I'm going to blow your damn head off," Dominique said, again raising the gun.

"Wait, wait, man. I have a wife and a kid. What's going to happen to them?" Ahmaad asked fishing for sympathy.

"Haven't you noticed Ahmaad? Laquan doesn't love you anymore. Not since she found out that you were cheating on her. By the way, she has known for six months now. I got her to agree not to say anything to you until Tashiana confessed to me about you guys. You know, Laquan has a lot to offer some lucky man. With you out of way she can meet someone who'll love her and treat her right," Dominique said.

"What the hell do you know about my wife?" Ahmaad asked angrily.

"Don't be mad Ahmaad. She needed someone who respected

her. I gave her a shoulder to cry on. Actually, I gave her more than that. Did she ever tell you why she bought that $250.00 dress? I took her to the All Gentleman's Club in Austin. You know about that club, right? Anyway, she wanted to be assured that she is just as beautiful as any white woman in this world. And you what Ahmaad, she is, but you wouldn't know that anymore because you're in love with Tashiana. I told her Tashiana had confessed her affair and we couldn't continue seeing each other. It broke her heart, but she'll get over it when she finds the right man. Just like she's going to get over you once she have planted you and moved on with her life," Dominique said, putting the barrel of the gum into a chair cushion to muzzle the sound.

In one last defying moment Ahmaad said, "You're sick man. You come in here talking this bullshit about how I'm breaking up your family, and all the time you've been sleeping with my wife. I say we're even. Lets forget the shit ever happened and get back to our lives. What do you say?" Ahmaad begged.

"I would never have known Laquan if it weren't for you forcing her into my life. Nope, we're not even. But, we are now," Dominique said pulling the trigger.

Ahmaad eyes stared in disbelief as the bullet smashed into his face, right between his eyes. Dominique watched Ahmaad body fall back onto the bed in slow motion. Although he knew Ahmaad was dead Dominique had to make sure. He walked up to the bed and put another bullet into his brain.

Dominique looked out the door, and seeing no one in the area he said, "Whoever's wife you choose to mess with in the next life, let me suggest you make sure he ain't sick." Dominique locked the door, closed it and slipped away into the night.

Tashiana went back to work, on Tuesday. Ahmaad didn't call her, until that Friday afternoon. Her secretary told her she had a phone call.

"Hello, Mrs. Goodman speaking." Tashiana answered not knowing it was Ahmaad calling her. She thought he was remaining true to his word about not trying to see her again.

"Hey Tashiana, this Ahmaad. Please don't hang up. I need to talk to you," he said quickly.

"I don't think it's a good idea for you to be calling me, Ahmaad. If I'm going to get over you, it has to be cold turkey. So, if you don't mind, I'm going to hang up now," Tashiana said her heart pounding in her chest.

"No, wait. I called to say good-bye," he lied to keep her from hanging up. He then continued. "And to let you know I still love you more than anything in this world. I'm willing to take the chance of being caught and killed, rather than let you walk out of my life without trying to keep you. You know I love you. Don't you?" Ahmaad asked, encouraged because she hadn't hung up on him.

"It doesn't matter whether you love me or not. I promised Dominique I wouldn't see you again, and I intend to keep that promise. So, say your good-bye and leave me alone," she said not convincing at all.

"I want to see you one last time. When we said good-bye at the motel it was under stressing circumstances. I want to say good-bye the way it should've been said." Ahmaad enticed her to agree.

"I'll have to think about it," Tashiana said, fighting the urge to agree with him.

"Please Tashiana. I'll never bother you again if you don't want me to. Just one proper good-bye is all I'm asking, okay? What harm could it do," he begged.

"I'll have to think about it," she repeated. "If I want to meet you again, for a final good-bye, I'll call you there at your office before I leave for home today," Tashiana said weakening.

"Okay darling. I'll be waiting patiently for your call," Ahmaad said and hung up.

After hanging up Tashiana admonished herself for being so weak. *You, Tashiana, are one stupid bitch. You're going to end up in divorce court if you don't let that bastard go.* She then turned right around and tried to convince herself otherwise, *but what harm can it do if I see him one more time, just to say good-bye?*

Subconsciously, Tashiana had already agreed with Ahmaad as he made his proposal, because she felt the affair was not giving the proper ending. It should not have been because of a note left on a motel room door. It needed to be ended, but not that way.

Meanwhile, Laquan called Dominique at his office. She had an intuition that something wasn't right because Ahmaad had been acting so strange the whole week.

"Dominique, why have you avoided me this week? I want to see you."

"I guess Ahmaad didn't tell you, huh?"

"Didn't tell me what?" Laquan asked.

"Tashiana confessed that she and Ahmaad were having an affair. I stopped by his office Monday morning and told him if I ever caught them together someone was going to get hurt. So that throws a wrench into the whole works. I don't know how I can continue seeing you, if me and Tashiana are trying to work things out," Dominique said, hoping she would see things his way.

Laquan had a different take on how things should be, and was not about to be persuaded that easily. "I don't see why that has to change anything, as far as we're concerned. They were seeing each other a long time before we got together. Hell, let them sit at home and worry about what we're doing for a change," Laquan said angrily.

It sounded tempting, but Dominique's mind was made up. "I don't know how I can possibly continue with this affair, if I want to get my life back in order."

"Oh, I see. Did you tell Tashiana about us?" Laquan asked, knowing he hadn't.

"Don't be stupid about this, Laquan. You know damn well I haven't told her anything about us." Dominique detected a " what if" in the way she had asked the question.

"Why not, you want to start your new life with Tashiana based on honesty, don't you?" It was more of a statement than a question.

"It's different with us, and you know it. We haven't been messing around long enough to become that attached. I don't see any reason to tell her anything about us. What she doesn't know won't hurt her," Dominique reasoned.

"It not them I'm concerned about and you know it. I've become very attached to you. I can even go so far as to say I love you. I don't know if I'm going to be able to let you go this easy. Maybe if we went some place nice and cozy, we could figure out a way to break this relationship off a more smoothly. Then, I won't feel I've been used, and is now being dump like last week's garbage," Laquan said sounding hurt.

He owed her at least that much he thought. "You're right, Laquan. I wouldn't like it if you called me and said, hey, this is it. I don't want to see you anymore. I'll meet you tomorrow evening at the Cove."

"Yes," she agreed eagerly.

"About 8 p.m.?" Dominique asked.

"I'll see you there lover," Laquan said happier than she had been all week.

It was Dominique turn to admonish himself. *Don't be a fool man. This is your chance for a new start with your wife, even if it is under duress right now. Don't blow it trying to make an ex-lover happy. Especially, since you're not in love with her.*

Meeting Laquan that final night was the only time he had ever been nervous about meeting her during the whole affair. Before he figured he had nothing to lose by being caught with her. Now, he stood a chance of losing the one thing he cherished more than anything else in his life, an intact family. He felt as long as Tashiana kept herself together, he would be able to deal with the heartache. *Damn life's a bitch, because you get smacked around every day of your life until you die,* Dominique sighed.

The same evening he was to meet Laquan, Shantel brought up her mother's affair for the first time since they had been told what was going on with their parents. She entered the den tentatively and asked, "Dad, can I talk to you a minute?" She wasn't sure if she should be asking him questions about it.

"Sure honey. What's on your mind?" Dominique smiled at his inquisitive daughter.

"I was wondering if you're going to be able to forgive mom for what she's done. And I wanted to know if you still love her," Shantel said.

I'm not going to lie to you, baby girl. My first reaction was to divorce your mom. But after thinking things over, I realized I still love her and want us to remain a family. As far as being able to live with the knowledge that your mom had an affair, is going to take a while to get over. Hopefully, with yours, and your sister's, and brother's help, it won't be too difficult. Right now, I don't trust your mom any further than I can see her. How do you guys feel about this whole situation?" he smiled, trying to make Shantel feel at ease.

"I personally think the whole situation stinks. Me, and Sheena, figured you'd accept what Mom did for our sakes. Did you know Mom was having an affair? Me and Sheena did," Shantel looked at him strangely.

"I figured something was going on, but hoped she would get over it and stop running around," Dominique admitted.

"Well, why didn't you say something to her? Or follow her to find out what was going on. If it was my husband, and I thought something was going on, I would've followed him and put an end to it," Shantel said, making Dominique feel guilty for not putting an end to the affair.

"I don't know what to say. You're one hundred percent right. If you love someone, you should do whatever it takes to keep the relationship sacred, even if it means spying into his or her private affairs. We do have a life outside of our marriage you know. Since I didn't follow her, I guess I'll have to learn to deal with it. Besides, why should you have to follow the person you love around town to see what they're doing, while at the same time you're telling them you have trust in your relationship," Dominique replied, giving Shantel something to think about.

"You want to know something, Dad? When I do get married, I hope the man is like you," Shantel said and hugged him.

"I just hope you find the right one, the first time around," Dominique said seriously.

After the embrace ended, she again looked at him sternly and asked, "Dad, are you having an affair too?"

"No, why do you asked?" Dominique said acting surprise she would ask him such a thing.

"You've been running around just as much as mom lately, and we know what she was doing. So we, Sheena, and me were wondering if you were doing the same thing to get back at her. And that's why you're not going to divorce her," Shantel said embarrassed.

"No baby girl. I would never do anything like that knowing how much it would hurt you all," Dominique lied, thinking of the upcoming rendezvous with Laquan.

"Good. I love you Daddy," Shantel kissed him and left the den.

After Shantel left the room Dominique sat back and massaged his temple. He had to convince Laquan their affair was over and done with. And it was best to end the affair without hurting anyone any further. He knew she probably wouldn't agree, but he had to give it his best shot.

Tashiana came into the den and asked if it was okay if she went over to Janet's house to pay her a visit. "Sure, I'll see you when you get home," Dominique had said without even looking up. Otherwise he would have notice the nervous look in Tashiana's eyes.

When Tashiana left the room he let out a deep sigh because he also had to deal with Janet in the near future as well. *Damn, I'll be glad when all this drama is over and done with*, he said to himself, getting mentally ready for the breakup with Laquan.

When Dominique walked into the Cove, Laquan was already there. She waved him over to her table. When he was seated she said, "I was beginning to think you weren't going to show. Now where have I heard that line before," she laughed, remembering him telling her the same thing on numerous occasions.

"I told you I would be here, but what I have to say you're not going to like," Dominique informed her not wanting her to think he could be persuaded to change his mind about them.

"Lets order a drink before you continue," Laquan interjected. "I hate to be dumped while my head's clear."

Dominique went to the bar and got the drinks himself. He wanted to get this confrontation over with as soon as possible. Once he was seated again he continued, "You know I care a great deal for you, Laquan. It's just that, we have a chance to start our marriages from a new beginning. Surely Ahmaad won't be running around anytime soon, knowing you know what he has been doing in the past. What do you say?" Dominique asked.

"To be honest with you Dominique, I no longer love Ahmaad. I love you. Besides, we both know Tashiana isn't the only woman Ahmaad has been sleeping with. I know you don't want to hear me say I love you, but it's the truth. I don't know if I can pretend nothing happened between us the next time we run across each other. Last night, all I could think about was what I would do if I lost you. I even thought about telling Ahmaad and Tashiana about us, hoping you would understand I only did it because I love you, and don't want to lose you.

Then I thought about sending Tashiana an anonymous letter, telling her you've been having an affair also. And that you knew about her and Ahmaad six months ago but chose to ignore it because you're in love with another woman. Now that you're actually dumping me, I don't know what to say, or do. Maybe after everything sets in, I'll be able to deal with it. Right now, I have to get out of here, before I embarrass myself," Laquan said, close to tears.

"I wish I could tell you I feel the same as you do, but it would be a lie. If there was any other way we could end this affair, without anyone getting hurt, I would. I'm sorry, for what I'm putting you through. There's just no other way," Dominique said, feeling sorry for her.

"If you don't see me again, I swear I'll tell Ahmaad everything. You know what he'll do, don't you?" she threatened.

Dominique knew what she meant. Ahmaad would go straight to Tashiana and tell her everything Laquan had told him. Regardless of the outcome, he was willing to take that chance. If Laquan actually followed through with it, It would only prove he knew less about women than he thought he did. He didn't think she was the type of woman who would put her business in the streets.

"Do whatever you think is right Laquan. As far as I'm concerned, this affair is history. I do care for you, but if you tell Ahmaad, or anyone else, anything about us, I'll never speak to you again as long as I live," Dominique hissed.

"I didn't really mean it Dominique. Don't be angry with me. I'm afraid I won't know what to do with my life if you're not a apart of it. I don't think I can ever be happy with Ahmaad again. You could see me every once in a while, couldn't you? Just to see how I'm doing. No strings attached," she promised.

"I'm sorry, Laquan, this is it. After tonight, I'm not going to see you anymore, other than when we meet in public. You do whatever you think is right for you. It won't stop me from caring about you, but either way, we won't be sharing any more dreams together," Dominique said remembering the no strings attached pact he and Jewel made back in the day.

Laquan wanted to say more, but the tears forced her to jump up and run from the club. Dominique didn't run after her for fear she would get the wrong impression as to why he would be comforting her. He thanked God that there was at least one woman he could figure out. He had a few more drinks before heading home. Halfway there, he decided it was too early to go home. So, he went to the club at Lackland to see what was so interesting about the place. It certainly held some kind of magic for Tashiana and Ahmaad.

While driving around looking for a parking spot after arriving at the club, he saw Tashiana and Ahmaad's cars in the parking lot. He started shaking as if he was having a seizure. *How in the hell can she do this shit to me?* he asked no one. Dominique almost hit several cars before he finally found a parking space.

Since Dominique wasn't a member of the club he had to purchase a membership card before he was allowed to enter. After purchasing the club card he walked around the club looking for them. He located them at a table in the back of the club. They were both teary eyed. Although they were sitting across from each other they may as well had been kissing

I guess you love the son-of- a-bitch after all, he said to himself, as he headed over to the table where they were sitting. Tashiana and Ahmaad were so engrossed in each other, neither one of them noticed Dominique until he reached their table. Ahmaad's back was to him. Seeing the panic in Tashiana's eyes, he turned to see what, or who had caused it. As soon as he saw it was Dominique he started to say something, but the words never made it out of his mouth.

Dominique felt teeth and bone give, as his fist smashed into Ahmaad's face. Blood gushed from his mouth as if he had suddenly turned on a faucet within himself. Dominique was on top of him before he hit the floor.

Tashiana was too stunned to move. She sat at the table, screaming with her hands over her face.

"I told you, you hard headed son-of-a-bitch, I was going to beat the shit out of you if I caught you with my wife," Dominique screamed, as he continued to beat Ahmaad's face to a bloody mess. Ahmaad's eyes and lips were already swelling, his nose twisted, and mis-shapen by the force of Dominique's blows.

The bouncers rushed over, and pulled Dominique off of Ahmaad's semi-conscious body, but not before he was satisfied with the job he had done on the no-good bastard.

Everything happened so fast, no one even thought about calling the base police until after he had been restrained. He didn't struggle with the bouncers. Instead, he turned to Tashiana and said, "When I get out of jail, I want you gone."

"Dominique, you don't understand. All we were doing was saying good-bye. That's all," Tashiana sobbed.

"Yeah, right," Dominique snarled. "Tell that to the kids, on your way out."

He was led to the manager's office to wait for the arrival of the base police. They also called the paramedics to attend to Ahmaad's battered face.

"I want to talk to my husband," Tashiana sobbed as she stumbled along behind them, as they escorted him to the office. She was told she had to wait until the base police arrived before she would be allowed to talk to him. Not once did she go to Ahmaad's aid. A quick glance in his direction was all the sympathy he got from her.

Dominique sat as if he was in a trance once he was in the manager's office. He was able to blocked out everything except the sound of Tashiana's uncontrollable sobbing outside the office door.

After the base police and paramedics arrived and had everything under control. Ahmaad was asked if he wanted to press charges against Dominique for assault. Already embarrassed beyond belief, he wanted nothing but to get out of the club as soon as possible.

"No, I just want to get the hell out of here," Ahmaad mumbled through broken teeth and swollen lips. He and Tashiana shared a stolen glance, but said nothing as he exited the club.

They explained to Dominique that although Ahmaad didn't want to press charges against him, they still had to make a report of the incident. He didn't care what they did to him. He answered their questions without showing any emotions. When they finished questioning him, he was told he could leave but he would be barred from the club for a year. Tashiana was waiting outside the office door when he walked out.

"Dominique, wait a minute?" Tashiana begged.

"For what? So you can tell me some more of your damn lies? Screw you, and Ahmaad, Mrs. Goodman," Dominique said, and ran from the building with Tashiana at on his heels.

"Dominique, please. I know how it must've looked, but you're wrong about the reason I'm here this time. Please talk to me," Tashiana continued to beg.

When Dominique reached his car he said, "I'll see you at home.

Dominique was so mad, he didn't know if talking to her that night would be the wise thing to do. Although he beat the shit out of Ahmaad, he blamed Tashiana for everything that happened. He wanted to beat her face in too, but knew that wasn't a wise thing to do. With all the family abuse laws on the books he'd only end up in jail, for real this time. He was a true believer that a man could do no more than a woman let him. He broke every traffic law in the books on his way home.

Catch me, and see if I give a shit, he said to invisible policemen.

It was 1:30 when he burst through the door, waking up the kids. He went straight to the liquor bar and drank a quarter of a bottle of the first thing he got his hands on.

All four kids came to the railing at the top of the stairs to see what all the commotion was about. Seeing their Dad's face as he headed for the den, they ran into Shantel's room.

After listening for a while and not hearing anything, Shantel ran into Sheena's room. "Do you think we should go down stairs and see what's wrong with dad?" Shantel asked her sister.

"Not me. He probably caught Mom screwing up again," Sheena theorized. "Besides, Mom will probably be home in a few minutes. Maybe we'll be able to hear what happened."

They waited at the top of the stairs for their mother's arrival. Sure enough, their Mom arrived a short time later, but went straight into the den where they couldn't hear a thing that was said.

Dominique had calmed down somewhat, but he still wanted to beat her within an inch of her life. He was sitting in the den with the lights out, staring into the darkness when she entered.

"Dominique, can I turn on the lights, we have to talk," Tashiana said tentatively.

"Go ahead. What do we have to talk about? Who you've decided to live with?" he growled.

"I know you won't believe me, but here goes anyway. Ahmaad called me at the office yesterday and said he wanted to say good-bye under normal circumstances, not the way it happened. What Happened? Last week after leaving a motel room, there was a note on the door. Someone told us to enjoy our last encounter together because we had been found out. We both panicked, and got the hell out of there. I told him before I left that I would never see him again. I was serious about not carrying on the relationship, but I didn't feel the way we said goodbye was under the right circumstances. So, I thought it would be okay this one last time. It's true I care for him, but it's you and the kids that I love, and want to share the rest of my life with. Plus I wanted to know if he found out who had left he note on the door. Please Dominique, believe me. That's all it was," Tashiana explained.

Dominique turned to her and said, "Maybe tomorrow I'll believe you my dear, not tonight. The only thing I believe right now is what I saw. So, we'll talk about this in the morning."

Knowing Dominique meant what he said, she went into the bedroom, threw herself across the bed and cried herself to sleep.

Hearing the door to her parents bedroom slam, Shantel tiptoed out to the railing to see if she could hear anything. She almost jumped out her skin when Sheena, along with Zelvina and Dominique Jr., came up behind her and tapped her on the shoulder.

"Don't ever do that again," Shantel whispered.

"Where's Dad?" Sheena asked.

"I think he's still in the den," Shantel answered.

"Mom sure has been screwing up a lot lately. What're we going to do?" Sheena asked.

"I don't know about you, but I'm going back to bed, and wait to see what happens in the morning." As usual, seeing the scared looks in the younger kids faces she said, "Come on, everyone can sleep in my room tonight."

"Good, cause I can't sleep in mines," Zelvina said.

Dominique sat in the den drinking the remainder of the night. The more he drank the sober he got. He thought about how his male friends would view him once they found out what had happened. Greg would understand if he decided to stay in the marriage, but the rest of them would call him a first class wimp, especially after what went down at the club.

Well, what the hell. I won't be the first, or only, wimp in the world to sacrifice himself for the good of his children. Who knows, maybe I can make her feel so guilty, she'll die an early death. At this morbid thought, he smiled to himself. *Then again, I may end up forgiving her and falling in love all over again. Either way, I keep the family intact, and hopefully, happy. After all, I'm not a damn angel myself, although she doesn't know it.*

Normally it took an act of God to get the kids out of bed on Sunday mornings. But after the happenings of the previous night, they were up at sunrise. They were sitting around the kitchen table eating cereal when their Dad entered the kitchen to make coffee. He looked terrible.

"Good morning Dad. Are you feeling alright?" Dominique Jr. asked.

"Yeah, I feel fine little guy. Why?" Dominique asked smiling.

"Because you look like you didn't sleep last night," Sheena answered for her little brother.

"I didn't, but it doesn't concern you nosy little rats," Dominique said and made a pot of coffee. He didn't say anything to them while he waited for the coffee to brew. After the coffee was ready he poured himself a cup and went back into the den.

Tashiana smelled the coffee, and came into the kitchen for a cup. She had slept, but very little. When she did manage to doze off, her dreams were filled with the incident at the club. She saw Dominique's look of utter disgust toward her, and Ahmaad's battered and bruised face.

"God, Mom, you look awful!" Shantel exclaimed, getting up from the table and going over to where she was busy pouring herself a cup of coffee.

"I know, but you don't have to rub it in," Tashiana moaned.

"Mom, what happened between you and Dad last night?" Shantel asked.

"I'll talk to you guys about that later. Where is your dad?" Tashiana asked looking around the kitchen.

"He came in the kitchen, made coffee, got himself a cup and went back into the den where he slept last night," Sheena said not wanting to be left out of conversation.

Tashiana hesitated before going into the den to face the man she had caused so much pain. She wondered if he could possibly love her after that bone headed move at the club. He had every right in the world to hate her for what she had done. When she walked into the room he looked up from his morning newspaper.

"I guess it's about that time huh?" he mumbled, and went back to reading the paper.

"What's going to happen to us, Dominique?" she asked. When she got no response from him she continued. "I know you feel I abused your trust in me after promising I would never talk to him gain, but for the first time since I met Ahmaad, last night was totally innocent. I felt I owed him, at least, a proper good-bye. You can understand that can't you?"

"I can't say that I can. Maybe if I have an affair, and fall in love with the bitch, I could. But as it stands right now, I haven't the slightest idea if I would have handled things as badly as you did. If you expect me to feel sorry for you, or Ahmaad, you're wasting your time. I should've killed the bastard. God, it felt good to beat the shit out of that cocky SOB. What's going to happen to our marriage? I don't know. I'll let you know in a couple of days. Maybe for the sake of the kids I'll be able to deal with this. Otherwise, we'll be going our separate ways. It's going to be hard dealing with the fact you actually fell in love with another man, while still professing your love for me. Every time I look at you, I'm going to wonder if you're comparing me with Ahmaad. Especially, since you went against your own word to never see him again after confessing to having the affair with him. He has to have some kind of hold on you, to make you go against your own word. What happens to us my dear is up to you. You have to decide who you want. I'll never share you with anyone, again. I thought I could at one time. I tried to convince myself that if I couldn't have all of you, I would be satisfied with what I could get, but I was wrong. It's all or nothing," Dominique finished.

"I told you, you're the only man I want in my life, from now on. I know I made a stupid mistake by seeing Ahmaad again, and I'm sorry. Are you going to hold this against me for the rest of my life?" Tashiana asked.

"To be honest with you, Tashiana, I probably will. But you know what they say, time heals all. Well, I get a chance to find out first hand, if that old saying is true. Yep, probably will, but I won't bring it up in your face every time we have an argument. Nor will I ever ask you to leave, in the future, because of what happened in the past. I'll leave it up to you whether you want to stay. Remember one thing though, don't expect too much from me for a while. Right now I feel I'll never be able to touch you again and feel good about it, because Ahmaad will always be in the back of my mind," Dominique said, so sadly it caused her heart to skip a beat.

"I'll be here when you change your mind. Matter of fact, I'm going to do whatever it takes to make everything up to you," Tashiana said, sitting on the arm of the chair.

He looked at her sternly and said, "I want you to know, Tashiana, I'll never shed another tear over this marriage."

Tashiana left the den to leave him with his thoughts. She felt blessed. At least they were not going to get divorced. It was going to be rough at first, but she knew in time, she could make him happy again. Her friends said she could charm the hide off of a rattlesnake. She went back into the kitchen with a smile on her face, and explained what had happened to the children. She agreed, when they all said it was a stupid thing to do.

Dominique knew he had to seek help in order to deal with Tashiana's infidelity this time because he couldn't shake the urge to kill her. So the next day he went to the one place he knew he would get sympathy, understanding, sound advice, and it was free of charge, the church.

Dominique circled the church several times before pulling into the church parking lot. He sat in the car contemplating for a long time whether talking to a Minster would help alleviate the pain and anger he felt toward Tashiana. He prayed to God to give him the strength to forgive her for her infidelity because he himself was not without sin, but it seemed his prayer was not answered. He couldn't dislodge the thought from his mind that killing his wife was the right thing to do if he was to save face with the world. He tried to justify his feeling by the thin line of reasoning that he had honored their marriage vows until she went astray a second time. The saying espoused by the church that the families who prays together, stays together came to mind. Dominique wondered if he was being punished because his family hadn't chosen a church to belong to, or because they didn't worship the Lord each Sunday.

Dominique belief was an individual could worship God without the guidance of a preacher, or belonging to a church. The bible says once you have accepted Jesus into your heart, you have been baptized, and you live as righteous as possible, God has a place in heaven reserve for you. And as far as sin goes, the bible tells us there is no man without sin. So Dominique had asked a local pastor how he could help save his soul when his own was not saved because he to sinned on a daily basis. Of course the pastor gave him a long drawn out answer, but Dominique was not swayed.

Dominique didn't really have a problem with the church, just with most of the preachers and their congregations who pretended that they were holier than thou, but could be found at the local clubs every Friday and Saturday night dirty dancing and getting drunk. Dominique never pretended, or tried to fool anyone that he was God's favorite child.

And he prayed for forgiveness every day of his life because he was a sinner. This day he decided that it wouldn't hurt if he asked for a few words of encouragement from a man of the cloth. He chose this particular church because several of his friends belonged to the church, and said Reverend Fredrick Gilroy was one of the best religious marriage counselors in the city.

Dominique got out of the car and walked up to the church, but hesitated at the door before entering. It had been a long time since he had last sat and listened to a messenger of God. He membered friends telling him he hadn't been to church in so long, the building would probably cave in the minute he stepped through the door. If his situation had not been so dire he probably would have laughed at the memory. When he entered the church Reverend Gilroy was standing by the door.

Reverend Gilroy happened to be looking out the door window when Dominique drove into the parking lot. He could tell Dominique hadn't been to church in a while by how long it took him to get out of the car, and his hesitation at the door before entering. Therefore, the minister knew whatever Dominique's problem was it had to be weighing heavily on his mind for him to seek relief from the church. The reverend had moved away from the door to allow Dominique to enter.

"May I help you young man?" the reverend asked.

"I don't know if anyone can help me, but I need to unload the burdens that is weighing on my mind," Dominique answered.

"Well, come to my office and tell me what's burdening you so," he said leading the way to his office. "Have a seat and let talk about it," the reverend said once they were in his office.

"I don't know where to start," Dominique hesitated.

"Start from the beginning," he said.

"Well, I've been married for fifteen years, have four beautiful children, and a pretty good job working for the government. I was feeling pretty good about my marriage and my life until a couple of weeks ago. That was when my darling sweet wife told me she was having an affair with one of the neighbors that live in the same housing area as we do. I met him on a professional basis one time, but it had nothing to do with my wife. Anyway, now I can't get this thought out of my head that the only way I'll ever be happy again is if I kill the both of them. I know it sounds crazy, but I can't get the thought out of my head," Dominique confessed.

"You're not crazy. That's the first reaction of the average man, or woman. It's hard for anyone to accept the fact their loved one has given themselves to some one else. The first thing you have to ask yourself is did you do everything within your power, as her husband, to make her happy. The second thing you have to ask yourself is do you still love her. If you do, then you have to ask yourself what will it take for you to forgive her. God tells us the hardest thing to forgive is the breaking of our wedding vows. What're the answers to the questions before you Dominique," the reverend asked.

"I thought I did everything expected of me as a husband. I spend time with her and the children at home. We go shopping, to the movies, and on picnics occasionally as a family. I get her something special every holiday that means anything to women, such as her birthday, Valentine's Day, our anniversary, and Christmas. And I give her the freedom to get away from the children and household chores every now and then. I do the household chores, cooking, cleaning, washing, etc., while she spend the time any way she chooses. Usually she spend that time window shopping all day with at the malls, or so I thought," Dominique said angrily.

"It sounds like you just described a made for television family. You mean you guys never fight about anything?" he asked suspiciously.

"Of course we fight. Most of the time it's about the amount of money she spends on the kids and the house. She buys the kids almost anything they ask for, whether they need it or not. The house is cluttered with so much stuff, like end tables, coffee tables, telephone tables, china cabinets, bookracks, decorations of all sort, etc. When I think it is impossible to put anything else in the living room or bedroom, she makes room for it somehow. And the other thing we fight about is my stinginess. I don't believe in wasting money on trivial stuff, like eating out all the time. Or her buying new purses every time she goes shopping. Simple thing like that,"

Dominique said.

"You know purses and shoes are very important to women, don't you?" he asked, but continued before Dominique could answer. "Why do you think she had the affair?" the reverend asked.

"She says it started when she thought I had cheated on her at a party a couple of years ago when she saw me and the so called town whore coming down the stairs together at a friend's party one night. She must've known I wouldn't do anything that stupid with her right down stairs. I believe it was just an excuse for her to justify her sleeping around," Dominique said.

"Did you give her any reason to think you may have slept with the woman?" the reverend asked.

"None that I can think of," Dominique answered.

"Okay. Do you still love your wife?" he asked.

"Yeah, I still love her but I don't know if I'll be able to forgive her this time," Dominique said without thinking.

"What do you mean this time?" the reverend asked.

"I didn't intend to open old wounds, but she had an affair while we lived in Alaska. I forgave her and we moved to San Antonio. So you see why I'm having the thoughts I'm having." Seeing the look on the reverend face Dominique added, "I know God forgive us every day for our sins, but I'm not God."

"Did you go out and have an affair when you found about hers?" he asked.

"I thought about it, but since we were moving here to San Antonio I figured no one knew about it so I lived with it," Dominique said.

"And now? Are you going to go out and have an affair now that she has betrayed you again?" he asked.

"That's why I'm here. I don't know what to do. The first thing that crossed my mind was to have an affair with her best friend Janet because she's always making passes at me when Tashiana isn't around. Then I get this overwhelming desire to hurt her and her ex-lover. I'm so damn confused. What do you suggest I do?" Dominique asked.

"Answer the last question. What'll it take for you to forgive her again?" Reverend Gilroy asked, sensing he intentionally avoiding the question.

"I don't know," was Dominique's simple answer.

"Did you tell her how you feel about her having another affair?"

"I told her I didn't know if I can forgive her this time. That she has to give me time to think whether our marriage is worth saving. She says she understands, but I think she's playing me for a fool. I've been a fool twice, I'm not going to be a fool again," Dominique said.

"What if she means it? What if she never cheated on you again? I assume that's the promise she made," the reverend said.

"Yeah. That's the promise she made, but how in hell am I suppose to believe her. She made the same promise before we left Alaska," Dominique informed him.

"Do you believe she's capable of changing?"

I guess anyone can change if they really want to. Do I believe she'll change, I don't know," Dominique said.

"The question is, are you willing to take the chance to see if she can change and be a one man woman? Are you willing to take that chance? What about the children? Have you considered what they'll have to go through if you decide to divorce their mother?" Reverend Gilroy asked.

"That was the main reason I forgave her the last time. I

didn't want my kids going through the roller coaster ride divorce causes. I know they're faced with the same possibility, but the circumstances are different this time," Dominique said.

"As far as the kids are concerned, the situation is the same. You're going to put them on that roller coaster ride through hell that divorces cause if you divorce their mother. Do you really want to put them through that?" Reverend Gilroy asked with a smile on his face. He felt he had something to work with now that he knew the welfare of his children was the upper most thought in Dominique's mind.

"No, I don't. But, I may not have a choice this time. You can whip a dog only so many times before he bites you in retaliation for your cruelty. I have some more soul searching to do. I figure with God's guidance, I'll make the right decision," Dominique sighed.

"You have already made one right choice. And that is to trust in the Lord to guide you during this difficult time in your life. Just believe He will lead you down the right path and He will. Do you want me to say a prayer for you and your wife, that your marriage may be saved if God think it is the right thing to do," the reverend asked.

"It can't hurt," Dominique agreed. After the prayer Dominique left the church with a renewed sense of what he wanted to do. And he made a promise to God that he would find a church home in which to worship Him.

When Ahmaad arrived home the night of the fight, and Laquan asked him what had happened, he lied and said three guys had jumped him when he left one of the local clubs on the eastside of town, and his face was the outcome of the encounter.

Laquan was told a couple of days later what really happened, by Mrs. Greenway. They happened across each other at the local grocery store. Mrs. Greenway was so pissed at Ahmaad for cheating on the both of them she couldn't wait to fill Laquan in on what had happened to Ahmaad.

"Why hello, Laquan. How are you holding up?" she asked.

"Hi, Mrs. Greenway. What are you talking about, how am I holding up. Did something happen that I don't know about?" Laquan asked.

"I'm talking about Ahmaad getting beat down by Dominique over at the club the other night. I hear he caught Ahmaad and his wife, Tashiana I believe her name is, together and he beat the hell out of him. What did Ahmaad tell you happened to him?" Mrs. Greenway asked, enjoying the wide-eyed expression on Laquan's face.

"He told me he got jumped by several dudes when he left some nightclub," Laquan answered.

"If I were you girl, I'd find out the truth. If he was sleeping with Dominique's wife ain't no telling who else he's sleeping with. I don't mean to pry into your personal life Laquan, but Ahmaad isn't being honest with you," Mrs. Greenway said, and continued her shopping.

That evening when Ahmaad came home Laquan asked him, "Didn't you tell me you got jumped by several guy after leaving some club?"

"Yeah. Why?" he asked.

"The talk in the streets gives a different account of what happened," Laquan informed him.

"Oh really? And what are the people in the streets saying happened?" Ahmaad tried to sound uninterested in the gossip going around about him.

"That you got caught with another man's wife over at Lackland and he beat the hell out you. It makes more sense than someone you don't know jumping you out of the blue for no reason. You never told me why they jumped you, or whether they tried to rob you, or what. I think you lied to me. You want to tell me what really happened," Laquan asked hands on hips.

"I told you what happened?" he insisted.

"So, you didn't get caught with Tashiana at the club?" she asked.

"Tashiana who?" Ahmaad pretended ignorance.

Laquan picked up the telephone and said, "Okay. I guess you won't mind me calling Mr. Goodman and asking him if he was the one who kicked your butt."

"Damn, alright. She was stalking me, okay. I've been trying to get her to leave me alone for over a year now. The only reason I was there is because she threatened to tell you about us. I swear that is the truth," Ahmaad said.

"You're a sorry, lying ass bastard, Ahmaad. I figured some man had whipped your ass about his wife, but I didn't know it was Dominique. You see Ahmaad, I've known about your affair with Tashiana for sometime now. So, you can save your little charade and lets talk about what we want to do as far as this sham of a marriage is concerned," she said, her anger getting the better of her.

"What the hell do you mean, you knew about me having an affair with Tashiana?" he asked unbelieving.

"Yeah. I've known about six months now. I never said anything to you because I've been seeing someone also. A man who cares for me, but isn't willing to make any commitments," she confessed.

"Who is the bastard? I'll kill his ass," Ahmaad said seriously, because of the pain of knowing while he was sleeping with other men wives, some man was sleeping with his.

"It doesn't matter. We're not going to see each other anymore. He suggested I tell you the truth and we try to work our marriage out. You want to know something Ahmaad? I don't even know if I love you any longer. Not just because of Tashiana, but also because of all the other women I've heard about you sleeping with, including with Mrs. Greenway and her daughter Lisa. I deceived myself into thinking everyone who ever told me anything about your cheating were liars, and you were telling the truth. Now I feel like a total fool. I don't know if I can continue living with the neighborhood dog," she said the tears starting to fall.

"You feel like fool. How the hell I suppose to feel? You just finished telling me, you not only don't love me anymore, but you've been sleeping with another man. Is it Dominique? Its Dominique, isn't it?" he demanded to know.

"No, it wasn't Dominique, although it should've been, because that would've been the perfect revenge. Me sleeping with the husband of the woman you were having an affair with. When I told him I suspected you two were having an affair, he said he would find out if it was true, and he did. I tried to get him to have an affair with me so as to punish you and Tashiana for you were doing. He said two wrong doesn't make a right," Laquan laughed.

"Okay, if it wasn't Dominique. Who was it?" Ahmaad persisted.

"Like I said, Ahmaad, you should be worried about this marriage. What do you want to do?" she asked.

"I'm sorry for what I did. I'm willing to give it another try if you are," he said.

"Okay, so am I. I hope you don't think this is going to be easy",
Laquan said sadly.

"I know," Ahmaad concurred.

Ahmaad had hurt her deeply. She would never forgive him for
it. She stayed in the marriage strictly for the sake of her child, and
to make Ahmaad regret the day he brought the pain, lies and deceit
into their lives.

Laquan had known from the beginning of their affair that
Dominique was too much in love with his family to let anyone
break it up, even Tashiana. She took comfort in knowing that
she helped him over the rough part of his life when he found out
about the affair. She could sense the love he felt in his heart for
Tashiana, even while he was cussing her name and she was lying in
his arms.

Ahmaad was so devastated over losing Tashiana it left him
impotent for several weeks. Laquan never knew because it was
a couple of months before she let him touch her again. He
discovered his impotent when he attempted one last rendezvous
with Lisa, before honoring the promise he had made to Laquan.
Lisa was laid out before him in all her glory and he felt nothing.
It didn't matter what she did to arouse him nothing worked.
Embarrassed, Ahmaad left the motel room vowing to never have
another affair. From that day forward he honestly tried working
things out between himself and Laquan.

Laquan on the other hand, had been pushed to the brink of
no return. She quickly became the talk of the town. Whenever
Ahmaad and Laquan got into an argument about her running
around, Laquan would threaten to take their son and leave, saying
if she left he would never see Ahmaad Jr. again. Ahmaad held

onto the hope that eventually she would forgive him for the affairs, he forgave hers, and they would get back to being the family they were before this whole sordid affair happened.

Dominique went out of his way on several occasions just to say hello to Laquan, and to insure she was okay. After several months of friendly conversation, they actually became pretty close friends, but they never shared another bed.

Several days after the fight at the club, Janet came over to the house to comfort Tashiana, and see how Dominique was doing. While Tashiana was upstairs she asked if he was ever going to see her again.

"Janet, you know the answer to that question as well as I do. I'm one of the unhappiest men in the world right now, but I don't think trying to find comfort in the arms of another woman is the answer. As much as I liked being with you, the affair is over. I hope you and Jeffery can find a way to make each other happy," Dominique said, then kissed her on the cheek and left the room.

Her eyes misted over, but she knew it would do no good to cry. She was happy that Tashiana hadn't lost him as well. Although they would never share another bed, she would be able to see him when she visited Tashiana.

Tashiana never found out it was Dominique who left the note on the door of that motel room. And she never found out about the affairs with Laquan and Janet. Dominique thanked the Lord for that.

It took a long time before Dominique could take his wife to bed without feeling Ahmaad's presence. Nor could he get used to her noticing other men on the streets. The kids accepted their Mom's infidelity with a grain of salt and continued as if nothing had happened.

Tashiana thanked almighty God for still having her family intact. She was encouraged that everything was going to work out because Dominique continued to fulfill his duties as a faithful husband and a caring father. The only indication he gave of how much Tashiana's affair hurt him was whenever a conversation about husbands or wives having affairs came up he always found an excuse to leave the room.

Although he caught some flak from Tillman about staying in his marriage, Dominique was thankful the majority of his friends at work respected his decision. They restrained themselves from asking a lot of embarrassing questions. It was long time before Dominique could talk to anyone about Tashiana's affair without getting angry all over again. His biggest supporter was Greg Farley. Dominique doesn't know if he would have been able to forgive and forget if for him.

When young married men come to Dominique for advice, when they suspect their wives are cheating on them, Dominique smiles and say, "Welcome to the new millennium in Blackville. Where cheating black wives is on par with their white counterparts, and black husbands are expected to deal with it rationally, instead of going off the deep end and killing someone."

Sometimes, Dominique wished for the good old days when revenge against a cheating wife wasn't left up to the divorce courts, or the Lord.